NOT IN THE SCRIPT

NOT
IN THE
SCRIPT

An if only *novel*

Amy Finnegan

BLOOMSBURY

LONDON NEW DELHI NEW YORK SYDNEY

Bloomsbury Publishing, London, New Delhi, New York and Sydney

First published in Great Britain in October 2014 by
Bloomsbury Publishing Plc
50 Bedford Square, London WC1B 3DP

First published in the USA in October 2014 by
Bloomsbury Children's Books
1385 Broadway, New York, New York 10018

www.bloomsbury.com

Bloomsbury is a registered trademark of Bloomsbury Publishing Plc

A CIP catalogue record for this book is available from the British Library

ISBN 978 1 4088 5553 9

Printed and bound in Great Britain by CPI Group (UK) Ltd, Croydon CR0 4YY

1 3 5 7 9 10 8 6 4 2

For Shawn, who changed my world when I needed a ride home

EMMA

"*Celebrity Seeker* claims that I'm dating Troy again," I say as I skim the pages of the gossip magazine. Tabloids are scattered like fall leaves all over Rachel's bedroom, and I want to rake them up and stuff them into trash bags. "How stupid do they think I am?"

I haven't talked to Troy since he shattered my car window three months ago. Rachel doesn't know anything about that, though. No one does, and I have to keep it that way.

"I'd feel bad for you, Emma, but some of us don't have any guys to ignore." Rachel has her back to me, admiring the collection of men who cover her otherwise lavender walls. Most of the space is taken up by carefully cut out magazine pages featuring a male model she calls The Bod. "And worse, the only guy I'm dying to date doesn't know I exist. Literally."

"I doubt he's worth dying for," I say. "If a boy looks like he belongs in a museum, there's a pretty good chance his head is solid marble."

Rachel huffs at me, offended, as if she actually knows him. Or even his name.

I leave her bouncy desk chair—great for girls with energy to burn—to study a close-up of The Bod's face. "At the very least," I go on with a teasing tone, "those puffy lips are airbrushed."

Chancing a peek at Rachel, I find her bright-green eyes narrowed at me. "You know," she says, "for someone who's on *People* magazine's Most Beautiful Young Celebrities list, you're awfully critical of beautiful people."

I suppose being my best friend for over a decade gives her the right to call me out on things like this. And Rachel is all about straight talk and honesty, which is usually a good thing.

My life doesn't always feel genuine, even when cameras aren't rolling.

Whenever I return to my hometown in Fayetteville, Arkansas, I expect the world to somehow seem real again, but work still has a way of taking over. Today especially, because a full five minutes haven't passed without me checking my e-mail. The final details for the new TV series I'm starting next month are being sent out today, including the casting choices.

The scent of coconut-and-lime body spray wafts toward me. Rachel snaps her fingers in front of my face. "Are you even listening?"

Yes and no. She's been going on about the endless charms of her paperweight soul mate. "All I'm saying is that guys who look like The Bod are usually the most overrated gimmicks on the planet," I tell her. "And crappy boyfriend material. Trust me."

I hear a screen door squeak open, and a canary-like chirp belonging to Rachel's mom instantly echoes in the house. Trina enters the room and says, "Oh, Emma honey, have *we* got a big surprise!"

For as long as I can remember, Trina has dressed like she's forty-going-on-sixteen. At the moment she's in black skinny jeans and a plum tee with a glittery fleur-de-lis stretched way too tight over her five-thousand-dollar chest. Trina's curly platinum hair matches her daughter's, but everything about Rachel's beauty is perfectly natural.

"You're just gonna die!" Trina adds.

My mother is right behind Trina and shoots her a *please stop* look, but I seem to be the only one who notices. Typical for her, Mom is wearing a white button-down shirt and gray tweed slacks, looking like she walked out of a Neiman Marcus window display. She wouldn't be caught dead in Trina's leopard print stilettos. But despite being polar opposites, they've been going out for regular lunches since Rachel and I first met in a community acting class.

I sometimes wonder if Mom only does it to stay on the good side of a careless gossip who might be too close to me. Or maybe Mom just wants to keep up on what's *really* going on in my personal life. She likely gets more from Trina, via Rachel, than she does from me.

Trina is still grinning so widely that every tooth in her mouth is showing, but my mom's smile seems fake, and her lashes are batting way too fast to be simple blinks. "I just heard from the studio," she says.

I only stare at her for a second. "But . . . why wasn't I on the e-mail list?"

"I'll forward you a copy, Emma. I always do."

That's not the point, and she knows it. I had asked her to tell the studio to put me on the direct list, and she obviously didn't. Like a lot of parents in this business, my mom became my manager when I landed my first big job, so *everything* goes through her. But now that I'm finally an official adult, I can hire a new management team if I want to, a team who would at least agree that I should know—before the rest of the world—what's going on in my career. Like me, Mom must realize this isn't working anymore, but she hasn't even mentioned the possibility of a new manager, like it isn't something I'd consider anyway.

As if she could never imagine me making a mature decision without her.

Mom tacks on a sigh. "We should head home so we can discuss this casting."

"I want to stay. Just tell me what the e-mail says."

"I'm dying to know too," Rachel adds. "We've been waiting all day."

Trina whispers something to Rachel, then Rachel looks at me with her mouth half-open, her eyes bulging. "Holy crap, Emma! You're gonna FREAK!"

Perfect. Now even Rachel knows before I do.

"Can we borrow this room for a minute?" I ask.

Trina and Rachel appear disappointed by the request but finally step into the hallway, whispering again. My mom shuts the bedroom door and pulls out her phone. "I had hoped we were past this nonsense," she mutters, "but you won't believe who's playing—"

I snatch the phone from her hand, open the e-mail from the studio, and read out loud. "Executive Producer Steve McGregor will launch the production of *Coyote Hills* in Tucson, Arizona, the second week of July . . . table read . . . camera tests . . . I'll go back to that later . . . Okay, here it is: one male lead is still in negotiations." Ugh. This is practically code for *casting problems*. "The remaining cast is as follows: Eden will be played by Emma Taylor. The role of Kassidy will be played by Kimmi Weston." I have no idea who Kimmi is, so I glance at my mom before going on. She's never heard of her either. "And the role of Bryce will be played by Brett Crawford."

I drop the phone.

I want to stomp on it. Scream at it!

Or possibly hug it and jump up and down.

I'm not sure which yet.

"You see?" Mom says. "This is why I wanted to tell you privately."

My arms are as limp as overcooked fettuccini, but I manage to scoop up the phone. "Okay, yeah. Him," I say, going for indifference. "A bit of a shock, but whatever."

Mom puts a hand on her hip. *Here we go.* "Emma, you know how tired I am of dealing with high-publicity romances," she begins, in full-blown managerial mode. "The last two years have been ridiculous, putting out one tabloid fire after another. You're at a crossroads here and have a chance to prove yourself as a serious actress. Brett Crawford is the worst sort of boy for you to get involved with, so don't even consider dating him."

Does she really think *I* would want to go through all that crap again? On-set romances are usually total disasters, and not just for me. Until last spring I was on a primetime drama that, despite sky-high ratings, was cancelled due to conflict on the set. I played the president's daughter, but the actor playing the president was caught having a real-life relationship with the actress who played the first lady—and unfortunately, she also happened to be our executive producer's wife. It wasn't pretty.

And it eventually shut the entire show down.

That was when Steve McGregor, the do-it-all executive producer/creator/director of *Coyote Hills*, called my agent to ask if he could meet with me to discuss his new project. It was the very day the cancellation of *The First Family* was announced, and I haven't received a bigger compliment in the six years of my career.

McGregor is responsible for more hit dramas than any producer in television—his shows don't even require pilots. I think his methods are brilliant, but some people say he's a nutcase. For one thing, he's already slated to direct about one-third of the first season, which either means the guy really is insane or he plans to live with a caffeine drip attached to his arm. McGregor is also notoriously secretive about who he's considering for his cast or I would have already known about Brett. And he rarely takes time to screen-test a pair of actors—who he's already familiar with—for chemistry. But I've worked with enough cinematic geniuses to know there's no use questioning them. You just go along.

"Listen, Mom," I say, trying to hide the likelihood that the pizza I had for lunch is about to land on her Jimmy Choo pumps. "This isn't a big deal. I had a silly celebrity crush on Brett when I was, like, eight." Well, it started about then, and went on and on. But his growing reputation as a guy who never commits, just loves whoever he's with at the moment, has definitely dampened my enthusiasm. "That's ancient history. I'm totally over him."

Totally may be pushing it. I might still watch his movies, a lot, and rewind certain parts that I think he's especially amazing in. But is it so wrong that I think he's the best actor of my generation? Isn't it natural that I would be attracted to someone with so much talent?

Mom gives me a thin, cynical smile. "I noticed just this

morning that your laptop wallpaper is yet another picture of Brett Crawford."

Yeah, well, about that . . . I also just like to *look* at him.

"The only time it's been otherwise in the last six years," Mom goes on, "is when you've been dating some other Hollywood hot-shot who thought nothing of dragging your name through the mud."

Why did she have to bring *them* into this? "It isn't my fault that they all cheated on me. *I* didn't do anything wrong."

Mom's icy expression melts a little, and I realize I rarely see this softer look on her face anymore. She has brown eyes, mine are blue, but we share the same dark hair and small-framed bodies. I've never felt like she's forced me into a life I don't want—I'm the one who got the lead in a first-grade play and begged her to let me become a real actress—but it feels as if she sometimes forgets that I'm not just a client.

It's all business, all the time.

"I know that," Mom says. "And your dad and your closest friends know that. But the majority of the world sees a girl who dates this same type of guy over and over, as someone who has very poor judgment. It just can't happen again."

How could she possibly think I pick losers on purpose?

When I first met Troy, who was my costar during the last season of *The First Family*, he was always smiling, laughing, joking around with me, surprising me with flowers or a dinner overlooking the ocean. But it isn't exactly easy dating professional actors—boys who can fake their way through anything.

I look my mom square in the eyes and say, "I get it, okay? I'm totally done with Hollywood guys. Can we move on now?"

Someone sneezes. Rachel and Trina are just outside the door

and have probably been there this entire time, listening. Mom breathes a familiar sigh of irritation. "We'll talk more when you get home," she says. "And perhaps you can find a new wallpaper for your laptop?"

I nod and return her phone. "Don't worry. I'll be . . ." Fine is what I'd intended to say, but a vision of Brett Crawford sitting next to me in a cast chair—with his perfect surfer tan, blond hair that always falls in front of his eyes, and a smile that puts a humming-bird in my stomach—enters my mind, and I can't speak.

"You'll be *amazing*," Mom says with a squeeze of my shoulder. "Steve McGregor didn't even consider another actress for this part, and he always knows what he's doing. You just need to focus on your career, not boys."

Mom leaves the room, and Rachel soon takes her place. She shuts the door again and says, "Are you freaking out or what? *Brett Crawford?* This is fate!"

"It's *ill*-fated, you mean." I collapse into her bed pillows and throw one over my face. I've had several chances to meet Brett. A few times, I've even been in the same room as him. But besides the fact that he's more than two years older and would have only thought of me as a silly little girl before now, I've intentionally avoided Brett because I don't want to know the real him. "I have a perfectly happy relationship with my laptop wallpaper version of Brett Crawford, thank you very much."

As things are, we never fight, he never cheats on me, and he doesn't . . . scare me.

"Brett was in television for the first several years of his career, so why would he want to come back?" I add. "He's been doing *great* in big-budget movies. He should stay where he is."

Rachel plops into her desk chair. "Don't you keep up with anything? It's amazing how much more I know about your world than you do."

It's not such a bad thing that Rachel always knows more gossip than I do; Hollywood is practically her religion. When we met, Rachel had already been doing commercials since she was a baby in a Downy-soft blanket, so she was quick to make herself my mentor. But a few years later, when we were twelve, we both went to an open audition for what turned out to be an Oscar-winning film, and I got the part.

It was a lucky break. Right time, right place, right look.

Since then, I've done whatever I could to get Rachel auditions for other major projects, but nothing has worked out. And tension builds with every failed attempt. A couple of months ago she straight out told me, "How did this even happen? You have *everything* I want."

Why doesn't she get that I wish she had it all too?

No matter how different things sometimes feel between us, though, one thing stays the same: Rachel is the only friend I have who's been with me all along—the only friend who keeps my feet planted firmly in the dark, rich soil of Arkansas. Even when I'm dressed from head to toe in Prada, with red carpet beneath me and cameras flashing from every other direction, Rachel is a constant reminder of where I came from. Who I really am.

I blow the silver fringe from her pillow off my face. "Are you talking about Brett's girl issues?" I ask. "Because, crazy enough, being a player only seems to *help* a guy's career."

"But it's more than just that," Rachel says. "According to insiders, Brett's been a pain to work with on his last few films. He misses call times and keeps the cast and crew waiting for hours." Rachel sounds like a newscaster as she presents a tattered tabloid as evidence. "Critics say he's lost his passion for acting, that he'll be nothing but a washed-up child star if he doesn't do something quick to redeem himself. So his management team must think television is his best bet. It's worked for a ton of other actors."

I've read some of this, but not all. "Everyone knows what a great actor Brett is—he's been nominated for major awards since he was *five,*" I say. "He's probably just burned out, and McGregor is smart enough to realize he'll push through it."

"Yeah, I guess I can see that. But back to the girl issues," Rachel replies and tacks on a sly smile. "You know what Brett's problem is? He just hasn't dated the *right* girl yet."

I toss a pillow at her. "The last thing I want to be is Brett Crawford's next 'throwaway party favor,' so don't look at *me,*" I say. Then I make a silent promise to put soap in my mouth for quoting a tabloid. Reporters tell plenty of lies about my own life, so I question everything I read, but I've seen enough myself to know that every once in a while they're surprisingly dead-on. In their pursuit of a quick, juicy story to sell, however, gossipmongers often miss the details that could *really* damage someone. "It's just that this is all sort of sad," I go on. "Brett has always been someone safe for me to crush on, but now—"

Rachel cuts me off with laughter. "Oh please! You *know* what's gonna happen. Brett will fall head over heels in love and change his whole life to be with you. So just flirt a little and see where things go."

"No way," I reply. She might understand if I told her how bad things got with Troy, but I can't take the chance of Rachel telling

Trina, who would go straight to my mom. Then Mom would freak out even more about me living on my own in Arizona, which is something I've had to fight for every day for the past few months. "I just need to get over Brett before we start working together. That's all. Or he'll be . . . well, a bit of a distraction."

"More like a tall, beautiful problem with a killer smile." Rachel turns back to her wall to swoon over The Bod in a western-themed cologne ad for Armani. "I can only imagine how distracted I'd be if I ever worked with *my* dream guy. Distracted by his perfectly toned arms, and his amazing green eyes, and his luscious mocha hair, and . . . gosh, I better not talk him up *too* much, or you'll want to start a collection of your own. But The Bod is all mine, got it?"

I probably sound just as ridiculous as Rachel does when I talk about Brett—I mean, when I *used* to talk about Brett—but I laugh anyway. "Yep, he's all yours," I reply. "Down to his last curly eyelash."

I have to agree with Rachel on one thing, though: The Bod, whoever he is, makes leather cowboy chaps look seriously hot.

JAKE

Chill, Jake, this is temporary, I tell myself as I pace outside Steve McGregor's production office in Tucson. If I get this job, I'll be locked into a four-year contract, but most TV shows bomb before then, so I might get out of it early.

For now, it's a perfect solution.

Coyote Hills will be filming less than two hours from my hometown of Phoenix, and the guilt has been killing me, being so far away all the time. If anything else happens at home—if things get worse—I can be there. And acting seems to be the quickest way I can ditch this pretty-boy modeling crap and keep making the money I need.

Still, I thought my agent was crazy when she said I should give it a try. "I got a B-minus in drama," I warned her. "I couldn't even memorize a one-minute monologue."

"Trust me, Jake, you'll be better than you think," Liz had

replied. "Acting isn't just an ability to recite lines. It's a talent for letting go of what your mind is telling you about reality and allowing the instincts of a character to take over. In that way, it's exactly like modeling."

I'd started to question that, but then I got her point. If standing around for eight hours in little more than leather chaps and a cowboy hat—and pretending you enjoy it—isn't acting, I don't know what is.

It's been six months since Liz hooked me up with a world-famous acting coach. Then McGregor called my coach a few weeks ago to say he was still looking for another male lead, and I jumped at the chance to audition.

Today is my third callback. The casting director gave me the same poker face as she did during my previous screen tests, but in the end, she smiled and said, "Loved it. Follow me."

She led me through a maze of halls covered with movie and TV memorabilia and told me to wait outside McGregor's office while they watched my final audition tape.

After forty-five minutes, the office door finally opens. "Mr. McGregor would like to speak with you," the casting director tells me. Then as she passes me on the way out, she pauses to whisper, "He's a little eccentric, but trust me, he can make you a star."

I've only taken my first step into the massive corner office when a man comes at me so fast that all I see is a blur of flaming red hair. "Here you are, in the flesh!" McGregor says. "And every bit as handsome."

Liz warned me about his thick Scottish accent, so I was expecting it, but I'm still not sure I understood him right. "Uh, thanks," I reply. "It's good to meet you."

At six-two I tower over McGregor by several inches. It doesn't matter, though—the guy oozes confidence. And he's probably held at least a dozen gold statues in the hand I now shake, so it's deserved.

The walls of his office are plastered with promotional posters and photo after photo of stars he's worked with. Oak shelves are stuffed with books and portfolios, and award statues are lined up in a glass case. It's like being in a museum. I don't dare touch anything.

McGregor motions for me to sit in a black armchair in front of his desk, then settles into his own chair opposite me. "Sorry for the wait," he says. "I was on the phone with your agent." This was their fourth call, which should mean I'm at least on the short list. "Mr. Elliott, it's taken some snooping around to get the full picture of you, but I've gained the impression that you didn't grow up hoping to be a model-slash-actor like so many others in this business." I hesitate before nodding. "What were your original plans?" he goes on. "Say, ten years ago?"

"Like . . . when I was a kid?"

"Isn't that when most dreams begin?" he asks. "As a child in Scotland, I wanted to run away to Spain and be a matador. But here I am in the US, red-inking a comfort list longer than the Great Wall of China." He slides a legal-size sheet of paper across his desk so I can see what he's crossed out: a steam shower and on-site massage therapist are just a few of the demands someone has made. "*Bull*fighting, indeed. How about you?"

"Well . . . I think I first wanted to be an astronaut, and then a baseball player," I reply, loosening up. "But then I got this crazy idea when I was in the third grade and took like twenty pairs of my mom's shoes, set up a store on the sidewalk in front of my house, and sold every last pair to the girls in my neighborhood. They didn't even care that the shoes were too big."

McGregor raises his bushy ginger brows at me. "I can't imagine why."

I shift in my chair. "Anyway, from then on, all I wanted to be was a businessman—buying, selling, making deals. Whatever."

That's still the only thing I want to do, but as my buddy Devin once put it, I traded my college plans for bronzing powder.

"I assume your mother got her shoes back?" McGregor asks.

I smile when I recall all her spiky high heels, in every possible color, but then I imagine where they are now—useless in her closet. "Yep. And it just about killed me to return all those quarters."

McGregor offers an amused nod. "So if your heart's set on business, how'd you get *here*?" He motions to his colossal glass desktop, nearly hidden by piles of folders, screenplays, set sketches, headshots, you name it. If it belonged in Hollywood, it was in this dude's office.

I'm the only thing out of place.

"My agent is my best friend's sister, so she's the one who . . . I guess you could say, *scouted* me." That's the uncomplicated answer.

For some reason, McGregor thinks this is funny. "Ah, yes, that's right. Liz told me she went searching for new talent in Phoenix and found you posing like a chiseled work of art in her own parents' driveway."

"I wasn't posing," I say with an accidental smirk. "I was playing basketball and just happened to be shirtless, like the rest of my friends."

It was a Saturday afternoon during my junior year of high school, and Devin's much older sister was visiting from New York

City. Liz watched me from the porch for over an hour, creeping me out a little, but I had no idea what I was really in for. She was a pretty smooth talker when she cornered me after we all went in for dinner, and the numbers she threw out for just a single day of modeling were more than a little tempting for a guy who couldn't afford a car, let alone save for college.

And that was before I *really* needed the money.

McGregor scans me with appraising eyes. "All right, let's get to the reason you're here." I like this guy. "Mr. Elliott, there are plenty of good actors out there, but too many of them need incessant direction, and I'm not a patient man. I want actors who don't need to be constantly *told* how to portray their characters—it's got to be second nature for them."

Okay, this is it. I just want to hear yes or no.

"Your audition tapes certainly prove that you can pull off the look and arrogance of Justin," McGregor goes on, "but deep down, can you connect with his darker side? Embrace him? *Become* him?"

"Well . . ." Is this a trick question? "To tell you the truth, Justin seems like an irresponsible mess."

"Precisely. Which is why I believe you're perfect for the job."

Huh? How could he have such a bad impression of me? I've always been prepared and on time for the auditions. And Liz said she'd told him I was her favorite talent to work with.

McGregor slaps the desk. "Ah, blast! Got ahead of myself. What I meant to say, before I insulted you, is that I look for suppressed traits in my actors that are likely itching to be unleashed. So as I said, it's their *second* nature I'm interested in."

"Uh, right. Okay." I'm still lost.

He leans forward. "Wouldn't you like to listen to that devil on your shoulder every once in a while? Be a rebel, a menace, a villain who never thinks of anyone but himself?" He waits for my reply, so I nod. "If what I hear is true, Mr. Elliott, you might enjoy a break from the maturity you seem to have found too early in life."

How much had Liz told him? "Sure. Who wouldn't?"

"Then you're about to get your chance," he says. "You have a raw talent I haven't seen in quite some time. Not only have I studied your audition tapes, I've also spent a great deal of time with your acting coach, discussing your potential and watching your impressive progression on hours of film. All I need now is to know if you're willing to take in this 'irresponsible mess' as part of your soul."

My soul would take in a nest of hornets if it meant I could ditch modeling, make more money, *and* live in Arizona. For over a year now, I've been constantly traveling between my mom's new place in Phoenix and the hotel of the week—usually in New York—for modeling jobs. Here, there, everywhere. It's corny and sentimental, but I miss having a *home*.

"Yes, definitely." I have to be careful not to sound overeager or I'll blow the upper hand in negotiations, which is always my favorite part of the process. "The details have to go through Liz, of course, but I'd love to work with you." I laugh. "At the very least, it'll be entertaining."

I worry for a sec that I've insulted him, but McGregor starts laughing too.

"And don't forget exhausting," he says. "Depending on your screen time in each episode, you'll be on set between eight and sixteen hours, three to five days a week. This leaves room for little else. But rather than dancing on tabletops for paparazzi, some young stars pursue more respectable interests in their personal time—college, for example."

Yep, he really has snooped around. "Good to know. But I'm cool with putting a business degree on the back burner." That part may be a lie, but I want him to know that once I sign my contract, I'll commit myself like I always do. I'll have to. "I should probably focus on not embarrassing myself on national television. Or *you*."

McGregor chuckles, his face turning splotchy. "That would be appreciated. However, if you're curious, perhaps you can ask"—he rummages through a pile of folders and sets a headshot in front of me—"this pretty girl right here how she managed to complete two years of college credit before the rest of her high school class even graduated."

I glance at the photo, then look up, stunned. "Emma Taylor did that?" Liz already told me that Emma is in the cast, but I figured a superstar like her would be too busy shopping on her days off to care about school. "I mean, she doesn't just do TV stuff, she's in a lot of movies too. How can she keep up?"

"Not sure, honestly. You'll have to ask her." McGregor brings out two more headshots. "Here are your other costars."

"Brett Crawford," I say. According to Liz, McGregor struggled with the decision to hire him, and Liz agrees that he's a gamble. "He'll definitely draw the women."

"Aye, and I'm counting on more than that," McGregor says. "He's phenomenal, that kid. I'm expecting Emmy buzz on Brett by episode three—five at the latest. If he shows up to work, that is." McGregor winks at me as if I'm in on some sort of joke. "I've got my fingers crossed."

I smile back and take a look at the caramel blonde in the other headshot. "Who's this?"

"Kimmi Weston, an impressive new actress I also found through Anne," he says, referring to my acting coach. "She's been a star student for several years at the Manhattan Academy for the Performing Arts, and far too talented to pass up. But she's perhaps been praised and applauded a tad more than was good for her."

He turns his attention back to the "comfort list" he previously pointed out, picks up a red pen, and crosses off *personal chef.*

I laugh, but I'm only half kidding when I tell McGregor, "Now I'm wondering what you'll say about *me* after I leave here."

"Whatever I want to," he replies and offers his hand across the desk. "Welcome to Hollywood."

EMMA

My mom stands by the front door of my new town house in Tucson, surveys the living room, and says, "I still don't like this."

She didn't exactly have a great time helping me shop for the furniture that was just delivered, but Rachel and I had a blast. Mom tried talking me into a boring cream-colored love seat and sofa set that looked like it belonged in my grandmother's house.

"I love it!" I reply and plop down on the cranberry-red sofa that I'd bought instead. It's a huge sectional with oversize pillows, and so soft and cozy that I think I might sleep here. "I can't wait to snuggle up with a big bowl of popcorn."

There's a giant TV mounted on my wall, and I just finished stuffing a black entertainment center with my movie collection— mostly romantic comedies because everyone is always happy in the end—while Rachel unpacked my kitchen stuff and my mom hung pictures. I finally gave in to Mom on those: poppies and tulips, in simple black frames. I'm going shopping again as soon as she leaves anyway. I'm out-of-my-mind excited to have all this space to myself, most of it begging me to fill it up with things I don't really need. I might even get a lava lamp.

Hot pink. No, orange. Maybe both.

Rachel lands beside me and kicks up her feet. "This will be the best couch *ever* for having tons of friends over."

Maybe that's what my mom doesn't like about it. She eyes us like she's imagining the room filled with kegs and shirtless frat guys. Not really my thing, but I don't remind my mom because it's kind of funny watching her face turn green.

Rachel seems to have caught on to Mom's crazy thoughts too, because she leans toward me—obviously fighting a smile—and adds, "Do you think Brett will like it?"

I should hit her, but I laugh instead.

Mom groans and closes the window blinds. "I'm not talking about your furniture. I still don't like the idea of you living alone. And in the desert, no less."

"But I'll be one entire state closer to home than California is," I say, which is where I lived while filming *The First Family*. My living arrangements are always a touchy subject. I haven't lived with my parents for more than a few weeks at a time for over three years. My dad was a professor at the University of Arkansas when I signed on to do *The First Family,* and since that meant I had to live in Southern California, Dad applied for a job at UCLA. He got what he called an "adequate" offer, but the University of Arkansas didn't want to lose him, so they counteroffered. A short time later he became a dean.

I ended up living with my aunt and her husband—both

architects in Santa Monica—only fifteen minutes from where *The First Family* filmed. My aunt was protective of me too, but in a less intrusive way than my mom is. I also had an on-set chaperone. But my mom still traveled between Fayetteville and Los Angeles every week or so for the first year, usually with my wild little brothers, Levi and Logan. Then the twins started kindergarten and things got even more complicated for my mom.

It was at about this time that I overheard my parents arguing, my dad telling my mom something like, "We also have two young sons who need our attention. We can't keep rearranging their lives just so their big sister can be a famous movie star."

That stung a little.

Dad has a more traditional idea of what a real career should be, so it wasn't until he looked over the numbers on my new *Coyote Hills* contract that he started taking his little girl's dreams a bit more seriously. And because I'm no longer a minor, the paychecks now go directly to me rather than a trust for when I'm older. Still, Dad's parting words when I left for Arizona were, "Spend wisely, Emma. This business is fickle."

My first big purchase was this town house, and even Dad agreed that it was a good investment. It smells like wet paint, new carpet, and an apple-cinnamon candle, which Rachel brought along as a housewarming gift. I'd asked her to help me move because I knew three days of shopping and organizing with my mom would likely lead to all sorts of stupid arguments, and Rachel is always a good buffer between us.

Mom has to be here because, according to her, I have no idea what kind of stuff I need to "set up an actual household." She also doesn't want me living out of boxes for the next several months, so we're trying to get everything put away in its proper place—wherever *that* is—before the weekend is over. And Mom was the one who got the utilities up and running, like the water, electric, city services, and the security system. She was actually right about me having no clue how to do any of that. But I probably could've handled the rest of it.

I jump off the sofa and reopen the blinds to let the sunshine back in.

Immediately out my window is a patch of prickly pear cacti. The plants have round padded leaves with needles that I wouldn't want to mess with, but they aren't nearly as impressive as the gigantic arms of the saguaro cactus. Saguaros are everywhere and as big as trees. The landscape here is seriously cool, except for the rocks that are used in place of grass. I'll miss the smell of a freshly mown lawn.

"I wouldn't call this place a desert," I tell my mom. "With all the trees they've planted on this property—and the waterfall at the pool—it's more like an *oasis*."

"I suppose," she replies. "But just so you're aware, there's an eight-inch lizard on your front porch." Mom says this as if it will send me running back to Arkansas. "And look, there's another one."

"Then you see? I'll be fine. I already have friends."

Rachel joins us at the window, and we all watch the brown gangly creatures scurry over the concrete, going no place in particular.

"Great," Rachel says. "I'm being replaced by two lizards who eat bugs, can't talk, and lose a limb whenever you frighten them."

"Nobody's perfect," I reply. "But I bet I can teach them to play fetch."

Rachel puts on a pout. "Then they *will* become your new best friends, because you know how bad *I* am at sports."

"Says the girl who almost won the hula hoop contest in the third grade!" I remind her.

She sighs and leans her head against my shoulder. "Darn that Jenny Perkins and her supernatural hips."

I give Rachel a tight, supportive squeeze. "I heard that her hips were actually mechanical and made of gold. Who could compete with *that*?"

My mom laughs, which is a nice break from her usual glares of disapproval. That is, until she says, "You two should try to act like grown-ups once in a while. You might like it."

Rachel scrunches up her face. "I did try it once—a few summers ago—but it gave me hives. I think I'm allergic."

Dang, I love this girl.

Rachel and I are always at our best when we're goofing around, like we did all the time before tabloids, audition opportunities, and award-show swag bags began to dominate our conversations. I realize we can't make jokes about hula hoops and lizards forever, but couldn't we somehow return to . . . a better balance?

Mom's phone rings, so I tell her Rachel and I will be finishing up the boxes in my bedroom, and we head for the stairs.

"Holy crap, Emma," Rachel says as soon as she sees what I'd already accomplished on my own. "It's like a giant marshmallow exploded in your room. What's with all the *white*?"

"Oh," I reply, having earlier thought the room felt perfectly calm and peaceful this way. But now that I look at it as a whole, I get what she's saying. So far I have a white four-poster queen bed with matching dressers, a white eyelet comforter set, and no kidding, swooping white curtains. I must have been in one of my clean-freak moods when I bought it all online. "I'll have to add 'brightly colored, fluffy pillows' to my shopping list."

"Yeah, that and a few new posters of Brett!" she says with a playful nudge. "I saw some seriously delicious ones the other day."

I'm sure she did, but she still isn't getting how desperate I am to desensitize myself to the *actual*, seriously delicious Brett. I'll be working with him in just five days.

"But why would I need *that* view when I already have this one?" I ask, and throw open my bedroom curtains to expose the gorgeous mountain range out my window. I had expected it to be totally flat here and covered by nothing but dirt and sagebrush. And, yes, there's plenty of that in Tucson—and it feels like the sun is a million miles closer than anywhere else I've ever been—but here in Sabino Canyon, I'm a full twenty minutes away from the hot pavement of the city center. I even have a river out my back door. "Check out that sunset!"

"Wow," Rachel breathes. "It looks like someone smeared orange sorbet across the sky. I have *got* to capture this on film."

Rachel has been getting into photography this summer and she's a real natural at it. She mostly just uses her phone to take photos of whatever inspires her, but then she manipulates them in ways that make them look like stunning digital art. Some of the so-called snapshots she's taken of me are better than magazine covers I've been on.

Her Twitter feed, which used to just be a constant stream of her latest thoughts on casting news, tabloid rumors, movies, and television shows, is now peppered with professional-quality images that she presents as perfect shooting locations for this or that upcoming film, or ideal mood-setting shots, such as this sunset. She's even chronicled my move to Tucson, which has been half-fun, half-annoying, but her followers have doubled this past week, so I'm okay with it. They'll soon see that there's much more than boring old me to stick around for.

"Marshmallows, 'seriously delicious,' and now orange sorbet?" I ask Rachel. "Either you didn't eat enough today, or your sweet tooth is acting up."

"Definitely hungry again. Didn't I also say that I wanted to eat bugs?"

I laugh. "I thought you were talking about the *lizards* doing that."

She considers this. "Oh yeah." She takes a few shots of the sunset from my window, says she can't see enough of it from this view, then races for the door. "I'm gonna be a while!"

With photos on my mind, I decide to start unpacking my big box of pictures. I unwrap the first frame to find a photo of Rachel and me in the English countryside last summer. We're standing in the color-infused flower garden behind William Shakespeare's home in Stratford-upon-Avon, and smiling like we'd found our motherland. I'd had a movie premiere in London earlier that week—for a historical-novel adaptation that I wished I could've lived in forever— so Mom let me splurge and bring Rachel along. The two of us spoke to each other in perky British accents the entire week, and my mother wanted to toss us into the Thames.

It was my favorite vacation ever.

We spent our days visiting dozens of sites that totally blew my mind, and at night we went to play after play in London's West End, and were awestruck by the quality of the acting.

I doubt I could ever perform live like that. I love that if I mess up on film, the director just says, "Cut! Go again!" and I can fix my mistake as if it never happened.

How great would that be in real life?

The next picture I unwrap is of my family. Levi and Logan, who are seven now, grin back at me with half their front teeth missing. I was an only child for over ten years, and I'm pretty sure my parents had meant to keep it that way. But whenever I get homesick, my brothers are almost always the reason. My heart twists a little, wishing they were here.

I unwrap the next frame, but it's the paper, rather than the picture, that catches my attention. Rachel packed some of these boxes for me, and although I'm grateful she sacrificed some of her tabloid collection to use as packing material, I notice the publication date on this particular issue of *Celebrity Seeker* and feel a stab in my side: March.

Everything about last spring was . . . ugh.

I tear through the rest of the box anyway and find the cover: EMMA LOSES TROY TO SAND SIREN. I never actually read this article, so I open the pages and force myself to do it:

Poor, poor Emma Taylor. Her eyes are probably red and swollen today after learning that yet another one of her boyfriends has cheated on her. Troy Dawson, her beau of six months, was seen at the Santa Monica Pier this past weekend wrapped around another beauty in a barely there bikini.

"He definitely wasn't trying to hide anything," reported an onlooker. "It was hard to tell whose hands were whose."

This shameless display in broad daylight supports recent rumors that the superstar relationship is on the rocks. "It's about time Troy moved on," said a friend of the young actor. "Emma is impossible to keep happy."

Another source claims she saw Taylor and Dawson arguing at a party the night before his fling on the beach.

"I could hear Troy screaming at Emma over the music. She kept trying to calm him down and saying that they should leave."

This isn't the first time Taylor has attempted to curb a boyfriend's appetite for wild parties. It also isn't the first time she's failed to curb a guy's appetite for other women. "For whatever reason, Emma can't keep a guy faithful," said a Hollywood insider. "And having three boyfriends in a row cheat on her, she's gotta be wondering if she's the problem, not them."

The conflict has yet to reach the boiling point. Taylor and Dawson still have another month of filming before their television series, *The First Family*, wraps for good. Heartthrob Dawson was brought on to play a love interest for Taylor's character this season, likely to distract viewers from the real-life drama taking place behind the scenes between another Hollywood couple.

That's when I stop reading because my eyes are burning, and I refuse to cry even one more tear over Troy Dawson. The story is right about us arguing the night before he cheated on me, but I wasn't trying to "curb his appetite" for anything. That particular night, another guy—who was one of my *Mountain Home* costars— gave me a big hug when he saw me. And then we had talked . . . too long, and too friendly, and too everything for Troy. He had acted overly possessive a couple of times before, but that night was the first time he yelled at me.

I knew I wanted out right then, but I decided to cool things off slowly to draw less attention to the breakup. My apology—explaining how I knew the other guy, and that he was *ten years* older than me—wasn't enough, though, and Troy thought he could teach me a lesson by showing up on a full-page tabloid cover, playing his own version of Twister on the beach.

That was nothing compared to what followed.

I refused to take him back, so for weeks after we broke up he left creepy phone messages, saying he was watching everything I did, and he proved it by listing specific places I'd been. Then after his last day of work on *The First Family*, he chased me for over an hour, with me darting my car in and out of crazy L.A. traffic. I thought I'd ditched him, but when I returned to my aunt's house, he was waiting in the driveway.

I unrolled my window just an inch to try to defuse the situation, but he immediately started swearing at me, saying how stupid I was being, that I had started all this by flirting with other guys. "Come on, Emma. Get out. Let's talk," he said, finally in a calmer tone. But he'd held my arms so tightly before we left the studio, I could already see bruises forming. So I was scared to unlock the door.

That's when he tried to put his fist through my window.

There was blood all over the broken glass, but I backed up and sped off again, too shocked and horrified to consider how badly he'd hurt himself. And I haven't seen him since.

I sometimes wonder if he's more freaked out about what he did than I am.

I realize I should've filed a restraining order, but I still can't get past what feels like the *equal* threat of the media. Even now, tabloids would slap together whatever pieces of the puzzle they could find, filling in the missing details with pure, tantalizing fiction. They would dig up photos of me looking weepy, terrified, or both—*poor, poor Emma*. And they would splash my face across every cover for weeks, alongside photos of Troy looking cruel and menacing. But they would likely have to pull those from acting clips, since Troy so rarely shows that side of himself in public.

He's always the charmer. Always the guy every girl wants.

Exactly the type of guy I'm fooled by.

"Emma," Mom says from the doorway, making me jolt and scramble to my feet. She eyes me suspiciously. "The studio just called. Brett Crawford has a conflict with his appointment with the costume department next Monday, so he'll be there during *your* time tomorrow morning. I just thought I should warn you."

What? No way.

"Let's reschedule," I reply. "I think I'm getting sick, and I'll probably be worse in the morning. My hands are shaking. See?"

They really are.

"We've been through this Brett thing—you're over him, remember?" she says. "And you'll have to meet him in a few days anyway. It might as well be tomorrow."

Why? So she can be there to stop me from swooning?

I fall back onto my bed like dead weight. "It isn't Brett," I reply, because it isn't, not really. I shouldn't have read that article, a stabbing reminder that being in the "public eye" gives tabloids the legal right to share my every mistake, mishap, and humiliation with the world, for the sake of *entertainment*. "I just suddenly feel like crap."

"Ill, Emma. You feel ill."

"No, I feel *crappy*." This is only a fitting. Costumes can work me in another time, right? "Why don't I just swap times with Brett and go Monday when he was supposed to?"

Mom comes over to check my forehead, like all good mommies

should do. "You *are* a bit clammy." Her dark brows pinch together. "But calling back after I've already said you'd be fine with sharing your time might make you seem high maintenance—and no one likes a diva. So I surely hope you're not faking this."

I wish I was. I would rather be known as a diva than *poor, poor, Emma Taylor,* the girl whose dating life is perfect fodder for the tabloids.

Rachel returns right then and immediately notices what my mother hadn't. "Oh my gosh!" she says, rushing for the cover of *Celebrity Seeker* and stuffing it back into a box. "I didn't realize *this* story was in the stack of tabloids I brought to your house. I'm so sorry!"

I shrug and shake my head, like it doesn't matter, and glance at my mom. I expect her to say something along the lines of "Heartbreak is *not* a legitimate reason to cancel an appointment." But she just walks over to my box of photos, finishes unwrapping the frames while Rachel sits on the bed and tries to cheer me up, then leaves the room with a big box of toxic waste in her arms.

"Thanks, Mom," I say as she shuts the door. And I mean it.

About thirty minutes later, Rachel presents me with a gift so awesome that I'm sure we'll laugh about it for years to come. She's used her mad photo-editing skills to cut off the head of the barely there bikini girl and put Troy's head in its place.

"Look at his scrawny little arms!" I say when I finally catch my breath. "But he looks surprisingly good in pink. And I love those itsy-bitsy polka dots you added."

"I'm glad you like it," Rachel replies. "Because I just anonymously posted it online, and it will probably go viral."

JAKE

Only a few weeks after my first meeting with Steve McGregor, I'm walking into Desert Productions Studios in Tucson. The entire cast and crew should be on set today. I check in with security and am escorted through the main doors to where a production assistant gives me a schedule and a hanging name tag: JAKE ELLIOTT, CAST.

A guy I recognize right away as Brett Crawford is talking on his phone just a few steps from me. "No, seriously," he says. "I *do* remember you! I just forgot your name for a sec."

While listening for a reply—I can hear a girl's high-pitched, flirty tone from here—Brett rolls his eyes and laughs. To himself, it seems. "Tonight? Ah, dang! I'm not in L.A., or I'd totally come over." He notices that I'm watching him and shakes his head at me with a look of terror on his face, as though he's trying to tell me *she's scary.*

Brett is so loud that even after I turn away and walk toward the main area of the studio, I can still hear him say, "Sorry, gotta go! They need me on the set . . . yeah. Yeah, of course. I'll call you later." Then somehow, he's right next to me again, slapping a hand on my shoulder. "Chicks, man. They're crazy. I have *no* idea how she got my number."

I stop and look at him. "Caller ID?"

"Nah. I've never called her. We hooked up at a party . . . I think."

This guy has mastered the art of first impressions. I start walking again, and he follows. "Was she ever alone with your phone?" I ask.

"Uh . . . I might've left it sitting around while I grabbed some drinks or whatever?"

"Then that's probably when she used it to call her own cell," I explain.

Brett thinks this over as if he's doing long division in his head. "Dude, I hadn't even thought of that," he says. "No wonder I get calls from girls I can't remember meeting."

Several minutes later, Brett is finally finished giving me a tour of his big-time-famous career—as a player, that is. When I spot the row of cast chairs lined up in front of what looks to be a classroom set, I take my designated seat, and Brett says, "Wait, I thought you were crew!"

Taking a chance that he can actually read, I hold up my name tag.

"Oh!" More laughter. "I didn't recognize you—fully clothed, I mean. You look different than you do in those Abercrombie ads."

"Armani," I say. For a second, I think I might punch him. I've only done a few shirtless ads, but they're all people seem to remember. Brett is making an attempt at male bonding, though, and I'm being a jerk, so I add, "Abercrombie requires full exposure of a guy's *eight*-pack, and I draw the line at six."

He finds this comeback hysterical—or if the last fifteen minutes is any indication, he laughs at everything anyone says to him—and starts into anecdotes he's collected during his *many* years of doing photo shoots. I turn my attention to more interesting things.

From the street the studio looks like a massive warehouse, but the interior is more like a gigantic house that's been turned inside out. The exterior walls of each set are rough with exposed two-by-fours, plywood, and electrical wires. Furniture and smaller props are scattered everywhere I look. The air is infused with the smells of duct tape, lumber, and . . . chaos.

Just from my viewpoint, I count over fifty crew members. The constant flow of movement reminds me of an amusement park on a busy day.

The crew hauls around equipment and props, and sets up cameras and lighting. Assistant directors and department heads are easy to spot—they're the ones talking nonstop and pointing fingers in all directions. Then there's Steve McGregor, shooting between sets like a torpedo. Two-way radios and earpieces are glued to pretty much everyone.

The only cast member I've met before today is Kimmi, and once was enough. She had caused the costume department to be an hour behind schedule when I showed up for my fitting. I'd overheard McGregor trying to calm the costume designer—he said it wasn't easy to dress a pit viper with legs—then Kimmi had stormed out of the room, nearly bulldozing me, and said, "These people are *impossible* to work with."

McGregor now stops in front of where Brett and I sit and scans over the cast chairs. "Where are the girls?" he asks no one in particular.

A production assistant appears out of thin air—PAs seem to be everywhere, all at once—with folded papers sticking out of both back pockets, a radio in one hand, and a clipboard in the other. "There was a transpo issue with Miss Taylor," he says. "We hadn't been cleared at her security gate to pick her up, and we had a wrong cell number. But we got it sorted out."

McGregor keeps his hard stare locked on the guy. "And Kimmi?"

The PA speaks into his radio. "Anyone have eyes on Kimmi?" A few seconds later the radio blurts something about heads flying because her dressing room isn't ready, and the PA replies, "Copy that." He starts to answer McGregor, then stops to motion in the direction of a tirade making its way toward us. "I think we just found her."

Kimmi emerges from a hallway, and even with all the noise, I can still hear her heels clicking on the concrete floor. "Good morning, Miss Weston," says the PA who's stationed at the entrance. She walks right past him, and he follows. "I just need to give you a name tag."

"You're kidding, right?" Kimmi says, as if he's asked her to put on Mickey Mouse ears. She's almost as hot as she thinks she is— shaped like a runway model, smoky brown eyes, flawless face— but the prima donna thing is always a deal killer for me. She's wearing an off-the-shoulder top, light pink with rhinestones, a tight black miniskirt, and stilettos, also with rhinestones. Also deal killers.

Brett turns around in his chair for a better look. "I think I know her," he says as Kimmi gets closer. When she finally stops in front of us and poses with a hand on her hip, Brett stands and opens his arms as though he's inviting her into a hug. "Hey, it's been a while!"

Kimmi's tight smile loosens, and she looks back at him, confused. "Sorry, but I—"

"The Hard Rock Hotel. Vegas. Remember?" Brett prompts her, followed by a grin filled with mischief. "We met in the hot tub. Just the two of us . . . it was a great night."

Yeah, clearly unforgettable, judging by Kimmi's narrowed eyes.

"*What?*" Her scorching glare shifts from Brett to the crew members who have stopped in their tracks after his bold announcement. They practically trip over each other as they get back to work. "I've never met you before," Kimmi tells Brett. "Let alone in a hot tub."

She seems not only humiliated by Brett's suggestion, but insulted. Brett, however, just appears stumped. "Are you sure?" He pauses, giving her a completely shameless full-body scan. "Huh. Maybe I just recognize you from your headshot in McGregor's office."

"Ya think?" Kimmi snaps. She glances around again like she's hoping the previous crew members are still close enough to hear *this* part of their conversation. But they're not.

Brett throws his hands in the air. "Jeez! It was a simple mistake. I'm sorry."

"Great. Then stop looking me over like that. It will *never* happen, got it?"

"Well, it's not like I was hitting on you anyway. So . . . whatever."

Kimmi doesn't reply. She just settles into her cast chair, to my right, then flips her highlighted hair to her other shoulder and starts digging through her Fendi handbag. "I hope you're at least more civilized than Brett," she tells me. "As in, not an ape."

I scratch my head, apelike. "Depends on who you ask."

Brett folds his arms. "Kimmi, Jake probably won't be interested in you either—not when the only curve on your body is your turned-up nose. But there's help for that, you know."

When Kimmi raises her head, she looks dangerous enough to pound Brett into dust. "Thanks for the suggestion," she says. "But I don't take advice from Hollywood has-beens."

Color seeps over Brett's neck. "Just offering my professional opinion."

This guy is begging for a harassment charge.

"Dude, are you *on* something," I ask, "or are you just naturally this stupid?"

He sits on the other side of Kimmi and grins at her. "Born this way. Sad, isn't it?"

"It's sad that you were born at all," she replies, and I laugh.

This girl can take care of herself.

McGregor's booming voice is behind us now. "Ah, Miss Taylor," he says, causing everyone to look. "So sorry about the confusion this morning. It won't happen again."

"It was actually *my* fault. My car got delayed in shipping, and I forgot to . . . ," Emma replies, and everything else is a blur. *Whoa.* Cameras don't do her justice—I can see the color of her famous cobalt-blue eyes even from here. She's in a white shirt, scoop-necked and kinda lacy, and tight jeans. Her dark wavy hair pours over her shoulders like hot fudge on a sundae.

I think of my poor friends in Phoenix who would sell their

souls to get within a hundred feet of Emma Taylor, and here I am, within ten . . . nine . . . eight . . .

She stops dead still, stares right back at me, and then gasps.

"Hi," I say. At least I think I do.

Emma keeps her eyes locked on mine and laughs. *Laughs.* "No. Freaking. WAY!" she says before coming around the row of chairs to sit to my left, her shoulders still shaking as she tries to calm down. "Sorry! I . . . *you*! . . . No . . . freaking . . ." She can't even finish.

"Way," I add, wondering what I have on my face that's so darn funny to look at. "You already said that."

Kimmi's hand moves to my knee, and she peeks around me to tell Emma, "I take it you guys already know each other. You hooked up in a hot tub too, huh?"

Emma stops laughing instantly.

"No!" she yelps, more to me than to Kimmi. Her face is bright red, and mine is probably the same color, because now I can't help but imagine myself in a hot tub with her. "We just . . . have a mutual friend," she goes on. "That's all."

"We do?"

Emma doesn't answer. Instead, she asks Kimmi, "Who said I was in a hot tub with him?"

Brett leans forward. "No, no, Emma. Don't worry. Kimmi's confused. I told her it was *you and I* who hooked up in a hot tub, but she's jealous, so . . ."

He appears to have noticed that Emma has gone from red to purple and is no longer breathing. Brett jumps up from his chair and in half a second, he's on a knee in front of her. "I'm joking!" he says, grabbing both of her hands. "I just thought I'd have a little fun with you."

"Because he has a *little fun* with everyone," Kimmi mutters.

Brett whips his head to her. "By any chance, do you have an off button?"

Emma slides her hands slowly out of Brett's grip. Then she looks back to me. "What exactly is going on here?"

"No clue," I reply with a shrug. "But I think it's safe to say that none of us have spent any time together in a hot tub."

She smiles. "Thank you! What a relief."

Brett notices that McGregor is heading back, then latches onto Emma's shoulders and says, "I can't believe we haven't met before. We have a *million* of the same friends, so we've gotta talk. I started following you on Twitter last night—did you see that?"

Emma just nods at him, looking a little shaken again. But why?

McGregor is in front of us now, grinning like a kid in a toy store. "Splendid! You've all met. What do you think of your new castmates?"

If Kimmi were a cartoon character, she'd have steam billowing from her ears, but she says nothing. Emma and I keep quiet too. Brett has plenty to say, though. "I can't stand *her*," he tells McGregor, pointing to Kimmi. "But the other two are cool. Can't wait to work with them."

McGregor's grin doesn't budge. "All right then. Moving on!"

EMMA

It would have been the best moment ever if Rachel had walked into the studio with me this morning to find Jake "The Bod" Elliott sitting in a cast chair, instead of being lovingly taped to her wall where he's supposed to be.

My mom had received the e-mail announcing the casting of the last male lead, but she'd said it was someone else who—like Kimmi—was new to major productions. I was still curious of course, but with everything I had to do to get ready to move here, and then unpacking, catching up on homework, and studying the first script for *Coyote Hills,* going online to search for the name Jake Elliott slipped my mind.

It will probably be a while until I can call Rachel, but she's gonna flip!

I'm dying to talk to her about Brett too, who—despite my best efforts to desensitize myself over the past few weeks—still made me light-headed when we met. And he's impossible to avoid. At the end of a studio tour, we enter a production room for our first table read, and McGregor instructs Brett to sit right next to me.

I can't put a complete sentence together.

I'm learning quickly that sudden stupidity is a pretty crappy thing to happen to you in front of the producers, directors, network execs, department heads, writers, and the entire cast—almost all of whom have smaller paychecks than I do and are likely wondering how a tongue-twisted airhead like me even got hired.

But it's Brett's fault that my brain is on vacation today. He won't stop talking to me.

It doesn't help that he's even more gorgeous in person: his eyes really are as blue as the Pacific Ocean, his hair is currently my favorite color of blond—as if the sun loves him so much that it decided to *live* in his hair—and his ever-changing facial expressions are beyond adorable. But why can't he just jump back into my dreams and stay there?

No more Hollywood guys, I remind myself. *It always ends badly. Always.*

Four long tables are arranged in a square, with twenty or so people around the outsides and about that many more scattered throughout the room. The first table read for a new series is a big deal, and just about everyone who plays a major part in the production is here. This is a chance for the powers-that-be to get a feel for how the actors plan to approach their characters, as well as an opportunity to get to know one another.

Kimmi looks over the variety of breakfast drinks—milk, juice, teas, coffee, and water—along with the fruit and pastry platters on the tables. She wrinkles her nose before turning to the first person she sees without a chair. "I need a Diet Coke," she says.

The guy, who is wearing a first assistant director name tag that Kimmi should be able to see as clearly as the rest of us, just stares at her a moment before leaving the room. First ADs don't typically go after Diet Cokes. On set, they're second in command. But Tyler returns with a Diet Coke anyway, and when McGregor notices this, he appears to be gritting his teeth. "It's time for official introductions," he finally says.

Once we've learned names and titles, McGregor asks everyone to open the binders in front of us and read the first two pages of the script for the first episode, just to ourselves. It's been revised a bit from the version I've been studying, but that's usually the case.

```
FADE IN:
INT. EDEN'S BEDROOM — DAY
Music blasting, we see EDEN as she slowly zips
a black leather boot past her knee. Her pleated
skirt is still inches higher. She looks into
a full-length mirror and likes what she sees.
Her father, CAL, walks past her open bedroom
door, backs up, and stops.


                     CAL
     There's still a dress code, Eden. Even for
                    juniors.


Eden smiles at the mirror again and unbuttons
one more button on her shirt.
```

                    EDEN
                   Uh-huh.

                    CAL
      It's the first day of school, and you already
          don't care if you're sent home again?

Eden stuffs her makeup, a brush, and a single
notebook into a large Louis Vuitton bag. Then
she plants a kiss on her father's cheek as she
passes him in the doorway.

                    EDEN
        I'm counting on it. There's a one-day sale
                   at Saks.

Cal's troubled eyes follow his princess down
the hall.

INT. COYOTE HILLS HIGH — CHRONICLE OFFICE — DAY
The new student editor of *The Coyote Hills
Chronicle*, BRYCE, sits eagerly in a chair,
organizing his desk. He lines up, perfectly,
a row of No. 2 pencils, then spots a silver
paper clip that is out of place. He moves it to
the appropriate paper clip compartment, one of
three, sorted according to size. The workspace
is all but sterile. Bryce looks everything
over and smiles. Both a butt and a backpack
land on his desk.

JUSTIN

I hear you get to boss me around this year.

Justin bites into a slice of buttered toast.
Bryce brushes off the crumbs that fall on his
desk.

BRYCE

You're the only one who volunteered to write
the sports section. So, yeah, I guess we're
stuck with each other.

Noticing Bryce's reaction to the crumbs, Justin
laughs and takes another messy bite of toast.

JUSTIN
(while he chews)
It's gonna be great, man.

EXT. COYOTE HILLS HIGH — FRONT STEPS — DAY
We see the inside of a large cardboard box.
It's empty. ZOOM OUT: reveal KASSIDY standing
above it, forcing a smile. In handwritten
block letters, the front of the box says PLEASE
DONATE YOUR EXTRA SCHOOL SUPPLIES TO NEEDY
CHILDREN. STUDENTS walk by, ignoring her.

KASSIDY
Um . . . anything would help, guys.

Kassidy hears a small thud below her. She looks
down, excited, only to find a used, stubby
pencil.

                    KASSIDY
        All right. I guess that's a start.

The ripping of paper from a spiral notebook
makes Kassidy look up again. A single sheet
floats down into the box. Written in the center
of the paper is a giant *L*.

Kimmi is first to speak. "Kassidy should at least flip someone
off as they walk away. Seriously, *who* will even relate to her? A
noble do-gooder? People like that have been extinct since the
Middle Ages."

"Interesting observation, Miss Weston," says McGregor. "Can I
hear some other opinions about Kassidy? I allow myself only two
pages of a script to hook the audience and introduce them to the
characters. So tell me, what have you already learned?"

Brett leans forward in his chair. "As that paper pointed out,
Kimmi—or, uh, *Kassidy*—is a loser with a capital *L*. At least that's
what everyone else thinks of her."

"Indeed," McGregor replies. "Mr. Elliott?"

At the mention of his name, Jake freezes and only his eyes
move as he glances around the room. Yep, everyone *is* staring at
him—just about every female in the studio, no matter her age, has
been staring all morning. I've even caught myself doing it a few
times.

I was wrong about his lips being airbrushed. Exactly as he is, Jake doesn't need a single pixel of digital enhancement. In fact, the combination of his dark brown hair, perfectly tanned skin, and jewel-like green eyes is nothing short of astonishing. Rachel will hit her head on the ceiling when I tell her that the 3-D version of The Bod is somehow, impossibly, even better. I mean, he's showing a lot less skin right now than usual, but still . . .

"Are you *giggling*?" Brett asks me.

I'm the one who freezes now. I guess I *was* giggling a little, thinking about delivering the news about Jake to Rachel.

But "Er, what?" is how I reply to Brett, because that's how girls who suddenly turn stupid talk. "Um, kinda?"

Jake answers McGregor. "Well, even on her first day of school, which might make another girl self-conscious or whatever, Kassidy is actually thinking about other, less fortunate people. So she's probably been into this peace, love, and happiness stuff for a while."

Huh. That's a smart observation. Could our Adonis actually have a brain too? He shrugs, and I notice the muscles on his neck and shoulders tensing. *Probably not.*

"You know, like she does charity work a lot," Jake says.

"Correct," McGregor replies. "And Miss Taylor?"

I realize I'm totally staring at Jake again, so I whip my head back to the producers' table. "Me? Yeah, sure. I love charity work. In fact, I'm starting my own foundation."

Someone puts his hand on my back and breathes into my ear. "He's still talking about Kimmi's character, not about *you*."

I turn to find Brett so close that our noses almost touch. I jerk away from him, and everyone laughs.

"Sorry!" Brett says. "I kinda have a problem with personal space. I ignore it."

My face feels like it must be fluorescent red—as in, glow in the dark. So much for making a grand announcement about the charity foundation I've been working on. The only problem is, I haven't come up with any unique ideas for what the foundation will support. There are plenty of worthy causes, but I want to do something that matters to me *personally*.

The most obvious choice, of course, is opening up a place called The Emma Taylor Center for Chronic Crush Detox. I can't possibly be the only girl in the world who keeps falling for guys who are just short of lethal, can I?

"Save the butterfly kisses for after work," Kimmi says, making me want to throw something at her. She's across the room, next to Jake, but I've been told I have a pretty good arm. "We need to fix my character," she goes on. "As I've expressed before, Kassidy needs more *dimension*. I'll be typecast for life if I play a friendless dweeb destined for the Peace Corps."

Everyone at the writing team table looks at one another, and McGregor chuckles. "That's one plotline we had yet to think of, Miss Weston. Thank you. I believe we'll have Kassidy try to save the dolphins as well. And while she's at it, a few gorillas."

"Oh yes, please do," Kimmi replies. "And don't forget to give me at least a dozen scenes where I can wrap my body around a tree."

"I hope she keeps talking," Brett whispers, motioning to the writers' table where pens are now dancing like happy little muses, taking notes. I just nod and gulp, because Brett keeps touching me—and his lips are, like, an *inch* away. "She's only digging a hole for herself."

His breath is warm and smells like peppermint Altoids.

"But Kassidy was forcing that smile, right?" I blurt out, trying to distract myself. "Which could mean she isn't entirely comfortable standing there with that donation box, but she's doing it anyway. That could say more about her than anything else."

"Because she has a higher purpose.than the rest of the high school scum," Kimmi adds.

"Perhaps she does," McGregor says. "She might even be the most important character on the show. Only time will tell."

Brett holds up a hand as if he's thought of something brilliant. "*Or*, Kassidy could turn out to be just as cliché as the actress who plays her. Resident diva, mean girl, ex-cheerleader who's stuck in her long-lost glory days. You name it."

"I was *never* a cheerleader!" Kimmi snaps.

She draws a sharp breath, poised to continue, but McGregor clears his throat and turns to Brett. "Mr. Crawford, cliché is the arsenic of television. Certainly you aren't meaning to imply that I've hired dull, predictable actors. If that were the case, *you* wouldn't be sitting here."

"Point taken!" Brett says.

The conversation continues about Kimmi and her character. I'm not sure how long, but when I look down at my binder, I've drawn about three hundred *X*s on a blank page. When McGregor switches to Brett's character, Brett nudges me. "Hey, Picasso, we're talking about your award-winning castmate now. Pay attention."

He's a player.

"Right," I say, not looking at him . . . ignoring him.

I begin to draw smiley faces instead.

The group comes to the conclusion that Brett's character, Bryce, is a perfectionist. He controls his world by placing its many pieces into tidy compartments. Each character has a connection to the semi-unsupervised and trouble-causing school paper, a central element for storylines in the series.

"You'll see as this season progresses," McGregor says, "that Bryce holds this group together with an astonishing ability to calm the storms of teenage life. He's certainly the most mature one of the group."

"Then no wonder you hired me," Brett says, making everyone crack up. "Since I couldn't be more like that."

Most people think McGregor was at least a little punch-drunk when he came up with his second-nature method for casting, but I like the theory behind it. I really do have a hidden vixen inside me that makes me want to stop being so appropriate all the time and ignore the potential consequences—which is likely the reason I'm attracted to guys who are bad for the *better* side of me. Does that mean Brett has a more responsible side of him wanting to get out?

"Now, Mr. Elliott," McGregor says, "let's discuss your character, Justin."

Jake sits a little straighter, but Kimmi doesn't even give him a chance to reply. "Wait a minute, I need to know something first," she says. "Why do all of these characters' names start with the same letter as the actors' names who play them? That's so weird."

Every time Kimmi phrases a question like this, the producers and studio execs narrow their eyes at her. Kimmi better catch on to that quick. She has the very false impression that because she's an actress, her face is higher on the totem pole than anyone else's. But a lot of these people were in this business before most of the cast was even born, and they have enough influence in this industry to kill our careers like bugs under their thumbs. *Squish.*

A gracious actor is a working actor—that's the best advice I've ever been given from an industry veteran. Or in layman's terms: don't be a brat.

Kimmi is lucky this time because McGregor seems amused. "Do you know, my dear, that I usually respond to that question by changing a character's name to something a little less appealing? Rather than Kassidy, for example, you could be called Kipper."

Kimmi's jaw literally drops.

"Ah, then maybe Karp. With a *K*."

She snaps her mouth shut.

"Or perhaps," McGregor goes on, "I could just explain that such a method of naming my characters helps me—a fading old man—to mentally attach the same first initial to one character and one actor. Yes, yes, I know that begs another question: What if I have two actors with the same first initial? Well then, I just change one of the *actors'* names—happens all the time in Hollywood." He has a playful gleam in his eye. "Jake over here used to be called Eddie."

"Yep, all my life, but then *Emma* screwed that up for me," Jake says. "My mom's having a tough time with the change, but she'll deal."

While my attention was on Jake, Brett had written something on my script: *Tucson is boring. Let's do something tonight.*

How can a heart flutter, stop, and then shoot into someone's throat in less than a second? I read the note again to make sure I didn't misunderstand.

"No?" Brett says. "Why are you shaking your head?"

I shook my head? Really? I said *no* to Brett Crawford? So easily?

"Justin is the type who likes to start fires, just for the fun of it," Kimmi says, so I guess we've moved on. But I didn't notice because I'm busy starting my own fire—burning Brett. My *former* laptop wallpaper guy. "He noticed that Bryce was bugged by the crumbs, so he took another bite of toast."

I write back: *Sorry. Tons of homework.*

Brett reads my reply and flicks my leg with the back of his hand. Then he turns to McGregor and says, "Justin doesn't just *start* a fire. He stirs it to see how hot it can get, and then he feeds it a gallon of gas."

"Exactly right," McGregor says. "Which leaves your character, Miss Taylor. What do we learn about Eden in the all-important first scene of the series?"

"Eden is a spoiled only child with nothing to do but shop and stick her nose into other people's business," Kimmi answers for me. "She justifies her bad habits by writing columns for the school paper on fashion and student affairs."

McGregor drums his fingers together. "Thank you, but in this first scene, we only know about the shopping bit of that," he tells Kimmi. "The rest isn't introduced until later."

"True, but I need a break. So there you go. That's what Eden is all about." Kimmi stands, but everyone else stays in their seats. She gives a little cough. "Is that okay?"

"It doesn't appear to matter," replies McGregor. "But I suppose we can take a twenty-minute break. When we return, we'll let Emma answer my question."

Before Brett can say another word to me, I grab my bag and take off. I need a place to hide—not just because of Brett, but because I have to tell Rachel about The Bod. She'll be so happy that she will put me into a good, normal mood.

But Brett's flip-flops are soon slapping on the concrete floor behind me. "Hey! What's up with you, Taylor?" he says. I pretend like I don't hear him and walk even faster, heading for the restrooms. When he speaks again, he's closer. Too close. "Why are you ignoring me?"

He stops just short of following me into the women's bathroom. My hand is already on the doorknob. "I just need to . . . um, make a call," I say.

"In the bathroom?"

I shrug and try to avoid eye contact. In his well-worn navy tee, Brett looks too much like a poster I used to have of him. He announced to the group earlier that his ultra-casual beach attire—including board shorts—is due to not hiring a housekeeper yet, who will eventually be unpacking his moving boxes. So this morning, he'd just grabbed something from the first box he opened.

Yes, Brett is extremely nice to look at, and oozes a confidence that always catches my attention, but I didn't picture him being so spastic; he can't sit still—constantly touching me, for example—for longer than fifteen seconds. Now that I think about it, he reminds me of a boy who used to sit behind me in the second grade and flip paper footballs at my back.

"Our dressing rooms aren't ready yet," I tell Brett, surprising myself with a complete sentence. "And I have to call my best friend."

"Oh, chick stuff." He brushes his bangs to the side. "Look, I'm sorry you got dragged into that hot tub crap earlier. It sorta got out of control."

I let go of the restroom doorknob. "Yeah. What was that all about?"

He hesitates, brushing his hair to the other side now, as if he isn't sure which side it's supposed to be on. "Kimmi will probably tell you a villainized version of it, so I might as well fill you in on how it really happened," he says. "When I first saw her this morning, I thought she was someone who I . . . well, once met in a hot tub. Then, you know, spent some time with in a really awesome suite at the Hard Rock Hotel—oops, I don't think I said that part before." He laughs, eyeing me like I should be laughing too. "Anyway, I was wrong. It wasn't Kimmi. But whoever that Vegas girl was, she must have *looked* like Kimmi."

I am *sooo* not laughing. This story isn't a far-fetched *Celebrity Seeker* article. I'm hearing it straight from Brett himself, and he's clearly not the least bit ashamed of treating girls like . . . throwaway party favors.

"Wow," I reply. "For once, someone really is as bad as the tabloids say he is."

"No, I promise, I'm not!" It's the first time I've seen Brett with anything close to a serious expression. "I've only been *half* that bad. And McGregor says I need to be a freaking choirboy now if I want to keep this job. But I've really been no worse than guys even you've dated. In fact, I could tell you things about them that—"

"Brett," I say, feeling something like ice cubes sliding down my back. Definitely not the good kind of chills. "If you've heard anything at all about my dating history, you'd know that it's a bad idea to compare yourself to my ex-boyfriends."

"Whoa, whoa, whoa," he tells me, holding his hands up between us. "Don't get the wrong idea. I figured that's why you were avoiding me, but I'm not saying all this because I want you to think I'm worthy dating material. I don't date girls I work with anymore. I haven't for years."

I relax again. "Neither do I. Date coworkers, I mean. Never again."

A smile jumps back onto his face. "I just hope we can hang out—with Jake too, or whoever. Well, not Kimmi. But I'm going to be *bored to death* in Tucson if you don't stop ignoring me. And it isn't fair for you to judge me as a potential *friend* based on my crappy dating record. Because you'll never hear anyone say that I'm a bad friend."

I swallow, a little ashamed of myself. This is Brett Crawford, after all, someone who I've studied, judged, and evaluated in more ways than I'd ever admit to him. Being his friend hasn't even crossed my mind until now.

"That's probably true," I tell him. "But if the tabloids have even been half right about you, I doubt that what you've been doing with girls can actually be called *dating*."

I expect him to laugh, but Brett's face turns serious again. "How would they know if I've ever really cared about someone?" he asks. "Why would *that* interest the tabloids? It would go against too many of the other stories they've told about me."

It seems like Brett wants to keep talking, but he doesn't. And I can't tell if my comment has made him sad, angry, or both. What I do know, however, is how it feels to be pigeonholed by the press as being so one-dimensional.

"I totally get that," I say, then hold out my hand. "So let's be friends."

Brett looks at my hand like he doesn't want to touch it. "Are you kidding?" he says, and pulls me into a bone-crushing hug.

For a moment I try to imagine that the guy with his arms wrapped around me is my computer wallpaper version of Brett Crawford. But I can't really picture him anymore.

It's like he just . . . never existed.

At last, I make it into the bathroom. I start to dial Rachel, but I realize I don't have enough time to tell her about Jake, listen to her scream for who knows how long, and then get back to the table read before McGregor sends a search party after me.

Besides, there's gotta be a more clever way to surprise Rachel.

JAKE

I'm freaking out a little. My cell shows three missed calls from my mom.

A year ago that wouldn't have bugged me. Moms do that kind of thing—call you over and over again until you pick up—but my mom must know I panic now. The last time I missed three straight calls from her number, I was on a catwalk in Paris.

When I called back later that day, her cell phone was answered by a neighbor who said he'd been trying to reach me because he had found my mom on the sidewalk, unconscious. It was the first time my mom ever really needed me, and I was halfway across the world.

While racing through the terminal to catch the next flight home, I was still shaking gold glitter out of my hair. That's when I decided that I truly, *passionately* hated modeling.

During our break from the table read, I head for somewhere

quiet. The best place I can find is a corner on the far side of the studio, away from the actual sets. It takes Mom five rings to pick up. "Good morning," she says. "I wanted to catch you before work to wish you luck, but you must've started early. Sorry if I interrupted."

I breathe easier. "Nah. I had to be here at seven. Everything okay?"

"Of course I'm okay." She says that, but her words sound more slurred than usual. She's probably just tired. "You're the one we need to worry about," Mom adds. "All this fame go to your head yet?"

That's one thing that hasn't changed a bit: Mom is just as sarcastic as ever. The fact that her stroke didn't affect her personality is all that should matter to me, but when her voice is different, and her face is different, and she can't move her arms all over the place when she talks, like she used to, I'm reminded every day that things will never be the same.

And I can only do so much to fix it.

"I'm just chillin' in a private cabana right now, surrounded by my entourage," I tell her. "And after work, I'm buying a high-rise penthouse so I can host parties every weekend. Which reminds me, I need parental supervision. When are you moving down here?"

I doubt either one of our opinions will budge on the matter of her living in Tucson now, rather than two hours away in Phoenix, but it's worth a try.

She laughs. "Jake, the only thing more pathetic than a young bachelor living with his mother is a mother clinging to her son. I'm happy here, and I'm also happy to be rid of you and your early morning trips to the kitchen in your boxers. So leave me alone about it."

I groan. "Fine. But you're missing out on my mad cooking skills."

"Thank heaven," she says.

We talk a bit longer, then I reply to a series of texts from my friends. It's still early, but they're probably already together, hanging out around the pool at Devin's house. When it's a hundred and ten degrees before noon on most days, swimming is one of your few choices for summer entertainment. It's either that or go to the mall, and we outgrew the mall years ago. Devin texts me first, but Mark and Sophie soon join what appears to be a coordinated attack:

Devin: Hey Fabio. Do you think she'll go out with me? Talk, dude. Tell me everything.

Me: About my job? It's okay.

Devin: EMMA TAYLOR you prick.

Me: Who?

Devin: I'm on my way to Tucson. You have two hours to live.

Mark: Ignore Devin. Emma will like me better. All her boyfriends have been blond.

Me: You actually pay attention to that stuff?

Mark: Yes, because I'm normal. You're a freak. Is she snobby?

Me: The blonde? Yes.

Mark: What blonde? There's a blonde?

Me: Yep. His name is Brett Crawford. He'll love you.

Mark: Elliott, I'm driving down with Devin to strangle your pretty-boy neck.

Me:	Stop obsessing about how pretty I am. It makes me uncomfortable.
Sophie:	You promised to text me a photo of Brett Crawford! I've been waiting all morning!
Me:	Sorry. He's wasted. Didn't think you'd want to see that.
Sophie:	LIAR! He so wouldn't do that at work.
Me:	He'd probably do that and a lot worse at work.
Sophie:	Crazy!!!!! Is he really drunk?
Me:	Nah. Just unusually stupid.
Sophie:	You've ruined my day :(:(:(
Me:	I'll make it up to you. Want to meet Emma Taylor sometime?
Sophie:	YES!!!!!!!!!!!!!!!!!
Me:	You'll like her.
Sophie:	Oops. I just told Mark and Devin that you're gonna introduce me to Emma. You're in trouble.
Me:	So I've heard. Remind them that they have Pixy Stix for arms.

I look up from my phone when a PA calls everyone back to the table read. The info dump this morning has been a bit overwhelming, but there's been plenty to hold my attention—one thing in particular.

Yeah, I might've promised Devin and Mark that I'd check out Emma for them and eventually talk them up or whatever. But that was before I met her.

EMMA

McGregor wraps at four, way earlier than we'll usually get to go home, which is great because I have a crazy anthropology paper due at the end of the week and I haven't so much as found a topic for it yet. I've been too busy moving and trying to get over my crush on a guy I hadn't even met—pretty lame, considering that all I really needed to do was meet him.

Brett's jabs at Kimmi throughout the day became seriously ridiculous, but when it came time to read lines . . . wow. He plays his part like Bryce truly is another side of him. In fact, for a first read, *everyone* was amazing. McGregor's smile was ear to ear by the end of it.

My ability to talk was at least kicked up a notch after my chat with Brett in the hall. But apparently my brain cells are still popping like soap bubbles because now I can't find my call sheet—an actor's daily bible—so I have no idea what time I'm supposed to be here tomorrow. And this only adds to the long list of idiotic things I've done today.

Every PA in sight already looks swamped, so I stop by the production office on my way out. A girl with spiky strawberry hair stands behind a desk. She looks like she's only a few years older than I am, but I can't tell for sure because she is hidden by stacks of folders. "Sorry to bother you," I say.

The girl straightens in a hurry, and I catch a glimpse of her badge—her name is Mandy. "Um, hi . . . Miss Taylor," she says with a wobble in her voice.

"Call me Emma," I reply, using an overly cheery tone. As Kimmi just proved in our table read, film crews put up with as much crap as zookeepers, so it's easy to understand why Mandy feels the need to be cautious. The majority of people in this industry are actually pretty cool, though; it's just that those who are the most obnoxious usually get the most attention. "I stopped by to give you my new cell number. And can I also have another call sheet?"

"Sure!" Mandy says, more at ease. There must be a method to the madness on her desk because just a few moments later, she pulls out a folder labeled CAST INFO. "Let's start with your number." She flips over the first set of papers, Kimmi's stuff. Jake's info is next, then mine. She writes down my new number and puts everything back into the folder. "Okay, a call sheet. Where, where, where . . ." After a minute or so of looking, she says, "Sorry, I'll be right back."

The second Mandy leaves, I snatch up the contact info.

Cast files contain private information like addresses and phone numbers, so they're completely off limits to all but a few crew members. But bios are part of each actor's set of papers, and I now know exactly how to tell Rachel about Jake.

She'll love me forever.

My heart races as I dig through my bag for my cell. Then I find just the main page of Jake's bio—I'm not stupid enough to give Rachel his address—and snap a picture of it with my phone. It turns out blurry. And so does the next shot. And the next.

What's the point if Rachel can't actually see the small photo of Jake in the corner of the bio, and read the details below it—his name, birthday, height, weight, eye and hair color, work history? *Crap!* I'm too set on the idea to give up, so I take a calming breath, hold really, really still, and try one last picture. It's perfect!

"Um . . . is that my bio?"

I whirl around to find Jake standing only inches from me. "Uh . . . *no,*" I reply, blindly stuffing his bio back into its folder. "It's mine. I was curious about what my agent sent over."

He's giving me one of those smiles that suggests he's flattered by my *interest.* "That's weird," he says. "Because I was just walking by the door here and saw you holding a sheet of paper with my name and face on it."

How immature would it be to kick him in the shin and then run?

Okay, Emma Taylor, are you an actress or what? Start acting!

"All right, you caught me," I say with a shrug. "I took pictures of everyone's cast bios so I can check them out when I get home. But now I feel totally stupid about it."

"Don't. That's actually a good idea," Jake replies, reaching for the folder that I've hidden behind my back. But I twist around so he can't get it. I have to return the folder to its pile before Mandy sees me with it. "What's wrong? Did your agent send a bad photo of you or something?"

"No! It's just that . . . you know, I'm a *girl.*" Jake is still reaching and I'm still twisting—one side then the other—and I'm now on the verge of giggling, which has already happened way too many times today. "So I don't want you to see how much I weigh. *Duh*."

This causes him to step back, and I take the opportunity to slip the folder into a stack of identical files. "Seriously?" he says. "You're about the same size as Tinker Bell."

That would have made me smile, but now I'm worried he'll think I really am self-conscious about my weight, and he might tell other people. Then I'll end up on a cover with a STARVING HERSELF! banner over my head.

Again.

I have very little time to clear this up. "Okay, I don't actually care about my weight," I admit. "And I really did take a photo of just your bio. But it isn't for me. It's for a friend."

Jake nods. "The classic 'it's for a friend' story."

Before I realize it, I've backhanded his chest—a totally flirty thing to do, which negates everything I'm trying to tell him. So now I have to explain even more.

"Get over yourself," I say. "Her name is Rachel, and she's been collecting your ads for at least a year. But she hasn't known who you are, which is why I couldn't stop laughing when I saw you this morning. It's just a funny coincidence that we've ended up working together." This is all said so quickly that I doubt Jake understands much. "That's the truth. I promise."

"So . . . this is the 'mutual friend' you said we have?"

"Exactly! You just haven't met her yet. She's amazing."

Jake leans back on the desk, his biceps tensing against the sleeves of his T-shirt, which is about the same color as his dark hair. He looks like a Hershey's chocolate bar, waiting to be grabbed off the shelf. And once again I notice that his lips are freaking unbelievable.

Holy crap, I'm totally checking him out again. *For Rachel. Only for Rachel.*

"Where does she keep the ads?" Jake asks. "In some kind of scrapbook?"

"No, nothing that formal." I can't tell if Jake truly wants to know, or if he's a little creeped out. But I hadn't meant to make Rachel look stupid. "They're just taped to her wall. Like, you know, posters."

Jake stays quiet, his eyes locked on me. "Darn," he finally says. "If a full collection of my work could be found in a single book, I'd love to get my hands on it. And burn it."

An embarrassing blast of noise escapes my mouth. It's my genuine laugh, the one I can't help when I'm caught off guard by something I find truly funny. Directors ask me for it all the time, but I can't imitate it on film, no matter how hard I try. Some things can't be faked.

"Didn't we just discuss your character, Justin, wanting to burn stuff?" I ask.

He nods. "Especially the cowboy ads. I'd torch every one of them."

"No, not those!" I beg. "Your boots were so *cool.*"

Jake is laughing now too. "The boots weren't the problem."

"Was it the hat?" He knows where I'm going with this— low-rider leather chaps, hello!—and he's shaking his head, looking a little desperate.

"That's a great place to stop," he says. "Right there."

Mandy walks through the door and jolts. Her expression

suggests that she's afraid she's interrupted . . . well, flirting, or something. "Oh! Do you need a call sheet too?" she asks Jake.

"No thanks, I've got one," he says, totally composed. Didn't *he* see how Mandy looked at us? "Emma's just saying how much she liked my photo shoot in cowboy chaps."

I hit him again. *Get a grip, Emma.* Gossip spreads so fast in studios.

"What do you think, Mandy?" I ask her. "Is Jake's big head gonna fit back through your doorway?"

Jake looks confused. "It's my *biceps* I'm worried about."

The same biceps I've been admiring.

I need to get out of here, right now. For several reasons. "Sorry, guys, I've gotta go. I have *so* much homework."

Mandy gives me a new call sheet, and I thank her. I'm about to say good-bye to Jake when he tells Mandy, "See ya tomorrow," and follows me out. "I've wanted to ask you about sch—" Jake starts to say, but I speak at the same time.

"Maybe you could sign a few of your ads, or whatever, for Rachel? That is, if you have some extra magazines sitting around."

"Nooo. Not a single one," he replies, walking a step behind me. "But I do have a whole box of headshots in my car. I guess I could sign some of those."

This gets me laughing again. "You keep a *box* full of headshots in your car?"

"Doesn't everyone?"

Wait, he could be serious. New actors are notorious for carrying around their headshots, especially in L.A. and New York, just in case they meet someone who's influential in the business. But Jake doesn't seem like the type to do that.

I glance over my shoulder, wondering if I've misread him—it wouldn't be the first time—and come just shy of smacking into the metal door that leads to the parking lot.

Jake reaches around me and pushes the door open just in time. "It's not what you think," he says, and I'm pretty sure he noticed that he saved me from a broken nose.

"Miss Taylor!" someone shouts. Jake and I both pause in the doorway and turn back. The transportation guys who picked me up this morning are walking toward us.

"Hey!" I reply with an awkward wave. "I'll be ready in just a sec, okay?"

Jake practically has his arm around me, propping the door open, and I feel the heat of the Arizona sun on my back. "I can run you home," he says, loud enough for the transpo guys to hear. They stop a few feet away from us. "I have to give you those photos anyway."

"Right . . . ," I begin, but I need a moment to think.

I don't get time, though, because one of the transpo guys immediately says, "Whatever, that's cool." And the other adds, "We'll see you tomorrow!" Then they stroll back down the hall.

Jake opens the door a little wider, and I step through.

"Are you sure you don't mind?" I ask as I follow him out to his car. It's a black BMW convertible—nice, but not usually the car of an egomaniac. I've taken rides in enough of those to know. I prefer to go totally casual in my red-and-white MINI Cooper. "I live in Sabino Canyon."

"No problem. I've heard it's nice up there." Jake pops his trunk and glances back at the studio. "One of those drivers looked pretty ticked off that I stole you. He might have a crush."

"Nah," I reply. "I'm sure they're both perfectly happy that

you've cut an hour out of their workday. Besides, it's a bad idea to date crew members."

"Yeah?" Jake says. "What about cast members?"

The way he looks at me, with just a hint of a smile, makes my insides flip over. *What?* I'm hopeless.

"Twice as stupid," I reply, showing zero signs of interest. None.

Jake shrugs and reaches for a box in his trunk. "Just curious."

JAKE

Emma has worked her way under my skin in one day flat, but I can't blame her for steering clear of guys she works with. It doesn't take being in celebrity circles to know how that's turned out for her in the past.

The sun is behind her, making her glow like some sort of offering from heaven, but I decide not to point that out. "So . . . which photos do you want?" I ask, flipping through a stack of my headshots. There are eight different shots—total overkill, but that's what the studio asked for—and I'm channeling an arrogant prick in most of them. "For your *friend*, I mean."

She smiles up at me, almost a full foot above her. "Maybe I could just give her the whole box. Or at least half. You seem to have plenty."

"Yeah, but as I said, it's not what you think." I better explain. "You see, the studio asked my agent to send a freakish amount of these things for fan mail purposes—like I'm gonna get any of that—and since I'm such a nice guy and happened to be in New York a week ago, I offered to deliver the first box myself because my agent was going sorta nuts with a new client named Trixie, or Pebbles, or some other variation on a breakfast cereal that I can't remember." I need to take a breath. "Anyway, I'm just doing my agent a favor."

Emma tips her head. "Is she hot?"

"My agent?" Liz is the female version of RoboCop—part human, part machine.

"No, Trixie or Pebbles," Emma replies. "And is that who taught you how to talk in such long sentences? It had to be a girl."

I laugh. "I have a bossy older sister who talks *nonstop*."

"Enough said." Emma holds out a hand, and I give her the stack of photos. She won't last out here much longer, on a blacktop in the middle of an Arizona summer. I grew up in the blazing heat, spent my entire childhood with red dirt in my hair, but it isn't easy on beginners.

Emma takes one of each photo and returns the rest of the stack.

We talk about our day for the first fifteen minutes of the drive, then compare Arizona—she's surprised when I tell her I'm actually from here—and Arkansas. "I'm still trying to get used to the idea that our household pests are cockroaches," she says, "and yours are scorpions."

Why are girls so easy to torment?

"I hate to tell you this," I say, "but we have a lot worse than scorpions here. Over a dozen species of rattlesnakes, for example. And Gila monsters are also rather deadly. Massive tarantulas. Bears. Mountain lions." The pink in Emma's cheeks is slowly fading. "In fact, I'm pretty sure that the only scary thing we *don't* have in Arizona is great white sharks."

Emma shivers but keeps her focus straight on the road ahead, giving me a perfect profile to look at. No wonder I've been in a daze all day.

I should probably pay closer attention to the road myself.

"But," she says, her smile returning, "Tucson also has the prettiest birds I've ever seen. Hummingbirds seem as common as houseflies, and a cactus almost always has a woodpecker tapping on it. I've even seen a pelican." Emma turns with an expression of disbelief. "A *pelican*, in Arizona. So overall, I can't help but love it here."

"Me too," I reply. From a distance the towering mountains give Tucson a different look than Phoenix, but the dry, hot air and desert landscape still make it feel like home. "My favorites are the bright-red cardinals."

"They're amazing, right? Like flutters of fire, shooting through the sky."

I can't believe we're talking about birds and I'm not bored out of my head. "You're kinda different than I thought you'd be," I admit. "In a good way."

She seems surprised by the comment and glances away. "People rarely think I'm anything like I really am." Her tone makes me wonder if I've hit a sensitive topic. I want to know more, but when she turns back, she says, "I suppose I judge strangers too. For instance, I told Rachel that you were most likely stupid, *definitely* a jerk, and worst of all, airbrushed."

"Good guess," I say. "But I'm only a jerk on Tuesdays. Stupid, occasionally. And airbrushed . . . well . . . there's no escaping that dark magic."

Emma laughs. "So true. Sometimes they even put a twinkle in my eye."

We're in Sabino Canyon now, at the base of the Catalina Mountains. There are a couple of golf courses in the distance and gated communities all along the road. The thing that really catches my attention, though, is the river—definitely a rare sight in the desert. And there are more leafy trees in Sabino Canyon than I've seen in all of Arizona put together.

Emma's phone beeps, and she ignores it. A few seconds later, I hear my own text message tone. My phone is on the armrest between us; we both glance down to find a message from Brett: **Dinner for the principal cast at 8. El Loro Feliz. Tanque Verde Rd.**

"Dang," Emma says. "I really need to work on a paper."

Dinner means I'll see her later on, but now is a better chance to ask about school. "McGregor told me you're already a couple of years into college," I say. "Shouldn't you have just graduated from high school?"

She nods. "I marched with my original class in May, but I actually finished about a year and a half ago. My last on-set tutor put me on an acceleration plan, so yeah, I'm almost a junior."

"But how do you go to school with such a busy schedule?"

"My classes are all taught online. You'll see me studying at work. Tons."

I graduated from high school early too, and have considered online courses, but it doesn't seem like they'd be the same. "Will you eventually have to take campus classes?" I ask.

"I need to choose a major before I'll know. It's taking me forever to decide because I want to learn about *everything*."

Emma motions to the entrance of *Paraiso del Rio,* just ahead.

I pull up to the front gates, and a security guard peers through my open window. "Good evening, Miss Taylor," he says. "Is this a guest we should expect on a regular basis?"

Emma gives me a scrutinizing look, but she doesn't get the opportunity to make a wisecrack. "Hi, I'm Jake Elliott, her best friend with benefits," I tell the guard. "So, yeah, I'll be here *a lot*."

He laughs and waves us on.

I punch the gas pedal, and Emma smacks my arm. "Now I'll definitely tell them to watch out for you. There's a reason I moved here; it's like Fort Knox."

She's right. Even after we make it past the guard, we're met by an additional gate leading into the next section of the community. I stop at the keypad and turn to her for instructions. Emma hesitates, then says, "Excuse me for a moment, but I'm gonna have to get a little up close and personal."

She releases her seat belt, plants one of her knees on my arm-rest, and leans all the way across me so she can enter the code. She isn't exactly indecent, but I can't help but notice the obvious. "Versace, huh?"

It takes Emma a few tries to get the code right. When the gate finally opens, she comes back through the window and pauses when our faces are even. "I don't recall giving you permission to look at my butt."

"Uh . . . sorry?" I reply. "I'll get my people to call your people the next time your butt is the only view I have." She sits back down, and I drive forward. "And I only noticed the label because I did some work for them a while back."

Why do I feel like I have to *try* to impress her?

"Cool," she says. "Did they give you freebies?"

"Of course—I always work free clothes into a deal. And I really like their ties."

She seems intrigued. "How often do you wear a tie?"

I shrug. "If I'm home on the weekends, I go to church with my mom."

Emma smiles. "My parents would freak if I wore Versace to

church. We go to this tiny country chapel outside of Fayetteville. The fanciest thing I'm allowed to wear is a feathered hat."

I picture her as a true Southern belle, not in a movie but in her actual life, and I have to resist an impulse to touch her. I try to keep a straight face when I say, "Only my ties are Versace. My suits are by Armani."

"Gosh!" Emma says, but it comes out like *gawsh*. Talking about her home has brought out a hint of a drawl, and it makes me laugh. "That's a serious clash of the Titans."

The recreation area of her community has a tennis court, a couple of pools under canopies of palm trees—one with a waterfall—and a fitness center. Next, we drive into the residential section, which has part of the river running through it. And . . .

"Whoa," I say. "Is that a running path?"

"Yep. Nice, huh?"

It's more than nice. "How long is it, do you know?"

"Two miles is what I've heard, but I haven't tried it yet." Emma shoots her hand out. "Right here. Number sixteen."

I pull in front of the Southwest-style town house she points to. "This is huge for just one person," I say. I've spent the past few days looking for a place to live, so I'm getting good at guessing size from the outside. The sooner I get out of my stuffy hotel room, the better. "Does your family live here too?"

"Nope. I'm on my own. And I love it."

I turn my engine off because I want to keep talking. "Do you have brothers or sisters?"

Emma's eyes are instantly brighter. "Seven-year-old twin brothers. My career is sort of on autopilot now, so my mom spends her days shuttling the boys between soccer, baseball, and basketball practices—whatever sport is in season. She has to keep them busy or they'll destroy the house. They're a hundred percent trouble, but still adorable."

"That's exactly what my sister says about *me*." How can Emma be so normal? Better than normal? "Do you need help with furniture, or boxes, or whatever? I could—"

"Thanks, but everything's pretty much done." She's already halfway out the door. "And I really appreciate the ride. Hope it didn't take too much time."

"Not at all."

She doesn't reply, just smiles and shuts the door. What am I thinking? Emma Taylor is way out of my league. But I like a challenge.

She turns back to say good-bye, then stops waving when she notices my license plate. "YA I NO?" She laughs. "As in, 'Yeah, I know I'm hot'?"

My friends haunt me wherever I go.

I lean out my window to say, "It was a stupid joke—a birthday present from my buddies." My mom thought the idea was so hilarious, she helped them with the online application. "Getting a new plate is at the top of my priority list."

Emma walks back to my side of the car, looks down at me with a lingering glimmer of humor in her eyes, and pats my arm. "That's your top priority, huh? Then what you *actually* need is a reality check."

Definitely a challenge. "I think I just met one."

EMMA

Oh, crap . . . how bad did I flirt with Jake? A lot? Only a little? I close my eyes tightly and pretend I don't have to ask myself that question. Besides all of my own reasons to keep my distance, Rachel would never forgive me for even *thinking* about Jake.

Not like this.

I collapse onto my sofa and watch my ceiling fan go around and around and around. *It was nothing*, I finally tell myself. When two people first meet, they kind of joke around, that's all. And Jake is easy to talk to.

That's another thing Rachel will be happy to hear.

I grab my bag off the floor and fish out my phone. But while I'm thinking through exactly what I'll say to Rachel, I also find myself zooming in on the details of Jake's bio. His modeling credits began a little more than two years ago with lesser-known labels, and then designers like Versace and Armani discovered him. With such a red-hot start, why would Jake switch to acting so soon?

And what was with all the questions? Hardly anyone, especially a guy, ever asks me about school or my family. Jake didn't even seem superficial about it. He's both an open book and an intriguing mystery. A mystery I sort of want to figure out.

Wait . . . no.

No. No. No.

I *don't* want to figure him out, because what if I like what I discover? What is *wrong* with me? Jake belongs in Rachel's fantasies, not my reality. I send her a text: **Are u at home or in public where you might break someone's eardrums?**

Rachel replies with: **Home. WHY?**

There's no changing my mind now, so I send her the picture of Jake's bio.

While waiting for her reaction, I steal a few glances at Jake's headshots and can't decide if I should tell Rachel that I was wrong about his lips being digitally enhanced. I already know it would be a bad idea to describe the rest of him.

My cell rings and I brace myself for hysterical squealing, but all I hear is quick, heavy breaths. "Model ID Hotline," I answer. "Can I help you?"

"Em . . . ma," Rachel says, still panting. "It's hiiiimmmm!"

"Uh-huh."

"How did you get this? I've looked *everywhere,* for *anything.* This has his name, his height, his weight!" There's a pause. "Oh my gosh, both of our birthdays are in December! And he's only one year older than I am! I *never* would've guessed that from his photos."

Me either. But Jake has a younger quality about him in person. He lacks the sharp edge of arrogance that's so common in his magazine ads, which makes him even more attractive.

"Dang, they didn't list his e-mail or phone number on here," Rachel says, instantly devastated. "I wonder if he's on Facebook. Do you think he tweets?"

I laugh. "No idea. But . . . he's in the cast of *Coyote Hills*, so I can ask him."

That's when I should've known to throw the phone away from my ear.

"Shut up! Shut up! No way!" Rachel goes on and on until she says she's dizzy. "What's he like? Tell me evvverything!"

It doesn't matter what I say. I could tell Rachel that Jake has the personality of a boiled potato and smells like sardines, and it wouldn't change anything. "Well, you were right," I admit. "He's actually pretty cool, and he even gave me a stack of headshots for you."

Another shriek. "Did he sign them?"

"Um—" Crap! We got talking and I forgot to have him sign the photos. "I wasn't sure what you wanted him to write," I say, already spinning lies. "You know, just your name, or *To my favorite fangirl*. What do you think?"

"Oh . . . that's a tough one," Rachel says. "I don't want The Bod—I mean, Jake—to think I'm psychotic. So I guess you could just have him write *Can't wait to meet you,* or whatever. How many did he give you?"

"Let me see." I thumb through the photos, and as I count out loud, Rachel's vocal pitch increases with each number. "Seven," I finish.

I slip my favorite headshot inside a side table drawer.

"Seven? I can't believe this!"

Neither can I. *Naughty, Emma.* I yank open the drawer. "Wait, there's one more."

The jubilation just keeps on coming. For probably fifteen more minutes, Rachel asks questions about Jake, and I try to answer them in the most complete way I can without revealing that I learned most of the information from a private conversation with him in his car.

I'm desperate to change the subject. "I met Brett today," I eventually throw in.

"Who?" Rachel asks. "Oh! Brett Crawford! Did you faint, or what?"

"Close. I couldn't even look at him for a while. But he followed me when we had a break, so I *had* to talk to him. Then things were okay. And after all these years of being gaga over him, it's nice to know once and for all that the real Brett is *totally* not my type."

"Whatever! He's like every other guy you've ever dated."

"Um, duh. That's my point."

"Don't *duh* me. Tell me about him."

I skip the part when Brett wowed the room during our table read, and instead talk about his immature comments to Kimmi.

"Okay, so he's stupid. No shocker," Rachel says. "But he wasn't a jerk to *you*, right?"

"No. But it doesn't matter."

"Of course it matters, because you already know you'll eventually date him. How could you not? So you've gotta make it clear, right from the start, that you won't put up with the same crap your other boyfriends gave you."

I almost laugh. As if *telling* a guy not to break your heart—or embarrass you in front of the entire world—would actually make him think twice about it. "Brett doesn't date his costars, anyway," I reply. "He straight out told me that today."

"But, Emma," Rachel says, her tone sweeter now, "if anyone can change his mind, it's you. And Brett's gotta be interested if he followed you around. So I *honestly* think if you just turn on your charm, he'll become whoever you want him to be."

She reads too many trashy romance novels. "Thanks for your vote of confidence, my friend, but I'm not interested in a makeover project."

Rachel sighs. "Fine. Then just promise that you'll find another date for when I come out for the premiere. Don't you think it would be so much fun to double?"

"To . . . *what*?"

"Double date, of course!" she says. " 'Cause you've gotta set me up with The Bod, right? Please, please, please! You have to!" I am dead silent, but Rachel doesn't wait for my answer before she continues. "I mean, it doesn't have to be a date to the premiere—I don't want him to feel weird about introducing me on the red carpet and stuff. But sometime that weekend would be perfect!" She squeals. "Oh my gosh! What if we, like, totally fall in love?"

Yeah, seriously. What if . . .

"Um, don't be mad at me, okay?" I finally reply. "But I just barely met Jake, so I should probably get to know him a little better before I ask him if he'll take you out."

Rachel is the one who's quiet now. Then, "Please don't put it *that* way. Say something more like, 'My best friend is coming out for the premiere and I *know* you'll love her.' "

"But he could have a girlfriend. I have no idea." Maybe he does. Jake sort of dropped a hint that he was interested in me, but . . . now that I think of it, he could've been curious about dating *any* castmate, not me in particular. "Or worse, maybe he's a player," I tell Rachel. "Don't you want me to figure that out first?"

"He didn't say he has a girlfriend, did he?" There's panic in her voice. "And you said that he's way cool, so why would you think he's a player?"

There's no possible way to talk her out of this. "Just give me enough time to scratch 'serial killer' off the list, okay?"

Rachel laughs . . . kind of. It's the nervous giggle she does when something isn't quite right. "I guess so. Just don't get to know Jake *too* well," she says. "You've always had that wicked little way of stealing a guy's attention from me."

"Oh, ha-ha-ha." A rock grows in my throat and drops to the pit of my stomach. "That hasn't happened since junior high."

"Maybe," she replies. "But only because we haven't hung out with the same guys since then. And remember, The Bod is all mine, so don't you dare forget it."

I couldn't if I wanted to.

JAKE

"Well, that was quick," the manager of Sabino Haven says as he hands over the key to my new condo. He probably thinks I'm leasing it on a whim, but I've already checked out plenty of other options, so this was an easy decision. "I don't get a lot of young kids looking for two-bedroom, wheelchair-accessible units," the guy adds with a smile. "But that's real thoughtful of you to consider visits from your mom. When are you moving in?"

"Soon, I hope." Most of my days away from the studio are already booked for the next few months because I'm still contracted for ten or so modeling jobs in New York. But I'm trying to free up a weekend to move my stuff down from Phoenix. "I'll at least have some furniture delivered this week."

"Sounds good," the manager says as he files away my lease papers. "And for marketing purposes, we'd like to know how you found us."

I gesture out the window. "I was dropping off a friend at *Paraiso del Rio* when the running path caught my attention." Living right down the road from Emma might make her question my motives, but Sabino Canyon feels like a private island, and I need somewhere to run. Treadmills do nothing for me. "I have to keep in shape for my job."

The manager pats his round belly. "A lot of good the path's done me, but you'll enjoy it. It follows the river through several attached communities, all secure." He joins me at the window where the setting sun paints the sandstone courtyard with orange and gold, and a giant saguaro cactus stands like a bouncer at the entrance. "Not bad, huh?"

"It's perfect."

Brett calls after I leave my new place to make sure I'll be at the dinner. He says McGregor tore into him for harassing Kimmi today—making her even harder to deal with—so Brett asked for all of our numbers, and this is his attempt at playing nice.

McGregor also told Brett that *El Loro Feliz* has the best Mexican food around. That's really saying something in Tucson, where a cantina can be found on just about every city block. And it's a good thing the place came with such a high recommendation because the inside looks more like a cheap tie-dyed T-shirt—red, yellow, and green—than a restaurant. The scattered plastic flowers don't help much, and the stuffed animal parrots are as cheesy as it gets. But the combined aromas of hot, handmade tortillas, sizzling fajitas, and fresh salsa . . .

They have me at *hola*.

I can't see Brett from where I stand at the entrance, but with a crowd in one corner it isn't hard to guess where he is. I hang back until all but one girl clears out. Her mom is taking pictures of her sitting next to Brett in a semicircular booth. His arm is around the girl.

"Hannah will be a senior this year," the mom says. Brett's grin grows even wider when the stick-skinny redhead leans closer. Her mom snaps another shot with her phone. "And she just dumped her boyfriend because he needs to grow up. Hannah is *very* mature for her age."

I sit on the opposite side of the table, watching for signs that this lady's shameless marketing of her daughter comes off as disgusting to Brett as it does to me. But he just smiles and takes it all in; Brett is probably the president of his own fan club. "Okay, gotta do some guy talk now," he finally says, dropping the hint like an anvil. "It was cool to meet you, Heidi."

"Hannah," both the mom and daughter correct him, giggling. They compare autographed napkins as they walk off.

"Dude," I tell Brett, "you need *help.*"

"You volunteering?" His hand shoots up. "Kimmi!"

The whole place turns to see who Brett yelled at, and most keep watching as Kimmi slinks toward us. She's wearing an even shorter skirt now, with a silver sequined top and a different pair of stilettos. Strings of diamonds hang from her ears. "I told you it was casual!" Brett says when she reaches our table. "You look . . . sparkly! Great, I mean."

"Save it." Kimmi motions for Brett to move so she can sit between us in the booth. I need to remember to stand first when Emma shows up, so she'll sit next to me instead of Brett.

Did I just come up with a *plan* to get a girl to sit by me? What am I, twelve years old? I grab a plastic pitcher from the table and pour myself a tall glass of water.

"I'm sorry about today, all right," Brett tells Kimmi. "You just . . . made me look stupid. In front of the entire crew."

"You made *me* look like trash!" Kimmi snarls. "Everyone knows you only hook up with bimbos. You couldn't get another type of girl if your life depended on it."

Brett appears genuinely offended and is dumb enough to turn to me for backup. I shrug at him. "Sorry, man. I've only known you for a day and you've already convinced me that you're all charm and no finesse. And cheap swagger gets you cheap girls."

"Exactly," Kimmi says, flipping her menu open. A waitress had dropped off menus and water during Brett's fan frenzy, but since then she's been huddled with three other waitresses, doing little more than glancing over their shoulders at our table. "And sorry to disappoint, but there *are* a few females left in this world who have some self-respect."

Brett's eyes flicker between us. "You guys are seriously messed up if you think I have a problem picking up women. Or even . . ." He thinks for a sec. "Or even *good* girls, okay? Whenever I want to."

Kimmi's attention turns to the waitress heading for our table with bowls of chips and salsa. "Jake," she says, "show Brett what you mean by finesse. Get her number, *without asking.*"

"No way," I reply. "I don't flirt on demand."

Brett laughs. "C'mon, dude. Let's see whatcha got."

I don't have time to answer before the waitress, different from the one who brought us menus, is at our table. "I need a Diet Coke," Kimmi tells her. "Light on the ice. With a straw."

"Sure." The girl looks at Brett and gives him a starstruck smile, but then she gives *me* a double take. I feel a little smug about that. Just a little. "How are you guys doing tonight?"

"You already asked me that," Brett says, attaching his famous laugh. "I'm still doing great—as always."

The waitress points to her name tag. "I'm Tara. Nikki was the waitress you met earlier."

"Oops! My bad," Brett says. The other waitress is about six inches taller than Tara, and her hair is six inches shorter. But both are in the blond category, so I guess that can be kinda confusing for a guy who goes through girls like breath mints. "I should've taken a closer look at your name tag," Brett adds, his attention obviously drifting lower than where Tara had pointed.

This guy needs serious intervention. Maybe I *should* show him a thing or two.

The waitress takes half a step back, her expression clearly saying, *Slow down, perv.* "Anyway . . . I'm a big fan," Tara says. "We all are, so we drew straws for your table."

"Lucky me," Brett replies. As Kimmi and I continue to scan our menus, Brett tells Tara why he's in Tucson. He does a decent job plugging *Coyote Hills*, but doesn't mention anything about Kimmi or me. The waitress keeps glancing over at me anyway, and every time I return her look with a subtle smile. Brett ends with, "Emma Taylor is on the show too."

Tara literally gasps. "No way! Is she coming tonight?"

"Nah," Brett replies. "She got out of it at the last second. She had to write a lame school paper or something."

Great. Then what am I doing here?

"I need my Diet Coke, *right now*," Kimmi says.

"And a steak burrito," Brett adds. "For me, not her."

"I want a side salad, low-cal dressing, with pineapple tidbits, not chunks," Kimmi says.

The waitress squints an eye at her. "Sorry, we don't have pineapple—tidbits *or* chunks. The salad has carrots and tomatoes."

"Just make sure the lettuce is crisp, or forget it," Kimmi snaps.

Tara writes it all down. When she turns to me, I give her a sympathetic sigh and say, "Hazards of the job."

I know Kimmi won't appreciate the dig, but this demonstration for Brett was her idea, so she'll have to be a pawn in it. Tara's smile grows wider. "I can't decide what to order," I go on. "It all looks *so* good."

"I'll show you my favorites." Tara leans over and takes her time about it. The way she describes every last ingredient and flavor, you'd think she was an infomercial chef.

Kimmi keeps squirming for her Diet Coke fix. Brett just crunches more ice.

"That sounds delicious," I say, as if the waitress has left me breathless from her perfect pitch of menu item #9—Smothered Nachos. Man, this is cruel, but it's for educational purposes. "And, uh . . ." I glance around. "I don't want to get you into trouble or anything, but if you could sweet talk the cooks into a little extra . . . I'm *really* hungry."

"You won't leave hungry, I promise," Tara says.

She struts off, and I give Brett a nod. "Done."

Brett spills salsa on his shirt. "Whatever. You didn't get her number."

"He will," Kimmi says as she watches the waitress. "So, what haven't I heard about you guys that's worth knowing?"

I really just want to get this dinner over with, so I look at Brett to prompt *him* to answer. And man, does he ever. He brags about his cars, his boats, his motorcycles, and surprisingly, his family. "My parents are my rock. They totally love me."

"How touching," Kimmi says.

Brett glares at her—his pretense of playing nice obviously wearing thin—and I would rather not referee a catfight, so I turn to Kimmi and bring up our mutual acting coach. "McGregor told me you were handpicked by Anne Mabley to audition for him."

Kimmi actually smiles, teeth and everything. "Of course. I've been her favorite student at MAPA from the day I started there. And since you studied with her too, you probably know that *five* of her students have gone on to win major film awards."

"And she thinks *you* are a future A-lister," Brett says.

My attention is still on Kimmi, waiting for her to reply, but then I realize where she and Brett are looking. "Anne said that about *me*?" I ask. "Why would she say *that*?"

"Good question," Kimmi replies. "She told me the same thing, which makes me curious. Why is she so sure of your success— are you really talented enough to put butts in seats, or is it just your abs?"

"His abs?" Brett asks. "Have you seen his pecs? They're crazy."

I've had my own doubts about my acting talent, but I give McGregor more credit than hiring me based on my . . . other assets. "Knock it off with the X-ray eyes," I say, laughing, but in truth, I'm annoyed. They're both staring at my chest. "I did a lot more than strut around to get this job, okay? And when did Anne talk to *you* about me?" I ask Brett.

"A week or so ago?" he answers with a shrug. "I'm close with about every big name in this industry—I know everything, about *everyone*." Brett glances at Kimmi before he goes on. "Which is why people usually try to stay on my good side."

"Is that your sorry attempt at a power play?" Kimmi asks.

"First you think I'm hitting on you, and now I'm making some sort of threat?" Brett leans forward and eases his grin. "And just so things are perfectly clear: With Emma Taylor in the mix, why would I go after *you*?"

It's great timing for the waitress to show up with our food because I act like the shock I get down my back is from seeing a plate of nachos—stacked to the ceiling—set in front of me. I play a watered-down version of my game, but Tara still walks off with a little sway.

Kimmi sips her soda, then says, "Emma isn't your type."

"She's female, so she's my type," Brett replies, ignoring his burrito that covers an entire plate. I dig into my nachos. "And I already know she likes me."

A chip gets stuck in my throat.

"What girl her age *doesn't* have a crush on you?" Kimmi says, as if Emma still wears pigtails. And Kimmi is what? Maybe a year or so older? "But she probably got over you the moment you opened your mouth today."

"Wrong," Brett snaps. "Didn't you notice how nervous she was around me? She was all shy and couldn't make eye contact." He points his knife at me. "How did she act with *you*?"

"She was fine. No problem." Now that I think about it, the way she acted around Brett, he might be right. It's surprising that any girl at all—with a brain—could like Brett Crawford, but *Emma*? "So, Kimmi, back to you," I say. "Where are you from?"

Both Kimmi and Brett seem shocked that I care. Maybe they aren't as dumb as I think.

"My family has homes on both coasts—Pacific Palisades and the Hamptons," Kimmi says, explaining plenty right there. She goes on for another fifteen minutes about her jet-setter lifestyle, then finally gets back to her family. "My father is in real estate, like my grandfather—they're in Dubai right now working on a high-rise project. And my brother is at Harvard."

"Like, where else would he be?" Brett pipes up with a mouthful of burrito. "And your mom is a tipsy socialite who shimmies her way from one Bloomingdale's to another."

Kimmi goes rigid. "Yes, actually. But she's usually more than a bit tipsy. Did you get *that* scoop from your Hollywood connections too?"

"I was joking!" Brett spits out, along with his food. "Is she really an alcoholic?"

"Come on, man," I say. "Do you chew on your feet all day, or what?"

Kimmi's eyes are stone. "Who cares? I hardly know her." She holds up her hand and waves over the waitress. "Jake, you have a job to finish."

It isn't easy to fake a smile with Tara this time. All the Emma stuff is blocking my mojo, and I'm stuck between feeling bad that Kimmi's mom has such a big problem and stumped because Kimmi doesn't care. Or does she?

The way I feel about my dad is just as cold. Or at least I treat him like that.

"So, how was your food?" Tara asks, handing us each a separate check.

Brett and I say it was great, but Kimmi just pushes aside her barely touched salad. Tara ignores her, wishes Brett good luck with his new show, and smiles at me as she leaves.

"Ha-ha, dude. You struck out!" Brett says with blasting laughter.

"I never strike out." I slide my check across the table. It says: *Dinner is on me. I'm off in ten minutes.*

"And that," Kimmi tells Brett, "is how a real man does it."

Brett finally looks up from the check. "Whatever. Nice snag, but you didn't get her number and that was the deal."

"Turn it over," I say, and Brett flips the check to see where Tara has written her name and number. "You can keep that as your consolation prize."

He crumples up the bill and chucks it at me.

My game ends here, so I leave a twenty-dollar tip and head to my car.

EMMA

The hair and makeup room is my favorite place in the studio: spinning chairs, sinks, long countertops, cabinets for supplies, lighted mirrors forever, and carts filled with gels, sprays, brushes, accessories, and endless cosmetics—in all imaginable colors.

Sugar and spice and everything nice.

On the morning of the second day, I walk in at seven thirty sharp and find myself alone with Brett. "Dang," he says. "Why do they bother putting makeup on you? You're even drop-dead gorgeous without it."

Brett Crawford just called you gorgeous, I tell myself, and my pulse stays the same. That's almost as freaky as realizing, just now, that I haven't thought of him once since my phone call with Rachel. But wouldn't that have been better than having Jake stuck in my head?

"Thanks," I tell Brett. "I'm kind of nervous after my visit to costumes."

Today will be filled with camera tests so McGregor can see if the styles for each character look right to him. Personally, I hope he makes a few changes, or I'll be wearing this same outfit for the entire first episode, which will take about eight days to shoot.

"Nice boots," Brett says. "I usually just see those on the Sunset Strip."

"My thoughts exactly," I reply. It's hard for me to dislike *any* pair of footwear, but somehow these black leather boots that go all the way past my knees make me feel like I'm not wearing anything at all. And there are still at least four inches of skin between the boots and my plaid schoolgirl skirt. "But it's this skirt I have the real problem with."

"I don't see a problem," Brett says with an even bigger grin.

I roll my eyes. "I guess I'm just grumpy this morning. Didn't sleep well and my call time was six thirty."

He roughs up his bangs. "I could've slept for another hour, but McGregor wants my hair shorter and re-highlighted. He thinks I look too much like a surfer."

"You California boys just can't help that, can you?"

Our hairstylist, Donna, walks in and says, "Forget California. I'm gonna turn you into a sun-kissed Arizona hottie."

"Is there a difference?" Brett asks.

"Is there ever!" Donna replies as she throws a cape around him. I already decided during hair and makeup tests that I like Donna a lot, but our makeup artist, who steps in behind her, frightens me a little. Madelyn is twice my size, in every direction, and crabby. Not exactly someone I want poking around my eyes. I've barely greeted her when she nearly chokes me with a cape, then yanks my hair into a ponytail. "Gentle with the locks," Donna tells Madelyn. "I've got something sassy planned today."

"You should do Emma's hair exactly like it was for that British movie last summer," Brett suggests. "All tossed and curly. She looked *good*."

Donna starts whipping up a color concoction for Brett and agrees that she liked my hair that way, but she's doing something different. Madelyn just grunts—who knows what that means? And I'm also unsure of how to reply to Brett, so instead, I bring up the director of the movie. "You've worked with Hugh Kramer before, right?"

"Yep. Can't stand the guy," Brett replies. I don't like Kramer much either, but he had talked as if he and Brett were as tight as Tupperware. "All Kramer cares about is box office draws. If he happens to snag a star who's also a good actor—like you—it's just luck."

I squint my eyes, making Madelyn huff. "Hold still," she says through gritted teeth.

"Sorry." I open my eyes wide again so she can blot off the liquid eyeliner mess I just made. "Thanks, Brett. I guess. And you're probably right. The horses did a better job than some of the actors in that movie, but I'm glad it did well anyway."

"Yeah, there's nothing like having your name attached to a box office flop. I mean, you can read a script and think it's gonna be a colossal hit, and then . . ." As Brett's hair is being wrapped in foil, we talk about the occasional disasters we've been involved in, and it's refreshing to speak so openly about the unpredictable, frustrating side of the business.

When Brett isn't being a spastic, potty-mouthed womanizer, he's not too bad.

"So when you're not working, what does a good girl like you do besides paint your toenails?" he asks. "Have you ever been to a motocross race?"

Wait . . . how had he gone from movies to toenails to motorcycles in a single breath? "Never even thought of going," I say with a laugh. Racing is one of Brett's hobbies that is supposedly—according to gossip—distracting him from being a serious actor.

"No way! You'd love it!" Brett looks hysterical now with his tinfoil-topped head, and we switch chairs so Donna can work on me while the color sets. "I've been racing for five years," Brett says, "but McGregor made me swear I wouldn't touch a motorcycle until we wrapped the season in April. He even put it in my contract."

McGregor's contracts are a bit intense. I can barely brush my own teeth without written approval. "Did you have to swear off anything else?"

"A whole list of stuff, which is sorta good for me right now, but it doesn't mean I can't watch someone else have fun. In fact, I'm going to a big race in L.A a couple of weeks from now. You wanna come?"

"Um—"

"Hey, don't get excited or anything. I already told you I stopped dating my costars," Brett says, all snarky. "We'll be with a big group—not in couples—so it'll be a blast."

The Los Angeles factor makes this easy. "Thanks, but I can't."

Brett glares at me. "You don't want to be seen with me, do you?"

Donna and Madelyn exchange interested looks, and I want to beg Brett to end this conversation. Studio employees sign strict confidentiality agreements, but *somehow* on-set gossip finds its way to the tabloids anyway. All I can do now is be honest.

"Okay, yeah, that's definitely part of it," I tell Brett. "It's nothing personal, but if we happened to be photographed together—with a big group, or not—we could still be labeled as a couple. That's just what happens if you work together *and* hang out."

"Sometimes, I guess." Brett falls quiet after this, so I let him stay that way. But after just thirty seconds or so, he looks back and says, "You won't believe what an idiot I was last night—I feel *so* bad. When we were at dinner, Jake asked Kimmi about her family, and I accidentally made fun of her alcoholic mom."

Did I hear him right? "How can you *accidentally* do that?"

"It just sorta happened, you know?" Brett replies. "I'm always saying and doing the wrong things, even when I don't mean to. I hate it. Anyway, I was thinking I could try to smooth things over with Kimmi. Payton Wilson is going to the motocross too, and I bet Kimmi wouldn't mind meeting 'Hollywood's Hottest Young Bachelor.' You'll come if she does, right?"

I laugh. "No! Adding her would just make it look like a *double* date."

Madelyn keeps passing between our chairs, getting another tray ready—probably for Kimmi, who should be arriving any minute. Jake won't be too far behind her.

"Then let's make it an unofficial publicity trip for *Coyote Hills*," Brett says. "I'll invite Jake too. McGregor will love it if we're all seen together. Early buzz—his favorite words. Well, besides 'Emmy winner,' and 'sizzling-hot ratings.' "

Kimmi's reflection pops into the mirror. "Where are we going?"

"L.A.," Brett says, all smiles. "We're gonna hang out with Payton Wilson. You in?"

Every part of Kimmi that can perk up does so, but her holier-than-thou expression returns in a hurry. "Whatever," she says, as if she's doing Brett, and even Payton, a favor. "Are you going, Emma?"

"Oh yeah, she's going," Brett answers for me. "She only gets to ditch us once a year, and she used up that pass last night."

"You're ready, doll," Donna says as she finishes the last dose of whatever ozone-killing fog she's spraying on me. "See you later on."

I stand, and Brett scans me—like *totally* scans me. "I wouldn't worry so much about your costumes. Every guy in the world's gonna have plenty of nice things to say about them."

"Great. What a relief." I tug my skirt as low as I can and wish there was just one more button on my way-too-tight white shirt. "This is one role that will definitely challenge me."

"How can *you* complain?" Kimmi asks as she examines the seat I just vacated. What does she think I left behind, an egg? "Look what costumes did to *me*."

She's in baggy capri pants, a bright-purple square-neck top, and sneakers.

"Well, like we talked about yesterday," I say, "Kassidy has a style all her own."

Kimmi rolls her eyes. "Who cares about her character sketch? I'll be wearing designer labels by next week."

A blast of laughter comes from Brett. "Good luck, sweetheart! The only choice *you'll* be making around here is what color of underwear you put on."

Wrong. I was handed a flesh-colored pair of Spanx this morning, due to my ultrashort skirt. "Not even that is a sure thing. Today, for instance," I say, and Brett scans me again, so I hit him. "Knock it off! Do you think girls don't notice that?"

"He *knows* they do," Kimmi says. "And speaking of behaving badly, I'll be surprised if Jake staggers in anytime before noon."

Jeez. Did he get wasted? The thought makes me feel kind of . . . disappointed or something.

"That dude is one serious pickup artist," Brett tells me, as if he's impressed. "He hardly said a word to this waitress last night, but he still ended up leaving with her."

Oh.

Not only is Jake exactly like every other guy in this industry, but Brett just gave him a slap on the back for it. My taste in men *totally sucks*.

"It's crazy what you can learn about someone in so short a time," I say with an amused little smile. I'm good at those. Ask any film critic.

Despite the mixed results of the first week on set, the second week is fantastic. There's been too much drama in my head for way too long, so I'm thrilled that McGregor runs the production like a conductor of a symphony and keeps me focused. Shooting scenes seems to go twice as fast as usual, and I love it. Somehow, I even feel comfortable as my character.

With everything, really.

Our crew is amazing. McGregor has pulled several people from other projects to create his dream team, and I give him kudos for that during a lighting setup.

"Thank you, lass," he replies, sitting next to me after raiding the craft service table. Crafty, as everyone calls the heavenly department that feeds us, keeps the whole set happy. Today, we even have freshly squeezed lemonade. And a catering company is still on its way with lunch. "And if you haven't noticed, I've also gathered a spectacular group of performers."

I glance over to the cast chairs, where Kimmi is flirting with Jake. She does that a lot, I've noticed, and Jake is either playing it cool or his mind is still on the waitress he met a couple of weeks ago. Brett runs past them, kicking a plastic cup like a soccer ball, and Jake jumps up to follow him.

"Talent, beauty, and a brilliant crew—my recipe for success," McGregor says. Then he narrows his eyes at me. "What do you think of Kimmi?"

To lie, or not to lie? "She's a great actress. As in, *really* good. But she's not very excited about her baggy pants."

I sip my lemonade, a delicious mix of sweet and sour.

"Ah, yes." McGregor sticks a carrot in his mouth, but that doesn't stop him from talking. "She'll adapt. I have some interesting things planned for her."

Actors are usually kept in the dark about future plots, but I want to see how much I can get out of him. "I'm sure the writers are working on cool storylines for *all* of us," I say. "Eden won't always be a self-absorbed gossip columnist, will she?"

McGregor thinks a bit before he answers. "This series is planned to progress well beyond the high school years," he finally says, "so the characters need to begin a fair distance away from where I'd like them to end up."

A typical brush-off. "I suppose there wouldn't be much of a story to tell if our characters were already perfect," I say.

"Precisely." McGregor looks to where Jake and Brett are now in a heated battle for the plastic cup/soccer ball. "Not that either of our male leads feel a need for improvement."

"So true," I reply. Jake is still a mystery to me. Ever since I heard about the waitress, I've been watching for signs that prove he's like Brett made him sound—because, of course, I want to warn Rachel if Jake is a player—but I just don't see any. Brett's continued lack of manners isn't so bad, though. My crush is buried for good. "Yet, surprisingly, I've known bigger egos."

McGregor nods. "You've dated some high-and-mighty fellows, haven't you?"

I stop smiling. "Yeah. A few too many."

"And not one of them deserved you. Many in this business are arrogant jerks only because they're allowed to be, so let's hope you taught those twits a lesson."

I doubt it. With Troy, pretty much all I've done is run away and cry.

A plastic cup hits my leg, and Jake runs over to get it. "Sorry! I missed!" he says, motioning to the two chairs set up as a goal. They're at least twenty feet from me.

"By a country mile!" Oh my. I never use that phrase outside of Arkansas.

Jake shrugs. "Someone must've moved the chairs."

It's hard not to laugh as Jake runs off, kicking the mangled plastic cup again. When I turn back to McGregor, his eyes are steady, as if he's already been watching me. "Don't think *that* possibility hasn't kept me up at night," he says.

"What possibility?" I ask, then my face gets hot—jalapeño hot. McGregor dropped a hint in contract talks that on-set romances make him bristle. "Oh, heck no! I've kissed enough frogs to know none of them turn out to be princes."

"Then perhaps you should spend less time in swamps."

"Well, sadly, I don't have a lot of variety in my dating pool," I reply. "But who knows? Maybe I'll one day meet a decent guy who walks into the studio by mistake."

McGregor's gaze has shifted to Jake. "Or might just *think* he doesn't belong."

JAKE

Most days at work, I catch Emma looking at me at least once, but the last time we had anything close to a flirtatious conversation was when I gave her a ride home that first day in the studio. Since then, she's only been available enough to not seem snobby.

What do I have to do to get her attention? Some sort of freaky, Hollywood mating dance?

Emma is being just "friendly" with Brett too, though, so I've decided she doesn't like him after all. And with every word he speaks, Brett adds another point in my favor.

"Eww, you sicko!" she tells him now, backing right into a camera to get away. "I didn't want to know *that*!"

"You asked me if I knew Bethany Parke," Brett says. "And I do. Really, really well!"

"At least you remember her name," I mutter.

He slugs me.

Tyler, the first assistant director, bellows, "First team, back to one!" so I have to focus again. In the scene we're shooting now, I'm stretched out on an old sofa in our newspaper office set—my feet kicked up and my head on a backpack—and I'm supposed to *look* relaxed, while also being constantly aware of where my arms and legs are and every expression I make. And I also have to pay attention to what everyone else is doing and saying. Otherwise, I'll miss my cues.

In modeling, a photographer only has to tell me "smug," and just thinking of kicking Devin's butt in basketball will get me through fifty successive shots. But McGregor's instructions for me earlier today were slightly more complicated.

"Justin, you rolled out of bed ten minutes before you had to leave for school," he began. "You took three of those minutes to shower, and the only item of clothing you didn't grab off your floor was fresh boxers. Got that?" I nodded. I've been there. "The next five minutes were spent brushing your teeth, using the toilet, and making your hair look casually perfect, pretty much at the same time. This was also when you remembered to get your backpack. You then took one minute to toast some bread and another full minute to butter it, because this is important to you. Understand?" I nodded again. "And then you grabbed a half gallon of milk and raced out the door. You drank a quarter gallon straight from the jug, and the remaining milk is now spoiling in your Jeep. All of this happens off screen, *before* this scene begins."

I would argue that none of it actually happened at all, but after two weeks of McGregor downloading this stuff into my head, I'm starting to get why these types of details help me better understand my character.

"Your only concern now, however, is getting Mario from the red planet to the green planet," he went on, pointing out the broken Nintendo 3DS I'm holding in this scene. "So when Kassidy drops her donation box in the hallway, and Eden and Bryce hear the thud and look toward the door, you do *nothing*. Nothing but keep pushing *ABXXA*, or whatever buttons you have to push to make Mario jump. And all you *hear* is *zing-zing, bling! Boing-boing, pop!* Is that clear?"

Nod, nod, nod.

McGregor says he'll only be using his "incessant direction" technique on me during the first few episodes. After that, I'm expected to *be* Justin and know exactly what he would think, how he'd move, and every expression he'd make in any given situation. Kimmi is getting the same instruction, which she hates.

Brett and Emma rarely get anything more than applause from him.

Scenes are shot out of order, which I've just learned is typical for most movies and TV shows, so even though we're now only filming scene five, we're almost finished with the first episode. In the script, this scene looked like the easiest so far—I have just two lines. But we're on hour *four* of shooting it. Lighting issues, a glitchy camera, and Kimmi—just being Kimmi—have all caused delays.

Take after take from different camera angles, I keep pushing *ABXXA*. My thumbs are stiff, my neck has a kink in it, and my eyes burn from concentrating on a blank video game screen. The funny thing is, I like it. All of it.

"Picture's up!" Tyler calls.

An assistant director repeats the command, and PAs echo it

throughout the set. A buzzer sounds to warn everyone within the entire studio that filming is about to take place.

"Here we go. Quiet down!"

"Rolling!" Tyler says.

"Sound speed!"

"Camera speeding."

Camera A slate is held up, and an assistant cameraman says, "Scene five Echo, take four." *Clap.* "A mark."

Camera B slate is clapped. "B Mark."

McGregor sits in front of his monitor. "And . . . action!"

I tap out *ABXXA*. No one cares what order I really hit the buttons—or that it usually only takes hitting *A* to make a game character jump—because at least from this camera angle, it doesn't matter. *Thud* . . . that's Kimmi dropping the box.

I just keep thinking, *Jump, Mario, jump.*

"Do you need some help?" Brett says, racing toward the set door. He exits for exactly three seconds, as McGregor has instructed him, then returns with the box in his arms. Kimmi shuffles in behind him, looking discouraged after a long hour on the front steps begging for school supplies—according to the script, anyway. I wouldn't know because I'm on the red planet trying to get to the green one. "You okay?" Brett asks Kimmi.

My cue. I switch my feet, left on top of right. *ABXXA* . . .

"Yeah, but all I got was a used pencil," Kimmi says. "Will you help me next time, Eden?"

Emma's *as if* laugh is my next cue.

"Jump, you midget, jump!" I shout at Mario.

Kimmi gasps. "Hey, don't be mean to Eden! It's not *her* fault that she's so short."

I pretend to pause my game, then turn my head to glare at Kimmi as though she has "Politically Correct" stamped on her forehead. "Chill out, will ya?" I say. "My vertically challenged victim is also *reality* challenged, so he doesn't freaking care what I call him. And I don't think Eden looks short at all in those nice tall boots."

Kimmi's eyes drift down Emma. "Guess not," she says, scandalized. Or at least that's the expression the script tells her to have.

"Cut!" McGregor calls. It's actually the end of the scene, anyway, but he says it like Kimmi ruined the entire take. "Miss Weston, you've got that uppity curve to your lips again when you look her over, as though you're smelling something foul."

Brett removes his shoe and sticks it under Kimmi's nose. "This, maybe?"

Kimmi shrieks, a totally new sound from her, and bats him away.

"And why is it that with two guys in this scene," Brett asks McGregor, "*Kimmi* gets to be the one who checks out Emma? That's cruel, man." He turns to me and adds, under his breath, "At least you get a view of her butt. I get nothing at all from this angle."

"Except for my *face*," Emma says, close enough to hear him. Then she shoots me a scowl over her shoulder and whispers, "I thought you promised to stop looking at my butt."

Whoa. Is she . . . flirting?

"Well, once again," I reply, still lounging on the couch, "it's the only view I have."

Emma laughs. "Move over, these boots are killing me."

I swing my feet off the couch and gladly make room for her.

"Don't get too comfortable," McGregor tells us. "We're going again. Three minutes." He guides Kimmi over to his monitor and plays back the footage. "Ah," he finally says. "I suppose it's not too bad."

"Good, then let's call that the martini," Kimmi replies, suggesting we should wrap for the day—I think. The set lingo is still a bit fuzzy. "I've gotta get out of here."

McGregor waves Tyler over to the monitor and has him take a look too. And Brett leaves the set for who knows what reason.

Emma and I exchange glances.

"It's only four thirty," she whispers. "Do you think he'll actually let us go?"

"Maybe. Isn't this the last scene on the schedule?"

She thinks for a sec. "Yeah, but McGregor could come up with a *ton* of things that need to be tweaked. We're just lucky he's so determined to keep his entire weekends free for his family, or we'd all be spending Fraturdays together. That's how my last show was."

"Fraturdays?" I ask.

"Oh yeah. And they'll still be necessary once in a while—probably for night shoots," Emma says. "We'll work for about sixteen hours straight, half of Friday and all through the night, until the sun rises on Saturday. So, you know, *Fraturday*. It's pretty much a big company pajama party because everyone is half-asleep and laughing at every tiny thing that wouldn't seem even remotely funny in the daylight."

"That doesn't sound too bad," I reply.

Emma smiles. "No, not usually. And it's definitely better than studying every Friday night, which is all I've been doing since I moved to Tucson. I'm not exactly looking forward to yet another quiet evening filled with textbooks."

With any other girl, that would have been a hint. I jump all over it.

"I won't be having any fun tonight either," I say. "I need to make a trip to Phoenix so I can start hauling all my stuff down here." Not bad. Here I go. "It would be great to have someone come along for the drive—you know, keep me awake? Just talk?"

Emma holds very still. "Is your . . . waitress friend busy?"

"Who?" I ask, then finally catch on. "Jeez. I can only guess what you heard about the waitress. But Brett and Kimmi just wanted to see if I could get her number without asking for it, which also led to her telling me when she got off work. But I went straight to my hotel—*alone*, by the way."

Emma raises a brow at me. "I definitely heard a different version of that story."

I shrug. "At least that explains . . . well, a lot."

"Like what?"

"You acting like I have rabies. Or at least cooties."

Emma laughs. "Subtlety isn't one of my gifts. But still, I better pass."

"Oh, c'mon," I say. "You've made it clear enough that you don't want to date me. So as long as we're both good with those terms, what's wrong with hanging out?"

I just keep smiling at her while she thinks it over. Her face is the color of Atomic Fireballs, as hot as the rest of her.

"You're not very good at taking no for an answer," she finally says.

"I haven't had much practice," I reply, which is true. "Besides, I need to ask you a few more questions about online classes. I want to start school."

"Really?"

"That last take looks great, folks. We can wrap!" McGregor calls, and everyone cheers. "Scripts for episode two are in your dressing rooms."

I glance back at Emma. "So . . . I'll pick you up at six?"

What is it about me that makes her so hesitant? "Okay. I'll go."

Sweet. I want to reply, but Brett is headed back our way. "Guess who's getting a girlfriend?" he says, and waves a script at Emma. "You might want to take a look at this."

That can only mean one thing.

EMMA

It isn't a date, I tell myself as Jake walks off the set. I used to hang out with guy friends all the time in Los Angeles. And I'm desperate for some fun right now.

Oh, please, who am I trying to fool? That little vixen in me tempted my better half into trouble, and I know it. But . . . Jake only wants to talk about school. That's all.

It isn't a date.

Brett flips through the script in his hands. "Guess who gets to kiss—"

"Shh!" It's obvious what the script says. "No spoilers."

"Okay, okay," Brett replies. "You ready for tomorrow?"

I've already heard Jake can't go to the motocross because he's moving into his condo this weekend, but Brett still swears that no one will think our group is in couples because Kimmi and I will be the only girls with four guys. "If I get there, Brett, and it's just the four of us—"

"Seriously, Taylor! How many times do I have to turn you down?"

"I just don't want it to *look* like a date."

"It doesn't matter what it looks like—McGregor jumped through the roof when I told him we were all going to L.A. to promote *Coyote Hills*." Brett is backing away from me, off the set. "And he's counting on you getting tons of attention with your big, pretty smile. We're supposed to tell everyone we see about the show."

I should've known he would get McGregor all hyped up. "Fine, I'll go on your fake publicity trip," I call as he moves farther away. "And I'll get *tons* of attention, 'cause I'm gonna wear a flashing billboard on my head that says: I GOT TRICKED INTO THIS!"

"Perfect!" he shouts back, and several crew members turn around. "Write this on your billboard too: Watch me make out with Brett Crawford! *Coyote Hills,* Tuesday nights, eight o'clock!"

I throw both hands over my face. *Great.* Brett is about to become my on-screen boyfriend. That shouldn't complicate things much.

While driving home from the studio in my finally delivered car, passing more sagebrush than I ever knew existed, I try to avoid thoughts of kissing—or strangling—Brett Crawford. I turn my air-conditioning on as high as it can go, but I still feel like I'm a turkey cooking in a hot oven.

The locals have assured me that if I can just make it through the scorching summers, Tucson's weather during the rest of the year is perfect. Meanwhile, I'll try to enjoy the random fluctuations between one-hundred-and-ten-degree weather and hammering downpours. The monsoon storms have been hitting every few days, and the lightning is insane—fifty bolts striking all at once.

Beautiful, but truly dangerous. Sort of like Jake.

When I finally remembered to have him sign his headshots for Rachel, three days after we met, Jake mentioned that he had leased a condo in my neighboring community. And when I was on the running path a few nights ago, I saw him get out of his car and walk into it. So now I know exactly where he lives, about four minutes away. Half that if I run.

This probably isn't something I should tell Rachel. Not yet, at least.

As I'm thinking about all of this on my way home, my mom calls to say, "Trina won't stop pestering me about making sure her daughter gets an audition for *Stars in Their Eyes*. Has Rachel been trying to talk you into making some calls?"

"Yes, and I told her I'd do whatever I could," I say. "What's wrong with that?"

There's a sigh of exasperation, as if Mom can't believe I still don't understand how things work. "Emma. It's one thing to talk to a few friends—once in a while—who happen to be working on a project you feel Rachel would be good in, but quite another matter to call people you don't even know and use your name as though it can buy you the Taj Mahal."

"Gosh, Mom. I don't take my celebrity status as lightly as you think." I'm not sure my plan to get Rachel an audition will work, but can't I at least try? This is the first year she's old enough for *Stars in Their Eyes*—a reality show that gives aspiring actors a shot at stardom. "Rachel is one-hundred-percent perfect for that show, and the casting director will know it the minute she auditions."

"Then let her stand in line like everyone else," Mom says.

"I just want to make sure she gets a *place* in line, okay?" A lot of people don't, only because they wear a scarf one of the screeners doesn't like, or something petty like that.

Another sigh. "These favors have gone on far too long, Emma."

I'm tired of arguing about this. Rachel is exceptionally talented and deserves a break.

I'm home by then, so I end our conversation and try to erase all thoughts of my mom and even Rachel from my head while I get ready for Phoenix. I love the way Donna has been doing my hair, with just a little more body than usual, so I'm careful with it as I shower and remove my stage makeup.

One of the things I love most about my town house is the walk-in closet. Not only does it have room for all of my clothes—except for the formalwear that I keep in Arkansas—but it also has enough floor space for my hopeless addiction: shoes.

I decide to wear my favorite slingback heels. Now for a *non-date* outfit to match. I start with dark jeans, then try on five shirts, all black, and give each a thirty-second evaluation. I finally choose one with cap sleeves and a neckline that doesn't show anything, um . . . flirty. I finish my makeup just in time for Jake's knock.

One look at him tells me I should slam the door and bolt it.

I've just discovered Jake's best look yet—freshly showered. His hair is shiny black because it's still a little wet, and it curls up in all the right places. And he's wearing a tight jade-green tee that's partially tucked in.

Couldn't he look bad just once? Just tonight?

We start with the usual chitchat—hi, hey, you ready, yeah—that happens whenever a guy picks me up. Only this isn't a date. Nope. When we get to his car, I even open my own door, and nothing feels weird about it. Totally casual.

Jake turns onto the canyon road. "It's gonna take a while to get there. You hungry?"

Crafty set out fresh peanut butter cookies as we left work, and I grabbed *three*. A paycheck is just a side benefit of this job. "I'm fine if you are."

"Good, because I promised my mom I'd pick up her favorite burger along the way," Jake says. "You aren't a straight-salad girl, are you?"

"Do I look like a rabbit?"

"No, but you don't look like you down a lot of burgers either."

"I love hamburgers," I say. "And pizza, nachos, popcorn . . . whatever."

"And bottled water," he says. I've noticed the same thing about him. He gestures to my bag. "How many did you bring along?"

"Just a couple." I pull out a bottle for each of us. "It's pretty much all I drink. I loved the lemonade we had for lunch today, though. I asked for the recipe."

"Cool, now you can open your own lemonade stand. You'll make a load of cash."

Okay, he's cute. I'll admit it. "Does this come from experience?"

Jake smiles. "My one and only sidewalk stand was a bit more creative than that."

"Oh my. A kissing booth?" I ask.

"I wish! I would've been in a lot less trouble. Instead, I sold all of my mom's shoes."

I gasp, truly horrified, and shift my Prada-clad feet far from Jake's reach. "You were an evil little boy."

For most of the two-hour drive, there's a lot of banter like this, but no flirting . . . not really, and small talk about life in general.

"How'd you get into acting?" he asks, finally coming around to work. "You like it, right?"

A coyote darts across the freeway ahead of us. I've seen more coyotes since I moved to Arizona than cats and dogs.

"I have a nice scripted answer for that," I reply. "But it's boring and superficial, and my real answer is on the edge of cheesy."

"Pour on the cheese," Jake says.

"Okay, you asked for it." I chug down some water for dramatic effect. "I started acting lessons when I was six, was in community plays and such, then began auditioning for professional projects when I was nine. I did a couple of commercials, small independent films, stuff like that. Then, just after I turned twelve, my mom heard that a big-budget production would be shooting right by us in Fayetteville—a movie about a pioneer family, settling in the Ozarks. The role for the girl my age was a huge one, so my mom admits now that she really didn't think I had much of a chance. But for months my friend Rachel and I got ready to audition, and then our moms took us out to Los Angeles for the big day."

"Rachel acts too?" Jake asks. "The girl I signed the head-shots for?"

"Yeah, but this is when she sort of slipped through the cracks," I say, my chest tightening like it always does when I think back on this. "We don't know if it was some bad food she ate or what, but the morning of the audition, Rachel was super sick. She still auditioned, but didn't do her best."

"And *you* got the part," Jake says. "You probably would've gotten it anyway."

"Maybe," I say, though it's likely true. The casting director told my mom during filming that they had hoped to find a small-framed girl with long dark hair, bright eyes, and a genuine Southern drawl. Totally me. "But try explaining that to your best friend when you get to go to the Oscars—*Mountain Home* went on to win Best Picture, after all—and she's at home crying her eyes out because it could've been *her.*"

Jake stares straight ahead at the road, and I'm glad because my throat is suddenly constricted. Rachel has never revealed this herself to me, but Trina told me all about her daughter's broken heart the night of the Academy Awards—how she had choked back sobs when I went up on stage with our winning cast, but clapped and cheered for me anyway.

"Rachel is a seriously talented actress, though, and she's just getting into photography and is already great at it," I say, having just realized how I made Rachel sound. "And she isn't nearly as blubbering and flu-stricken as I just described her. She's also smart and pretty. Really, *really* pretty."

"Thanks for the sales pitch," Jake says with a laugh. "When you finish telling me what *you* like about acting, maybe you can tell me what *Rachel* likes about it. If you really, really want to."

I scowl at him but move on. "All right, this is the cheesy part: When we were shooting *Mountain Home*, take after take, I couldn't imagine how it could end up like anything but a jumbled mess. And the days were *sooo* long and hardly exciting after a while."

Jake nods as I talk, likely because he's having similar thoughts at work.

"But," I continue, "when I saw myself on the big screen, it felt *amazing.* It was incredibly cool to watch myself pretend to be someone so different from me. And I was stunned that I'd actually made the audience believe this pioneer girl was a real person. So it's not actually during production that I love acting, but the rush I get when I see the finished product."

"That's not cheesy," Jake says. "Everyone should do something they can be proud of—whatever gives them that same sort of buzz."

"Isn't modeling like that for you?"

"Not even close," he replies. "The runway stuff is awkward, but it's not like my buddies beg for tickets to Fashion Week. And if they did, they wouldn't be there to see *me*, anyway." Jake drums his fingers on the steering wheel. "It's the print work that bugs me. For weeks before an ad comes out, I can already hear my friends' voices in my head. I know exactly what jokes they're gonna make."

Jealousy has to play into it, at least a little, when his friends tease him. But it surprises me that Jake truly sounds humiliated when he says this. He's so good at modeling. But like fame, success means something different to everyone.

"I get that way about tabloids," I admit. "I take it all more personally than I should."

"But no one really believes those stories."

"Oh yes they do!" I reply. "*Celebrity Seeker* could run a bogus piece about me buying the entire country of Austria, and within ten minutes, there would be hundreds of people online trying to guess why I chose Austria rather than France. Or, heck, why not all of Europe?"

"With that kind of imagination, *you* should be a tabloid reporter," Jake says, so I smack his arm. "But your friends and family are cool about everything?"

Good question. "Rachel is great. She comes to most of my premieres and award shows. And my mom . . . well, she's also my manager, so sometimes those roles clash."

"That's understandable," Jake says. "What about your dad?"

"My dad? Hmm . . . he's a different story altogether. Proud of me, yes, but he kind of acts like my career is a fluke. Most of our conversations include him reminding me that the bubble will pop one day, and that I better have something 'of worth' to fall back on."

"Is that why you decided to go to college? So you can eventually do something else?"

"No, I just don't want to be one-dimensional." We're talking about me way too much. "What about you? How did you get into all this?"

Jake tells me how his agent found him playing basketball—I would have signed him too—and later suggested he might like acting better than modeling. "Don't take me wrong, because so far, I'm loving it," Jake says. "Acting is the hardest job I've ever had, and every day is a new challenge. But being a celebrity for the long haul . . . I don't know. It just isn't who I am."

Then who is he? "What would you rather do?"

"Business, for sure. Negotiating deals, all that stuff. Selling my mom's shoes was just the beginning." He exits the freeway. There are mountains in the distance, but the most immediate view of Phoenix is the jutting up of tall buildings, ten times more than can be seen in the Tucson skyline. "I drive my agent nuts because I never want to sign a contract without a dozen rounds of negotiating. But besides the pay, the deal-making is the only part of modeling I've liked."

"So you want a business degree?" I ask, and he replies with a happy nod. I almost laugh, tempted to tell him more about my dad's job, but I decide to wait. I can, however, offer Jake a bit of advice since he's already said he wants to talk about school. "Well, most general requirements are now available online. And we usually don't work from mid-April to early July, so you could take a few campus classes too."

"That's what I've been trying to figure out since we talked a while ago," Jake says as he pulls into The Hamburger Hut parking lot. "I'm just not sure where to start."

He stops in front of a large drive-thru menu board, and I tell him, "I guess I could point you in the right direction, but I don't work for free. You'll have to buy me a burger."

Jake gives me such an incredibly cute smile that my whole body goes limp. I need to plaster NO TRESPASSING signs all over him.

"You're an easy girl to please," he says.

I can't help but laugh again. "You're the first person who's ever told me that."

He leans a bit closer and twirls a lock of my hair between his fingers . . . that's all.

But it's enough.

I grab my bag, open the car door, and practically sprint out of it. "I'll meet you on the other side of the drive-thru," I say, and head straight for The Hamburger Hut restroom so I can stare into the mirror and remind myself that I will *not* fall for Jake Elliott.

JAKE

If Emma had any mercy at all, she would have worn a frumpy dress and put her hair up in a librarian bun. Instead, she looks good enough to be on a movie screen and is just as untouchable. Right before she reaches the Hamburger Hut door, she pulls out a big white hat and sets it low, almost over her eyes. Man, that's one face that should never have to be hidden.

Once I've picked up our food, I find Emma waiting at the end of the drive-thru. We talk a little more about school, then she asks, "Does your mom know I'm coming?"

"Yep," I say. "But don't worry, I clarified that this isn't a date. She's still excited, though, because . . . well, she's a fan."

"And she wants a hamburger."

"That too." We'll be at my mom's place in a few minutes, so I can't put this off any longer. "Okay. I, uh . . . need to tell you something."

Emma eyes me suspiciously. "All right."

I suck in a breath. "My mom had a pretty serious stroke about a year ago that left half of her body paralyzed. Her face is looking better every day, but she's in a wheelchair now, and the doctors doubt she'll regain any more movement." Emma just listens quietly, her arms wrapped around her waist, and I can tell she doesn't know what to say. No one ever does. Not even me. "Anyway, I just don't want you to feel uncomfortable when you see her, and it makes *her* uncomfortable when people don't know what's wrong. Her speech is still a little slurred, but she's fine, you know . . . mentally. So just talk like you normally would."

Emma nods. "I can't imagine watching one of my parents go through that."

We pull up to Mom's gated community, and I enter the code. "It's been a tough year, to say the least. And it doesn't help that she acts like it isn't a big deal, like she can take care of things on her own. But my mom didn't recognize any warning signs before her stroke, so it freaks me out, thinking that something like this, or worse, can happen again."

The doctors aren't sure why it happened in the first place. It "just did."

Not only did the stroke come out of the blue, but the timing was horrible. I bought my BMW—straight off the lot, with every possible option—just before then, and had thought I'd been so responsible by saving cash for it. I didn't count on having more important things to spend my money on, like the new house my mom needed, or her home health care and physical therapy. My sister had recently left for her study-abroad program in Italy, and I was already registered to start at ASU, planning on doing just a few modeling jobs a month. But everything changed overnight, and Liz went after the Armani contract so I could keep up with all the expenses. College had to wait.

While I wind through the roads of my mom's neighborhood, Emma and I talk about lighter topics. I don't want to show up with a solemn expression on my face or Mom will think I've been "feeling sorry" for her again.

Emma grabs the bag of food when I park in the driveway, and we head for the front porch. "This house looks new," she says. "It isn't where you grew up, is it?"

"Nope." I unlock the front door. "We had a two-story house a few miles from here, but my mom has to live in a rambler now."

We barely make it past the entry when Mom comes around a corner in her motorized wheelchair. "Get out of the way, Jake," she says. "I can't even see her."

"Hello to you too." I step to the side and introduce them.

My mom's eyes light up. "My goodness, it's really you," she says.

Emma hands me the hamburger bag. "It's great to meet you, Mrs. Elliott."

I doubt I'll ever adjust to the way Mom's life is now. It kills me to think of how trapped she must feel in that chair, with the use of only one arm and one leg. She used to run for miles every morning. She loved it.

"You two must be starving," Mom says as we make our way through the living room and into the adjoining kitchen.

"Only one of us is starving," Emma says. "There was rumbling from the driver's side all the way up here."

"Even *if* my stomach had been rumbling," I tell her, "you wouldn't have been able to hear it because you were talking too much."

Emma laughs—a sound that's starting to make me smile instantly—but both she and Mom ignore my jab. "This boy of mine takes in food like a black hole," my mom says as she parks her wheelchair at the kitchen table. "I can never feed him enough."

"I get the feeling that I won't be allowed to speak during this meal," I say.

"I've raised Jake to be quite intuitive, haven't I?" Mom asks Emma.

I sit next to Emma and help divvy out the food. She smiles at me. "Intuitive, and a few other things," she says. "Jake keeps us very entertained at work."

Mom shoots me an accusatory look. "You're not teasing the girls again, are you?"

"Me? Never." I take a monster-size bite of my burger.

"It sounds like he's always been a lot of trouble," Emma tells my mom. "Jake says he once sold all of your shoes."

"Yes, but that was the least of his mischief," Mom replies. I can understand her slurred words perfectly because I know her so well, but I wonder if Emma is picking up on everything. "I can't imagine that he's told you the worst of it."

"Well . . . not about my little stint in Folsom," I say. "If that's what you mean."

Emma tosses me her familiar smirk. "Prison, huh?"

I nod solemnly. "You know those tags on mattresses that say it's a crime to cut them off? I got a bit carried away one day."

"I see," Emma replies. "Then that explains why McGregor felt you had that *America's Most Wanted* look he was after."

EMMA

"*America's Most Wanted*," Mrs. Elliott repeats, her laughter more robust than I expected. Her appearance is almost the opposite of Jake's; she's petite—and looks even more so in her wheelchair—with fair curls that rest on her shoulders. She definitely gave Jake his green eyes, but his height and dark hair must've come from his dad, who I don't see any hints of around the house. "Jake is always needing new friends to put him in his place, so I'm glad you met."

Mrs. Elliott seems far too young, maybe fifty, to have had a stroke. The left side of her body seems fine—strong, even—but the right side has very little movement. When she smiles only half of her face responds, but both of her eyes totally light up. And even though her speech is slow and a bit slurred, I can understand her okay.

I'm guessing Jake got his wit from her too. She seems like one of those *cool* moms.

"We all do our best to keep Jake humble," I say. "It isn't easy, though. Not many actors walk into a studio with the natural talent he has. The whole crew has been talking about that."

"What set are *you* working on?" he asks me. "Pretty much all I've heard is, 'You're looking straight at the camera again. Watch that cord. Missed your cue.'"

I shake my head in his mom's direction. "Maybe for the first few days, but he's caught on really fast. It's kind of confusing for a while and there's a lot to get used to—stuff all over the floor that you have to watch out for but not notice, and crew members everywhere that you can't look at. Then there's a boom mic right above your head that you have to ignore. And sometimes you're even saying your lines into thin air, pretending that someone's actually talking back to you. It can make you feel kind of psychotic, having conversations with invisible people."

"I can't understand why. I do it all the time," Mrs. Elliott says. "Oh! Hello, Charlie!"

I turn around to see who she's waving to, and Jake laughs louder than I've ever heard him. "Did you really fall for that?"

"Jacob!" his mom says, obviously trying to hold back her own laughter.

I throw my hands over my face. "I thought that, you know, you must've had a brother named Charlie."

"Sorry," Jake says, still laughing. "I only have a sister."

"Well, I don't see her anywhere, so she must be invisible too."

"Amber is in a study-abroad program in Italy," Mrs. Elliott explains. "She came straight home after my stroke, but when I regained my senses enough to realize my kids had put their lives on hold for *me*, I snapped the whip and sent them away again."

I'm convinced now that there isn't a father in the picture. But where is he?

Jake's more somber eyes meet mine, and he says, "Amber applied three times for her art program in Florence—it's a once-in-a-lifetime thing. She'll be there for another year or so."

"Yes, and she wouldn't be there at all if it wasn't for her younger brother," Mrs. Elliott says, and Jake freezes, his hamburger half-way to his mouth. "I won't allow you to be humble about *that,* Jacob. Her scholarship doesn't cover even half of her expenses, and she'd never stay put if you weren't constantly convincing her that you're taking care of me. Which you *are.*"

"That's . . . um, wow," I say. If Jake is trying to pull off some elaborate hoax—to fool me into believing he's the best guy on the planet—his mom is in on it.

Jake's attention lingers on his mom for a second; then he shifts it back to me. "I only help Amber out because she drives me nuts if she's around here. There's some of her work, though." He motions to a pair of paintings behind the sofa. "Pretty good, huh?"

"Amazing, actually." I leave the table to take a closer look at two oil paintings of shorelines, each with a lighthouse. If I didn't know they were painted by Jake's sister, I could've easily assumed they were from a seaside gallery in Santa Barbara or Monterey.

Hanging between the paintings is a matching quilt. "Oh my gosh," I say, noticing how complicated the pattern is, almost like a glass mosaic with tiny pieces of coordinating fabrics pieced together, but it's done to perfection. "Did Amber make this too? Quilting is a big thing back home, but I've never seen anything like *this*."

"My mom made it," Jake says, and I turn around with a grin. It's hard to hold this expression, though, when I see that Mrs.

Elliott's smile has a hint of sadness in it—she can't quilt anymore. "She's made a hundred or more quilts as cool as that one, mostly for others."

"I had another one three-quarters done when this darn stroke happened," Mrs. Elliott says. "And as soon as I get my right arm working again, I'll finish it." She looks over at Jake. "I go to a terrific physical therapist a few times a week."

"Mom likes PT," Jake says, "because she thinks her therapist is cute."

Mrs. Elliott doesn't look the least bit embarrassed. "And he's single, and always easy to talk to," she says. "Which reminds me, I should increase my visits."

"I don't know, Mom," Jake replies. "He seems a little too serious for you."

"Son, at my age, I'm lucky to meet a man with his own teeth and hair."

Jake laughs. "Then I guess you better grab him before anything falls out."

I take another look at the wall and say, "I've never quilted, Mrs. Elliott, but I do know how to sew a bit. So if you wouldn't mind teaching me the basics, I'd love to come another time and help you finish the quilt you're working on."

All she needs is an extra hand, right?

"Would you really?" she asks in a tone of disbelief. "It's an awfully long way to drive."

"No problem," I reply.

I turn back to find Jake staring at me, a slow smile developing on his face. "I, uh . . . I'm gonna load up my boxes," he says. "You two can talk about quilting, but not about me. Don't talk about *me*."

"So, about that time he spent in prison," Mrs. Elliott says as Jake walks off. But we really do end up talking about quilting, and she glows as she explains the process. From choosing fabrics to cutting each tiny piece and setting up the frame, to threading needles and stitching one careful stitch at a time—it all sounds exhausting. But it's clear that quilting means as much to Mrs. Elliott as acting does to me.

It isn't just a hobby, it's part of who she is.

How would I feel if by some bad twist of fate, I couldn't do what I love most? The thought makes me a little sick inside, and I have to swallow down a lump in my throat so I can talk again when Jake returns. "All right, we're ready to go," he says.

Mrs. Elliott and I express how nice it was to meet each other, and I tell her that I'm entirely serious about helping with the unfinished quilt. Then Jake and I head for the front door.

"It was good to meet you too, Charlie," Jake says with a cheerful wave to the invisible man behind his mom. "I always wanted a brother."

I smack his arm. "That's the last time you'll ever tease me about Charlie."

"I seriously doubt it," he replies.

Once we're in the car, Jake tells me how much he wishes his mom could at least quilt. He says he's hired a housekeeper who not only cleans, but prepares meals that Mrs. Elliott can just heat up, as well as two home health nurses who alternate days caring for her physical needs—including taking her to appointments—and Jake has promised extra pay to all of them if they'll help his mom quilt once or twice a week. But so far, nobody has.

No wonder he gave me that smile when I offered.

The longer we talk, the more I realize how expensive Mrs. Elliott's care has to be. I also try to imagine how things would be for her if Jake didn't have the job he has. How many people in her situation need long-term nurses or someone to make them meals or clean their house? Let alone a friend who can help them enjoy activities they can't do on their own. Are there enough organizations out there that provide services like this?

Hmm . . . a cause that matters to me. I'll have to think this over.

"You know," Jake says, "there's a club down the street here that's so dark and crowded, no one would recognize you—you're in the mood for some fun, that is."

I don't smile and nod on purpose. It just happens.

We pull up to a dance club a few minutes later, and I scan the square three-story glass building and the massive crowd waiting to get into The Cage. "Do you think we could use a back entrance?" I ask.

Jake opens his door. "I'm way ahead of you."

While we walk through the parking lot, just a few inches apart, I put my hands in my pockets because I'm suddenly hyperaware of them swinging by my sides. Jake does the same thing at exactly the same time, and we both laugh.

"Awkward much?" I say.

"No, actually."

We stop short of a back entrance, guarded by a bouncer. "Wait here and keep your head down," Jake tells me. "Let's hope I'm a better actor than I think I am."

In L.A. I can sneak into a club without much fanfare, but I doubt Phoenix has a lot of people trying to avoid recognition.

Jake pays the guy, and when he returns, he whispers, "All right,

I told him that my bitter ex-girlfriend is standing at the front entrance, and he totally understood."

I smile and drop my head as we pass by the bouncer.

We have to feel our way down a pitch-black hallway and keep bumping into each other. The club music is our only compass until we find the dance floor. It's jammed with bodies, and the flashing colored lights make it impossible to get a clear picture of anyone. "Great place, huh?" Jake says, leaning down so I can hear him over booming hip-hop.

"I love it." The tempo is so intense my heart feels like it's pumping with the downbeat. Jake takes my hand—only so we won't get separated—and we weave through body after body until we find a small space to dance. It doesn't take long for me to loosen up because Jake isn't too touchy at all. And whenever a slow song plays, we always take a break.

I shake off all thoughts of this being a bad idea and just have a good time.

We're there for about two hours before we both show signs of being too tired to stand, let alone dance. Jake asks me if we should leave after the next song, and I agree.

But the next song starts, and it's a slow song. I take a step to go get some water, and I guess end the night a few minutes early, but Jake hooks a finger around one of my belt loops and pulls me back. "Hey, we're just friends, remember? I think we can handle it."

He's right. I'm being ridiculous.

"Are you sure?" I say as he settles his hands on my waist. I move mine to his shoulders and try to ignore my racing pulse. "I've heard that nine out of ten girls pass out when they get this close to you."

He holds me a bit tighter. "Even if that were true, you'd still be the *one* who didn't."

In different circumstances, he might've been wrong about that.

When the tempo picks up again, he takes my hand and leads me through the crowd, into the dark hallway, and out the back door. He lets go when we reach the parking lot—sort of abruptly, in fact. I take a deep breath while a fresh breeze cools me off.

As far as I could tell, not a single person recognized me.

Jake seems to be distracted by something and keeps glancing toward the club entrance as we walk. Maybe he really does have a bitter ex-girlfriend waiting in line now.

But it doesn't matter. Just before we reach his car, a smile takes over my entire face, and I tell Jake, "I've had more fun tonight than I've had in forever. Thank you."

JAKE

"Elliott!" My name echoes across the parking lot. *I knew it.* I had thought I saw Devin pull up to the club just as we walked out of it.

"You better hide or things might get crazy," I tell Emma, hurrying to open my car door. Her eyes widen, and she jumps inside. I shut the door and lean against it.

"Jake, my man!" Devin says, coming over with Mark. "You said you wouldn't be up until tomorrow." He motions to Emma, who I hope keeps her face hidden. I shift, trying to block the light from the street lamps. "But no wonder you didn't call."

"It was a last-minute thing," I say, unwilling to share Emma. Not tonight. "I have to make another trip for my stuff anyway."

"I don't get you," Mark says. "You're loaded. Hire some movers."

"It's only boxes," I tell him. "I bought my furniture in Tucson."

Devin cranes his neck for a better look. "Who's the chick?"

I don't budge. "No one you need to know about."

"It never is," Mark says with a hand on my shoulder. "We've done all we can for you."

"Yeah, everything but take a hint when I want you to get lost," I say, and they laugh because they think I'm joking. I promise to call when I'm back in Phoenix tomorrow, and we part ways. I have some explaining to do.

"Cute friends," Emma says once I'm in the car. "I could see them in the mirror."

"Sorry I had you hide, but those guys have been bugging me nonstop to set you up with them. Especially Devin, the one with the brown hair." I drive toward the main road. "So imagine what it would've looked like if they'd seen us together—in Phoenix."

A date, for one thing. Which is exactly what Emma wants to avoid.

"Got it." Emma glances out the window, and there's silence in the car for about ten seconds before she adds, "Setting me up might actually be a good thing, though. When Rachel visits me for the premiere, I was hoping you could take her out. So I guess we can double that weekend, and you know, I'll go with Devin." She looks back. "Is that okay?"

Is she freaking kidding? No, it isn't *okay*. "Sure."

Silence again. Then, "You'd tell me if you didn't want to do that, right?"

"I always say what's on my mind," I lie.

"Just checking," Emma says. "The premiere is, like, ten weeks away though, so if Devin starts dating someone, or whatever, it wouldn't be a big deal." Was there some subtext in there? "But don't get me wrong. I'm sure he's cool."

Nope, no subtext. She'll go out with *Devin*, but not with me.

Devin pretty much lives the life of my dreams anyway, always has. Perfect family with plenty of money, and he's flying through school and loves telling me about it. He's been my best friend since junior high, but we're still big-time competitors when it comes to just about everything. I would have rather set Emma up with Mark, who's a bit of a goofball.

I turn on the stereo. "Yep. Devin's the coolest guy I know."

"Is he the one whose sister is your agent?" Emma says, *still* talking about Devin.

I just nod and focus on the road again.

"Oh! I forgot to tell you! McGregor let some interesting news slip." Whatever it is, Emma sounds excited. "You and Kimmi have a big make-out scene coming up!"

No way. "Please tell me you're kidding."

She smiles up at me, the joke obvious now. "That wouldn't be so bad, would it?"

"Not bad at all. For Kimmi."

Emma laughs and my tension eases. "Oh, please. You can't be *that* good."

There's a glimmer in her eyes that makes me want to say, *Try me.*

"With a room full of people watching, screen kissing is far from romantic, anyway," she goes on. "My first kiss happened on camera, and it took about a dozen takes and four camera angles to get right. I was so nervous that the director had to close the set."

"Seriously?" I ask. "How many guys have you kissed since then?"

Emma about jumps out of her skin. "Excuse me? That's a little nosy!"

"On set, of course. That's all I meant." I flip on the car light to get a better look at her. "You're blushing."

Emma checks in the visor mirror. "Nuh-uh."

She *is* blushing. "I'll guess. One . . . two . . . three . . . am I getting warmer? Four . . ."

"Oh, fine!" she says. "Eight."

"I figured you'd know. Girls always count—we're nothing more than numbers."

"Whatever! That's such a guy thing."

"Really?" I ask, feigning shock. "So, how many guys have you kissed *off*-camera?"

Emma covers her face and neither of us can stop laughing. "You're cruel."

"And you're trapped in a car with me, going . . ." I look at the speedometer. I'm only at fifty so I speed up. "Going sixty-five—for another two hours—and I'm a pretty patient guy. So just get it over with."

She keeps laughing and shaking her head. "All right, but you'll be in the hot seat next."

"Fair enough." I don't have anything to hide.

"Dang." Emma draws a long breath. "I ended up dating three of those eight guys I had to kiss at work, and thanks to the tabloids, it isn't hard to guess who. But the first time I kissed any of them was on set. So that kind of took away from the *real* sparks."

"No sparks, huh?" I say, feeling a few sparks myself. "That's sad."

"I guess so," she replies. "Okay, my turn to pry. Kimmi is all over you, but I can't decide if you're playing hard to get or if you're really not interested. Which is it?"

This is easy. "I can't stand snobby chicks. Too high maintenance."

"Don't tell me you haven't dated any of the models you've worked with."

"Of course I have, which is exactly why I avoid girls like Kimmi."

Emma looks out the window again. "You never know. You can't help who you fall for."

EMMA

Jake and I didn't get back to Tucson until two thirty in the morning. Then we talked in his car until after three. He had me in a giggle fit the entire time—saying all the right things to embarrass me, but not going so far that I was offended. My sides are still sore from laughing when my alarm buzzes at seven. It takes me a moment to remember why I set it; it's Saturday.

Motocross. Brett. Kimmi. Lots of noise.

Brett picks me up in his electric-blue custom truck, with just a bench seat in the front, and we head to Kimmi's place. She jumps in, scooting me right next to Brett, so he says, "Hey, honey," with the tone of a total hick, and gives my knee a squeeze.

Seating is also an issue on our flight to Los Angeles. When Brett bought the tickets there were only two seats left in first class so he had to buy one in coach as well, which he'd "unintentionally" attached to Kimmi's name.

I offer to take her place in coach, since she refuses to sit there, but Brett says, "Kimmi and I will fight the entire ninety minutes, and the air marshals will come after us."

He has a good point, so I end up next to Kimmi in first class.

She's too busy with demands on the flight attendants to talk to me for a while, but when she's finally settled in and has reapplied her lip gloss, she turns my way and says, "I've been meaning to tell you that you pull off the tramp act better than I'd thought you would."

"Um, thanks?" Is she referring to the way I play my character, or saying that I'm acting like a tramp as myself? I choose the safer path. "I don't think Eden is exactly what she seems. I've heard some girls dress that way because they're looking for any attention they can get, so I bet deeper issues will come out as her story unfolds."

Kimmi's mouth parts as if I've directly insulted her. "Just because a girl isn't ashamed of her body doesn't mean she has issues. *Or* that she wants attention."

A touchy little nerve there. "Of course not. I'm only speculating about my character. You're doing an amazing job with Kassidy, by the way. Are you okay with the costumes now?"

Kimmi closes her compact mirror with a snap. "I'm wearing them, aren't I?"

"And I'm still stuck with being Look at Me Barbie."

I expect another snarky comment, but Kimmi offers me what could actually pass for a real smile before uncoiling her earbuds and plugging them into her ears.

A few minutes later, a flight attendant hands me an airline napkin with huge scribbled words on it: *Come back here. I'm bored!!!* My gosh, Brett needs a full-time circus to entertain him. "He ran out of room on the napkin, but he wants me to tell you he has a deck of cards," the flight attendant says. "And an empty seat beside him."

"All right, thanks," I reply, a bit put on the spot. I turn to talk to Kimmi, but she already has her eyes closed.

Brett sees me coming down the narrow aisle and waves. He isn't the only one who notices me, though, so I stop several times to return greetings from passengers. As usual, I feel rude for not having more personal what's-your-name, where-are-you-from conversations with every one of them.

"I'm impressed," Brett says when I finally reach him. "You lasted longer with Kimmi than I expected."

There are three seats on his half of the row, but he's sitting in the middle one, so I still have to sit right next to him. I choose the window. "I plugged *Coyote Hills* all over the place while we were boarding," he adds. "And I told everyone this is a publicity trip, so don't worry about your whole *we're-not-a-couple* phobia."

"I won't," I reply. "You have a deck of cards? Let's play."

"Nah, I just wanted to give you an excuse to ditch Kimmi." Brett leans closer. "I need to ask you something."

"Okay, but you might want to lower your voice from sonic boom?"

"Sorry, I only have two volumes: loud and deafening," he says. But then he at least *tries* to whisper. "Look, I just want to make sure you're serious about keeping things casual, even in private, because I've had a feeling since we first met that you have a thing for me, and—"

"What? No, I don't!" I jerk away from him, my face instantly burning. Then I catch myself and hush my own voice. "Why would I do that? Have a thing for you, I mean. Because I don't. Never did."

"Wow, you really do have it bad," he says, laughing and moving closer again. "Or *did* . . . which is it? Present or past?"

How did he figure this out?

He hums the theme from *Jeopardy*, waiting for my answer. And there's no escape—not without a parachute—so I finally look directly at him and say, "Past tense, Brett. *Very* past tense. So wipe off that silly grin."

"I knew it!" he says, pointing at me in triumph, and I slap his hand down. "But you're already over me? Since when?"

"Since the day we met and I discovered you were a total perv," I say, almost laughing myself. "And you have no social filter whatsoever. Like now, for example, you're sitting here all full of yourself, and you're not the least bit bothered by how stupid you're making *me* feel. You really can't see what's wrong with that, can you?"

"Um, sort of?"

There's no stopping me now. "You've been treated like a movie star since you were four, and allowed to say *whatever* to *whomever* you want. So sixteen years later, you still have the maturity of a four-year-old."

"Ouch," Brett says, and leans back against his seat. "Let me hear it then, straight out. What do I do that's so immature?"

Fine, he asked for it. "For a start, the way you talk to girls, and about girls, is disgusting. I want to rinse your mouth out with toilet bowl cleaner," I say. "You need to think about things before they come blasting out—especially if they have anything to do with . . ."

I whisper, even quieter, half a dozen of his favorite ill-humored topics.

"That stuff's not so bad. Aren't you gonna tell me I have to stop talking about—" I slam my hand over his mouth before he can get anything out. But then he calms down, and says, "Okay, the truth is, I *know* I need to grow up. You're about the hundredth person to drop that hint lately. Even my parents have been getting irritated with me, which is . . . weird."

Brett's parents are known to pamper him, big time. "Well, I can tell you're at least trying to be nicer to Kimmi, so keep that up. It's a good start."

He reaches across me to close the window shade, with a bit of a bang, before he speaks again. "It would be a whole lot easier if someone would just tape my mouth shut, or at least write a script that dictates *exactly* how I should behave. I could follow that, no problem. But instead, I get crap from almost everyone—people judging me, hating me. I don't remember the last time someone other than my mom or dad gave me a compliment that wasn't related to . . . well, you know, the way I look. Or my acting, which is nice, but kind of doesn't count because that's me pretending to be *someone else.*"

I'm listening intently but am too astonished to interrupt him.

Brett pushes both hands through his hair. "I mean, how many roles have I played—since I was a kid? Twenty, at least. And I swear, a bit of each character has hung on to me, so now I'm just a sloppy conglomeration of all these people who . . . who don't even really exist." He looks at me, still completely serious. "Is this making any sense? Because what I'm saying is"—Brett motions with his hands to indicate his entire body—"how much of this *freak show* is really *me*?"

Wow. "I totally get where you're coming from," I tell him. "You've actually just voiced something I've been trying to put into words for years. That's a compliment for you, right? And I actually gave you another one a minute ago—I said I was impressed by your effort to get along with Kimmi. So there, that's two in just one day, from someone other than your parents."

Brett grins, his entire demeanor changing in an instant. "No wonder I like you, Taylor. But not *that* way," he says with a nudge. "Now stop touching me, or you'll make people talk."

Maybe this trip won't be so bad after all.

Payton picks us up at the airport in his black Escalade, and Kimmi sits in the front seat, where he has a perfect view of her long, beautiful legs. She actually seems nervous, fidgeting with her bag and such. Payton is, after all, sort of a marvel to look at—dirty-blond hair, killer brown eyes, just a shadow of facial hair—the guy is a perfect image of a mega movie star.

I already know the other guys too. Gabe and Aiden are members of a boy band who can barely sing, but girls scream so loud at their concerts no one notices. They hit on me every time I see them. But they hit on everyone.

The California weather is great as usual—overcast enough to keep the sun from beating down, but still warm. Brett gets lost in the races pretty fast, but once in a while, he leans over to tell me something "super cool" about this special engagement event. He also makes sure that I notice, over and over again, the unique roars of each souped-up engine, which really only sound like a whole lot of noise to me.

Kimmi seems put out because Payton isn't paying more attention to her. She's left the bleachers several times to make "important calls," but I suspect that she keeps leaving just so she can make another grand entrance, which is usually when Payton talks to her the most.

Dirt is spraying everywhere, and we're in the front row, so the exhaust from the bikes is mixing with the dirt to make my bare legs look like I've been mud wrestling. Brett keeps laughing about the state of my legs and offering to clean them off.

"Thanks, but no," I tell him. What was I thinking, wearing shorts?

Brett returns his attention to the riders who are lining up for the next race right as my cell buzzes in my back pocket, so I sit on the bench and read a text message from Jake: **Devin says yes. He'll take you out if you really want him to. And my invisible brother Charlie wants to go out with you too. Do I get commission for setting up these deals?**

I laugh, just to myself, and write back: **One date for me = one hamburger for you. Fair?**

Once I send that, I notice my stomach doing back flips. Not good. And Jake's message had a typical friend tone. But *my* text was flirty.

Crap! Someone needs to invent a way to unsend text messages.

Jake is taking an unusually long time to reply, so I stand again and yell like everyone else, having no clue who I'm cheering for. When the engines die down, everyone starts talking about dinner plans. I hear a word here and there, and I fight the urge to check my cell when it buzzes again.

What if Jake flirts back? What if I've started something I can't stop? I finally just grab my phone and read his message: **Darn.**

Only one burger then, for the Devin deal. I tried to find Charlie to tell him the good news, but he's disappeared again.

I stifle a laugh and put my phone away before Brett notices who I'm talking to. Then seconds later, he latches on to my arms and turns me toward him. "I'm guessing that big smile means you're cool with 99."

"With what?" I ask.

"Club 99," he says. "Sara Roberts is having her birthday bash there tonight."

"Awesome. Let's go," I rush to say. Then something dark trickles into me . . . if this is a party for Sara, Troy might be there. He's the reason I know her. "Oh, wait. I'm actually staying at my aunt's tonight, and promised I'd be there around seven," I tack on, which is true, except that she isn't expecting me at any particular time. "And that's only an hour from now."

"Are you serious? Your curfew is at *seven*?"

"Not my curfew, but—" I give myself a mental shake. I can't outrun Troy forever. At some point I'll have to face him, and it might be better if it's in front of a crowd, where he always plasters on his phony smile and looks like the hottest hookup in the room. "Never mind. I'll just call her and—"

"Hey! Get lost, will ya?" Brett yells. He lets go of my arms and leans over the guardrail. "Do your job! The race is *behind* you!"

I peek over the rail too, and my head spins.

"Brett . . . that isn't a motocross photographer." The guy taking pictures of us is a sleazebag named Craig Paddock, and he's on my list of most despised paparazzi. But he has on an actual press pass—probably fake—so there isn't anything we can do about him.

Gabe has an idea of his own, though, and starts undoing his belt as he turns his back to Paddock. "I'll give him a shot he can make a million on."

Brett scoots past me. "No way, dude," he says, stopping him. "I promised McGregor I wouldn't get caught within fifty miles of bad press."

Paddock points his camera toward the motorcycles to keep up his ruse, and goes off thousands of dollars richer. His profit depends on which shots he got, and how much gossip a reporter can dig up to attach them to.

We attract so much attention at the end of the race that security has to escort us to the parking lot. Paddock is around for all of it, of course, snapping pictures like it's his only daughter's first day of school. And right in the middle of the chaos, Kimmi links an arm with mine and says, "How do you deal with this, Emma? It's crazy!"

"Just smile and hope you don't have anything between your teeth," I reply, thinking Kimmi picked an awfully convenient time to become my best friend. There's nothing better for a starlet than to be seen with the A-crowd.

That's when it hits me . . . Paddock was tipped off.

For young Hollywood, Club 99 is the most popular hangout in Los Angeles. There's always great music, good food, and if the only thing you do here is people watch, you'll have all the entertainment you need.

It's eight by the time we start mingling with the star-studded crowd. I get a lot of "Where have you been?" types of questions, since I haven't hung out in L.A. in a while. But I'm also asked a dozen too many times about who I'm dating now that Troy and I are over—as if I *have* to be dating someone new—and everyone acts like we just barely broke up. I remind them that it's been over four months.

In dating time, isn't that like a decade?

The main part of the club is oval shaped and decorated in shades of blue, with platinum accents. About thirty semicircular booths line the walls. The center is open for dancing, but the music is low for now, and the lighting is still bright. Almost everyone is huddled around a table with drinks, appetizers, and a massive chocolate fountain.

Sara Roberts is a media darling, and seems to love it, so photographers are everywhere. I've already heard that Paddock was turned away at the door. That's a pretty good sign that security is running a tight ship, but even respected photographers can cause plenty of trouble.

"I'm surprised you didn't recognize that photog at the race," I tell Brett. At first he was sitting on one end of our large booth, with Gabe and Aiden on the opposite end and me in the middle. But then I was scooted closer to Brett by his buddies, who reminded me that we still have to fit Kimmi and Payton in here. "Craig Paddock? Forked tongue, big red horns. No?"

Brett waves to a pair of twittering girls across the room. He's already named them Glamour and Glitter because the club lights are bouncing like lasers off their gobs of jewelry and threatening to blind us. "I can't tell one photog from another," he says. "They always have a camera hiding their face."

It's never hard for *me* to spot Craig Paddock. Before he snaps shots, he usually says something snide, like, "Emma darling, why do your boyfriends keep cheating on you?" Those were his exact words a few months ago, during all the Troy fallout. In response, I gave Paddock a look halfway between mortified and fuming, and he captured it. The shot was then attached to a story with the head-line: EMMA HAS BREAKDOWN! STARVING HERSELF!

Apparently, the photo Paddock took proved I was starving myself because all I had in my small grocery bag was a few stalks of celery. In reality, my aunt and I had been making a nice pot of stew when I realized I forgot to pick up celery, so I ran down to the corner market for it. But Paddock was waiting outside for me when I left the store, and that's how I became a poster child for starving children.

"Why was Paddock at the motocross, anyway?" I ask Brett, still trying to keep some distance from him. "It's old news that you guys go to those races, and you don't usually take girls. So why did he show up *today*?"

"How do you know we usually don't take chicks? You would've had to ask around," Brett says, and then he laughs like a play-ground bully. "You really *did* like me."

"Did, Brett. Keep the emphasis on *did*," I hiss. "And I swear if you ever tell another soul, I'll shave your head in the middle of the night."

"Emma," he says, all patronizing, "I've already told you that you shouldn't expect to be anywhere near me in the middle of the night. Take a hint."

I elbow him. "Get serious," I say, whispering again so Gabe and Aiden won't hear. But they're already busy scoping out their prey for the night. "I think Kimmi might've tipped off Paddock.

She totally lit up when he asked her name, and she told him all about being in the cast of *Coyote Hills* like it was a practiced reply. So I'm sure she set it all up to get attention."

"But isn't that the point of our trip?" Brett says. "Kimmi's definitely been leeching, though. Look how she's hanging all over Payton, and he's having to introduce her to everyone."

It's true, but in the absence of motorcycles to get Payton's blood pumping, he doesn't seem to mind Kimmi hanging on him. "Remember how she kept making all those phone calls today?" I ask Brett.

He thinks about it. "You're probably right. But photogs are all over here anyway, so what does it matter?"

"Because Paddock sells to the dirtiest tabloids." Brett's attention seems elsewhere when I say this last bit, so I peek around him to see what he's looking at. "Oh, it's Bethany Parke. You should go say hello."

Brett turns back. "Yeah, I probably *should*. But she can be annoying."

"What? I thought you . . . liked her." This is the polite way to interpret the type of relationship Brett told me he has with Bethany.

"I like her all right," Brett replies. "But I can like her just as easily *tomorrow* night."

I nudge him toward the edge of the booth. "Excuse me, please. I'm gonna go throw up."

Brett laughs and wraps an arm around me. "Darn it, Taylor. Am I being naughty again?"

Kimmi and Payton finally slide into the booth. "Hey, you lovebirds," Kimmi says. "Everyone's begging us to dish on the hot new couple."

Brett and I both sit straight up. "We're just talking," I say.

Kimmi's glossy pink lips curve into a smile. "That's not how it looks. And someone wants a minute with you, Emma." She motions in the direction of the food. "He asked if I'd pass along the message to meet him by the back door."

My entire body stiffens before I even dare to look. Troy's eyes lock on mine as he pops a chocolate-covered strawberry into his mouth.

On the outside, I only glance away. Inside, all power shuts off . . .

Total blackout.

"This should be interesting," Brett says.

I fumble for my phone but can't get a grip on it. "I need a taxi," I whisper.

Brett lifts one of my hands. "Whoa. You're shaking."

I can barely speak with my heart blocking my throat. The thumping is in my neck, my chest, my ears. "It's nothing. I just . . . I need to leave."

Brett reaches across the table. "Payton, keys. Now!"

I hear Kimmi and Payton whispering, sense some movement. "*Please,* I just want a taxi," I repeat. "If Troy asks, I'm staying at the Four Seasons."

I don't want him to find me. Anywhere. Ever again.

"Okay, okay." Brett says. "We'll get you out of here."

But Troy is at our table before we can stand. "Hey, guys, what's up?"

I squeeze my hands together and force myself to raise my eyes. I hate being this scared of him, but all I can see right now is his fist hitting my car window.

And blood on shattered glass.

Kimmi's voice pierces through the high-pitched static in my ears. "I passed along the message, Troy," she says. "But Emma is with someone else tonight. *Obviously.*"

Brett speaks next. "We'll have to catch up later. Our food will be here any minute."

"I just need to talk to her for a sec," Troy says. "C'mon, Emma."

Brett laughs. "That's just wrong, dude. Like Kimmi said, Emma is with me tonight."

"Do I look like I care?"

My skin flickers between fire and ice.

Payton stands. "Get lost, Troy. Seriously. You had your chance with Emma."

"And now Brett gets a turn?" The tendons in Troy's neck are flexed, ready to snap, as he faces Payton. My mind shouts at me to do something, stop this, but my body won't move. "Maybe you oughta tell your buddy here that Emma's *traditional values* won't exactly fit into his brand of lifestyle, you know what I mean? He'd have a much better time with one of the other ten girls he has here on tap, than with this coldhearted bit—"

Brett shoots from the booth, I scream, and Troy falls to the floor—all at once.

Cameras flash like lightning, and the entire area clears. I'm under the table before I know it, my hands over my face. The yelling and scuffling goes on and on, sounds of fist against flesh. Then the worst of it seems to be over, and someone is suddenly under the table with me. "Your face is a mess. Put this over you." I peek between my fingers to see Kimmi holding out a black dinner jacket. "Follow me."

I can't believe I'm desperate enough to trust her, but I take the jacket anyway and crawl out. Bouncers have finally pulled Troy and Brett apart, but there's still plenty of noise and commotion. With my head partially shrouded, Kimmi leads me through the buzzing crowd and stops outside the women's bathroom.

She takes the jacket back. "Go in here. I'll keep everyone out."

"What are you doing?" I ask. How does Kimmi benefit from this? "I mean, thank you, but . . ."

"You looked *pathetic* under that table." She holds up the jacket. "And I ripped this off the manager, who was also being pathetic."

Kimmi shoves open the bathroom door, and I step inside.

Mascara and eyeliner are smeared all over my face. I really am pathetic. How could I have let things with Troy get so out of control? And now that Brett is involved in this, he'll also have to worry about running into my explosive ex wherever he goes.

At least twenty minutes pass while I attempt to calm down. Then Kimmi returns to the bathroom and says, "The police want to talk to you."

The police? *Crap. Crap. Crap.* This can't be happening.

Kimmi hands me her makeup bag, and adds, "I told them Troy is a disgusting, cheating, prick of an ex-boyfriend who obviously has anger-management issues." My mouth parts in disbelief, and she rolls her eyes. "I knew *you* wouldn't say it, so someone had to."

I half whimper, half laugh. "Can I hug you?"

"Not a chance." She disappears again.

I fix up my face the best I can, and then an officer leads me out to the parking lot. When I see the siren lights and camera flashes cutting through the darkness, I want to push an emergency eject button—fly away, run and hide, pay someone else to be Emma Taylor. At least for tonight.

I'll never forgive myself if Brett gets arrested. McGregor might even fire him.

I scan the group and see several people being interviewed by officers. When I finally spot Brett, I release the breath I've been holding—he isn't in handcuffs. But neither is Troy.

I've witnessed plenty of fistfights at clubs, and the police are rarely called. So why are there *six* squad cars here? I realize the answer as soon as I see the grinning faces of the reporters and photographers. One of them, at least, must've called the cops as soon as the fight broke out and made it sound like a much bigger deal than it was, so they'd have a *bigger* story to tell.

From the looks of it, the police were expecting a full-blown riot.

I answer the officer's questions—he doesn't ask me to reveal anything more than what was said to provoke the fight—and when I'm finished, Brett walks toward me. I'm so relieved to see a smile on his face that I throw my arms around him. "Are you okay? You must hate me!"

"No way!" he says. "I'll get nothing but respect for this."

"But you said that McGregor warned you about bad press." I take a closer look at his left eye. It's swelling fast. "I'll call him right now and explain what happened, so he doesn't have a heart attack when the news hits."

Brett motions to all the cameras and squad cars. "Relax. I don't see a story here."

I sense Troy watching us and dart a glance his way. His icy-blue eyes shoot shivers through me, and as usual, I cave under the weight of his stare and look away.

Pathetic is right. Am I really going to let him keep scaring me like this?

I ask Brett to wait where he is and go over to the officer who interviewed me. I tell him I want to talk to Troy, but emphasize that he may try to get me to leave with him and I don't want to be out of the officer's sight.

"No problem," he replies. "Just glance my way if you need me."

When Troy sees me approaching, he ditches his arm candy and comes within inches of my face. But before he can draw a breath, I tell him, "What could you *possibly* have to say to me that was worth making yourself look like such a jealous, desperate freak?"

Troy is used to me taking whatever crap he dishes out, so my sudden aggression throws him off. "I . . . uh," he begins, then his face darkens again. "I want to make sure we're clear on something: you better keep your mouth *shut* about what happened to your window." He holds up a hand. "I have scars all over my knuckles, thanks to you."

I've got to hit him where it hurts, and he's just provided all the ammunition I need.

"Then let *me* be clear about something," I say, about to lie through my teeth. "I know a reporter who's dying for a career-making story, and I'd love to help him out. I've already given him a copy of the security tapes from a house that had a perfect view of my aunt's driveway—betcha didn't consider cameras *that* day, did you? And he thinks the public will be *really* interested in seeing one of Hollywood's 'it' boys try to punch his fist through my car window. And I've also passed along your messages. You know which ones—talk of you following me wherever I go, watching my every move. Sort of creepy, don't ya think? And yeah, if you're wondering, my reporter friend is only waiting for my go-ahead, or for something else to make him trigger happy. In fact, he thinks this story could skip the tabloids and go straight to primetime news. Then you'll definitely be a household name, won't you?"

Troy blinks a few times. "That's blackmail, Emma. And it's illegal."

"No, this is called self-defense, which is actually *encouraged*. So if you ever threaten me again, in any way, the next time you see your pretty face on a magazine cover, it will have the headline STALKER printed above it."

I don't need to wait for Troy's reply. I've just delivered the performance of my life, and his stunned look says enough.

JAKE

Emma leaves a message Sunday afternoon. She says, "Don't believe anything you see or hear about this weekend until I tell you about it myself. Tomorrow, at work."

She must not have checked the schedule, because I have Monday off. When I don't hear from her by nine that night, I give in and call her. She doesn't pick up, but sends me a text right away: **On the phone with my mom and publicist. For 50 more hours. Ugh. Sorry.**

Tuesday morning, when Emma is on location somewhere else, I walk into the sound studio to find Brett in the foam-padded booth. The whole left side of his face is black and blue. "Ouch," I tell the sound guy.

He shrugs. "Never a boring day with this dude."

"Hey! I can hear you!" Brett says.

"No, you can't," the sound guy replies with a laugh, just then turning on his mic. He tweaks a few more controls on the massive mixing board. "Okay, let's go again with that last line . . . we're rolling."

Brett looks back to the jumbo TV on the wall and watches himself walk across a football field with Kimmi. I remember it being really windy the day they shot this scene, so the mics probably didn't get a good take.

If there's just a word or two missing, we can usually do "wild lines" right on set, where a few retakes are done using a boom mic. Then everything is patched together during editing. But when full lines are missing like this, we come into the actual sound studio for automated dialogue replacement. The tricky thing with ADR is to match the pacing of your words to the exact movement of your mouth, and the tone of your voice to the emotion your character is supposed to be feeling. It takes some getting used to, but I kinda like the process.

This sound studio is also used by the Foley artists—actors who re-create the crunching of gravel under boots, the dropping of books, slamming of doors, just about every background noise imaginable. Watching them work could entertain me for hours— each footstep, creak, and thud is performed with choreographed precision. And they do it take after take until they get it perfect, just like the actors on set.

Sound editing is way more complicated than I ever could've guessed.

There are three beeps and Brett goes back to his mic. "Just drop it, Kassidy," he says. "It isn't worth investigating."

The sound guy checks and double-checks the recording. "Got it," he tells Brett. "You're almost as good as one-take Jake here."

I was hoping he wouldn't remember the nickname he gave me last time.

"I hate you, man," Brett says when he comes out of the booth. "Everywhere I go: Rah, rah! Jake is *great*! If I had pom-poms of my own, I'd shove them down your throat."

"I think I saw some in a prop box a few days ago," I reply. "But if we're gonna fight, I like my chances. You look like a pretty good punching bag."

"Oh, this." Brett rubs a hand over his face. "You know what happened, right?"

"Kimmi?" I ask.

"That was my first guess too," the sound guy says. "I'll be back in five."

He leaves the sound studio, and Brett tells me, "You obviously don't watch the entertainment news *or* go online—it's been all over the last couple of days. And the tabloids are out today." I just shrug, so he goes on. "Emma and I went to a party at Club 99 Saturday night, and Troy Dawson spotted us getting cozy in a booth. Emma refused to talk to him, but he wouldn't leave her alone, so I . . . had to take care of things."

I have no idea how long I stand there, mulling over the words *getting cozy,* before I process the rest of what he said. "Whoa. Seriously?"

Does Emma's no-dating policy only apply to me?

"Yeah, man. Totally nuts," Brett says. "But I've never seen anyone so freaked out. Emma started shaking like an earthquake when she saw Troy, and I had to wonder why, you know?" The possibilities make me sick enough to stop thinking about my wounded pride. "So when Troy wouldn't back down, I snapped. Even McGregor told me I did the right thing."

He probably did. I clap him on the shoulder. "I guess that makes you a hero. A butt-ugly one right now, but still."

Brett and Emma? I don't get it. But Troy making Emma so nervous . . . that bugs me even more. What did he do to her?

Studying a script for at least an hour every night doesn't fit well with my regular workout schedule, so now I do my core work while memorizing lines—which is why I'm in the middle of crunches, and only wearing gym shorts, when Emma shows up on my porch Tuesday night.

"Um . . . *hello*," she says, her wide blue eyes finally darting from my bare chest to my face. "I saw a sign today that sort of worries me. That river behind us is called Rattlesnake Creek, so does that mean . . . ?"

"Didn't we already have this talk about Arizona?" I ask.

"Yes, but I didn't expect snakes to be . . . you know, waiting outside my kitchen door. Like stray cats."

"Well, if you're worried about them going hungry, you could always toss them a few raw eggs," I say, not sure if I should invite her in or not. After thinking about her and Brett all day, I'm leaning toward *not*. But I also can't stop thinking about the way Troy must've treated her. "Other than that, you just have to be careful. Stay on the path, watch where you step."

Emma shivers. "Holy. Freaking. *Crap*."

I shrug. "I guess, if it would make you feel better, I could try to . . . I don't know, herd them back into the mountains? I might've done a merit badge for that in Scouts."

Emma laughs and she has me, right there. I can't stay away from her.

"Actually, could you just go running with me?" Her hair is pulled into a ponytail, and she has on a tight gray tank and navy running shorts. She's looking way too pretty for actual exercise. "I want to explain all this crazy L.A. stuff."

"Sure," I say, even though I'd rather die a slow death than hear any more about it. "But we agreed that Friday night wasn't a date, so there's really nothing you need to *explain*."

"I get that. It's just that I wasn't on a date with Brett either." Emma reveals a rolled-up tabloid she's been holding behind her back. "And I at least want my friends to know the truth."

I scoop my shirt off the floor and pull it on. "The press made a big deal out of nothing—guys fight over girls all the time. They'll be buddies again by next weekend."

"But they weren't really fighting over me," Emma says, opening the tabloid to expose two full pages of pictures that suggest otherwise. "And this 'hot new romance' crap is silly."

I point out a photo of Brett and Emma nestling like turtledoves in a booth. Brett was right about getting cozy. "I wonder where they got *that* idea."

This earns me a stabbing glare, so I hurry to add, "Sorry, but—"

"Jake, it was wrong for me to believe someone else's interpretation of you and the waitress, wasn't it?" Emma backs me up through the doorway of my condo and shuts the door behind her. I gulp. "So, please, just let me separate fact from fiction so you don't make the same mistake. Believe it or not, even pictures can lie."

I kinda like this alpha-Emma thing she has going on. "Whatever, that's cool."

"Good. Then read this first." Emma hands me the article:

Brett Crawford was seen cuddling with his new flame, Emma Taylor, in several hot spots this past weekend. According to sources, the couple met just over two weeks ago on the set of the upcoming television drama, *Coyote Hills*.

A source close to the young stars revealed, "They were totally in their own world, oblivious to anyone else." Others agree that this is the real thing, not another one of Crawford's weekend flings.

After an exciting day at the motocross, where the pair was anything but ashamed to show affection, they attended the birthday party of a common friend, Sara Roberts, held at Club 99. This was where trouble broke out.

According to eyewitnesses, Taylor's ex, Troy Dawson, saw her kissing Crawford in a private corner booth, and approached the couple. When Taylor refused to speak with him, Dawson began slinging insults, berating her *traditional values* and telling Crawford that he would have a better time with one of his "other ten girls."

Crawford leaped from the booth in a flash, sources say, taking Dawson to the ground. A short fistfight later, with a frightened Taylor crouching under the table, all were released without any charges.

Taylor was later seen crying on Crawford's chest in the club parking lot. A friend of the couple confirmed that Taylor later spoke with Dawson to ask that he give her some room in her new relationship. "He looked seriously ticked off," said the insider. Taylor was reported to have then walked calmly back to Crawford's waiting arms.

With this hot new romance, we see a refreshing change in Crawford's choice of women. Perhaps a girl with "traditional values" can turn this once golden boy back into the star we all used to adore. Here's to love, and to the beginning of a new celebrity couple—Brett and Emma. Or, as we'll now refer to them: *Bremma*.

I only skim the story because I already read it at a grocery store on the way home from work. I hand the tabloid back to Emma, never wanting to touch it again.

"Want to know how much of that is pure garbage?" Emma asks. I nod, grab my running shoes by the door, and sit on one of my massive beanbag chairs. "In a nutshell: most of it's true," she goes on, sending a shockwave through me. "All but the important parts, which is usually the case with stories like this."

"Okay. Which parts?" I ask.

Emma sits next to me, but on the floor. I don't have a couch in my living room. Just two beanbags, a pimped-out entertainment center, and a single lamp—everything is pretty much black.

"I'll explain using these pictures," Emma says. She points to one from the motocross where she's facing Brett and he has his hands on her arms. Her smile explains enough. "This photo actually features a cameo appearance by *you*, because I'd just read your text about your invisible brother Charlie, and it made me laugh. Brett didn't know we were texting and was only asking me about dinner plans. But you know him, he can't talk without touching."

"Oh," is all I say to that, lost in thoughts about her massive smile in the photo being because of *me,* not Brett. I point to one of the shots from Club 99. "What about this?"

Our arms keep brushing when we move. Her skin is warm.

"We weren't even close to kissing in that booth. From any other camera angle, that would've been obvious," she replies. "But there isn't nearly enough sting in a caption that says, 'Brett and Emma were whispering.' We were trying to decide if Kimmi had tipped off the photographer at the race so she could be seen with our group and get some personal publicity."

This detail alone gives Emma's story more credibility. "Do you think Kimmi could've been one of the sources for the article?"

"It's possible." She looks up at me with those eyes that could make me believe anything. "But some reporters attach any label they want, to quote practically anyone. Like a 'source close to the couple' could mean someone who just happened to be sitting a few tables away from us—not an actual friend. And a *friend* could mean someone who 'seems to have our best interest at heart.' Oh, and my favorite: the *insider*. I swear a person can be anywhere *inside* the state of California, but tabloid reporters make it sound like a stranger is living inside my own head because he's so *well* informed. It's a stupid play on words."

"But still a lie." There's something more important I want to know. "Did you really talk to Troy? I'm guessing he might be a . . . jealous, possessive creep?"

Emma bites her lips together, but doesn't look away. "With a very short temper," she finally says. "I didn't see it at first—not at all. But then a couple of months into our relationship, he started acting all broody if I said anything more than hello to another guy.

Then that turned into accusations, and then after the beach bimbo stuff happened and I wouldn't take him back, it got . . . scary, if you want to know the truth."

She eyes me as if she's trying to gauge my reaction. I wonder if she can tell my gut is twisted into a knot. "How scary?"

Emma takes a breath, exhales. "I need to keep this a secret, all right?" she says, and I offer a solemn nod. "The last week of filming, Troy lost control outside my trailer and wouldn't let go of me until he'd said every cruel thing he could think of—he actually left bruises on my arms. I finally broke away and took off in my car, but he followed me. And . . . long story short, it ended when Troy shattered my driver's-side window, with his fist."

"He . . . *what*?" I don't know what I'd expected to hear. "Did he hurt you?"

Emma shakes her head. "I was okay. Better than he was. And I told everyone that someone shattered my window at the beach—apparently trying to break in to the car. But after the fight at Club 99, I threatened to make all of this public, and more, if Troy doesn't leave me alone. I wish I would have done it sooner. It felt great."

My tension eases a bit. "What made you confront him now?"

"Kimmi, if you can believe it," Emma says. "She told me I was pathetic for hiding under that table, and I thought, 'Yeah, I *am* pathetic.' So I finally decided to stand up for myself."

"Good." I feel an urge to hug Emma—more like keep her safe or something—but decide I better hold off. "Thanks for trusting me. I won't tell anyone, I promise."

"I didn't even tell Brett what I said to Troy," Emma reveals with a smile. She then lifts the tabloid again. "This full-page photo was taken of a brief hug I gave Brett when I saw that he hadn't been arrested. So I didn't go back to his 'waiting arms' like the article says, and I never cried on his chest. I left the club, stayed with my aunt, and flew home the next morning. Since then, I've been on the phone with my mom and my publicist, trying to clean up the mess." Emma sighs. "In summary, Jake, there is no *Bremma*—just a touchy-feely friend who risked a lot to kick someone's butt for me. Brett definitely has his faults, but I'm grateful for what he did."

"Me too," I reply. But why did Brett himself tell me they were "getting cozy" in that booth? I stand and help Emma off the floor. We leave through the front door and head toward the running path. "So, let me get this straight," I go on. "As long as guys agree to your *just friends* clause, like me, you'll . . . cuddle with them?"

She laughs. "No! Brett only had his arm around me for a few seconds."

"And his hands all over you too. *But,*" I say before she corrects me again, "I'm not the kind of guy who passes out affection like samples in a bakery. So if I ever act the way Brett does, you should know that it actually *means* something."

Emma smiles, then whips her head in the opposite direction like she hadn't meant for me to see her reaction. Now I know for sure: she likes me.

We reach the paved trail and pick up our pace.

"I've already figured that out about you," she replies. "But as far as hanging out goes, this tabloid crap with Brett makes everything more complicated."

"Why? Brett shouldn't care if we're all just friends."

"Brett isn't who I'm worried about," Emma says. The rush of the river is loud, so we have to run only a foot apart to hear each other. "With the media saying I'm with him, imagine what would happen if I'm seen with *you*—out dancing or something."

On Emma's side of the path, we're approaching a full-grown tarantula resting on a boulder. I try to calculate the odds of her: 1) screaming and jumping into my arms, or 2) never running with me again. I play it safe and distract her before she notices the spider. "Even if you *were* dating both of us," I say, "it's normal to play the field, like everyone else our age."

We pass the tarantula without incident, and Emma shakes her head. "*Normal* girls can date lots of guys at once, but not me. Tabloids can't make money on innocent stories. In their world, no one goes out just to have fun. There has to be a scandal involved."

"But you can't cheat on someone if you're not even together," I say. "And if you're so worried about that, why'd you just knock on my door?"

Emma grabs my shirt and jerks me to a stop. "Because . . ." She faces me and takes a moment to slow her breathing. "Maybe I like hanging out with you. So if you're still cool with that—and not dating, or *cuddling*, or anything in that category—then we just can't be seen together."

I am, without a doubt, the biggest sucker on earth. "Okay. I'm in."

I wonder how long it will take Emma to notice she hasn't let go of my shirt yet. In fact, both of her hands are now holding onto me. She drops them seconds later. "Good," she replies as she glances down the running path, lit only by scattered landscape lights. "How about a race?"

"Seriously?" I ask. "You really think you have a chance?"

"Heck yeah. But I've gotta tie my shoe first." She leans over for a sec, then shoots back up and takes off. "Or not!"

I start after her, but almost fall on my face. Emma untied both of my laces. It's pretty fair to say I'll be chasing her for a while.

EMMA

Within minutes of leaving Club 99, I had called my publicist to tell her *almost* everything that happened—nothing about what I said to Troy. But even then, she kept saying, "We need your mother in on this."

My impulse was to shout, "No way!" But I knew that "I'll tell her tomorrow morning" was as much as I could delay it. First, I'd wanted to see how the story unfolded on the gossip sites, which often hint at the direction the tabloids will take. And before ten that night, news about the fight was everywhere—and the bottom line? Brett and I are "in love."

Unfortunately, Rachel saw the gossip site stuff pop up at the same time I did and immediately told her mom, who then sent a text to my own mother, who then called me at my aunt's house at midnight. She was crazy mad because I had not only put myself in a situation to make it even *look* like I was dating Brett and—just slightly worse—incited a fight, but because I'd also committed the cardinal sin of calling my publicist first. As Mom reminded me, it's *her* job to discuss damage control with my publicist, not mine.

Mom calls all the shots. *She* gets to decide how stupid or innocent I come out looking. If I had another manager, I'd surely have more say in this. And I'm sick to death of my opinion being so irrelevant. I want to be more than just the *face* of Emma Taylor, Inc.

But how can I fire my manager without losing my mom too?

After a few weeks of lecturing me, she finally chills about the events in Los Angeles. And the tabloids continue to spin the story in a way that brings positive attention to *Coyote Hills*—making McGregor happy—so in a backward sort of way, Brett's plan to promote the show has been a huge success. And he's more than a little pleased with himself.

"All right, you two," McGregor says, speaking to Brett and me on the library set. "I need some *steamy* chemistry in this shot. Your fans are expecting sparks, so let's see 'em!"

In a cast chair to the side of me, Kimmi laughs and whispers something to Jake. He then whispers something back, and I can only imagine what they're saying. Jake finished his last scene a while ago and is heading to New York on a red-eye flight later on, but he's had to stick around for a meeting we're having once we wrap.

If I can only make it through this last camera angle, we can get out of here. The crew is currently testing some rearranged lighting on the stand-ins.

"You ready for some more fun this weekend?" Brett asks me. McGregor suggested earlier this week that Kimmi and I go back to L.A. with Brett for a Dodgers game. "We'll be with an even bigger group this time. And no hand-to-hand combat, I promise."

"You've also promised that your hands won't be all over *me*."

"Right, but I've conveniently forgotten that," he says. "Fair warning."

"Last looks!" Tyler calls.

Within seconds Brett and I are being poked and prodded by vanity weapons. I have no idea how anyone in show business can possibly be arrogant when it takes a full squadron of hair and makeup artists to hide their flaws.

"First team, back to one!" Tyler says.

Brett and I return to our starting positions, and the stand-ins leave the set. I try to regain my focus, saying the first line in my head over and over. If I can get that out right, the rest usually flows with ease. But I'm doing some serious come-hither stuff in this scene with Brett, while Jake is sitting just twenty feet away.

Acting or not, it all feels awkward. And I can't stop asking myself why.

"I'll give you a million bucks if you wear that shirt this weekend," Brett whispers, referring to the ultra-low V-neck I have on. I only roll my eyes at him. He pokes my stomach. "Just trying to get a sign of life from you. Any reaction at all."

"I could break a few of your ribs," I reply. "How's that?"

"Picture's up!" Tyler says.

"Picture's up!"

"Quiet on set!"

Tyler scans the set. "Rolling!"

"Sound speed!"

"Camera speeding!"

The boom mic is lowered to right above our heads, and a slate is held in front of me. "Scene four Delta, take one."

The slate is clapped. "A mark."

"B mark."

"And . . . action!" McGregor says, and I summon my inner temptress.

For at least the tenth time, I circle the back of Brett's chair—all sultry-like—trailing a finger over his shoulder blades. "Bryce, if you study for that biology test any longer, Mr. Adams will think you cheated. You can't get *every* question right." I push his books aside and sit on the library table in front of him. "Live a little. Come to the party."

"Uh . . . maybe?" Brett says, sliding down in his chair and darting his eyes away to look at his rich-boy loafers instead of my legs. Costumes has me in *another* short skirt. "But you need to study for the test too. So just come to my house instead, and we'll, um, yeah . . . study." He adds an uncomfortable sigh, squirming in his seat as I lean forward to weave my fingers through his hair. I have to fight back laughter every time we get to this part—Brett is so great at playing a good boy; *being* a good boy is a different story.

A few lines later, McGregor yells, "Cut! Cut! Brilliant! Let's go again, just like that." He gives me a playful shake of his finger. "Naughty, naughty girl, that Eden is! She needs *someone* to buy her presents now that Daddy is broke. And Brett, way to play the loser, lad."

"Going again. Back to one," says Tyler.

We do this same shot three more times, then McGregor wraps filming for the week. "Now, first team, gather round," he adds. "And anyone else can listen in if they'd like to. We're one big family."

We all settle into our cast chairs—Jake's almost always ends up next to mine, and we're not the ones making the arrangement—and McGregor is joined by a woman in a gray pantsuit and a stack of folders under one arm. "I'd like to introduce you to our publicist, Vicky," McGregor says. "She has some exciting news."

Vicky tells us she works directly for the network and will be launching a major *Coyote Hills* campaign next week. "With the curiosity that has followed recent events, we need to strike while the iron is hot," she says, sending a cheerful glance my way, on one end of the row of chairs, and a smile to Brett on the opposite end. We obviously aren't a real couple, but Vicky couldn't care less. I know that look: *Keep stirring up that gossip, kids. Stir, stir away.*

"The hits on the network website have tripled over the past few weeks, and we've received thousands of e-mails asking about the series," Vicky continues. "So we've decided to launch the official *Coyote Hills* website a bit earlier than anticipated, and we need your immediate help." She has a folder for each of us. "A copy of everything here has been sent to your managers, but I'd like to personally explain our plan."

I open the folder and flip through the contents. Brett seems as surprised as I am by the top page—a question and answer form. "I'll be happy to tell you my favorite foods," he says. "But what I do in my spare time is hardly a secret."

Vicky nods. "That may be true, Mr. Crawford, but we only know what the press tells us, don't we? We want these cast spotlights to be in your own words. Your fans should feel as though they're having a personal conversation with you." She turns to McGregor, who is beaming proudly. "The network executives all agree that *Coyote Hills* has the potential to be our highest-rated show, and we're planning some special events to give it a gentle shove in that direction."

Brett laughs. "There's no such thing as gentle promotion. You just shove."

"Quite right," McGregor says, then raises his hands as if parting the Red Sea. "Our premiere at The Sonoran Events Center will be spectacular! As you know, we'll be inviting Hollywood to *us*—giving them a taste of the authentic environment in which *Coyote Hills* takes place. And the weekend prior, rather than holding a typical press junket, we'll be having a day of food and fun with the media. They'll get to know each one of you as a best friend, at my ranch!" He waits for applause.

"Yeeee-haaaw!" Brett says, twirling an invisible lasso above his head.

Kimmi's sour expression doesn't change. "Let me guess: we'll be posing on horses."

"Forget horses," Jake says. "I want to ride one of your bulls."

He looks entirely serious, which makes me smile. Big time. *Stop it, Emma.*

McGregor's brows pinch together. "Sorry, lad. I can't risk your handsome face." His arms fly back into the air. "But! We'll have all sorts of glorious entertainment—the screening of the pilot being the main event, of course. And by the time the press leaves the junket, they'll be so enamored with the series and its actors, they'll spread your praise from here to Moscow. Now, please, get these packets to the production office by Monday. Busy, busy weekend for us all—which reminds me . . ." McGregor turns to Brett. "Did you pull something together for the Dodgers game?"

"Oh yeah! Watch for us on the jumbo screen."

"Excellent! Look cheery for the cameras, will you?" McGregor's eyes shift to me. "It doesn't matter if the two of you aren't the lovebirds they make you out to be—quite relieved that you're not, honestly—but you're attracting some wonderful attention for the show. And you as well, Kimmi. I must say, Payton Wilson was a fine pick. Buzz, buzz, buzz!"

"Jake won't be there," Brett says, throwing a wad of paper at him. "Again."

"Mr. Elliott does enough promotion by donning cowboy chaps— and little else, mind you—in ads throughout the world." McGregor grins at Jake, who then hurls Brett's paper cannonball at him.

McGregor clutches his chest, mortally wounded. After a quick recovering breath, he says, "All right, have a great time in L.A. this weekend, but I'm begging you, please behave."

I've never been put into the *please behave* category before.

Los Angeles won't be half as scary now that Troy isn't an issue. Both his manager and attorney called me at the studio a few days after the Club 99 fight to apologize *on behalf of* Troy. It's a major relief to know he's taken me seriously, and more so to know that he feels desperate enough to involve his management team. They'll have a bigger influence on him keeping his cool—at least for the sake of his career—than I ever could.

"Can I just double-clarify something?" I ask McGregor. Then I turn my head in the direction of the crew members standing behind us because a few of them have admitted to getting calls from tabloids. "Brett and I aren't even close to really dating, so if anyone contacts you for some sort of inside scoop, please share *that* with them."

"In other words, Emma is in love," Brett quips, and I shoot him a look that implies the opposite. "So just say 'no comment' and they'll get the picture."

"But the *wrong* one, I'm afraid, because I don't even *like* Brett at the moment."

Everyone laughs. I'm sort of faking it.

"Oh, you two are just so cute." Vicky literally giggles. "Which brings us to our next item of business. Our research shows that the target audience for *Coyote Hills* is more involved on Twitter than any other social network, so we'd like to ask that every cast member becomes involved there. A tweet or two a day would be just fine, perhaps a little teaser about your character, or a humorous anecdote that took place on set. And we'd *certainly* like to see our cast interacting with one another. Some witty banter would go a long way in providing a glimpse of the genuine chemistry that exists among this cast."

"Here, here!" McGregor says. "Now one of you, I've noticed, is not yet on Twitter."

Jake, who's been slowly sliding deeper into his chair, says, "Ugh."

I throw a hand over my mouth to stop a burst of laughter. Jake *hates* social media.

McGregor tips his head as if he's considering something. "You know, Mr. Elliott, your delivery of that line just convinced me that you'd play a *fine* caveman if I ever have a need for one. Meanwhile, I expect to see you on Twitter."

Jake's chin is still dropped, but he turns toward me just enough to furrow his brows and whisper, "Maybe modeling isn't so bad."

I can't stop laughing.

Vicky then lays out the promotion schedule between now and the premiere, and we're finally dismissed. I stand, but Jake stays in his chair next to me, so I plop back down. When everyone else has scattered, he tells me, "I'll be back from New York Sunday night. Want to . . . teach me how to tweet?"

We've gone running a few times now, so getting together

outside of work isn't such a surprising request, but it's usually more of an impromptu thing.

"Sure," I reply. "I need to talk to you about something, anyway. An idea that I'd like your opinion on."

"Hmm." He waits a moment before adding, "Then maybe you should make dinner for me too. I think better on a full stomach."

Miraculously, I keep a straight face. "Can't you just eat before you come over?"

"Why would I do that if you're gonna cook for me?"

Sheesh. I'm in trouble. "The only thing I'm good at is spaghetti. Which is pretty dull."

"Not if you top it off with . . . let's say, peach cobbler? I'll bring the ice cream."

"Oh! So now it's dinner *and* dessert?"

"And I'm sure I can think of something else," Jake says, and walks off.

I'm left in my chair staring straight ahead. *Something else?*

There are ten of us at the Dodgers game the next day—a few who are friends I haven't seen in forever—and I get the chance to casually ask about everyone's managers. When it comes time to make the change, I'll have to do it fast. I can't be calling around Hollywood saying, "Hey, I'm ditching my mom. But don't tell anyone, 'kay?" The news would make it back to her in less than an hour.

Best-case scenario, I'll have a chance to discuss this with my mother civilly before I officially hire someone else. Worst case? She'll never talk to me again.

Even Kimmi and I get along pretty well on game day. Payton pays *plenty* of attention to her this time, so she's in a great mood. And Brett sits next to me during the game, but he's flirting up a storm with my friend on the other side of him. At one point, he turns to ask me, "She's kinda hot, right?"

I have to laugh. "Yes, Brett, she's actually *beautiful*. And she's also a very *good* girl. So if you ask her out, behave yourself."

"Yeah, she's definitely giving me those 'behave yourself' vibes," he says. "But . . . I kinda like that sometimes. What's her name?"

"You're joking, right?" I don't know how Brett keeps shocking me this way, but his density is astounding. "Look, I could either *tell* you who she is, or there's a thing called *con-ver-sa-tion*, which is what normal people do when they want to get to know someone. So turn back around, formally introduce yourself—yes, even though your cute little face is hard to mistake—and ask who she is and where she's from. It's a great starting place."

Brett smiles. "And *then* I can hook up with her?"

I want to pull out a chunk of his hair. "Your Prince Charming lessons are over. I quit."

Paparazzi follow us everywhere once we leave the game. They throw out comments like, "C'mon, Brett and Emma, just one kiss!" But Brett handles it perfectly. He only laughs and says, "You'll have to watch *Coyote Hills* if you want to see that kind of action."

I just smile and wave.

The idiots still get everything wrong. Not only did they miss Brett's flirting marathon with *someone else* at the game, but he bounced between calling me "Taylor" and "Dude" the entire day, not "Emmalicious" and "Babe," which is what one online gossip site reports on Sunday afternoon—a site that Rachel reads constantly.

On a phone call that evening, I try to explain things to her as they really are, but she thinks the tabloid version of my life is more exciting. "I'm telling you, Emma," she says, "you guys would make the perfect Hollywood power couple. Just go for it."

"Um, no. How about we never discuss that again?"

"Fine," she says. "But speaking of men . . ." She giggles, and I tense up because I'm currently making dinner for the boy who's about to be the focus of this conversation. "Jake is on Twitter now! Brett started following him, and I totally freaked out when I saw who this new only-here-for-the-food guy was. But why did he choose *that* handle? What does it mean?"

I'm a little confused because I thought I was supposed to help Jake set up his account tonight. "Give me a sec," I say, and open my app. Yep, it's Jake all right: @onlyhre4thefood. I laugh because his profile photo just shows the back of his head. "Well, he was kind of forced into the whole Twitter thing, so I think he's saying, 'I'm only here because I have to be.' "

"Oh. Well, I want to direct message him, but he isn't following me yet," Rachel says. "So do you think it would be, like, *really* forward for me to text or even call him, or just *kinda* forward?" During my three seconds of silence, Rachel groans. "Okay, I won't. I just thought he might want to talk about what we should do on our date."

"He's not really the plan-it-out type," I reply. "So maybe I could send you some links to cool stuff out here, and you can decide what we should do. I haven't seen much either."

"All right. Thanks," Rachel says. "But while we're on the subject of what type he is, I went to your parents' house like you told me to and tried on a few of your dresses for the premiere. And none of them really . . . well, I want to look *gorgeous* when he meets me. So when you work with a designer this time, could you maybe say you can't decide between two dresses and borrow both? I would love something in gold." I drop my spoon into a bubbling pot of spaghetti sauce and splatter it all over myself. "They won't get too mad, will they?" she goes on. "If I wear one and you wear the other? Because that would be twice the red carpet advertising."

She can't be serious. The dresses usually cost at least twenty thousand dollars apiece, which Rachel knows as well as I do. I'm lucky to be offered just *one*.

"I'm really sorry," I say, "but I can't do that. And I thought you wanted to wear my dress from the New Year's gala."

"Well, I tried it on and my butt looks flat," Rachel replies. "And my chest does too. So how would you like *your* dream guy to see you and be like, 'Whoa, is she ten years old?' Because that's exactly what he's going to think, and he's The Bod. He's perfect, so I've gotta look perfect too. Like a model. With a nice round butt."

I'm already at a loss for words when The Bod himself knocks on my back door. We've been meeting there at night because the running path goes behind both of our communities, and the fewer people who see us together, the better. At least the majority of my neighbors are nice retired couples who don't seem to have a clue who I am, which suits me just fine.

I race to the door so Jake won't knock again, but only part the curtain and motion for him to wait a minute. "I understand that, Rachel, I do," I tell her. "But I can't do any more about the dress issue. I have some good news for you though! You ready?"

"Yes! Always! What is it?" She's probably already guessed.

"While I was at the game yesterday, I talked to a friend, who has a friend who's on the crew for *Stars in Their Eyes*." Rachel screams, and I feel slightly less guilty for smiling at the faces Jake is now making through my kitchen window. "Anyway, this friend of mine is going to make some calls, and hopefully we can get you a foot in the door at the auditions. And you'll be amazing! I totally know you'll make it on the show."

A few minutes later, Rachel likes me again, and we say good-bye.

I throw the back door open. "Ever heard of Windex, buddy?" I ask Jake. "'Cause you're about to wipe off every one of those blowfishes you just put on my window."

"You're the one who left me standing out there," he says. "For like, twenty minutes."

I laugh at his pouting. "Five. I was talking to Rachel. And if you can put the water on the table without making another mess, you can clean the window later."

Jake heads over to my fridge, sets his small carton of ice cream in my freezer, then takes out some bottled water. He juggles the bottles in the air a few times before sliding them across my small round table, narrowly missing the salad I already placed there.

He's in a plain white T-shirt. Yummy.

Food, Emma. Focus on the food.

I return to stirring the sauce, but he's suddenly right behind me. "What's next?"

"Can you grab the garlic bread out of the oven?"

"Garlic?" he asks. "So much for that *something else* I thought of."

"Exactly why I made it," I say, but have to tell my imagination to stop drawing that picture for me. Erase it. *Now.* "You're here because we need to talk about a business proposition and tweet—nothing more. Well, maybe one or two things more, but not . . . that."

Jake peeks over my shoulder, and I can feel his warm breath on the back of my neck. Why is he teasing me like this? "Dang," he says. "I even brushed my teeth."

I push him toward my oven mitts. "Are you ready to hear my idea?"

"Yep, shoot."

I've been excited out of my mind to talk to him about this. "Do you remember our first day on set, when I awkwardly announced that I was starting a charity foundation?"

"Yeah, I do." He slides the garlic bread onto a plate. "What's it for?"

"Well, it's taken a while to figure that out," I reply, "but your mom was the one who put me on the trail of a solid idea. And you were a lot of help too."

Jake raises his brows. "Interesting. So . . . you're setting up a support group for friends and family of chronically arrogant boys?"

"No, you dork! Though that isn't a bad idea either." I hand him the bowl of spaghetti and shoo him toward the table. "Okay, now sit down and act like a guest."

He relaxes into a chair and, in a formal tone, says, "Jake Elliott will now be playing the role of the guest, which he's very happy about since takeout is getting old."

Wanting to get settled before I dive into the foundation, I hurry and place everything else on the table and sit across from him. I scoop a mountain of pasta onto his plate, but he sneaks even more when I turn away for the sauce.

"Back to the foundation," I say when our plates are full. "I hope this isn't too nosy, but suppose you didn't have the money to pay for your mom's medical care and rehabilitation. Would her insurance and other benefits be enough to cover the expenses?"

Jake leans back in his chair. "Not even close. She was self-employed before her stroke, so her insurance was minimal. And government programs never provide as much as you think."

"So without the job you have, how do you think things would be for you guys?"

He considers this. "Well, I'd still be working just as hard somewhere else, but for a lot less money. There's no way I could've bought her a new house. And her home care and rehab bills alone are in the thousands every month. So if I couldn't pay for all that, things would be *very* different. Especially for her."

"That's what I figured," I say, "which is why I'm starting a foundation that will not only offer financial aid to the physically disabled, but social support as well." Jake's eyes are wide open now. "It will provide funds for motorized wheelchairs, prosthetics, physical therapy, home health care—things like that. And I'm also hoping to organize a network of volunteers who are willing to help these people learn new hobbies, or continue old ones if they can't do them on their own anymore. Like quilting or painting, or whatever."

I've been doing tons of research on this and even used it for a sociology paper.

Jake doesn't say anything. He just smiles and moves a hand across the table . . . then slowly lifts my own hand and slips his fingers under my palm. A shower of chills races through my body. We're both quiet.

"You blow me away sometimes," he finally says, and lets go. He'd only held my hand for about five seconds, so maybe he didn't mean to hold it at all. Maybe it was just meant to be a long sort of touch. Or maybe a nudge? Like when you're telling a friend she did a good job, and you nudge her. But with your hand?

No, that's stupid. *He held my hand.*

There's a slight possibility that I might have a goofy grin on my face. "Well, as I said, you and your mom were the ones who gave me the idea. And I know the foundation can't help *everyone,* but I hope it can at least do some good."

Jake takes another slice of garlic bread. "It sounds great. But you'll eventually need more money than your own for this, right?"

"Right. That's where you come in," I say. "Once the foundation is up and running, I'd love it if you could help me get a good start on the donations, because you like the business side of things. I figure that between the two of us, we know a lot of deep pockets with big hearts."

"Yeah. I'd like that," he says.

"Thanks!" Gosh, I'm smiling a lot. I take a bite of spaghetti.

"Just let me know when you're ready." Jake leans back in his chair again, his hands behind his head. "*Emmalicious.*"

"Ugh. You read that?"

"Just trying to keep up like everyone else."

I pluck an olive out of my salad and throw it at him. "You're officially banned from reading tabloids, paper or otherwise. That crap was only posted online a few hours ago."

"But you see, my friend Sophie reads all that stuff," Jake explains. "And she called me as soon as my plane landed tonight. She thinks since I know you guys, I should be obsessed with *Bremma* too."

Sophie?

"When, really, it makes you less interested because you know the truth?"

"Sure. Whatever," is all he says. He takes a bite of spaghetti and chews as he smiles. I chuck another olive at him, and he swallows. "You don't have to get violent! I just think you're blind to what's going on: I'm pretty convinced that Brett really likes you."

I laugh. "No way! Don't tell me you're buying into this too! Brett doesn't like me that way *at all*. In fact, yesterday at the Dodgers game, he wanted my help to hit on one of my friends. And by the end of the game, I was like, 'Stay the heck away from her!' because he told me all sorts of sick ideas he had to make this good girl turn bad. Does that sound like something a guy would do if he was interested in *me*?"

Jake hesitates before he answers. But why? What is there to hesitate about?

"No. Not usually," he says. "But that bum just became my worst enemy. Look at this."

Jake hands me his phone with his Twitter app on the screen. "I thought we were setting up your account *together*," I say in a teasing tone. But I'm sort of wondering if someone else helped him. Not that he actually needed help. It's just . . . who is Sophie, anyway?

Jake shrugs. "My flight was delayed today. I was bored."

I turn my attention back to his phone. "Whoa. You set this up *today*? But you already have over three thousand followers."

"Yeah. Scroll down and you'll see why. All the way to the beginning."

It takes me a while to get through hundreds of tweets—99 percent of them from women. I can't help but pause on a few because some are very . . . suggestive. Then at last, I reach the conversation between Jake and Brett that apparently started this landslide of female *charm*:

Brett Crawford @actorincognito
@onlyhre4thefood #WTH man?! Your profile pic is of the
BACK OF YOUR HEAD!

Jake Elliott @onlyhre4thefood
@actorincognito And yet I still look better than you.
#gofigure

Brett Crawford @actorincognito
Hey lady friends! Go say hello to my new #CoyoteHills
castmate @onlyhre4thefood! He's single! #pleaseretweet

That isn't the worst of it: along with this last tweet, Brett attached
Jake's Armani ad with the cowboy chaps, then posted several more
of Jake's ads with the same message.

"My, my," I tell him. "You've got some very aggressive *fangirls*."

Jake takes his phone away. "I don't think this is what Vicky
meant by 'friendly banter.'"

"It's exactly what she meant." I step away from the table to
check on the peach cobbler. Jake follows me, and I have this crazy
urge to reach back for his hand. But I don't, of course. "Ready for
dessert?"

"Yep. It smells delicious."

That's when I notice the oven clock. "Oops, I forgot! My dad's
gonna call you any minute."

Jake stands perfectly still and silent. Then, "*Huh*?"

"Sorry! I meant to tell you earlier," I say, and grab Jake by the
shoulders. For a beautifully tanned Arizona boy, his face is looking
pretty pale right now. "Relax. I told him that you want a business

degree, but have to do most of it distance ed. That's all. So he's just going to give you some ideas on how to juggle the course work."

"Because he's a dean?" Jake's confused expression is sort of adorable.

"Of the College of Business. At the University of Arkansas."

He smiles. "You've never mentioned the *business* part of that."

"Yeah, well, I didn't want to until he agreed to give you some advice."

Jake's cell rings and the sound startles me like a freight train just blasted through my kitchen. But it's perfect timing because my hands are still on his shoulders, and his own hands have somehow found their way to my waist.

And I want them there.

JAKE

Only a father with some serious parental instincts could sense when a guy is eyeing his daughter the way I'm looking at Emma, hundreds of miles away from him. Why else would he pick that very second to call? But Mr. Taylor has nothing to worry about. When my cell rings, Emma steps away from me—*fast*. I clear my throat and answer, "Hello, this is Jake."

"Jake, Bob Taylor. Emma told me you want to be a businessman."

Brisk and to the point. I straighten up. "Yes, Mr. Taylor. Thanks for calling."

Emma snickers at my formality, so I lightly step on her foot as I walk off to her living room. For the next fifteen minutes, Mr. Taylor fires questions at me, I try to come up with impressive answers, and then he gives his opinion on what I should focus on first. At the end of the conversation, he says I can call whenever I need "further assistance." I thank him for his time, and he tells me, "Happy to help. Good luck."

And that's it.

I return to the kitchen to find Emma scooping peach cobbler onto some plates. "Your dad had some great advice," I say. "Thanks for thinking of that. Really."

Emma hesitates before she replies. "He didn't give you his lecture about acting only being a career for the narcissistic, did he?"

"Well, yeah," I lie. "But I just said, 'I'm sorry, I couldn't hear you. I was talking to myself.'"

Emma laughs and hands me a plate of cobbler. The ice cream on the side is already melting from the heat. I mix it all together and shovel a huge spoonful into my mouth. "Dang," I say after a few seconds in heaven. "Does my mom pay you to be nice to me? Dinner, the call from your dad, and now *this*?"

Our eyes meet, and Emma smiles. "I can't help but feel sorry for a guy who doesn't have much going for him."

I tug on a lock of her hair. What I really want to do is kiss her.

McGregor is steaming mad. We're filming on the classroom set when A-10 fighter jets start flying over the studio into Davis-Monthan Air Force Base, and they aren't just a sound issue, they're making the cameras shake. The scheduling guy tries to defend the oversight, saying that he's dealing with the military, who doesn't find it a top priority to inform a television studio of its every move.

"Well, why not?" McGregor snaps at him. "I didn't become a US citizen for nothing!"

That's when we're told to chill somewhere off set until we can resume filming. Emma and I end up in Brett's dressing room, eating an early lunch while Brett tells us about some of the strangest stuff he's seen in his nearly two decades in the entertainment industry. And things turn a little crazy when he gets to the story of Mr. Piddles, the cat.

"We worked together in *Southside Runaway*," Brett says. "So I'd have to act all nuts while I told this cat my life story, right? Like how my character left an abusive home, joined a gang, became an addict—all this dark stuff. But the cat's real owner, Gustave, who insisted on being on set with the animal wrangler, kept bursting into tears, so we'd have to stop filming. Gustave would then rush over to Mr. Piddles, stroke him, and say"—Brett imitates a heavy French accent here—"'Ahh, you mus' stop deez 'orrible talk! My 'iddle pussycat eez too upset!'"

"Seriously?" I say. "Mr. Piddles licks his own backside."

"Oh no, not this cat. Mr. Piddles had a litter box that was covered by a blue satin tent. And when he'd done his business, he'd strut out from under the tent, and Gustave would clean him off with warm rose water and a washcloth."

Emma laughs so hard that her plate full of salad, chips, and a sloppy joe sandwich slips off her lap and lands face down on Brett's dressing room floor. Between gasps, she says, "Why . . . would . . . *anyone* name a cat Mr. Piddles and then treat him like a princess?"

While she tries to catch her breath, I start cleaning up the mess.

Brett tosses me his napkin. "Gustave said he rescued Mr. Piddles from a shelter and kept the name to prevent an identity crisis. When I suggested that the name probably came from the cat *piddling* all over his former owner's home, Gustave actually slapped me."

"Sometimes you deserve to be slapped," Emma says, still laughing. Then she notices me cleaning up and drops to her knees. "Thanks, but I'll get it."

Her spilled plate could almost go unnoticed in here. Junk is scattered all over Brett's floor—scripts, fan mail, candy wrappers. The cleaning crew probably has to wear hazmat suits.

"Poor Mr. Piddles," I say, still helping Emma.

She sneaks me a smile that could melt an icecap.

"Don't worry, he had therapy," Brett says, munching on his chips and spraying crumbs as he talks. "A therapist called every day, one o'clock sharp, on Mr. Piddles's cell phone. Yep, that cat had his very own cell."

Now I know he's joking. "You're making this up."

"I'm not." Brett turns to the laptop on his desk. "I'll prove it." A few minutes later, we're all staring in awe at Mr. Piddles's personal website. He looks like a plain black cat—other than the fact that he's sitting on a powder-blue pillow with silver fringe and resting snugly in a cast chair. Scrolled across the backrest in glittering calligraphy, it says *Mr. Piddles*.

I also notice what appears to be a bejeweled cell phone tucked under the cat's paw. "Wow. Nothing in Hollywood can shock me now."

"Just wait until you work in feature films with some 'up-and-coming' big shots," Emma says. "They're usually worse than those who actually *are* stars."

"Kimmi Weston, for example," Brett adds. He snatches up a mini-football and tries to spin it on his finger. "She won't be around long, though. Most actors who are prettily packaged but talentless never last."

"Don't bet on it," says Emma. "She *is* talented, and McGregor has high hopes for her."

"Yeah? Well, *I* hope she steps in front of a truck," Brett replies with a menacing smile. His effort to get along with Kimmi seems all but forgotten lately. "Why are you so nice to her, anyway? She walks all over you."

Emma shrugs. "What's the harm in pretending like I don't understand her snide remarks? Catfights only make things worse. Besides, it's fun to play naive."

"So you're . . . *acting*?" I ask. Something about this doesn't sit well.

"Why not?" Emma replies. "You do it in real life, right, Brett? Every once in a while?"

Brett puts on a pitch-perfect face of a guy who's never even considered it. "Why would I want to be anyone but myself?" he says, and I can't help but think right then that Brett Crawford isn't an award-winning actor for nothing. He might even be smarter than he *acts*.

Emma laughs. "Do you really want me to answer that question?"

"Only if you sit on my lap while you tell me," Brett replies.

"Sorry," Emma says, "but I've gotta run and get more food to dump on your floor."

"Me too!" I follow her out.

"Hey!" Brett calls after us. "Grab me another napkin."

I peek back into his dressing room. "How about a washcloth and rose water?"

He chucks the football at me. "How 'bout I tell the tabloids you've traded in your leather chaps for pretty dresses?"

"Oh! You'd look *great* in a strapless!" Emma says as she strolls off. Lacking a comeback for either, I shoot the football at Brett's head and run to catch up. "But, seriously, if you ever *do* give up your cowboy chaps, I want them," Emma adds. "They'd go for a fortune on eBay."

"Yeah?" I ask. "I bet you already sold the silverware I used the other night."

Emma gasps. "How did you know?"

I lean closer. "Paparazzi . . . they're everywhere."

She tries to trip me. "Now you're being mean."

"You weren't just making fun of *me*?"

"Nah. I know you'd never give up your chaps."

We have to stop flirting once we leave the empty hallway. The sloppy joes have been replenished, and now there's a massive tower of fruit, a cheese tray, and a platter of brownies. There are a few more tables too, with chicken, fish, and vegan choices. How can actors be expected to stay in shape with so much food around a studio?

Kimmi steps between us at the table.

"Hey, you're off the phone!" Emma says, all cheery. "We're hanging out in Brett's dressing room, discussing the sad plight of the male model. You should join us."

"Who'd want to miss *that*?" Kimmi replies.

When we get back to Brett's dressing room, he's throwing darts. "You throw like a sissy," I tell him. "Give me those." I take his darts away, step back another foot from where he stands, and let a dart fly. It doesn't hit dead center, but it's pretty darn close.

"I'll give you fifty bucks if you can do that again," Brett says.

"I'll do it for free." I throw another dart, and it hits the bull's-eye.

Emma whistles. Brett slaps me on the back. "That's insane!"

"I'm not surprised," Kimmi says. "Jake hits every target he aims at. In modeling, he became a hot item in like, what, a few months? Then he landed a job the rest of us needed *years* of training for. And don't forget his gift with women. Have you spent much time with your waitress friend, Jake, or was that just a one-night thing?"

She knows *nothing* about me. I've worked my butt off to be good at whatever I do, and if life ever starts feeling too easy, the rug always gets ripped out from under my feet. But I don't care to explain that to Kimmi. And we met that waitress *months* ago, so why bring it up now?

"I left that restaurant thirty seconds after you did," I reply. "Alone."

"Interesting," she says. "Then who do you spend all your time with?"

Kimmi's eyes shift, and she gives Emma a thin, poisonous smile that makes my skin crawl. *That's* why she brought up the waitress—to see Emma's reaction in front of *me*.

She knows about us.

Everyone is silent for a good four seconds, but Emma doesn't flinch. "Sorry, Kimmi," she finally says. "Nothing exciting to report on this side of the room."

Brett has gone straight from laughing to looking seriously pissed. He *does* like Emma, but I have to be careful how I talk to Emma about it. She'll never give me a chance if she thinks I'll just be another possessive creep like Troy.

"You know what?" Brett says. "We were having a blast in here before Kimmi showed up. I can hardly wait for our Labor Day trip to Lake Tahoe. Three whole days with the Ice Queen!"

Emma flicks the center of his forehead. "Play nice, Brett. You two are like kids fighting over a tricycle."

Kimmi snickers. "Yeah, Brett, grow up."

"She wasn't just talking to me," he says.

"Whatever." Kimmi opens the door. "I have to call Payton. I'm inviting some of my own friends to Tahoe, so he needs to book an extra houseboat."

Once she's gone, Brett shuts the door and bangs his head against it, popping off a curse word with each hit. He finally ends his R-rated rant with, "I can't believe Kimmi and Payton are actually dating!" He looks over at Emma. "Please, I'm *begging* you, come to Tahoe. I'm gonna *die* if you don't . . . no, it will be Kimmi who dies, because I'm gonna push her overboard."

Emma laughs. "When the police ask, I'll be sure to tell them that I've never heard you fantasize about Kimmi's death. Twice, just today."

"Please, you've gotta come. I'll do anything." Brett is right in her face.

She backs away. "I've already told you. I have plans."

Yep, she does. Emma is spending a day with my mom that weekend, talking over ideas for her foundation while they work on the unfinished quilt.

"What's so important that you won't cancel?" Brett asks. "If you have a secret boyfriend, you better tell me before word gets out. I need to be ready to look like a brokenhearted sap."

Emma tilts her head. "You know, Brett, that's tempting—it would be hilarious to see you stumble through a role like that—but I'm trying to start up a charity foundation, and that takes priority over sunbathing."

"Oh. Boring," he replies. "Then, Jake, you should come with me."

"Thanks, but I can't. I already have plans with my own buddies—we play in a basketball tournament every Labor Day weekend."

"Whatever. Then I'll have to talk Payton out of taking Kimmi," Brett says as he tosses the door open. Then he slams it shut, and Emma and I make eye contact.

We're alone, which rarely happens on set.

"This is convenient," I say, gathering some darts. "We've got a few details for Phoenix to work out." I take aim and get a dart off, but it's a few inches from the center. "I'm thinking you should just stay the whole weekend." Another dart. Closer. "There's no way you and my mom can get that quilt done in just one day. And you guys have a *lot* of foundation stuff to discuss."

Bull's-eye.

Emma is smiling up at me with a hand on her hip, so I know something sassy is on its way. "Running together is one thing," she says. "Dinner was pushing it. But spending *three days* with you in Phoenix? Hello? That would be a pretty major date."

"Eh, I don't know about that," I say as I pluck darts out of the board. "I'll be playing basketball pretty much the whole time, and you'll have a quilting needle in your hand. Just how close do you think I'll want to get to you?" Emma is still smiling, but now she's shaking her head. "I'll stay in a hotel, and you can stay at my mom's," I offer. "How's that?"

"No way. If anything, I would stay in a hotel."

I can't believe I'm getting somewhere. "Trust me, Emma. My mom would rather have *you* as her guest than me. I eat too much and I make a mess."

Emma snatches a dart. "Then when would we even . . . hang out, or whatever?"

Her first dart hits the wall, and I bite back laughter. "I guess if you really want to, we can do something between, uh . . . my last game of the day and when I go to a hotel?"

My team rarely makes it past the first couple of games in the tournament, but Emma doesn't need to know that.

"Depends on what you have in mind." She takes aim again and hits the door.

"How about dinner and a movie?" I ask. "Then cuddling on the couch while we watch late-night TV?"

She laughs. "Yeah, sure. Because that's nothing like a date."

"Okay, fine. I'll settle for half of that." I hand her one last dart and jump out of the danger zone. "No movie. And we can skip dinner too."

EMMA

Labor Day takes forever getting here, but once it comes around, I'm so nervous to spend the weekend in Phoenix that I drive about twenty miles an hour up the freeway.

When I reach his mom's house Saturday morning, Jake is already at his first tournament game. This past week, Mrs. Elliott and I spent a couple of hours on the phone discussing the general idea of my foundation, so now—as we work on her quilt—we iron out the details of providing financial and social support for the disabled.

Mrs. Elliott has also talked this over with her physical therapist, who specializes in cases like her own. He's offered to meet with us at his office Monday morning, when it's closed for the holiday, to give me a better sense of what questions to ask on an eligibility application. I already have a law firm doing the paperwork, and Jake is gathering a list of people to call when it's time for donations. McGregor has helped with names too, so everything is coming together perfectly.

And since Rachel loves all things Hollywood, I've asked her to help out by searching the Internet for celebrity-sponsored charity events. I hope to get some good ideas for what could be successful moneymakers, while at the same time be entertaining enough to draw a crowd.

Jake's mom warns me in advance that her home health nurse is coming for about a half hour—and might ask a lot of questions if she sees me—so when she arrives, I hurry out to my car that's hidden in the garage and use the time to call Rachel. She's called four times since I've been here, and answers on the first ring with, "Why haven't you been picking up your phone? Where are you?"

In Jake's garage. And you?

"I'm working on foundation stuff," I say. "Did you find any event ideas yet?"

"Any . . . what?" She pauses. "Oh yeah, events! I forgot again. I've been crazy busy."

Seriously? I asked her three weeks ago. And at least five times since then.

"And I get *so* distracted every time I go online," Rachel says. "My Twitter followers are so fickle, it's driving me nuts. I have to post something exciting every few hours or they drop like flies. I just tweeted about the new *Coyote Hills* website, though, and people are really excited about that. The Bod's cast spotlight is awesome! He loves Oreo shakes! Cute, huh? And basketball is his favorite sport. His favorite color is black—so hot. And he grew up right there in Arizona! No wonder he's got such a great tan."

More and more, I don't want Rachel to meet the real Jake Elliott. She can keep The Bod, he's all hers. But *Jake* . . .

"What do you think about *my* spotlight?" I haven't seen it myself yet, because I hadn't heard the site was up. "We wrote them ourselves. Was I too silly?"

"Hold on, I'll read it." Twenty seconds or so pass. She'll be entirely honest, like always. "What's up with your favorite foods being sushi and veal piccata? That sounds sort of—"

"*Huh*? I . . . I swear I wrote pizza and popcorn."

"There's nothing about pizza. No popcorn." Rachel says she's going to keep reading, and I'm pulling up the site too, but it doesn't look right on my phone and I can't find the spotlights. "Did someone hijack your profile, or what? It also says you want to learn how to play golf, but you hate golfing."

Golf? If Mrs. Elliott wouldn't have thought I was being murdered in her garage, I would have screamed my head off. "I've gotta go!" I tell Rachel and hang up before she can reply. I then call my control-freak *momager* who obviously tweaked a few things before she sent my "own words" to the network publicity office.

"Really, Mom?" I say the second she picks up. "Veal piccata? What's so wrong with pizza, huh? I sound like a priss!"

I had wanted to sound normal. I *am* normal.

"Calm down," she snaps. "You love veal piccata. You order it every time it's on a menu."

"Oh, I get it. Pizza isn't sophisticated enough for my public persona—unlike veal piccata or golf. Which is *your* favorite sport, not mine. And never mind that ninety percent of the fans who will be surfing the *Coyote Hills* website are a lot closer to my age than yours and won't even know what veal piccata is. You changed my answers, Mom. You changed me into *you*!"

The mudroom door opens, and Jake peeks into the garage. *Crap.* Had he heard me? He waves and squints through the dark—only the interior light of my car is on. I cover the phone, open the car door, and ask him, "Will you please bring out your laptop?"

I put the phone back to my ear when Mom is midsentence. ". . . didn't change everything. I kept *tennis* as your favorite sport. I only put golf for the question that asked what new skill you'd like to learn from a pro, because you had written—"

"Snake charming. Yeah, I know. It was supposed to be funny."

"Well, it wasn't," Mom says. "We're trying to change your image here, from being a young girl who flits from one train-wreck relationship to the next, to being a serious actress. It's time you start behaving like an adult."

"Oh, all right!" I say. "If you want me to behave like most of the other girls my age, then I have a *ton* of crazy stuff I've gotta go try. See ya!"

I hang up. She calls right back, but I send her to voice mail.

Jake pokes his head into the garage again, and I wave him over. He sits in the passenger seat with his laptop. He's close enough for me to tell that he's changed his shirt, because I smell the scent of fresh fabric softener. It's all I can do to resist snuggling right into him.

"Did you just want the laptop, or do you want me too?" he asks. "My next game isn't for another hour."

"Good. Stay," I reply. "I think I want . . . well, what I *need* is to fire my mom. Or actually, just the manager part of my mom. But I don't know how. Or when. Or anything."

And the tabloids use my love life as their personal ATM.

And my *best friend* keeps forgetting to do the one favor I've asked of her in years.

It seems like Jake is the only person in the world who treats me like a real flesh-and-blood girl—not just a TV character.

I slide my hand next to his and hook our pinkies. Just our pinkies.

No big deal. Right?

He stares down at our hands. "Oh . . . kay," he finally says. "What happened?"

I would tell Jake to go to the *Coyote Hills* website—because I still want to see what else my mom changed—but then he would have to let go of my hand. So I just tell him about the fight instead. In less than a minute, we're holding hands for real, and the argument with my mom suddenly seems humorous.

"She's been trying forever to get me to like golf," I say, "which is so stupid, because I suck! The last time we went to her country club, I hit more trees than grass."

"Then you definitely don't need professional help. I mean, I've golfed my entire life, and I can rarely hit a tree. It's so much easier to hit all that grass."

I try to smack him, but with our hands still connected, I'm a little off and hit the laptop instead. "Ow!"

Jake laughs and lifts my hand, but a split second before it reaches his lips, he stops. "Oh yeah," he says, and lowers our hands back to his knee. "I shouldn't do that. I forget sometimes."

"Me too." *Did I say that out loud?*

Jake looks back, his eyes wide open. "Really? You want me to kiss you?"

For hours and hours. I've wanted him to kiss me for a few weeks now, no matter how hard I try to push the idea out of my head. We just . . . can't.

"Nice gulp," he says, catching my reaction.

My cheeks are on fire. "Thanks," I reply. "I've been gulping a lot lately. Because, you know, you keep looking at me like . . . like you are right now."

"Like I want to kiss you," he says. "Yeah, I'll admit that's happened a few times. And it's probably good to get it out in the open."

I feel sort of tingly all over. I might even be hovering above the seat.

"I agree, but, um . . ." I suck in a bit more air. "If . . . well, if we do that *now*, for example, I'm afraid I might regret it. And then we'll both feel stupid. So we just . . . better not."

"Kiss, you mean? Which for some reason is a bad idea?"

"Lots of reasons," I say. "Such as, I'm not ready for another boyfriend."

"And you don't want to date another guy you work with."

Gosh, it's really hot in this car. "And my best friend likes you."

"The one who's never met me?" Jake asks. "And thinks I'm made of paper?"

"Yep, that one. Then there's also the little detail that everyone thinks I'm dating Brett, not you—which I'm not. Dating either of you, I mean." *Ignore the fact that I'm holding your hand and have a butterfly farm living inside me.* "But especially not Brett."

Jake looks hesitant to reply, but finally speaks again and the tension breaks. "I can't help wondering what things might be like if you and I were the ones who were first spotted together, when we were at The Cage. Then the gossip would be all about us, and . . ." He laughs. "Well, I'm guessing we wouldn't need to hide in my mom's garage to have a conversation."

While I think over the possibilities, I lean against Jake's shoulder . . . because I've wanted to for so long . . . and what's the harm in doing it for just a few seconds? Except that the mudroom door opens and Mrs. Elliott peers into the darkness. She clearly sees us, then hurries to close the door again. I sit straight up. "Um, wow . . . bad timing."

Jake pulls me back against him. "Don't worry about my mom."

"You've told her we're still just friends, right?"

He shakes his head. "She hates it when I lie."

His green eyes look down, and I look up. "Jake . . ." is all I get out.

"Hey, I'll go along with all this other stuff," he says, "but we should at least be honest with each other. You've gotta know this is going somewhere."

"Of course I do." But it's hard to trust my instincts—the feeling inside me that says our relationship wouldn't be the same type of ever-changing roller-coaster ride I've been on before: happy, super happy, not so happy, fight, more fights, lots of crying, done. Because with Jake . . . I don't want it to end. "But wherever we're going, I need to get there slowly," I tell him. "Like, snail mode."

"I get that. And I'm still cool with it, I promise." Jake combs his free hand through my hair, and I fight to keep my eyes open. It's bliss. "Just remember that after we work through *your* long list of stuff, we'll still need to tackle all the reasons I don't want to date *you*."

I pull back, my insides collapsing into a big hot mess. "Not that I'm all crushed and mortified, but what . . . *reasons* are you talking about?"

Jake shrugs. "They're actually pretty straightforward. One, you confuse me. Two, you frustrate me. And three . . ." He smiles and holds my hand just a little tighter. "I sometimes wish I'd never met you."

I laugh. "Oh. Is that all?"

"Yep, that's it."

My legs don't recover from feeling like jellyfish until a full ten minutes after Jake leaves for his next ballgame. The home health nurse is gone by then, but to delay a run-in with Mrs. Elliott as long as I can—she might as well have just caught me playing with matches in her garage—I study the family photos along the hall. Most are of Jake and his sister, Amber, at various ages. Jake has always been unusually cute. His toothless grin as a kid reminds me of the mischievous smiles my seven-year-old brothers now have.

The photos leave one question still churning inside me: Where is Jake's dad? Whenever we've talked about our families, Jake has always avoided discussing him. Mrs. Elliott hasn't mentioned him either, but the most obvious topic we've avoided this morning is her son. And there's no dodging it now.

Mrs. Elliott looks up from her quilt when I enter the living room; she's probably been picking out my knots. Once we're finished, she plans to donate the quilt to the rehabilitation center where she stayed after her stroke. "I, um . . ." *Want to bury my head in the ground like an ostrich.* "I was hoping to clarify what you just saw."

"I've been instructed to keep my mouth shut about you two." She zips her lips.

I smile and relax a bit. "Jake says I shouldn't feel stupid, but I can't help it. Not until I explain a few things."

Mrs. Elliott motions for me to sit next to her wheelchair. "Then get on with it, but please don't feel stupid. I know you're 'just friends' . . . most of the time."

"That's a great way to put it," I reply, walking around the quilt frame to collapse onto the couch. "I have a million reasons for avoiding anything more than that right now. I just don't seem to have enough sense to stay away from Jake."

"Don't be so hard on yourself," Mrs. Elliott says. "He's always had this effect on girls. The funny thing is, you're the first one to have the same effect on him. And my goodness, he's a mess. It's actually nice to see."

Firecrackers go off inside me. I should feel guilty for making Jake "a mess," but here I am, all giddy, and dragging his sweet mother into it. "The problem is," I explain, "I might never get my head on straight. But I don't want you to think I'm just playing games with him."

"Not at all. No one knows their future. That's what makes life so fun." We talk a while longer as we keep stitching, and then Mrs. Elliott yawns. "I think I need a nap, if you don't mind."

"No problem." I try not to imagine the disaster of a quilt she might wake up to.

"You could always go to Jake's game," she says.

My needle sticks into something hard. "That's a tempting idea, but, well . . ." I press my thumb against a finger so it won't bleed. "I don't want to put him in an awkward situation."

"Oh, I'm sure if you're recognized, he'll think of something," she replies. "And you certainly have permission to use my name in any bit of fairy tale you'd like to make up."

This is another one of those times when I should just say no, isn't it?

"The tournament is only a few blocks down the street," Mrs. Elliott adds, backing her wheelchair away from the quilt frame. "You could walk if you'd like to. I have a map."

There are six courts at the massive city park. With my white floppy hat and oversize sunglasses in place, I walk along the edge of the bleachers and search for which game Jake is playing in. At last, I spot him sitting on a bench with a few other guys, and figure the tournament must be behind schedule. Lucky for me.

I scan the bleachers for a place to sit, on the opposite side of the court. There's a single seat here and there, but I make my way to where there's a bit more room near the top. Two guys and a girl soon ask if they can squeeze into the remaining space next to me. I place my bag on my lap and scoot over, blending in with the rest of the crowd.

"You two need to chill out," the girl tells her friends. Her short black hair is spiky and cute, and she's wearing an ASU T-shirt. I wonder what brand of vitamins they take here in Phoenix, because *everyone* is beautiful—especially one of the guys she's with, who has light brown hair and dark eyes. Wait . . . something about him seems familiar. "I'm sure you'll both get a chance to go out with her."

"But just think, Mark, I'll get to kiss her *first*," says the brown-haired guy.

He gets slugged by his buddy, a white-blond, stocky guy. "I don't want your leftovers!"

"Why not? You've liked them before."

I watch all this out the side of my sunglasses while I drink from a water bottle.

"Ack! You guys are sick!" the girl says. "Emma Taylor's kissed way hotter guys than either of you, anyway."

I swallow wrong and cough like both lungs have exploded.

The girl whips her head around. "Are you okay?"

"I'm fine." *Gasp.* "Really." *Gasp.* I take another drink. "Thanks."

The Cage. Jake's friends! That's where I've seen these guys before.

Crap. *Double crap.* I have to get out of here. One more cough and I'm breathing again, but my bag has fallen off my lap and everything that used to be inside is now scattered among four pairs of feet.

I grab my wallet first—it has my driver's license under a clear cover on the outside—then stuff my *Coyote Hills* script back into my bag. My cell starts ringing, and I look around for it. But then I hear the girl say in stunned, slow words, "How do *you* know Jake Elliott?"

Only then do I notice that she's holding my ringing phone, and Devin and Mark are also staring at the caller ID on the front of it. And since my phone says in bright, bold letters that *Jake Elliott* is the one who's calling me, it's impossible to talk my way around this. I release my breath and take the phone. "Oh, is that him? We, uh . . . work together."

My phone stops ringing.

They all look at each other, and then everyone's focus shifts back to *me*. "No way!" the girl says. "I didn't recognize you!"

I tug my hat a little lower. "That's kind of the idea."

"Ouch," Mark says, running a hand over his buzz haircut. "Did you happen to hear what we just said? Because . . . yeah, that might've sounded sorta bad."

"Just a little," I tell him, unable to suppress a smile. "So which one of you guys gets to kiss me first? I got a bit lost around the *leftovers* part."

Devin half raises his hand. "Uh, hi there, I'm Devin. I was supposed to go on a date with you next month, but now I'm just hoping you don't have a hit man on speed dial."

I laugh. "Nah, I only make that call *after* a guy passes me off to his buddy."

"Sorry, that was just stupid guy talk," Devin replies, moving the girl out of the way so he can stand by me. "Which Sophie here is totally used to."

"But still disgusted by," Sophie informs me. "Don't worry, though. Devin's really okay. I mean, he's not as cool as Jake, which I'm sure *Jake* has told you. And definitely not as athletic as Mark. But Devin gets the best grades, so if you're into geeks . . ."

Jake is calling me again. Devin stops scowling at Sophie and looks down at my phone. "Oh man, can I answer it?" he asks. This situation really can't get any crazier, so I hand over my phone. Devin changes his voice to sound like a girl—me, apparently. "Hey, Jakey! OMG, you'll never guess who I just met. Devin is, like, so hot! And his muscles are *way* bigger than yours. I'm giving him a back rub right now."

Silence, then I can hear Jake laugh. "*What*? How did *you* get Emma's phone?"

"Dude, she followed me here. Total stalker."

I grab my phone. "They sat right next to me," I tell Jake, hoping to somehow save this very telling situation. "Which is funny, since the reason I came to the game was because you said you'd introduce me to Devin if I could make it." Devin grins and reaches around Sophie to hit Mark. "You know, because we're doubling the weekend of the premiere," I tell Devin, but close enough to the phone that Jake can hear too, and go along with the charade I'm trying to pull off. "And I was in Phoenix anyway, interviewing Jake's mom for a foundation I'm working on."

"Ri-i-ight," Jake says. "Oh, gotta go. My game's starting. Don't believe anything they tell you—unless it makes me look good, of course."

Once I'm off the phone, Devin is yanked out of the way by

Mark, and Sophie scoots past both of them to stand next to me. "Devin gets to spend a whole day with you," she says, "so Mark and I want to at least get to know you for thirty minutes."

"Okay, cool." I switch places with Sophie so I'm now between them. "I'm really not that exciting, though. People usually write every clever line I say."

Mark and Sophie laugh, and Devin wants to know why, but they won't tell him.

Once Jake's game starts, it's hard to watch him—but not too closely—and also pay attention to Sophie and Mark. Time flies, though, because the game only goes to twenty-one points. One of Jake's teammates hits the winning shot, and Sophie and I cheer. But Devin and Mark curse.

"They're just mad because they lost both of their games this morning, which means they're out of the tournament," Sophie explains. "So now they have to buy Jake a shake at The Hamburger Hut." She pokes Mark in the ribs. "Because he *isn't* a loser."

"Just to clear things up," Mark tells me as we all walk down the bleachers, "Sophie's not really flirting with me—she's my cousin. And she's already dated Devin. And Jake breaks every heart that gets within a hundred miles of him, so Sophie stays clear of him too." *Ugh.* That's likely a warning I should listen to. "Sophie just likes to annoy us."

"Yeah," she says. "And to remind Devin why that sweeping romance we once had, when we were fifteen, was the best week of his life."

"*You* dumped me, remember?" Devin says. "Why rub it in?"

"Why not? Someone has to keep you guys humble."

"Uh-huh," I say, suddenly distracted. The game had been shirts and skins, and Jake is only a few feet away from me now. Shirtless. I've seen him in this glorious state a few times before, but never in the high afternoon sun—with a freshly glowing tan, and having just poured a bottle of water down his chest. *Washboard abs* doesn't begin to describe the view.

I'm sweating more than Jake is.

"Put your shirt on, you show-off," Devin tells him.

Jake swats his head. "How was your back rub?"

Devin looks at me with mock fondness. "Amazing."

"Why didn't you tell us she'd be here?" Sophie asks Jake, and he shoots me a quick glance for help. "A little warning would've been nice."

"Actually, it isn't his fault," I say. "He knew I'd be coming to Phoenix this weekend to interview his mom, but I wasn't sure how much time I'd have today."

"Not so fast," Devin says. "We have a rule around here: Jake has enough good luck for all of us, so whenever anything bad happens, *he* has to take the blame for it."

Mark nods. "Jake's the only one out of a bunch of our buddies who hasn't had a thing for you at some point. Then we're all sitting around Devin's pool a while ago, and Jake tells us, totally casual, 'Hey, I got this acting gig, and you'll never guess who I'll be working with.' Anyway, there's not a lot of love for this dude around here anymore."

"Not that there ever was," Devin puts in.

"Eh, don't take it so bad, guys," Jake says. "You wouldn't want to spend your days with this diva anyway." I put a hand on my hip, and he goes on. "I mean, one minute it's about a pedicure gone bad"—I try to hide my newly polished toes, which I'll admit I'm sort of obsessive about, but I can't—"and the next, she's complaining because her lettuce isn't crisp enough."

"That's Kimmi!" I swing my bag, and he jumps out of the way.

"Really? I get you two confused," Jake says, now channeling Brett. "But before you stab me with your eyebrow pencil, Mark and Devin owe me a shake, and they'll buy one for you too. Wanna come along?"

Why not? The most awkward part of being discovered here is over. And I like these guys.

JAKE

The Hamburger Hut is pretty much empty, but we still sit in a back corner away from any windows to lessen Emma's chances of being recognized. She goes straight for the two small tables I pull together while Devin orders fries and shakes—Oreo for me and banana cream pie for Emma. I sit directly across from her.

This place has been around forever, and the way it looks now isn't much different from when I was a kid. The black-and-white-checkered floor is the same, and the booths that line one side of the restaurant have shiny red vinyl, with thick chrome edging on the tables.

The only big difference is that it's missing the long bar that used to run in front of the kitchen. About the time I started high school, I remember walking in and having my entire body go rigid when I saw that the owners had torn it out. My dad and I sat up to that bar on high spinning stools countless times, usually after one of my Little League games. It was kind of our thing to come here. Having that bar ripped out made me feel like someone had thrown away my best childhood memories with the trash. But now, I'm glad it's gone.

I wish the memories of my dad would go away too.

My friends fill the restaurant with a ton of noise. Everyone asks Emma questions over the top of each other, curious about the true nature of a celebrity's life. Sophie talks more than anyone, which is typical. "You actually do your own laundry and stuff?"

"Except for normal things that most people take to the cleaners," Emma says.

Mark wants to know about a fifty-foot trailer, and I tell him, "Emma has a dressing room that's twenty-by-twenty feet, but I only have a twelve-by-twelve box." I can state the exact dimensions because Kimmi measured all the dressing rooms for comparison. "Our producer likes his principal cast to be inside the studio, where he can yank us onto a set himself if he needs to."

"My dressing room is only bigger because female cast members usually have longer wardrobe racks," Emma clarifies. "That's all."

"But my clothes are bigger. And I have bigger feet that need to walk around."

"So true," Emma says. "But there's a *sprawling* desert right next to the studio, where you can walk for miles and miles."

I already want to get out of here. Things changed for us in Mom's garage, and I'm dying to be alone with Emma again. *Snail mode* is slow, but it's better than being parked at a stop sign.

"Do you have your own hairstylist and makeup artist?" Sophie asks.

Emma might be thinking the same thing I am because her eyes

stay locked with mine a little too long before she turns back to answer Sophie. "Some actors put that in their contracts. But every project I've worked on already had a great hair and makeup team."

"It must take an army to get Jake ready for the cameras," Devin says. "Between his buckets of bronzing powder and gallons of sculpting gel . . . sheesh, the studio must need a separate storage unit to hold all that."

I pretend to yawn, like Devin's jokes never bother me. Then I steal the cookie from the top of his own Oreo shake—he always saves the best for last—and toss it into my mouth. He swears and slugs me.

"You can bug Jake whenever you want to," Sophie tells Devin. "I need Emma to tell me if Brett Crawford is a good kisser."

Wrong question in front of the wrong guy.

If it wasn't in the script, I wouldn't know if Brett and Emma have kissed or not—I've never had to be on set for one of those scenes. And if I can get away with it, I won't watch them kiss on TV either.

Emma gives my foot a tap, so she must've noticed that I shifted in my chair. "Do you mean Brett's on-screen or off-screen kissing?" she asks Sophie. "Because, despite media reports, I only have experience with one, and it might spoil the show if I tell you which."

"I don't care," Sophie says. "I just want to know if he's as good as he looks."

Emma hesitates, then explains to Sophie what she once told me—that screen kissing is different from the real thing because so many people are watching, and it's pretty much choreographed. "Who knows what Brett kisses like in real life? Well, *plenty* of girls do, I'm sure," she adds. "He's probably a bit spastic, though, if you want to know the truth. But on set, I haven't really paused to evaluate him. If he did a bad job, it would be McGregor who'd say, 'Cut! You're drooling down her chin.' And we'd have to shoot it all over again."

"And over and over again, until you get it right?" Sophie asks, and Emma nods. "That's so weird!" Sophie goes on. " 'Cause what if Brett was your boyfriend in real life, but you had to kiss some-one else at work—like Jake—right in front of him. That would be *crazy* awkward! He'd probably get totally jealous."

So close, Sophie. Just reverse that.

"Time's up," I tell her before this subject goes too far. "No one else is getting a word in, and Mark and Devin will go home in tears if you keep talking about Brett."

"Oh, sorry, guys!" Sophie says. "You can flirt now."

For the next thirty minutes or so, Mark continues to make a good effort with Emma, but Devin is suddenly way off his A-game. In fact, he's paying more attention to *me*, and all I'm doing is lis-tening to everyone else. Then, even though I'm sitting just twelve inches away, Devin sends me a text:

Devin: Dude. You're whipped! How long have you been dating her?

Me: Whipped? How couldn't I be? But not dating.

Devin: You haven't even asked her out? You chicken.

Me: I've asked. She's declined. Technical difficulties.

Mark is still completely hypnotized by Emma, but Sophie notices our phones semi-hidden under the table and pulls out her own. She starts up a group text between the three of us.

Sophie: OMG, Jake! You like Emma!

Devin: Took ya long enough, Soph. I figured it out the second you started talking to her about kissing Brett. Jake was squirming like a guppy.

Me: No way. This chair is just uncomfortable.

Sophie: Jake, I'm SO sorry I said all that crap. I just barely noticed your puppy dog eyes a few minutes ago when she was telling Mark about her foundation. You have to promise I can be your best man or something, K? I'll even wear a tux. And I want to be your nanny too cuz you guys are gonna have the most beautiful kids in the history of ever.

I'm on the verge of cracking up but Emma and Mark are now talking about his wrestling team, so I don't want them to think I'm laughing at what Mark is saying. I can tell Devin is barely holding it in too. But I should probably abstain from this text conversation, anyway, or I might say too much.

Devin: Soph, they aren't even dating. Jake says she doesn't want to. Do you buy it?

Sophie: No! LOL! Jake, did you flex for her? Have you smiled like REALLY big so she can see how insanely straight your teeth are?

Devin: Yeah man. That should do the trick. Just don't mention your Batman boxers. Not cool. Sooo not cool.

Sophie: Seriously, Jake? Batman? Superman is way hotter.

Devin: True. And you've already got those buns of steel.

That's when Sophie loses it, and Mark turns and grabs her phone. "This better be good." He's silent for a sec as he scrolls through the messages, and I hold my breath. I doubt the content will surprise him; I'm just wondering what he'll say to Emma. "What the . . . why don't you guys ever talk about *my* buns of steel, huh?"

Everyone laughs, including Emma who still has no idea what's going on.

Mark turns to me when she isn't looking and flips me off, but he doesn't mean it. No matter how much I push and shove with my friends, in the end, we're thick as blood. I should've given Mark and Devin more credit—known they'd be cool about this. Why doesn't Emma think Rachel will understand too?

"Okay, I've obviously missed something," Emma says.

Mark leans over to whisper to her, but he's laughing too hard to speak quietly. "Jake has Batman boxers."

"Oh!" Emma says, and hurries to turn away from me as if I'm actually sitting here in my underwear. "That's . . . crazy. I took Jake for an Iron Man sort of guy."

"And I voted for Superman," Sophie says.

Soon we're all talking about which superheroes we'd want to be.

Devin eventually nudges me and says, "I've gotta show you something in my car." I follow him outside. Then he gives my head a swipe. "Why did you set me up with Emma?"

"You really think I wanted to?" I ask. "I could've dealt with *you* being pissed off if I didn't, but Emma's best friend has a thing for me, so Emma asked me to take her out. Then she thought of the even dumber idea that we should double, because I'd already told her that you wanted to go out with *her*. So now I just need you to . . . I don't know, punch me in the face, but then I'm hoping you'll be my wingman anyway. Or that day is gonna be painful."

"Whatever. That's cool. And the rest? Does Emma like you or not?"

"I don't really know," I say, because I figure it's only okay to admit how *I* feel. "She has a full constitution of reasons for not dating me—including this Bremma thing that the media has made up—but very little of it makes sense."

"Then under all that Hollywood hotness, she's just a typical girl. And when do chicks *ever* make sense?" He has a point.

When Devin and I get back inside The Hamburger Hut, Emma asks my friends to help keep her visit to Phoenix a secret. She tells them straight out that it's because of this couple crap the tabloids invented about her and Brett, so things might get messy if people start talking about her hanging out here with *me*, even though she's only working on her foundation.

My friends all promise to keep quiet, and I'm not too worried about Devin and Mark, but . . . "I've gotta bribe Sophie," I tell Emma once we're in my car.

I pick up my phone to make the offer: "Hey, Soph. I forgot to tell you that I have some extra tickets for the premiere and after party—a ton of stars will be there. So if you can help me keep our other idiot friends from telling even a single person that Emma was in Phoenix today, I'll let you decide who gets the tickets. And you can have one too. You cool with that?"

Sophie's scream just about shatters my bones.

* * *

We're back to my mom's house by eight, and while I shower, Mom and Emma work some more on the quilt. I return to the living room in gym shorts and a T-shirt, and even though I'm hardly camera worthy with my hair still dripping wet, Emma's entire face lights up. She's never looked at me this way before, not like I imagine my own expression to be when she catches *me* looking at *her*.

I don't know how, but something has definitely changed.

"Isn't *Star Trek* on tonight?" I ask Mom. She loves watching reruns of old TV favorites, and I need to take advantage of that. I check the time. "Yep, liftoff is any minute now."

"Jake, dear," Mom says, "please don't confuse a space shuttle with a starship."

"Yeah," Emma adds. "It's an insult to future technology."

"Oh, jeez. Don't tell me you're into all that geek garbage," I reply, but really just to keep teasing my mom. I've been known to watch a few episodes myself.

Emma answers with the Vulcan salute.

"You're the one who refused to wear anything but a spacesuit for a full year of your life," Mom reminds me. She looks back to Emma. "He once went door to door in it, informing the neighbors that I'd started up a daycare—which I *hadn't*—and for a dollar, I would watch their kids for an entire day."

"I was business-minded even at five," I explain. "And I wanted more friends."

"Makes perfect sense to me," Emma replies.

"All right, Jake," Mom says. "Remember that you have a hotel expecting you. Don't leave any later than midnight."

"One thirty," I reply.

Mom glares at me. "My roof, my rules."

We've played this curfew game plenty of times before. "How about one?"

"Don't worry, Mrs. Elliott," Emma throws in. "I'll fall asleep long before then. Jake's just going to help me figure out my classes for next semester, then if there's any time left, we might watch a few YouTube videos of him prowling the catwalk."

"Uh . . . I don't think so," I say. Has she already watched them?

"That should be fun," Mom replies as she heads for her bedroom. "If you need me, I'll be hanging out with Captain Kirk. That darn tractor beam keeps breaking."

Once she's closed her door, Emma says, "I love tractor beams. They can snatch whatever they want, right out of space. Like this!" She grabs my hand and pulls me onto the couch, right next to her. "Pretty cool, huh?"

Oh yeah. "Do you take the magic of the movies with you *everywhere*?"

"Always." She reaches for my laptop on a side table, and I notice that her oversize shirt slips to the edge of her shoulder. This chick is into torture. "Where should we go first? School or the catwalk?" Her fingers type out YouTube.

I steal the laptop and ask, "Do you already have some new classes in mind?" I've finally started three of my own: finance, economics, and business management. I study whenever I can at work, and since I'm on planes at least eight hours a week flying between Arizona and my remaining modeling jobs, I get plenty of homework done on my flights.

Life is pretty darn good. Especially today.

"I've finally decided to major in psychology," Emma says. "My dad should at least think it's academic enough, but my mom . . . well, she wants me to study history and politics, because that will make me *refined* enough to discuss sophisticated topics."

"And you'd rather talk about anxiety and depression?" I ask.

"Heck yeah!" Emma replies. "Psychology will teach me about a ton of interesting topics. I want to know why humans do what they do, and why they're afraid of certain things, and how they get through all the crap that happens to them." She takes a breath. "I mean, I already know the techniques of acting. But the best actors can dig deep inside the heart of their characters and connect with them—figure out *why* someone would do something like sit and cry rather than face their problems. And academically, psychology is the best way to understand that."

"Then it sounds perfect for you." I love it when Emma gets this excited. Her big blue eyes are brighter right now than the lamp that's next to her, and none of her smiles on film even come close to what the real thing does to me.

We spend the next half hour or so going through Emma's classes for next semester, then she brings up the videos from last year's Fashion Week in New York that someone posted on You-Tube. I happen to be in a few of them. "I'll make you a deal," I say. "You can watch those runway clips if I get to google your name and check out all forty-five million links. Fair?"

"Forty-five *million*? Whatever."

She obviously hasn't looked for a while. "Want to see?"

"Um . . . no," she replies. "Why did you google me, anyway?"

"Why did you look me up on YouTube?"

"Because you won't do your runway walk for me." She's tried several times to get me to do it on the running path. "I've got it down pretty good now, though. Watch!"

I'm perfectly fine with her trying to imitate my walk. She struts back and forth with her cute bare feet, and in her baggy—but still smokin' hot—sweats that are rolled up a few inches above her ankles. And I tell her stuff like: *Your arms are swinging too high. Slow down. Walk backward. Diagonally. Now walk on your hands.*

Emma rolls her eyes and starts beating me with couch pillows. I play along just long enough for her to give me hints that I'm getting *too* physical for her comfort, and then I snatch away her weapons. I have to know something.

"So how long are we talking here?" I ask. "Three, maybe five years? Until we can actually date, in public?"

She sinks into the cushions. "I'd never expect you to wait that long. But I keep making one mistake after another with guys, and I don't want *you* to be the next one."

Nice sucker punch. "I definitely don't want to be a mistake."

"We're getting to know each other really well this way, though," she says. "And if things had been any different, I doubt we would've spent this much time *talking*."

I laugh. "True. Very true."

She quickly gets serious again. "And I need a chance to tell Rachel what's been going on before anything really changes between us. But I don't want to tell her until after the premiere because she's really looking forward to coming out here. And I'll feel less guilty if I can explain things face-to-face, so she'll . . . hopefully understand."

Why should Emma feel guilty about *any* of this?

"So I'm guessing this means that little rule we talked about in the car will stay in place until then?" I ask, and my stomach sinks when she nods. "All right. I can handle that. But some things"—I

slide my hand along the couch and slip my fingers between hers—
"are getting impossible to resist."

Emma smiles and inches closer. "Friends hold hands, don't they?"

"I don't do it with *my* friends," I say, "but I'll take your word for it."

EMMA

By the time I've showered and dressed the next morning, Jake is home from the hotel and in his mom's kitchen, burning pancakes. And he was apparently in a hurry to get here because he's still in the same gym shorts and T-shirt from the night before, and his hair looks like a hurricane hit him. The crazy thing is, he's never been so irresistible.

He turns from the griddle and catches me watching him. "Hey there. You hungry?"

"Starving."

"Good, because—dang!" Jake hurries to shovel off the pancakes. "How'd I burn those?"

"They were already burning when I walked in here," I say. "A full minute ago."

"Nuh-uh, really? But look, this other batch is perfect." He holds up a serving platter stacked with neatly round pancakes. I suspect

Jake only added half the required amount of water, though, because they're twice as dense as they should be. Either that or he accidentally followed a recipe for pound cakes. "I guess I was just thinking about . . . well, you. So you can't blame *me* for burning them."

"When it's obviously my fault," I say. His eyes are so amazing—jade green this morning. The exact color seems different with everything he wears.

"Jake!" Mrs. Elliott hollers from her room. "Answer the phone, please!"

Without really looking, Jake reaches around me to pick up the kitchen phone. Then just a few seconds after he says hello, his face loses all color. He turns away without even a signal to me, walks out to the back patio, and closes the glass door. To keep busy, I start cleaning the kitchen, but my mind goes wild trying to make sense of his reaction.

Mrs. Elliott finally comes in and asks, "The call was for Jake?"

"Yeah," I reply, doing my best to sound casual. "He's on the patio."

Mrs. Elliott then turns sort of pale too, and makes her way to the counter to check her caller ID. "I'm gonna skin him alive!" she says, and my heart rockets to my throat. "Not Jake. His father," she goes on. "He's been calling every weekend, trying to catch Jake. But he always makes things worse. And he's already done enough damage, so I told him to back off for a while."

His dad. The one topic Jake continues to skirt around.

His silhouette is now on the other side of the sheer window panel—the phone in one hand, dropped to his side, and his other hand resting on the door handle. "Maybe you should talk to him alone," I say. "I'll finish getting ready."

I leave the kitchen before Mrs. Elliott replies. About twenty minutes pass before Jake knocks on Amber's bedroom door, where I slept. "Breakfast is ready," he says, sounding normal. The smells of eggs and bacon now waft down the hall, and when I reach the kitchen, Mrs. Elliott is already at the table, and Jake pulls out a chair for me.

He's smiling but still has a vacant look in his eyes.

"So, you were saying last night that you like Sophie?" Mrs. Elliott asks me.

As we all talk about Jake's friends, he glances at his mom's plate over and over again, and I can't figure out why. She hasn't started on her pancakes yet, but she's making her way through the scrambled eggs and bacon just fine.

I watch closer as she finally attempts to cut her pancakes using the side of her fork—totally impossible because they're as hard as Frisbees—then saw through them with a table knife, like I've been doing. But the top of her stack keeps sliding to the side, so she has to set down her knife, pick up her fork again, and go back and forth like this, one utensil and then the other, until she finally has a bite-size wedge.

Jake puts his own utensils down, and that's when I realize what's going on: his mom can't use her knife and fork together because she can only use one hand. But she doesn't seem nearly as bothered by this as Jake does. He reaches for her plate to help, but Mrs. Elliott shoots him a glare and says, "Thank you, Jacob, but I can feed myself."

Jake looks at her with an expression of dejection, then wipes his mouth with a napkin. "I'll, uh . . . be back in a minute."

I can only watch as he stands and walks out the patio door again.

"He's having a rough morning," Mrs. Elliott tells me.

"Should I go out there?"

She hesitates. "If you'd like to. But don't take it personally if he's snippy."

Outside, I find Jake staring blankly at the warm morning air. "Hey, you have a porch swing," I say, not daring to sit next to him. I think back to yesterday in the garage, and how he gave me an opportunity for privacy if I wanted it. "You can talk to me," I say, "or I'll go back in. I'm fine either way."

Jake scoots over and motions for me to sit. "We need freaking chain saws to eat those pancakes," he says. "Why didn't I just make omelets, or oatmeal? My mom could've easily eaten *those* with one hand." He pushes his fingers through his hair. "You'd think that after a full year, I'd be used to this. But I even put the fork on her paralyzed side. Did you *see* that?"

I construct a careful reply before I speak. "I'm sure the only thing that really matters to your mom is that you thought to make her breakfast. And I bet you do it every time you're here."

A smile tugs at Jake's mouth, but he doesn't reply. He just takes my hand and strokes his thumb over the top of it, clearly still agitated. As the seconds pass, though, his touch becomes more gentle, and it's almost painful for me to resist an impulse to lay him down, rest his head in my lap, and play with his hair until all his worries go away.

He clears his throat. "I doubt it will ever get easier to see my mom like this. She used to be the one who rushed off to help someone, no matter what they needed. But now, well . . . nobody's here for *her*. My mom's friends have all moved on, and the person who owes her the most—my dad—has done nothing more than send a cheap bouquet of flowers and a stupid get-well card. I hate him for a lot of reasons, but mostly for that." Jake looks away and brushes flour off his shorts. "That was him on the phone."

I nod. "Why did he call?"

"Who knows? He's probably run out of gambling money again and wants to hit the jackpot the easy way—using *me*." Jake lets go of my hand and leans forward on his elbows. He's silent for a bit, then finally goes on. "It's hard to believe now, but my dad used to be super cool. When I was a kid he came to my ball-games, we built forts in the backyard, chased lizards—all the stuff that makes growing up fun, you know? Then everything just . . . stopped. Not overnight, really, but his weekends in Vegas got more frequent, and soon he was gone three or four days at a time. Then he lost his job, then he lost another one. And eventually, he left and didn't come home for weeks. And Vegas is only five hours from here."

Imagining all this makes my throat tight, and I don't trust myself to reply.

I'm not surprised when Jake's own voice sounds even more strained when he speaks again. "We talked on the phone once in a while, and he always said he'd be home soon. One summer my mom couldn't convince me to go anywhere—not even to the park across the street—because I was afraid my dad would come home while I was gone and I'd miss him before he left again. I kept up that kind of crap until I was about twelve. That's when I finally figured out he'd been lying to me, for *years*."

Jake falls quiet again, so I say, "It must've been an awful time for your mom too. Especially watching *you* suffer."

"Yeah, it was bad. And Amber was as messed up as I was, but my mom just put on a brave face and got a job. She did transcription work at home, so she'd be around when we were out of school. Then my dad borrowed against our house without my mom knowing, and we almost lost it because he wasn't paying his part of *anything* anymore. He just kept making things worse and worse for her, and they finally divorced."

"And now?" I ask.

"He's been around here and there, but not much," Jake replies. "Then a couple of years ago, once I started showing up in magazines, he called me with a sob story about being laid off. He said he'd been kicked out of his apartment, all this garbage, and for some stupid reason, I believed him. So without telling my mom, I sent him what he wanted: five thousand bucks—almost everything I'd saved after my first few months of modeling. But it didn't take long for my mom to figure out what I'd done, and when she did some research, she discovered that my dad had been doing *just fine,* living it up in some swanky casino that gave him a room as long as he kept spending his money there. He'd just needed some extra cash to enter a high-stakes tournament." Jake looks back to me with an expression of utter torment. "I doubt you've ever fallen for a scam like that."

I'm already thinking of a time when I did. "When I was fifteen, my aunt Ivy from Fayetteville called to tell me her daughter was having problems breathing at night and needed surgery on her sinuses, but they didn't have good enough insurance to cover it. My aunt explained the situation first, then asked for my mom. As they talked, I sat there and cried my eyes out, thinking one of my favorite cousins was going to die. My mom was acting funny about it, though, so I begged her to stop being selfish, and she finally told my aunt that yes, I could help out, and she sent the money."

"Let me guess, your cousin didn't have surgery?" Jake asks.

"She did, actually," I reply. "She got an amazing—but totally unnecessary—nose job, and won the Miss Fayetteville pageant."

Jake surprises me with laughter. "How did your aunt expect to get away with that?"

I shrug. "We went to visit my cousin after the surgery, and she had no idea what I was talking about when I asked if she could breathe better. She didn't even know what a sinus was." My mom still brings up this occasion whenever she wants to remind me that she's always right about *everything*. "When my parents confronted my aunt, her excuse went something like, 'Emma has her fame and fortune, and this is the only way my daughter can get hers. You owe it to your family to take care of them.' Which is ridiculous, right? I would've happily paid for a life-saving surgery, but I didn't owe my cousin a new *nose*."

Our families haven't spoken since. It's a typical Southern feud.

"It's bad enough when *anyone* takes advantage of you, but so much worse when it's a family member," Jake says. "So whenever my dad calls and says in his fake, cheery voice, 'Hey there, Jake! How's my boy doing?' I just want to say, "Funny you ask, Dad, because I'm actually doing everything *you* should be doing, and I hate you for it." Jake clenches a handful of hair in his fist. "I know that's cold, but my dad's a smart guy—he has a freaking master's degree. But he *chose* to live this life, and dragged the rest of us down with him. So why should I give him that chance all over again?" Jake is still gripping his hair, so I ease his hand away and hold it. "At the same time, I'm tired of hating him. Avoiding him.

Pretending like he doesn't exist. I need to get over everything he's done. Maybe even forgive him. But how?"

I'm not sure if he's looking for advice or just venting. Still, I take a chance and say, "I totally get why you don't like to even think about your dad, but I doubt you'd feel so conflicted about it if you truly hated him. And pushing him away doesn't seem to be working for your own peace of mind, right? So maybe you could start talking to him for only a few minutes at a time—try having a normal conversation for just *that* long. But when it comes down to it, Jake, earning back your trust is up to him."

"Yeah, true. And I should probably try that. It's just that I have a hard time trusting *anyone* now," he says quickly, then seems to regret telling me this. "I kinda, well—" He starts tugging on a loose string at the hem of his shorts. "I get what you could call a knee-jerk reaction whenever people seem too good to be true. I instantly doubt them. I doubt that *anything* good can last. And I'm usually right."

Jake glances back for a sec, giving the impression that even I fit into this category, and I can't let him believe that. "At least you don't have to worry about *me*," I say, "since I'm nowhere near too good to be true. I think I've made it perfectly clear that I'm a pain in the butt."

He laughs and wraps an arm around me, his entire body seeming to relax. "You, Emma Taylor, cause me *plenty* of pain. But don't count on scaring me off so easily."

I nestle into him, the two of us fitting together so perfectly it's as if we're custom made for each other. "Well, as you can see," I reply, "that's exactly what I'm trying to do."

I've always thought that when I one day found myself feeling like this, I would wonder if it was the real thing—if it was something genuine enough, like Jake said, to last. But I realize in this moment that there isn't a single questioning *if* in my head.

I'm falling in love with him.

I return to work on a Tuesday, the dreaded day each week when the tabloids tell me what's going on in my life. They are way off as usual—and on a scavenger hunt to figure out why I didn't go to Tahoe with Brett—but for once, I couldn't care less. They can speculate and lie all they want, just as long as they don't bring Jake into it.

The only flaw in my grand plan is that the tabloids *are* hurting Brett, most of them suggesting that he's fooling around and making me cry all day long, begging for his attention.

During Wednesday's lunch break, the first time I work with Brett after Labor Day weekend, he waves a stack of tabloids in my face. "Great, I'm on covers as a playboy again! And I don't deserve it."

"That's unusual," I reply. Then I realize he looks genuinely devastated, so I take the tabloids away from him and toss them into a nearby trash can. "Brett, they're just as stupid as they've always been. Why would you let them bother you now?"

He plops down into his cast chair, pushes his fingers through his hair one way, and then the other. Then he stands back up again. "Because you know that I'm *trying*," he says, and grabs me by my shoulders—his trademark move. I guess it could be worse. "I'm being good. Better than good. I'm bored out of my *freaking mind* here in Tucson, but I'm playing the part of McGregor's choirboy anyway. It doesn't matter though, does it?"

"Sure it does. They'll eventually catch on," I reply, but I also have my doubts. "And you've told me yourself that you want to change, so you're not just doing this for McGregor, and especially not for the tabloids. It's for your *own* happiness, right?"

Brett nods and gives my arms a squeeze, making me suddenly aware of Jake's presence. He's been studying in his dressing room during lunch but is now filling his plate at the food table. He doesn't seem to be *watching* us, just glancing around a bit, but I still slip out of Brett's hold and return to my own plate.

The following Tuesday, while we wait for an issue with the library set to be resolved, Brett waves a fresh tabloid in front of me. "Guess who the bad guy is *this* week?"

I take the paper, which he's already opened to a particular article: A VENOMOUS EMMA TAYLOR? "What the . . ." I begin, and Brett just motions for me to read it.

Don't cross Emma Taylor if you know what's good for you— that's the warning making its way around Hollywood's dating circles. A source close to Troy Dawson, Taylor's ex, claims Dawson won't go anywhere he suspects Taylor might show up. "Troy would kill me for saying it, but it seems like he's suddenly afraid of her," said the friend.

And now it appears that the girl formerly known for her mild Southern manners is also using a few scare tactics on her most recently departed, Brett Crawford. The two had planned a getaway to Lake Tahoe together before Taylor suspected he was cheating on her and canceled. "Emma's on attack mode," an insider said. "Brett wants her back, but she either talks trash to him or ignores him altogether. The set of *Coyote Hills* is a war zone right now."

This is unfortunate for Executive Producer Steve McGregor, but our studio source tells us that all the on-set drama is only increasing our chances for some hot and steamy TV.

Crawford's camp insists that the couple maintains a close bond, while Taylor's publicist declined to comment on her very uncharacteristic behavior. But one thing is crystal clear to everyone around her: sweet little Emma Taylor is all grown up.

So watch your backsides, boys, a new queen bee has left her hive and she's not just a lot of buzz anymore—she's out to sting someone.

I have to admit that I like the part about Troy; it isn't *my* fault that he's so transparent. But the rest of the article is totally absurd, so I crumple it up and throw it back at Brett. It bounces off his chest and hits the floor.

"What is *wrong* with these people?" I ask. "How can last week's tabloids say I'm desperate for you to love me, and this one claim I've transformed into a killer black widow?"

"Queen bee," Kimmi says. She's pacing to the side of us while talking on her phone, and apparently eavesdropping as well.

"Whatever," I reply. I'm glad Jake isn't around to see how irritated I am because I've been pretty calm about gossip lately. It's hard to ruin my mood these days; I sort of flutter around like I have wings on my back.

But in a butterfly sort of way, not a queen bee.

Brett grabs the tabloid article off the floor, flattens it in his lap and scans it. "They've made *me* look like a pansy, scared that a chick who doesn't even weigh a hundred pounds is gonna do what, say mean things to me?"

"She weighs more than that," Kimmi says. "I've peeked."

"Get lost!" Brett replies. He jumps out of his cast chair, steals Kimmi's cell, and ends her call, which is clearly just to annoy her since she can now eavesdrop even easier.

"Oh, look, Kimmi! A Diet Coke!" I say, but she ignores me and whacks the side of Brett's head. He whimpers and rubs the spot, making me laugh. "I have no idea where that article got this war zone stuff. We all get along perfectly fine."

"Exactly! That's my point," Brett says, missing my sarcasm. "We're tight, right? So you should come with me to that charity auction this weekend. I won't even sit by you. We'll just casually chat and laugh once in a while—no touching, I promise. And we'll be with tons of friends. Then these stupid rumors about you being a hormonal diva who hates me for hooking up with every random chick in sight—which I haven't done even once since I moved to Tucson— will disappear. You'll be in L.A. the night before the auction anyway."

We're doing official publicity now. Brett must have checked my schedule.

After several minutes of this, I realize he's right. We just need to be seen having a friendly conversation. So I agree and invite a bunch of my own friends to come along. Jake can't go because he'll be in New York as usual, but Kimmi plans to come, which surprises Brett.

She ended things with Payton in a pretty spectacular way in Tahoe—something to do with a league of Laker Girls who showed up on their boat, one of which ended up in Payton's cabin—and according to Brett, Kimmi is now desperate to avoid him.

*   *   *

Brett must be right because Kimmi doesn't show up at ι̵
after all, but it turns out to be a lot of fun and gives me son̵
for a future fund-raiser for my own foundation. I auction off ̵ ̵
movie scripts with my personal notes in them, and Brett donates
ten pairs of worn-out jeans with his autograph on the back pockets. We hopefully throw the tabloids way off by smiling and
laughing together, and Troy even walks by me once and casually
says, "Hey."

And I say it back, as confident as I've ever felt around him.

By the end of the day, I'm happy I went. And the best side
effect? The next flock of tabloid articles contradict one another so
completely that people are starting to question every article since
Bremma began. Hooray!

But my mom . . . holy crap. She's been asking way too many
questions about boys, and after this weekend in L.A., she finally
traps me into a conversation I've been trying to avoid. "Yes, Mom,
Troy was at the auction," I tell her. "And there wasn't any drama
at all."

A long pause. "All right, well, that queen bee story is still both-
ering me."

This is the third time she's brought it up.

"Your dad and I have been talking, discussing how quickly you
left Los Angeles after *The First Family* wrapped, as well as your
other odd behaviors during that time. Changing your number and
such. And now we wonder if . . . if you might've been scared of
Troy for some reason—not the other way around, as that article
suggested." I remain silent, surprised that she'd connected so much.
"Emma, please be honest with me. I'm truly worried. And your
dad . . . well, he's jumping to all sorts of conclusions and ready to
beat that boy to a bloody pulp."

"What? *Dad*? No . . . no, listen. Troy just . . ." My heart is on hyperdrive.

"I need some answers," Mom says. "And quickly."

"He sort of stalked me, okay?" I blurt out. "After we broke up. It started with a lot of weird phone calls, then he chased me in my car once. And then—" Dad *will* freak if he finds out about the window episode. Under his business suit, my dad is still a good ol' country boy, and Southern justice is no joke. "Then after the fight at Club 99, I told Troy that I'd tell the press every crazy thing he did if he doesn't leave me alone."

I guess I have a bit of the dirty South in my blood too.

I wait for my mom to berate me for how poorly I handled the situation, but she stays quiet for so long that I wonder if we've been disconnected. "Why didn't you tell me?" she finally asks, almost whispering. "I would've helped you. Somehow."

"Because you and Dad were right about him," I reply. From the beginning, my parents said that Troy gave them *bad vibes*, but I was flattered by his sweet words, and his thoughtful gifts, and I liked how his confidence made up for my lack of it. And who listens to their parents, anyway? "I felt stupid, you know? And I was afraid you'd call the police. I'm sorry, but I didn't want to go through the media frenzy that would've created."

"So instead you put your *life* in danger?" Mom says. I'm on the phone with her for another hour after that, being reminded that I am naive, that I am irresponsible, that I shouldn't "take the law into my own hands." And I should never, ever keep secrets from my mother, because she obviously manages my life so much better than I do.

But she does seem to genuinely care as she lectures me this

time, and not only about my career. At least this part of the conversation feels sort of nice.

Just when I think we're wrapping up, Mom asks if Rachel knows any of this, and I say that she doesn't. "Good. Keep it that way," Mom replies. "A rumor just reached me that her mother was approached by *Celebrity Seeker* a few weeks ago. Trina denies speaking to them, but that's suspiciously close to when they learned about you having a crush on Brett—laptop wallpapers and all—for the last decade. Besides Rachel and Trina, who else knew about that?"

I had asked myself the same question. Rachel seemed as surprised as I was when this information was added to one of *Celebrity Seeker*'s post–Labor Day articles, as an "online extra." But Trina would have also known about my previous obsession with Brett, just by being around me for so long. And Brett himself knew, but I've never told him about my laptop wallpaper collection. The only fallout I really cared about, though, is that I'd then felt a need to tell Jake the truth.

It was awkward, and more than a little embarrassing, but he was cool about it.

"Mom," I reply, "I'm sure I've told a lot of friends over the years. Girls talk about their crushes all the time without thinking about who's going to gossip about it."

She sighs. "*You* can't afford to not think about what you say," she reminds me. "There are too many people out there who could betray you for money and attention."

"But what am I supposed to do, judge every person I meet by their potential to stab me in the back?" I ask. "I wouldn't have any friends at all."

This ends our conversation because she doesn't have a good answer. Days later, though, I still can't stop wondering if Trina could be a source for *Celebrity Seeker*. I can totally see it.

But Rachel? No way. I'm the only traitor in our friendship.

Right?

JAKE

Brett is messing with me. Whether or not he's doing it on purpose is still to be determined, but either way, he's pissing me off.

When Emma finally admitted that she'd had a decade-long crush on Brett, I had laughed it off as if it were funny—at least while I was with her. And it really wouldn't be a big deal if she wasn't going on all these California trips with him. But Brett always returns with stories that don't quite mesh with the way Emma repeats them to me.

What she doesn't know is that it was actually Brett who first told me about *Celebrity Seeker*'s discovery of her "obsession" as they called it—a full two days before she did.

"See, dude, I told you!" Brett had said, pointing out the online article that he'd pulled up on his phone. I'd been studying in my dressing room that day, for a business management test, and it seemed like he tracked me down just for this. "Remember when we went to dinner at *El Loro Feliz*, and I was convinced that Emma had a crush on me? Well, she admitted it the day we went to the motocross, but made me promise I wouldn't tell anyone. It's common knowledge now, though, so I can tease her about it all I want."

I still figured it was all garbage, but I took his phone anyway and scanned the article, throwing in some laughter for good measure. "Isn't this written by the same tabloid that you called *total crap* just a week or so ago—something about Emma not going to Tahoe with you because you'd been cheating on her?"

"Well, yeah, that article was all lies," Brett said, taking his phone back. "But when we're in L.A., Emma is a different chick. She's tempting me to break my number one rule—don't date your costars—and just go for it. Or at least I'm starting to ask myself, why not?"

Had his "why not" been more than a rhetorical question, I would have given him more than a few answers to it. That is, if I were actually allowed to talk about what's been going on between Emma and me.

Since we're not officially together, it wouldn't really be *wrong* for her to be flirting with Brett just as much as she flirts with me. Wasn't I the one who told her it was normal to play the field? But haven't Emma and I . . . haven't we already agreed that we're more than friends? That we like each other *a lot*?

Brett has to be exaggerating. That's all.

The one thing I know for sure is that I'll be in an eternal state of limbo with Emma if I don't do something to move things forward, right now. I come to this conclusion one night when I'm in New York, and I call her before I can think better of my impulse. "I just finished my very last, totally humiliating modeling job," I tell her, "which included enough hair gel to hold up the Brooklyn Bridge. So guess how I want to celebrate."

"Go to Disneyland?" she asks.

"Close! I want to go on a date."

Emma laughs. "Wow. That's . . . ambitious."

"With you," I tell her. "A real one, where we actually call it a date. This Friday, the night before the press junket. But don't worry, the same rules will apply. I'll be good."

With only a week to go before the premiere, kissing Emma now could definitely mess everything up. I may not understand her concern for Rachel's feelings, but I'm doing my best to respect it. Well . . . the no-kissing part, at least.

"Oh," she says, then there's silence while I wait for the verdict. Yeah, it's stupid to make her *call* it a date, since we've pretty much been dating for months anyway, but it's about time she recognizes that. "What do you have in mind?"

Sweet. This might actually happen. "I want to pick you up, at your front door—not on your back porch—and I want to take you, in an actual vehicle, to somewhere other than the river that runs behind your house."

"Hmm. Maybe," she replies, which isn't exactly the enthusiasm I was hoping for. Why does everything have to be such a process with her? Why can't she just *go*? "There's a bit of a problem with that noble idea, though, because my mother thinks Rachel's mom is now a source for *Celebrity Seeker.* So if you and I are seen together before I tell Rachel about us, there will be heck to pay. And I—"

"Don't want to take that chance," I say. "See, that's the part I'm having trouble with."

"Jake, it's not that I don't want to," Emma hurries to tell me. "I'm just afraid that—" She draws a breath. "Okay, you're right. I'm being stupid. This Friday?"

I'll take that as a yes. "Yep, Friday. I'll pick you up at eight."

All right, so we've booked an official date. That's progress. But the next morning on my flight back to Tucson, I'm still a little ticked off that I had to talk her into it. More like *guilt* her into it. So with a wounded ego and my emotions in overdrive, I somehow get myself into a situation on the plane that leads me into a bit of a trap—with Miss Texas.

By the next day, I know I'm in trouble. And by that night, when Emma apologizes to me for "being so paranoid," I realize I've made a serious mistake.

When Friday finally comes around—the day of our date—I completely zone out, thinking everything is over. We're shooting outdoors at a high school football field, and even though it's now October, today is so hot it feels like fire is falling from the sky. The principal cast is taking cover under a production tent, and I'm stuffing my face with rocky road ice cream.

"What's up with you today?" Kimmi asks Emma, who also seems distracted.

Emma jolts as if she's been asked something too personal. "Um. Well . . . the junket is tomorrow. And the premiere is only a week away. I always get nervous before this kind of stuff."

Or maybe before she goes on a date with a guy she's not supposed to be seen with?

In a skintight peach tank top and black running shorts, Emma has her feet propped up on a small table and looks impossibly delicious as she rolls a cold water bottle down the back of her neck. I'm starting to think self-control is overrated.

"Why?" Kimmi asks, chucking her full bowl of ice cream into the trash. "You've seen the rough cut of the first episode. And even in that state, it was good. Amazing, actually."

"But it's impossible to predict audience response," Brett says. "Are you nervous, Jake?"

My head whips away from Emma, and I know he's caught me staring at her. "I wasn't until I had a crazy dream last night," I say, grasping for the only reply to hit my brain.

"Interesting," Brett says. "Spill, dude."

Emma sits straight up in her chair. "Cool, a dream! Let's analyze it."

I wipe my mouth with a napkin and say, "It's kinda lame, but have you ever had one of those dreams that for some idiotic reason, you forget to get dressed, but you keep walking around anyway, while people gawk at you?"

Everyone nods with understanding smiles, even Kimmi. "When I finally wake up," she says, "I always try to figure out why I spent the *entire day* being laughed at, and didn't even *think* about putting clothes on."

Brett gazes at her in wonder. "Wow, you dream? I thought only humans did that."

She gives him an appropriate-for-the-moment hand gesture.

I glance around at the crew members in the tent with us and lower my voice. "But this dream was different. I showed up at the studio—*au naturale*, remember—but instead of people staring at me, they just acted like I was supposed to be that way for the scene, even though everyone else was completely dressed. And when I freaked out, McGregor said, 'Deal with it. It's your job. We need this for ratings.' Then the episode aired, and there I was, in all my glory on national television. The censors went crazy—fining the network millions—so the series was canceled and everyone blamed *me*."

My audience laughs, but I don't think the dream is all that funny.

"I know exactly what your dream means," Brett pipes up. "You're afraid people will see you for who you really are—that soon, all your faults will be exposed to the world. And you can totally count on it. I mean, I made a few mistakes that the tabloids blew out of proportion, then within a matter of months, my job offers were cut in half. It's as if everyone thinks I can't act anymore just because I haven't grown up as fast as I should have." Brett shakes his head, glancing to where McGregor is planning out a shot with the director of photography. "That's why *I'm* nervous about the premiere. I don't want critics to say that McGregor's 'risky hire' was just as dumb as they thought it would be."

The surrounding mood has taken such a sharp turn that the rest of us are speechless. Brett stands and scans our faces. "Jeez, who died?" he says. "And why is this taking so long? We're roasting out here." He leaves the tent and treks over to McGregor.

"Uh . . . how did my dream inspire those deep thoughts from Brett?" I ask.

"Deep thoughts from Brett? What an oxymoron," Kimmi says with a curt laugh. "He's asked for the attention he gets—good or bad. There's no such thing as privacy when you're in this business. I knew that when I started acting, and he should've thought of it too."

Emma narrows her eyes. "He was four. I doubt he considered paparazzi."

Kimmi is getting ripped to shreds in the tabloids right now, so

I don't get how she can defend them. Since Payton ended up with someone else in Tahoe, the rumors are that Kimmi threw a major hissy fit, then tried to get back at Payton by hanging on *several* other guys. So in the worst kind of way, Kimmi is getting all the A-list attention she's ever wanted.

"That reminds me, Emma," she says, "I need something to wear for the junket tomorrow. Want to go shopping after work?"

Emma's jaw literally drops. "Um . . . sure," she replies, nice and slow.

My own shock and instant agitation would be hard to miss. Emma and I aren't leaving on our "real date" tonight until eight, and we're scheduled to wrap by four, so she has plenty of time to shop. But Miss Texas told me something about knowing Kimmi, or knowing *of* her maybe? I wasn't really paying attention, but now I regret that. Should I try to get a few minutes alone with Emma to explain things before Kimmi does?

Then again, maybe she needs to hear a rumor about *me* once in a while.

Kimmi and Emma finalize their plans, and we're called back to first positions. We all go to our marks on the track, joining a group of extras playing other students in our gym class. But before we even rehearse the scene, McGregor leaves his monitor and comes over. "This needs something more," he says, roughing up his wiry red hair. "Mr. Elliott, your shirt's gotta go. That'll add some heat."

Everyone on set snaps their heads over to look at me, including Emma. My response is much more delayed, hesitating as McGregor and I have a staring contest.

Finally, I give him a rigid nod and pull off my shirt.

McGregor seems pleased as he walks away, but he suddenly

spins back. "On second thought," he tells me, "this episode plays during November sweeps—you know how important *those* ratings are. So let's have you do this whole scene *au naturale*!"

Everyone cracks up, and Brett takes off like a bullet—he obviously told McGregor about my dream. I shout one threat after another as I chase Brett down and tackle him to the grass. McGregor's laugh is the loudest. "Costumes, makeup, and hair again! Go!"

EMMA

Kimmi and I drive separately and meet in the courtyard at *La Encantada*, an open-air mall with upscale shops and cozy boutiques. Typical for Tucson, the two-level buildings are earthy colors and blocky, but softened by wide arches over entrances and pathways. The shopping plaza is in the resort area of the Catalina foothills, not far from where I live.

We're mostly inside while we shop, so my sunglasses and big floppy hat would only raise suspicion. I've gone to my Plan B of disguises today: a baseball cap with a ponytail sticking out the back, and small reading-type glasses with tinted rectangular lenses. I've also taken off most of my makeup on the way here. People rarely recognize me this way, and I pay with cash whenever possible so no one sees my name.

The stone walkways of *La Encantada* weave from one store to another, and Kimmi and I make our way through nearly all of them. We spend a good hour just swinging handbags around in front of mirrors, and then see who can walk best in the highest pair of heels. I doubt that *friend* is a label Kimmi wants me to slap on her, but at the moment, she kind of feels like one.

She's even asking my opinion about what she should wear to the junket. This is a shocker in itself, but Kimmi really surprises me when we're in a very girly boutique, and she holds up a light-pink baby doll dress. "Is this *America's Sweetheart* enough?" she says. "Or do I need to cover up entirely?"

"I love it!" I reply. "It has a shy and innocent feel, but it's flirtatious at the same time." I actually like the dress so much that if she doesn't buy it, I will. The bottom flares out just a little and hits right above the knee—several inches longer than what Kimmi usually wears—and the top has a scalloped neckline with capped sleeves. A whisper-thin lace covers the silk shell. Kimmi has already considered dozens of dresses and skirts, but everything she's tried on has all been very non-Kimmi-like. "Don't take this wrong," I add, "but why are you worried about looking so . . ."

"Chaste? Prim? Completely opposite of what everyone expects?"

"I was thinking of a word closer to *modest*," I reply. Kimmi gives me her usual roll of the eyes, and I finally catch on and laugh. "That's why you wanted *me* to go shopping with you, isn't it? You need my expert, prudish opinion."

Kimmi drapes the dress over her arm and strolls off to a changing room. "Just to make things clear," she says, "I don't need fashion advice from anyone." She steps into a stall and closes the door. "It's just that the tabloids are *wrong* about me being a 'tantrum-throwing tramp,' so I need to change a few million opinions. Immediately."

"Oh."

"Tahoe was such a joke," she says. "Sure, I might've been a little too flirtatious with a few guys, and been a *bit* too vocal when I confronted Payton, but I wasn't about to hide under a table like someone else I know and cry my eyes out. Because who cares if he brought along the Laker Girls for his own entertainment?"

A part of me wants to say, "I know how it feels to be cast aside like that," but it's hard to imagine having a serious conversation with Kimmi. Still, I allow myself a moment of empathy. The only time I've ever seen a glimmer of light in her eyes—before we went shopping, at least—is when I last saw her with Payton. She had liked him a lot.

"Does that surprise you?" Kimmi goes on. "That I'm . . . well, *usually* not a wounded, raging, blood-sucking skank?"

Those insults didn't come from the tabloids. "Not at all," I say through the stall door. "I'm just shocked that you'd confide in me. That you're talking to me at all, really."

Kimmi opens the door, looking even better than I imagined she would in the pink dress. "What do you mean?" she asks. "We talk all the time."

"No, we *speak*. And you *tell* me things, like how pathetic I am."

She walks around me and strikes a red carpet pose in front of a full-length mirror. "But look how much good I've done for you. You wouldn't have been so blunt a few months ago."

"Maybe not, but if you want the truth, you've never scared me." Both our tones are matter-of-fact, not snippy or defensive. We could just as well be talking about different brands of designer jeans. "You look great in that dress, by the way."

"I know," Kimmi says and blows a kiss to her reflection. "But you *should* be afraid of me. Care to guess how many reporters have asked me for dirt on you? And I happen to know a super juicy secret that I could twist into making you look however I want to."

It's obvious that she knows Jake and I spend more time together than we let on, but I'm not about to admit it. "The tabloids tell plenty of lies about me. One more wouldn't matter."

"Oh, but this isn't a lie, so it could hurt you even more." Kimmi turns to see how the back of her looks. "Super hot, right? All I need is some killer heels." She returns to her stall. "What do goody-two-shoes girls like you wear on their feet these days?"

"Whatever we want," I say. "I bare it all, every single toe."

Kimmi peeks out from behind the door and gives me a smile, a real one. "Good comeback, Barbie. See what hanging around me will do for you?" Her large brown eyes disappear as she slips back into the changing room. "And now, for keeping my mouth shut, you owe me. I need to know how to be cute and bubbly, and utterly darling at the junket. Then you need to tell me how to make the press believe that the Tahoe stories were only a faulty attack on my upstanding character." When I just laugh at her, she adds, "Oh, I see. First, you want *me* to spill what I know about *you*."

I glance around the store, rechecking for anyone close enough to hear us. "Okay, I'll take your bait," I whisper. "Why haven't you dished out the dirt you think you have on me?"

Kimmi opens the door and motions for me to join her in the stall. She only has on a skirt and bra, but this isn't much less than what she typically wears. "Besides the fact that I know McGregor would likely fire me," she says, "you're a hard person to hate, and that's incredibly irritating. If it wasn't for all your 'Hey, Kimmi! How was your weekend?' crap. And daily kissing up, like, 'Oh my gawwwwwsh! I totally love your earrings!' Then I would've already told everyone you were hooking up with Jake. Like, months ago."

I keep my expression as blank as possible.

She pulls on her shirt. "Brett is suspicious too, I can tell. So if an idiot like him can figure it out, it won't be long until *everyone* knows. Just thought you'd want a heads-up."

My mind fills with a whole lot of cursing.

"You and Jake are about to cause all sorts of fallout," she says. "You already know about Miss Texas, right? Because she has every Tri Delta house in the country talking about their date, and I doubt she'll back down quietly."

A vision of Jake with a gorgeous, big-haired blonde in cutoff shorts flashes through my mind. Ugh. "I'm sure any girl who's ever dated Jake is bragging about it right now," I say, my voice barely holding steady. "To her sorority sisters and anyone else she knows."

There's a pause. "Your naïveté astounds me," Kimmi says, then her snide tone disappears. "Jake didn't date her in the *past*. He met her on a flight from New York last weekend, and they're meeting up in Texas this Monday."

I sit on the chair behind me.

"Didn't you hear Jake today?" Kimmi adds. "Making sure he still has Monday off?"

Jake did double-check his schedule today, but there's no way he would go out with someone else, not when we're so close to dating—for real now.

"Kimmi. Jake and I . . . we're not *together*. Okay? He can date whoever he wants to."

She's quiet again as she studies me. The truth of what I've just said, as well as the sting of it, is probably evident on my flushed face. Jake and I really *aren't* together—not officially. We've never even talked about being exclusive, and . . . maybe he's been going out with other girls all along. How would I know? We hardly ever have a day off together, and his weekends are usually spent in New York, surrounded by models. Hot, *gorgeous* models.

And beauty queens, apparently.

"Whether you're a couple or not, you like him—that's obvious," Kimmi says. "And his eyes follow you across every room you enter, which is why I don't get this Miss Texas thing. Most guys are scummy, two-timing pigs, but Jake seemed different." She shrugs. "Guess not."

With barely a wisp of air in my lungs, I reply, "How did you hear about . . . her?"

Kimmi swings her handbag over a shoulder and steps into her shoes. "I have tons of friends who are Tri Delts, and news travels fast when a fellow sister is dating a celebrity."

"Right." But . . . wait. I've fallen for this sort of story before. I can't believe anything about Jake without talking to him first. He's definitely given me enough chances to explain my own version of rumors.

What if this *isn't* just a rumor, though? What if it's true, and Jake really did ask another girl out, and likes her enough to fly to Texas to see her again? Technically, he wouldn't be doing anything wrong, not when I've been so clear about us not getting serious until I'm ready. And didn't he once tell me that you can't cheat on someone if you're not even *together*?

As Kimmi pays for her dress, I stay in the changing room and try to think logically. Do I feel betrayed . . . yes, no . . . maybe a little? It's probably jealousy, more than anything. I may not be ready for a real relationship, but I sure as heck don't want anyone else having Jake. And I know him well enough to realize that Miss Texas, or any other girl he'd be interested in, must be worth his time. So, what it really comes down to is this . . . I may have competition.

What am I going to do about that?

JAKE

The moment I see Emma wearing a fake smile, I'm convinced that Kimmi told her about Miss Texas. I should've flat-out said no when that chick's pageant director called Liz to ask if I would "escort the lovely girl" I met on the plane to a state luncheon with the governor of Texas. But the call had come too soon after I'd asked Emma to go on a real date, and she'd acted like she was only doing me a favor. So I'd told Liz, "Sure, why not? It's just a luncheon."

Pride is a beast. I've stooped to an all-time low by trying to prod Emma forward with jealousy, and now I'm freaking out, knowing I can't wait any longer to admit it.

I'm ten minutes late picking Emma up for our date. Trying to ease my previous demands, I go to her back porch, rather than marching through her front door like I'd wanted to, and we walk down the running path toward my place. Emma seems a world away—not mad, exactly, just . . . distant.

When we turn the corner of my building, she pulls me back and points to the parking lot. "Yeah, I know," I tell her. "It's Brett's truck. I borrowed it."

"Why?"

"You'll see," I say, and lead her to the passenger side.

As soon as I sit in the driver's seat, Emma tells me, "Just a little FYI: Kimmi has figured things out about us—she told me so—and she thinks Brett is suspicious too."

I start the engine. "And you said . . . ?"

There's total silence, then, "I didn't really deny anything. I just kept her guessing."

Emma waits for my reply, but when I only back out of the parking space, she adds, "As a matter of curiosity, what reason did you give Brett for borrowing his truck?"

"I told him I had to pick up some new furniture," I say. I hadn't planned on borrowing it, but when I saw that Brett drove it to work, a particular vision of how I could make this date just a bit better popped into my head, so I'd asked if we could switch cars for the night. "He didn't question me at all."

I half hoped he would.

Emma nods. "Kimmi has to be wrong about Brett, though. If he knew about us, he'd come right out and say it like she did. He doesn't have a single thought pass through his head that he doesn't tell the whole world about."

Don't act possessive. Play it cool.

"Maybe he's waiting to see how serious we are," I say. "To figure out if we're actually dating . . . or just flirting." I shoot a sideways glance at Emma. "He's not the only one who's wondering that, you know. And I'm not talking about Kimmi."

Emma trails the tip of her finger down my arm. "I haven't even *started* flirting with you."

Okay, I'm smiling now. "Maybe you should give it a try. Just to see if I like it."

The farther we get from the city, the more relaxed things feel. And since Emma doesn't bring up Miss Texas, I decide not to ruin our date by announcing how immature I am. But I'll still have to tell her about my attempt to make her jealous *before* the luncheon on Monday.

It takes half an hour to travel up Mount Lemmon and find a campground that has a perfect view of the sky. I grab a bundle of firewood and other necessities from the truck, and we sit on a log next to a fire pit for an hour or so, roasting marshmallows and eating smores.

"My dad used to take me camping," Emma says, then hurries to blow out the flames on her marshmallow before it turns to ash. "It was my favorite thing to do as a kid."

"Sorry to get your hopes up," I reply, "but I didn't bring a tent."

Emma kicks my giant hiking boot with her pixie-size sneaker. "Then what's under the tarp in the truck, huh? A UFO? Nuclear missiles?"

I steal the marshmallow off her stick and toss it into my mouth before she can stop me. "You watch too much television."

"I'm *in* too much television. It's obviously warped my mind."

"That's for sure." I wrap an arm around her and give her a quick kiss on the crown of her head. Then I freeze, stunned by what I'd just done without thinking about it. Emma holds as still as I do. "We, uh, better hurry and put this fire out," I say, standing. "There's a meteor shower tonight, and we have front-row seats."

Emma stays on the log and looks up at me, the light of a thousand stars reflected in her eyes. "So *that's* why we're in the middle of nowhere?" she asks. "I thought we were just hiding from the army of reporters who are in town for the junket."

"That's only a bonus." I kick dirt on the fire, a little nervous now. "The higher our elevation, the better we can see the meteor shower. And Arizona is one of the best spots on earth to watch one."

I'm relieved when I glance up from the embers to find her smiling. "How convenient," Emma replies, and she offers a hand so I can help her off the log.

When we reach the truck, I pull off the tarp and reveal the giant beanbag chair that I brought along. The second I saw Brett's truck at work today, my imagination had easily replaced my previous vision of Emma and I watching the meteor shower from the separate bucket seats in my convertible to getting a heck of a lot closer in *this*.

Emma laughs and shakes her head at me. "If you're thinking what I think you're thinking, Jake Elliott, you might leave disappointed."

I lift Emma into the back of the truck and climb in behind her. "Did you say *might*?"

"Same rules, remember?" she says, and pushes me onto the chair. I sink into the foam and pull her next to me. She laughs. "Don't you have *two* of these?"

"I can't remember. Do I?"

I stretch my arm around her back, and Emma rests her head on my shoulder. For several minutes we watch streaks of light soar across the sky and fade into darkness. Meteor showers are common in Arizona, but it's been a long time since I took the time to watch one. The sky is perfectly clear tonight, the air fresh and crisp, and about twenty degrees cooler than in the city.

I try to focus on this, instead of the heat that I'm *actually* feeling.

Same rules, same rules, I remind myself, but Emma doesn't help my self-control one bit when she rolls to her side and inches her hand over my chest. "Your heart is pounding like there's a boxing match inside it," she tells me.

"Uh . . . yeah. Pretty much," is all I say.

The longer we lie there, almost motionless, the more restless I feel. In the silence of the night, I swear I can hear her heart racing too, and I'm dying to know what she's thinking.

Emma bolts straight up. "Shoot. I forgot to call Rachel."

What? She was thinking about *Rachel*?

I don't want to make an issue out of it, so I just lace my hands behind my head and wait while Emma takes her cell from her back pocket and makes the call.

"Hey, sorry to just leave a message," she tells Rachel. "I know you'll be off work soon, but I wanted to let you know as soon as possible that our casting director approved you as a featured extra! The scene shoots on Monday after the premiere, though, when you're supposed to return home, so we'll have to rearrange some things. But that's awesome, right? Bye!"

Emma tosses her phone to the side and settles beside me again. But this time she's flat on her back, with only our arms touching. "So, where were we?" she says. "Oh yeah. Falling stars. Look! There's another one!"

I clear my throat. "Uh . . . tell me again: why don't we just set Rachel up with Devin?"

Emma props up on an elbow, her expression more serious than I'd expected. "Because Devin isn't the one who's taped to her wall," she replies. "But I'm telling Rachel about us before she goes home next week. I promise."

I nod. What else can I do? Except for . . . maybe this.

"Blame it on me, okay?" I dare to touch her cheek, trail my fingers slowly over her soft skin, and through her hair. "Tell Rachel I couldn't help falling for you, no matter how hard you tried to push me away. That I can't imagine being with anyone else, ever again." I pause for a breath. "And that you turn me *inside out* every time I even think about you."

Emma just stares at me for a sec, her timid smile not quite matching the intensity of her eyes. Then she plants both hands on my chest and leans closer. *Much* closer. "Don't move," she says. "I need to get something out of my system."

Her mouth goes straight for my neck, shooting a million watts of electricity through me. Her lips move down to my collarbone, up to my ear, and set fire to everywhere in between. But she avoids me when I can't hold back any longer and turn toward her.

"Just watch the stars," she whispers.

"I can't. My eyes are in the back of my head."

She laughs but keeps at it, slow and deliberate now and driving me *insane*. I'd expected heat, but this is a freaking inferno, and there's no way that I can—

"Okay, I better stop," Emma says, scooting completely out of reach.

What? "We didn't even—"

"I know." Emma gets a better look at my eyes, which are no doubt both wild and confused. "But we can't yet, remember?"

"Then what was *that*?"

"Oh . . . well . . ." She covers her face with her hands. "I just . . . like I said, wanted to get that out of my system."

"Then, wow. Glad I could help." I sit straight up. "Call me crazy, but I sorta took that as a sign that something had changed and you wanted to kiss me."

"I do! But I'll feel too guilty about it if I don't tell Rachel about us first, and—"

"And *what*? Ask for her permission?" A bomb explodes inside me. "Why is everyone else's happiness more important than your own? Or mine, for that matter? You're making me feel like a lap-dog. *Sit, Jake. Stay, Jake.* But I'm stopping at *beg*, okay?"

I've really got her attention now. "You said you were all right with this," she replies.

"To a point, Emma, but this is crazy. You shifted out of 'snail mode' when you pulled that trick a few minutes ago, and it isn't exactly easy for me to hit the brakes in the middle of a freeway."

"Then I guess this is where Miss Texas comes in," Emma snaps. "Did you just look at a map and say, 'Hmm, everything is big in Texas, I think I'll start there?' "

"Why *shouldn't* I date?" I shoot back. "At this point I'll settle for anyone who's willing to admit that she's going out with me."

Emma grabs the front of my shirt by one hand, and then the other. "All right then, I'm dating you," she says. "Feel better now?"

"No!" I begin, but then I see her tears and the rest gets stuck in my throat.

Emma's hands slowly lose strength and let go. "What more can I do, Jake?" she says. "I've gone against every rule I made for myself by getting this close to you, all the while knowing that when this ends, it will hurt *so* much more than ever before. Not only will the tabloids torture me for months to come, but every day when I see you at work—year after year—I'll feel the pain of it all over again." She darts to the tailgate, jumps off, and keeps moving. "So if you can't understand why I'm finding every excuse I can to drag my feet, then you'll have better luck with Miss Texas. Her website says she's determined to end human suffering."

"I don't want . . . *her.*" It comes out so quietly that I doubt Emma can hear me over the tears she's trying to choke back.

She reaches the passenger door, but just before she opens it, she stops and stands still. I already regret most of what I've said, so I don't trust myself to keep talking. Instead, I lean over and just rest my hand on the side of the truck bed. Then I wait.

At least a full minute passes before Emma even glances at me. I can tell she has something important to say, but what?

Is this the beginning or the end?

EMMA

What just happened? We don't fight. Ever. It's obvious that we've reached some sort of fork in the road where we need to decide if we'll turn left or right, but where will we end up? Some directions would be nice. Maybe a few helpful street signs like, Three Miles to Peace and Happiness. This Way to Misery.

One Step from Heaven.

Jake is still sitting in the beanbag, but his hand is resting on the side of the truck bed. I reach out and take it. "I can't believe I just said that. Any of it. I'm so—"

"Don't apologize," he says, holding onto me as though he'll tumble off a cliff if he lets go. "I deserved it. The Miss Texas thing was set up by my agent, and I agreed to it because—"

"Let's not talk about her," I reply, even though I'm relieved by even this partial explanation. "Not now. This is about *us*."

"Right," Jake says. "Then can I at least admit that I totally set myself up for rejection tonight, knowing you weren't ready for this? I even took you into a dark, scary forest. Coaxed you into the back of my truck . . . what a creep. I'm really sorry."

How could he think any of this is *his* fault? I'm the one who keeps coming up with new rules and regulations, and changing them whenever I feel like it.

"It actually isn't your truck," I say, "and this is *so* not a forest. We had to kick at least fifty tumbleweeds out of the way before we built a fire."

I imagine us in a real forest, surrounded by trees that tower a hundred feet into the air. I can practically smell the pine needles and the damp, rich soil. We're older in this alternate universe, like it's years from now, and we're past all of this frustration and uncertainty. We have a future together, I can feel it.

We just have to make it through the space between *here* and *there*.

"Still," Jake says, "I promised to behave myself and be patient while you figured stuff out. So I'd call this a pretty epic fail."

"But you're right about me trying to keep everyone else happy," I admit. I've been programmed this way. Brainwashed to believe that, whatever the cost, I need to impress the critics, entertain my fans, appease my mother, smile at the press. Even if they treat me like crap. Especially if they do. "And the funny thing is, Jake, you're the only one who seems to truly care about *my* happiness."

He doesn't reply to this, just hoists himself over the side of the truck and lands next to me. I want to melt into him, beg him to forgive me for being so high maintenance. And for something else almost as embarrassing.

"So . . . I just totally jumped you," I say. "Sorry about that."

Jake laughs and leans against the truck, arms folded. "I obviously feel violated, but don't get any funny ideas that I won't want you to do that again, some other time. You know, whenever you want to."

Just thinking about it makes me flush with heat, and I suddenly can't stand that he's not touching me. What felt fine and natural only an hour ago—to talk like friends do, a few feet apart—now feels awkward and wrong.

"Well, what did you expect after you told me that I turn you inside out?" I ask, because that's what his words had done to *me*.

"If I'm honest . . . yeah, I hoped for exactly what happened, but with a bit more participation on my part." Jake finally reaches for my waist and gathers me closer. And thank heaven, because I thought I'd have to make the big move myself. Again. "But it was all true," he goes on. "As for what I said *after* that—"

"You had a right to say that too," I reply, wanting to be even closer, feel his warmth all around me. "And I should've reacted to it with a lot less drama. I think I did some sort of a leap off the tailgate."

Jake nods. "It was pretty spectacular. I could see that you've had some ballet."

How does he do this to me? Make me laugh when I should still be crying. Make me want to toss all of my fear and doubt into the starry night sky and believe this can last. Give me hope that there's something better than what I've had before.

Aren't a lot of couples happy for decades? A *lifetime*?

My pulse is racing again, my breath too quick. I'm nervous and still a little scared, but I move my hands up his arms, trail my fingers along his neck and through the back of his hair. I can't turn back after this—I'm choosing Jake over Rachel, doing this without my mother's approval, and not caring what the opinion of the world might be.

It's a decision I'm making on my own.

"All I really should've said," I tell Jake, "is that I'm trying to get to where I need to be to make this work. So please don't give up on me."

He leans in. "And all I really meant to say—" His lips brush over my cheek, and I close my eyes, almost dissolve. "Is that I couldn't give up even if you wanted me to."

"Good, because . . ." I'm barely capable of speech. I wait for him to look at me. "Because I don't think I can spend another minute of my life without you."

In the moonlight, I only see a whisper of a smile before his bottom lip catches on mine, and we're gone. I am lost and then found again. My fingers get tangled in his hair, eager for passion, while the rest of me begs to slow down and enjoy the sweet and gentle touch of a perfect first kiss.

It's several minutes before Jake eases up, but I don't want him to, so I chase after more. He smiles against my lips and says, "I guess I forgot that I wasn't supposed to kiss you."

I steal another one. "Oops."

We don't say much after that.

JAKE

I get Emma home by three, which is pretty impressive, considering. She was right about us talking too little if we ever started kissing, but that's okay.

We can talk again in a week or so.

Brett is unfortunately the first person I see in the morning. He forgot that he had an appointment for his truck at a detail shop today, so he's knocking on my door at 8:30. By nine, I'm already dying to see Emma. But how early is too early to appear on someone's back porch?

I decide to call instead. One problem though—it isn't Emma who picks up. It's Brett, and he's laughing when he answers. "Hey there, Jake."

I'm silent, trying to figure out what the heck is going on. It was funny when Devin answered Emma's phone, but what is *Brett* doing with her? I only left her a few hours ago.

"Looking for someone else?" he adds.

Finally, I come to my senses, realize what's happened, and quickly formulate a cover story. "Emma lost her phone on set yesterday," I reply. "But a PA found it after she left, and I offered to take it to her. But I guess I must've dropped it somewhere when I was moving my furniture . . . in your truck, apparently."

"Yup. In the back," Brett says, and I can't tell from his tone whether or not he's buying this. "I heard it ringing when I was telling the detail shop what I wanted done."

"Sweet," I say, but still on guard. "Emma would've had my head if I'd lost it."

I'm already sprinting down the running path toward Emma's before I'm off the phone with Brett. If he's a snoop—which I wouldn't put past him—Emma's phone will tell him whatever he wants to know about us. Our text messages spell things out in plain English.

Emma opens her door in sweats and looks better than ever with long wet hair cascading down her back. "Miss me already?" she asks, motioning for me to come in. "I was just about to head over to ask if you found my phone. I must've left it in the truck."

I step into her kitchen and shut the door. Emma immediately wraps her arms around me and looks up. I kiss her once, then again, because I'm afraid things are about to get a little tense. "Yep, it was in the truck all right," I say. "You tossed it aside after you called Rachel."

Emma thinks for a sec. "Oh yeah. And I meant to tell you why I remembered to call her back *right then*," she says, and doesn't let me interrupt to tell her that it's irrelevant at the moment. "You see, I'd been wishing that I had already told her about us, so I could just . . . well, kiss your face off and not feel so conflicted about it."

I smile now, distracted. "Let's try that out a little later, okay? Right now, you might want to disable your phone, because Brett has it."

It takes her a moment to process this. "*What*? Really?"

I explain my call with Brett, and how it was dark when I took everything out of the truck, so I'd missed her phone. I expect Emma to flip, but she only looks mildly concerned. "Oh my. There's not a lot of wiggle room with that kind of evidence," she says. "But don't worry about my phone. I have a passcode on it. Besides, your cover story was perfect."

Perfect is a stretch. I'm hoping for plausible.

I pull out a barstool and take a seat, bringing her along. With me sitting and Emma standing in front of me, our eyes are almost even. "This might surprise you," I say, "but I'm beginning to see some sense in hiding our relationship a while longer. It's kinda fun sneaking around."

"I agree," Emma replies. Her waist is so small, it almost fits between my hands. "And right now, you're all *mine*. I don't want to share you with the world, or answer everyone's questions about how, where, and when I fell for you." She kisses me, then tips my head and brushes her soft, warm lips along my cheek until she reaches my ear and whispers, "Because I'm still falling."

Coherent thought is impossible past that point.

I stay at Emma's until the last possible second. Then I race home, shower and dress, and head off to McGregor's ranch for the press junket, where the principal cast has to be by three o'clock. I feel like I could do anything right now—break through brick walls if I needed to—and realize while I'm driving that this is the perfect time to make a phone call I've been putting off.

So I do it. I call my dad, and we just talk for a few minutes—about school, and work, and how mom's doing. And it's not so bad.

Relieved to finally have that over with, I try to prepare myself for the questions reporters might ask today. The network publicist gave me a list of possibilities, but who knows? Maybe reporters have even heard about my upcoming "date" with Miss Texas by now.

I explained everything to Emma just before leaving today—how I'd sat next to Miss Texas on a flight last weekend. How we talked, but I hadn't acted the least bit interested or asked for her number. Then her pageant director called my agent the next day, and I was feeling desperate for attention from Emma, so I agreed to go. "Anyway, I'll cancel," I told Emma. "It was stupid and immature, and I'm sorry."

"It's too late to cancel," Emma had replied. "Besides, I trust you entirely, Jake, and I never thought I'd trust a guy again. Not like this."

That was the best thing she's ever told me.

Still on cloud nine, I pull into McGregor's massive ranch. It has to be hundreds of acres, with long rows of stables and an all-out equestrian arena. Every rock, cactus, and terra-cotta pot is in its perfect place. I imagine his hired help mucking out horse stalls with radios on their hips and call sheets in their pockets.

The Southwestern mansion fits McGregor's personality perfectly. The great room is about the size of a luxury hotel lobby, with windows covering the entire back wall—from the wide-planked wood floor to the A-framed vaulted ceiling. On the other side of the glass is a tiled patio with a barbeque pit, and round tables topped with orange umbrellas. The decorating has a rustic feel, with over-size furniture in dark leathers. The Scottish Highlands might be in McGregor's blood, but the guy has the heart of an American cowboy.

The place is a flurry of busy bodies—both press and studio people walking, talking, setting up. And I've barely spent a full minute inside McGregor's home before the man himself swoops in on me like a bat. "Afternoon, lad," he says. "A word, please. This way."

He shoots down one of two main wings at his usual breakneck speed, and I follow. We reach what must be his office, but find a throng of reporters and cameramen in front of the doors. McGregor groans and snatches his radio. "Send Miss Taylor to my study instead," he says into it, and a missile hits me square in the chest. McGregor notices my reaction and arches a knowing brow at me while he waits for a radio reply. "We can't even go in the *study*?" he asks the radio now. "Fine. Direct her to the kitchen."

We continue farther down the hallway, passing one elaborate room after another, all packed with people. Emma is already wait-ing in the kitchen when we arrive. Her mouth parts when she spots me behind McGregor, and I confirm her concern with wide eyes and a small nod.

McGregor waves for her to follow, and we keep walking, straight out a back door and toward his glass pool house. Once we're all inside, swallowed up by warm chlorine-infused air, McGregor points to yet another door. "In there, please."

It turns out to be a bathroom—large, and apparently used for changing too—but still a bathroom. At least one of us should laugh, but no one does. McGregor shuts the door behind him and looks at each of us with his piercing, analytical squint. "My, my, I didn't see this coming so soon," he says. "But mind you, I *did* see it coming, didn't I?"

His focus falls on Emma who takes a step away from me, obvious as it is. "I don't know what you've heard, but we're just—"

"Good friends, are you?" McGregor says. "You forget, my dear, that I'm hailed as one of the best producers in show business for a reason. We considered over a hundred seasoned actors for the role of Justin, but no one, Miss Taylor, was a match to play opposite you until I happened upon this young man." He gestures to me, staring at him like an idiot. "I knew you two would sizzle on screen before you even met. And upon learning more about your personal lives, I also realized the chemistry might find its way *off* set. But that was a possibility I had to accept."

"Right, well . . . um," is all Emma says.

"It's only the timing that surprises me," McGregor tells her. "I'd expected to have a while longer before I had to deal with this—given your recent dating debacles. But Jake is a far cry from the numbskulls you've been linked to in the past, so I doubt that you *personally* have reason to worry."

"Uh, thanks," I say, also at a loss for an intelligent reply.

"However, let me make one thing perfectly clear." There's a definite change of tone in McGregor's voice. "The only drama I allow on my set is when cameras are rolling. So with Brett in the middle of this, it had better not get ugly—especially not today—which is why I called this urgent meeting."

In a bathroom?

Emma shakes her head. "There's never been anything real with Brett."

McGregor sighs. "When it comes to the heart, lass, things often seem more real to one than to another," he says. Why has everyone but Emma noticed that Brett's feelings for her have changed? "And Mr. Crawford had quite an interesting story to tell today. You see, he arrived an hour early to spend time in my game room with some of the most influential members of the press. And while I happened to be present, a cell phone jingled in his pocket—yours, he announced to everyone. He then pulled me aside a few minutes later to admit the 'humorous' circumstances in which he had found your phone in the back of his truck."

I see right through this: Brett had only told him why he had Emma's cell phone so McGregor would either confirm or dispute my lie about how I'd ended up with it.

"I knew your side of the story had to be a fib, Mr. Elliott," McGregor tells me. "If a PA on my set found a lost phone, no matter who it belonged to, he would forfeit his job if it was delivered anywhere save the production office. But for the sake of peace, I chose not to expose your lie to Brett, which now makes me part of it. So I expect that the pair of you will at least have enough respect to be honest with *me*."

Emma and I exchange glances. She surprises me by stepping closer and latching onto my hand. "Okay, you're right," she says. "But we wanted a chance to figure things out for ourselves before everyone else offered their opinion. And I especially don't feel like I owe the *press* an explanation. They're the ones who got it wrong about who I liked."

McGregor folds his arms and smiles. "Well said, Miss Taylor.

Now let's hope you can show that sort of strength when the real storm comes for you, which will no doubt happen. And it certainly doesn't help that we're on the cusp of introducing a story arc that might hit a bit close to home. Perhaps Jake told you about the snippet we filmed after you left yesterday?"

Emma turns to me. "No, actually. He didn't."

And for a good reason. "It was foreshadowing," I say. "That's all."

"Foreshadowing of what?" Emma's eyes widen and shift to McGregor. "A love triangle? No . . . not now. *Please*. There wasn't even a hint of that in the script."

McGregor taps the side of his head. "No there wasn't, lass, but it's been in *this* script for over a year now. You see, Justin and Eden are destined to become the true epic romance of this series—the setup of Bryce and Eden as a couple is only to create future tension. We have years ahead of us to entertain our audience with the ups and downs of it all. So yesterday, I had a spark of inspiration to tease the idea using a bit of close-up work, just a faint smile on Jake's face as you pass him up on the track. Only a few takes and a simple editing job, and it'll be perfect."

Emma expresses her opinion by shutting the lid of the toilet and taking a seat.

"The plotline won't be in full swing until the end of the season," McGregor says, "but what would a teen drama be without a heart-wrenching love triangle?" Neither of us answer, so he opens the door. "All right, stay put until I give you the go ahead. I'll have you leave one at a time."

The moment McGregor is gone, Emma says, "He's wrong, you know—about Brett. But this will be a mess once news of what's really been going on leaks. Everyone will think McGregor developed the love triangle plot straight from our real lives." She finally takes a breath. "Why didn't you tell me about that impromptu shot you did yesterday?"

"I guess I thought you'd overreact," I reply, hoping to charm her with a smile. "I just didn't expect it to happen in a bathroom."

"Me, overreact?" Emma stands, latches onto my belt loops, and pulls me toward her. My knees give out when she goes up on tiptoes and kisses me before I'm ready. I consider locking the door, ditching the junket altogether.

"Are you two done fooling around?" McGregor asks, knocking just half a second before cracking the door open. He peeks inside, gets a look at Emma's mortified face, and chuckles. "Kidding— only kidding. You first, Jake. Go."

EMMA

This isn't a good day for me to speak in public, let alone have my comments recorded for worldwide distribution. I am much too giddy and can hardly focus on anything but Jake. Every thirty seconds or so, I have to remind myself that I'm sitting at a long banquet table covered with live microphones, and am surrounded by dozens of cameras and reporters.

Seated from left to right are: McGregor, Brett, me, Jake, and Kimmi. We're each a few feet apart—close enough that if I stretched out my arm, I could touch Jake, but too far away to be sneaky about it. That doesn't stop me from an occasional sigh, though, or laughing because Jake also keeps grinning for no apparent reason.

I'm sure we both come across as being *very* excited about *Coyote Hills*.

A female reporter asks, "I'm curious, Mr. Elliott, do you have a girlfriend?"

"Well, that depends," he says. "Are you free tonight?"

The reporter, who is at least in her fifties, turns a bright shade of scarlet while everyone else laughs and claps. Kimmi even makes a convincing cougar sound into her mic.

She had thrown me off with the Miss Texas stuff yesterday, but I still gave her advice on handling the media. I'd also tossed in a few tips she didn't ask for, such as: "If you want lasting attention in Hollywood, you can't blend in with the rest of the starlets—the ones who are trying *too* hard to be famous. You have to let your talent speak for itself. And if you can manage it, Kimmi, stop being such a diva. It's annoying and makes work miserable for the rest of us."

"So," was all she said. She might have pretended like I hadn't told her anything useful, but she still follows my advice to the letter at the junket, acting gracious, approachable, and as if she's generally a pleasant person to be around. The reporters seem stumped, hopefully thinking—as Kimmi wants them to—that the tabloids are wrong about her.

When I'm asked about my relationship with Brett, I speak into the mic with confidence. "We've never been more than good friends," I say. "A few photographers have just caught moments of us laughing or goofing around and made us into some kind of grand love affair. I guess people just see what they *want* to see, no matter what you show them. It's sorta funny!"

I don't find tabloid stories the least bit humorous, of course, but I smile through my answer anyway, and glance over to see that Brett looks like I've thrown him under a bus.

He grabs his microphone without even being addressed. "Show me some love, guys! I've just been dumped during a press junket!"

Brett gets all the laughs and fake expressions of sympathy he hoped to solicit with that comment, so in the end, it turns out okay. We really have become good friends, so I hate keeping the truth from him. When I first saw Brett today, and he returned my phone, he was his normal, goofy self. If he suspected Jake and I were together, wouldn't that have been the perfect time to say it? What could he possibly gain from—for the first time ever—*not* speaking his mind?

Jake and I do a great job making up for lost time following the junket. And on Sunday too, until he flies out to Texas. He returns late Monday night, and between then and Thursday—the day of our premiere—we're together every spare second.

And it isn't close to enough.

All of this is something a girl would usually be *dying* to tell her best friend about, but when Rachel arrives Thursday morning, I have to keep it all locked inside. The moment she sees me in the airport baggage area, she runs up and without any sort of hello, says, "Did you *see* those pictures of The Bod with Miss Texas? He was all laughy and smiley."

Yeah, I noticed. But what was he supposed to do? Glower and scowl at the cameras? "Jake just smiles a lot. You'll see," I tell Rachel, throwing my arms around her.

She looks darling in a white flouncy shirt, light-blue skinny jeans, and high-heeled leather boots. "Miss Texas posted the photos online, like they were a couple or something," she says, practically wiggling out of my grasp. "What if he *likes* her, Emma? My life is over."

Ugh. *There are worse threats to your happiness than Miss Texas.*

As we gather her luggage, I try to calm Rachel down, but it's pointless. "Let's go shopping and forget about him for a bit, okay?" I finally say, desperate to do anything but talk about Jake. So straight from the airport, I drive to *La Encantada* and distract Rachel with my credit card. I feel sick, trying to buy her friendship, her forgiveness, her silence—all of it. But is this really so different from what I've been doing for the last six years? Always wanting to make up for what I have that she doesn't? Will it ever be enough?

I don't know. But tonight, I want Rachel to feel like the star she deserves to be.

I've hired Donna and Madelyn to get us ready for the premiere, and we need time to shower before they arrive, so Rachel and I only have a few hours for lunch and shopping. During the drive to my town house, renewed chatter about The Bod takes up 99 percent of our conversation. "Does he look the same in real life as he does in pictures?" Rachel asks. "Does he look older, younger, thinner, or what?"

I'm tempted to remind her that The Bod has a real name too, but letting her call Jake by her pet name for him makes everything feel less *real* for me. "Flesh, paper, or plastic," I say, "he's pretty much got the same bod."

"Ohhhh! I can't wait until he comes in plastic!" Rachel squeals. "I bet when he does a big blockbuster, they'll make an action figure of him. Then I can have an entire shelf in my room with cute little Bods on it."

I wouldn't mind a miniature Jake for myself, to be honest.

"I have so much in common with The Bod," Rachel goes on. "We're both actors, have December birthdays, green eyes, and our parents are divorced. Are we meant to be, or what?"

Rachel only knows about Jake's parents because a reporter who interviewed him at the junket did some pretty invasive research beforehand and asked Jake to confirm that his parents are divorced, which ended up in a well-circulated article. The question wasn't malicious, really, but why was it relevant? This has been Jake's first exposure to his private life going public, and it's made me feel very defensive, wanting to protect him from what I know will only get more intrusive as he becomes better known.

"I think divorce is one of those topics you're supposed to avoid on a first date," I tell Rachel, hoping to wipe that off her list of things to probe Jake about. "Maybe you should stick to things like his favorite movies, or the classes he's taking."

"Well, movies, duh. But charm him with talk about *school*? Really?" She says this like it's the lamest thing I could ever suggest. "Whoa! You just ran a stop sign."

"I did?" I glance back. The sign was right in front of Sabino Haven, and I guess I had just wanted to get past Jake's condo. "Oh, no worries. That stop sign is actually out of order."

"*Everything* has been out of order since you moved here," Rachel says, missing my joke. "I feel like we don't really talk anymore— like you hardly call me. It makes me sad, you know? I've really missed you."

It's true that I've been calling her less and less, especially these last few weeks. But the more I talk to her, the more I have to lie, and I hate it. "I've missed you too."

Just after my community guard waves us past the gate, Rachel's cell rings. She answers the call, listens for only a few seconds, then screams, "I got it! *Stars in Their Eyes*! I got it!"

I scream then too. Things had worked out great getting her in front of the right people who make the casting decisions for the reality show, and that was all Rachel had needed. Famous actors and coaches are mentors on the show, doors will now be opened for her at feature film auditions, agents will take serious looks at her . . . this is huge!

I pull my car over by the pool so I can pay closer attention and cheer along with Rachel in earnest, as she's told all the details and passes them along. I feel a bit selfish for also celebrating the moment for my own reasons: not only will Rachel have something to think about besides Jake this weekend, but I will no longer have to be the constant medium between her and Hollywood. That will only matter, though, if our friendship survives this whole Jake thing.

I'll know soon enough.

My dad texted me a few times when Rachel and I were talking, so while Rachel showers, I step out my back door and call him. He says he's with my mom at his campus office—the boys are at soccer practice—and they want to wish me luck for tonight.

Ever since I told Mom about what happened with Troy, Dad feels he should be more involved in my life. "I sure wish I could be there," he says. "You know how much I love those Hollywood egofests."

He's missed more of my events than he's made it to, but Mom usually comes to everything. This time, I told her I would rather her make a fuss over my brothers instead, who have a tournament starting tomorrow. Besides, having her in town right now would have complicated things even more.

Dad passes the phone to Mom, and I tell her Rachel's news. "It's about time she found something of her own," Mom says. "She's been living through you far too long."

We talk about Rachel for a few more minutes, and then I realize I've gone so far down the running path, I've reached Jake's condo. I take a deep breath and close my eyes against the high afternoon sun, its light a beautiful red glow. "Mom, can you put the phone on speaker?" I say. "I need to talk to both of you for a sec."

"Oh, brother. What's happened?" she asks, and I just wait, debating with myself. Should I tell them? "All right, you're on speaker. Go ahead."

"Okay," I begin, still unsure. "I think you should be among the first to know that . . . well, I've been dating someone, pretty much since I moved here. And it isn't Brett."

Dad's sigh sounds like relief. "It had better not be."

"Who, Emma? Who is it?" Mom asks.

I catch a glimpse of a large white egg that Jake set near his front porch last night to see if a snake would come out from under a rock or wherever and eat it. My bet had been yes, so I'd insisted that the test happen at *his* place, not mine.

He's such a boy. I love it.

"It's Jake," I tell my parents. "The guy whose mother inspired my foundation." Mom knows at least this much about Jake, but I had previously made it sound like I'd just casually met Mrs. Elliott when she was visiting Jake at work. "I've had a lot of reasons to keep our relationship a secret, but I wanted to tell you guys before—"

"The one with all the college questions?" Dad asks.

I laugh at the excitement in his voice. "Yep, that's him."

"Then you certainly have *my* approval," Dad says. "What are you all tight-lipped about, Judy? You said yourself that you think he's handsome."

I nervously kick pebbles around the riverbank, waiting for my mom's reply. "How he looks has nothing to do with this," she finally says. "There are other issues involved here, Bob, and you couldn't possibly understand them."

"Good grief, I have a PhD. I think I can—"

"The tabloids will go absolutely crazy with this, and *Rachel* practically expects to marry that boy," Mom says. "This is bad, Emma. Haven't you considered how Trina will react? She could make a fortune selling this sort of story to *Celebrity Seeker.*"

"Oh, who cares?" Dad says. "Trina is a loon. The last time I saw that woman, she was wearing a rhinestone-studded tank top. With matching boots."

I wait through another minute or so of my mom explaining to my dad all the problems I've just created. Then Dad tells Mom something about Jake being very polite and sounding smart when they talked a couple of months ago, and Mom says she has to leave and pick up the boys. "Okay, thanks for calling!" I half laugh to her because I think she's forgotten that I'm still on the phone.

At least Dad is on my side . . . which makes me think he might understand about something else too. I wait until I hear my mom close the office door, then say, "Hey, Dad, I need your advice."

I picture his ears perking up. He takes the phone off speaker. "Sure. What is it?"

"Well, I . . . need to hire a new manager."

Silence. "To replace your mother?"

"No. To replace my *manager*," I say. "Mom and I rarely talk about anything but business anymore—you saw what just happened. Jake is a *personal* matter, and the type of guy any mother would want her daughter to date, but Mom immediately turned him into a PR disaster. And this sort of stuff is pretty much a daily issue."

"Right. I've definitely noticed the tension and have been thinking this through for a while now," Dad replies. "I'm just not sure you understand your mother's viewpoint. Or mine, for that matter. We allowed you to enter a very grown-up world at just twelve years old. There was a lot we felt we had to protect you from early on, and we knew your mom was the only one who could do that. And yes, she's been rather aggressive. But in our eyes, Emma, you're still our little girl. We haven't been around to witness you growing into the young woman we only get to see every once in a while. So continuing to have control over your career might just be your mother's way of holding on to that small bit of your childhood we still have left."

Is he really telling me to keep her as my manager? "But—"

"*But,*" Dad interrupts, "you're right. It's time for her to let you go. Let you take charge of your career, *and* your life. I'll talk to her about it."

I'm not so sure about that. "Thanks. I think I should be the one to do it, though. I guess I just wanted . . . your blessing?"

"You have it. And I like this Jake guy too."

"He'll be happy to hear that!" We say good-bye, and I return to my town house.

Rachel is wrapped in her robe and sitting at the kitchen table when I walk in. She's flipping through a binder and looks up with a huge grin.

"I have a surprise for you," she says, and lifts the binder so I can see the cover. There's a photo of the orange-sorbet sunset I remember from when she helped me move into my town house, and *The Emma Taylor Foundation* is printed in beautiful scrolling letters across it. "I know the foundation doesn't have an official name yet, so I just put that. But here you go!"

I open the thick binder to find page after page of material from at least fifty fund-raising events. "This is *amazing*!" I say. "It must've taken you forever!"

Rachel shrugs. "Three or four days. I wanted to make up for putting it off for so long. There are some really great ideas, though."

"I'm sure there is! Thank you, thank you, thank you!" I set the binder down and hug her so tightly she's afraid I'll squeeze her guts out.

While Donna and Madelyn primp us for the premiere, we tell them about the fun we had growing up together, and how we once turned the sidewalk in front of Rachel's house into the Hollywood Walk of Fame. We spray painted silver stars on thirty or so sections of concrete, then wrote our names with black permanent marker on each one of them.

We had to scrub that sidewalk for weeks.

Once our hair and makeup is done, we change into our dresses. Rachel's golden hair is long and curly, which goes perfectly with the elegant gown she's wearing—flowing layers of indigo-blue chiffon. I'm glad she chose this dress after all. I wore it to a New Year's gala and felt like a princess. Tonight, I don't feel like a princess at all; I feel unusually grown-up in a crimson sheath by Valentino.

Except for the knee-high slit in the front, my dress clings to every curve of my body. The back is open all the way down to my waist, joined by only a pair of thin laces. The front covers quite a bit more, thank heaven, but with my hair off my bare shoulders, there's a lot more exposed skin than I'm typically comfortable with. Still, I feel pretty.

Rachel has taken photos of us at every stage and has live tweeted all day, so #CoyoteHills is trending big time. McGregor will be so proud. But I momentarily freak out when Rachel posts a picture of me in my dress, and within minutes, this tweet shows up that tags both of us:

Kimmi Weston @SoooooOverIt
Excited to wear matching dresses with my #BFF
@EmmaTayAllDay! #twinners #psych
(@Crazy4Hollywood—she freaked for a sec, didn't she? lol)

I laugh and tell Rachel, "Who would've guessed? Kimmi has a sense of humor!"

Rachel turns from my full-length mirror, her eyes wild with panic. "That's great, but I need you to focus now. I only have one chance to make this first impression, and I look awful."

"No you don't!" I reply. "You're *gorgeous*. And you're a natural star, Rachel, so just enjoy tonight. Don't worry about a thing."

Tears are pooling in the corners of her eyes, but she nods. "I'm just so nervous."

I've forbidden myself from feeling guilt this weekend, but I'm consumed by it right now. What could I have done differently? Been honest from the first day I met Jake? Said, "Hey, Rach, you know that Bod guy? You're right, he's amazing. Can I have him?"

Rachel gets excited again as a limo takes us to The Sonoran Events Center, but the moment we pull up to the red carpet, she digs her nails into my arm. "Emma! He's standing right by your door! I can't . . ." She starts hyperventilating, gathering only enough air to tell the limo driver, "Hit the locks!" And the doors click.

But Jake already knows it's us—our limo is scheduled to arrive last—so he tries to open my door. I take Rachel's hand. "You'll be fine," I say, attempting a soothing voice. "Jake is just a regular guy." Her face is as white as the teeth she's now gritting. I search for anything to prove my point and stop her panic attack. "In fact, he's absolutely disgusting sometimes. Just last week he had a belching contest with Brett, and Jake burped the entire alphabet."

Rachel recoils like she's swallowed a slug. "Eww!"

Yep, that does the trick. But she'll likely stop breathing again once she gets a better look at Jake in his Armani suit. I can hardly breathe myself.

I give Rachel's hand a squeeze. "He won't have much time to talk, but don't take it personally. He has to do all the red carpet stuff. So just say hi, then come find me."

I unlock my door, and Jake opens it. We're surrounded by throngs of fans, reporters, and photographers lining the red carpet—flashes everywhere. But once I step out, his eyes sweep down my dress anyway, and he whispers, "A new and improved way to torture me?"

My mouth smiles on its own. "Would you please help Rachel out too?"

He only nods.

I want to peek when he meets Rachel, but a StarTV reporter—who I happen to dislike quite a lot—approaches me, and I have to turn on my publicity personality. "Oh, hi!" I say, adding an air-kiss as she swoops in for a hug. "It's so nice to see you."

Her StarTV cameraman is also someone I don't trust. He's known for getting his video footage as unethically as he can get away with, and the only reason he isn't considered to be as scummy as regular paparazzi is because he works for a legitimate network.

Rachel joins me a few minutes later, and I introduce her as my best friend, as well as the one to watch on the upcoming season of *Stars in Their Eyes*. After a while, she catches another glimpse of Jake across the red carpet. "You said The Bod looks the same in real life as he does in photos, but he doesn't," she whispers. "I mean, is that shirt and jacket really necessary?"

We both laugh. *Forgive me, Rachel. Please.*

Walking the red carpet is always awesome. I'm used to the work itself, on set, but the glamour side of stardom never feels even close to normal.

Six years of this, and I still can't believe it's happening to *me*.

Hundreds of people are crowded along the red velvet ropes, many screaming, waving, holding out objects, or even arms, for autographs. Others just smile, happy to be here like I am.

The first episode is thrilling to watch—as usual, it seems like a miracle that all of those bits and pieces we filmed came together to create not only a cohesive story, but compelling entertainment—and the audience is totally into it. Jake looks so unbelievably gorgeous on the big screen that, once again, I find myself wondering if he escaped from Mount Olympus to play this part. And his acting is equal to anyone else's on the show. His comedic timing is perfect, and Jake's more serious moments make me wish he was sitting next to me so I could lean over and whisper, "You're *brilliant*. You amaze me."

I'm hoping I can sneak away to say hello to Mark, Devin, and Sophie, and especially Jake's mom. I want to ask her how it went when she delivered the quilt we finished to her rehabilitation center.

As we walk into the ballroom for the after party, Rachel asks me, "Why is Jake's mom in a wheelchair? Do you know what happened?"

I'm searching for a way to answer when Sophie notices us, comes running, and throws her arms around me. I almost tip over in my heels. "I hope it's okay if we're on a hugging basis now," she says. "I have a big surprise for you: Devin and Mark and I want to be your first foundation volunteers! We've even talked about starting a campaign for it on campus—I bet we can get a ton of students to sign up. What do you think?"

I pull back from her, stunned. "Really? Yes, definitely. Thank you!"

"No problem!" she says. "We can't wait. We're starting this week, by the way, with Jake's mom. We do things here and there for her, anyway, whenever Jake asks us to run over. But we're getting more organized about it now. Like, Mark is going to take her trash out Wednesday mornings, then Devin will bring it in that night. And they're both in charge of keeping her yard in good shape. And I'm going to quilt with her every Tuesday afternoon."

I can't even speak because I'm so choked up with gratitude. I just keep smiling, nodding, and hugging her. And then I come to my senses again and recall that Rachel is standing next to me, and now giving me a very strange look.

"Oh, you're one of Jake's friends?" she turns to ask Sophie. "And he told you about Emma's foundation?"

Sophie starts to speak, but then her eyes widen and she looks to me instead. I can almost hear the question she's holding back: *Why doesn't your* best friend *know that you hung out with us in Phoenix?* And then it seems to hit her—Rachel is Jake's date for tomorrow.

"Uh, yeah," Sophie tells her. "Exactly. I guess the whole cast is getting in on it. Everyone wants to help out as much as they can."

"Of course they do. Everyone always wants to help Emma." For some reason, the way Rachel says this doesn't sound like a compliment. "But I didn't know that Jake was—"

"This is my best friend, Rachel!" I barge in, with all the grace of a socially challenged hippo. "She made an entire binder for me filled with ideas for fund-raising events. And she'll also be on the new season of *Stars in Their Eyes!*"

This changes both the topic and energy quickly, and Sophie and Rachel talk for at least fifteen minutes while I pretty much just stand there, smiling and holding my breath.

The live band is on the other side of the ballroom, drawing most of the crowd. Kimmi is here with a few of her friends, but I haven't noticed any of her family members. She seems perfectly happy tonight though, and was full-out grinning when the press junket material made it to the public a few days back, using words such as "charming" and "easygoing" to describe Kimmi during interviews.

Jake isn't too far from me, and it's hard to resist running over.

I want to dance with him, and sappy or not, I wish we could just hold hands and walk around together.

Sophie nudges my arm. "You've *got* to introduce me to Brett!" she says. "He's coming over here! And . . . whoa! That's Payton Wilson! And . . ." As Brett and his wolf pack approach—some of them more notorious than anyone we've hung out with in L.A.— Sophie and Rachel take turns naming each one.

Hardly knowing each other, but neither seeming to mind, Rachel and Sophie grip hands and jump behind me, all giggles, like little girls standing in line for cotton candy. I'm tempted to ask Rachel if she's forgotten entirely about Jake, but would rather not remind her.

"Fair warning—they're *wrecked*," Brett says, reaching us a few steps ahead of his buddies. The lights are just bright enough to see that his friends have obviously had their own party before they joined this one. I'd noticed about a dozen empty seats around Brett during the premiere and figured they must've been saved for the friends he invited, who never came. His parents were with him then—he introduced us on the red carpet—but they hurried off after the screening to catch a flight to Rome. And then these guys finally decided to show up.

It takes forever to introduce everyone, mostly because the boys are drunk and the girls are unbearably starstruck. I want to pour buckets of ice over everyone's heads. Never mind that the guys are slurring half of their words, can't Rachel and Sophie smell the alcohol that's practically seeping through their pores?

Rachel finally asks why Brett's friends missed the premiere. "Happy hour at Crazy Pete's!" Payton says, and both Rachel and Sophie continue to be mesmerized by his every word. Hollywood's

Hottest Bachelor is barely standing, but hey, he's still talking to them. "There are some seriously wild girls in Tucson! And after *we* showed up, they all called their friends, and things got awesome!"

"They tried to get everyone in here," Brett tells me. "But go figure, not one of the thirty girls was on the guest list." He seems truly embarrassed by the state of his friends. Or maybe Brett is just bummed that he missed the *real* party. "Unfortunately, these guys were."

I laugh. "I wonder who invited them."

They're lucky that only studio photographers are allowed into the party, for better control over which photos make it to the press. This behavior isn't all that unusual for most of them, I suppose, but it surprises me to see Payton like this. He's a pretty solid guy on most occasions.

Brett's friends dance like lunatics and hang all over us, and more than a few grab my butt, so ten minutes into it, I want to shower. Rachel is having a blast, though, and still forgetting about Jake. After Sophie and Brett dance for a while, Rachel ends up with Brett. I'm just a few feet away, trying to provide a buffer between Sophie and a couple of creeps who could be big trouble if she isn't careful.

Rachel turns from Brett to tell me, "No wonder you're in love! He's *so* cute."

"Rachel!" I say, loud and rude, but she had been even louder.

Brett is still just on the other side of her, so I crane my neck to see if he heard what she said, but he's facing away from me, so I can't tell. "What's wrong with you?" Rachel snaps.

"I'm *not* in love with Brett," I hiss through gritted teeth. "You know that."

"Jeez, get a grip," she says. "I was joking."

My mouth opens, but nothing comes out. Brett's face is suddenly between us. "What's the deal with Jake? He just swept in, grabbed Sophie, and took off."

Had *Jake* heard what Rachel said? I hadn't even noticed him.

Rachel whirls around and screeches, "Emma, he's dancing with Sophie!" She spins back. "And I was being *nice* to her. What a wench!"

"Ouch!" Brett says. "You must be the friend who Emma's setting up with Jake."

"Do you see any other friends with me?" I ask.

Brett shrugs. "Guess not. Let's dance."

"I can't," I reply, and catch Rachel by the hand as she tries to storm off. "Jake doesn't like Sophie, okay? They're just good friends."

"But he asked *her* to dance when I was standing right here!" she whines.

Then Brett lets loose a string of curse words, and says, "Payton is so wasted, he's hitting on *Kimmi* again." He then runs after Payton, who is chasing after Kimmi, who is leaving the ballroom with her arm outstretched and a *talk-to-the-hand* signal firmly in place.

I want to scream until I pass out. Why do I feel like I'm babysitting toddlers?

Rachel and I stay where we are, and as she pouts and I inwardly groan, everyone else laughs and twirls around us. We're wallflowers planted in the middle of a room.

When Jake finishes dancing with Sophie, Devin dances with her, and Jake goes back to standing by his mom. But he keeps glancing over at us, looking like he would rather be at a dentist appointment. He finally walks our way, and Rachel begins to hyperventilate again.

Jake makes brief eye contact with me before smiling at Rachel and asking her to dance. I turn away, not wanting to watch them walk off together, even knowing how much Jake would rather dance with me. This whole thing is beyond agonizing, and it's my turn to pout.

Here I am—Emma Taylor, big-time movie star—and I'm big-time alone at my own premiere. Where are the paparazzi when they could *really* catch me having a meltdown?

I fan myself as if I've been dancing and laughing with everyone else and make a beeline to the main foyer. Brett is walking into the ballroom as I'm walking out. He spins back around. "Killer party, huh?" he says. Sarcasm isn't usually his thing.

"It's okay," I reply. There are only a few stragglers in the hall, so I don't have to put up too much of a front as I go straight for the dessert table.

"Oh, come on, Taylor. You're just as miserable as I am," Brett says, following after me. "But at least *your* friends didn't show up smelling like a frat house."

I offer a courtesy laugh and stack three thousand calories onto a small plastic plate. The ice has melted in the punch, watering it down, so I head for a drinking fountain instead. Brett waits until I pretty much drink the thing dry before he speaks again. "You've gotta see this cool room I found—it's an atrium, filled with huge fruit trees. It's crazy."

The band is still playing the slow song Jake and Rachel are dancing to, so I shrug and head down the hall. Me, my cookies, and my fake ex-boyfriend.

The atrium is brilliant white, the lights so intense that it takes my eyes a minute to adjust. The peaked ceiling and three exterior walls are made almost entirely of glass. The windows look out to mostly darkness now—except for a silhouette of what appears to be hedges—but the daylight view is probably of the courtyard where we walked the red carpet.

"Check these out," Brett says, motioning to the massive lemon, orange, and lime trees that are scattered around the atrium with their vibrant-colored fruit nestled in large canopies of leaves. The scent of citrus is almost intoxicating. And it's quiet in here, perfectly calming.

Brett was right about this being a good place to escape.

He ignores a DO NOT TOUCH sign and wraps his entire hand around an orange. I laugh, the sound echoing a little, and say, "I bet they put that sign there just for you."

He pulls his hand back as if it requires all of his effort. "I've never been good at following rules. Until lately, I guess." Brett turns to me, his eyes looking their brightest blue with this white room as a background. "I've changed a lot since we met, don't you think?"

Overall, he really has chilled out. "You've been calling girls by their right names all night. So that's *something* to be proud of."

I pop a bite-size cookie into my mouth and wait for his reply, but Brett just drops his head and sweeps away a fallen leaf with his shoe. Maybe he's being serious.

"Emma, my friends in there, acting like that, being so stupid . . . that used to be *me*," he says, his gaze still on the floor. This is such surprising sincerity coming from him that I step closer, kind of puzzled. "I was the guy in the center of it all, partying harder than any of them," he goes on. "You don't know how bad things got . . . I wouldn't want you to know. But I'm done. I'm sick of it. And my friends are just getting worse—getting into stuff even I wouldn't have tried. *Dangerous* stuff."

He raises his head, and I get a shock down my spine when I see tears in his eyes. He's truly worried about them, which he should be. I've just never seen him this concerned about . . . anything, really. "Brett, you've made a lot of good choices lately, so maybe you—"

He cuts me off. "Payton is like my brother, you know? And Kimmi brings out the worst in him. He needs to grow up, like I'm trying to do. He needs someone . . . someone like you."

I hold up a hand. "Whoa, um . . . no. Definitely not me."

Brett finally smiles. "Nah, I didn't mean it like that. Payton just needs to find someone *like* you, to give him a reason to change. Because . . . well, you've gotta know this by now . . . because that's what you've done for *me*. I'm crazy about you."

I wait for him to laugh, but after a few seconds of staring at his hesitant smile, I glance away, stunned and embarrassed that I hadn't listened to Jake—to McGregor, to anyone. I look back up at Brett to apologize for misleading him, but his lips suddenly press into mine, and I can't talk . . . I can't move.

My arms drop and my plate falls to the floor. "Brett . . . *stop!*"

I sink to the floor to pick up my cookies, to get away.

Brett stoops too, and takes one of my hands. "Oh man," he says. "I didn't think you'd freak out like this. We kiss all the time."

I pull my hand back. "Only on set, where it's fake."

"It hasn't *felt* fake," he replies, sounding desperate to explain himself. "And your friend, I just heard her say that you . . . that you're in love with me."

The bright room seems to twist around us. "But I'm not. And you've told me all along that you didn't want to date me."

"Yeah, I know things started out that way," he says. "The more I was with you, though, the more I liked you. But I knew you'd never want me the way I was."

"Brett, I'm . . . I'm sorry . . ." I can't finish, so I just leave the atrium, my legs moving at a much slower pace than my racing heart.

JAKE

No girl should ever look as good as Emma does at the premiere if she expects a guy to keep his distance. But once we're at the after party, her smiles seem forced. I thought we were past this, but has Rachel still found a way to make Emma feel guilty about us?

When Sophie doesn't have enough sense to push away a couple of Brett's lowlife buddies, I have to go over like a protective big brother and snatch her off their menu. And while I dance with Sophie, Rachel just stares at me—her shoulders rising and falling as if she's about to bawl. So for my best performance of the night, I ask Rachel to dance. But instead of getting a wink of approval from Emma, she spins around and leaves the ballroom.

Things actually go downhill from here. I prefer the deathly nervous Rachel I met at the limo to the Energizer Bunny mouth she turns out to be. And one dance isn't enough, oh no. She talks me into another. When she tries for a third, I tell her my mom is tired so we have to leave. Then on my way out of the building, I catch a glimpse of Emma racing into the women's bathroom, but she doesn't see me.

Brett is right on her heels before she enters the door, so as he passes me, I ask, "What's up with Emma?"

He whips back around, his face red. "You know chicks. I can't give her enough of what she wants, so she's hitting the stalls to cry about it."

What does *that* mean?

With Rachel staying at Emma's, I don't dare call or text, so I spend a long, sleepless night trying to figure it all out.

When Devin and I pick up the girls the next morning, Rachel already has the whole day planned out at Old Tucson Studios, which is famous for Western films. In Rachel's seemingly rehearsed words, "This will give us a chance to walk in the legendary foot-steps of Jimmy Stewart and Ingrid Bergman."

I'd rather walk in the legendary boots of Harrison Ford and Bruce Willis, but whatever.

Emma had her sunglasses on when I first saw her today, and she doesn't take them off a single time during our hour-long drive. She won't even speak unless she's directly addressed, which leaves me to deal with Rachel on my own.

As we approach the gates to the studio, Rachel whips out her phone and says, "Okay, guys, I'm live tweeting this whole day, so let's pose here at the entrance!"

"No way," I reply before I can stop myself. And then I scramble for a polite explanation. "Sorry, but I'm really uncomfortable with social media. And I've already posed for a truckload of cameras this past week. Can't we just . . . I don't know, relax today?"

Rachel laughs, then suddenly realizes I'm serious. "Oh my gosh, really? But I told my followers—I have like, ten thousand now—that I'd share every little detail, so . . ."

She shrugs, and I feel like I've been hit in the stomach by a wrecking ball. I don't want this day to suck for her. I turn to Emma for help, but she's gone off to the ticket booth.

"Jake's just being modest," Devin says, and I give him a look because this isn't a good time for his jokes. "You know my sister is his agent, right? Well, she's *really* protective of Jake's face— something to do with . . . the more it's seen, the less it's worth? Anyway, he's gotta be careful or my sister gets ticked."

"Ohhhh," Rachel says. "All right. That makes sense. Then I'll just have to take photos of everything *but* Jake. Which is . . . darn." She glances back to me. "Can I take just a few pictures of you, if I don't post them?"

I'm about to agree, even though I think she'll likely burn the photos later, but Devin scrunches up his face, and replies, "That *might* be okay, but you'd probably need written permission from my sister, and she's out of the office right now. In Milan, I think."

"Yep, Milan," I say, which is the only true detail about this story. How could I have forgotten that my wingman is a Level-Five Master of BS? But Rachel buys all of it, so once we begin our two-hour tour of the studios, she's happy again. She snaps photos like crazy and her fingers are flying to get *every little detail* up on Twitter.

And I'm being nice to her in every way I can, without flirting.

I actually would have enjoyed the tour if I wasn't dying to know what was wrong with Emma. Devin is confused too, so once we're on our own for a sec, about to eat lunch, he says, "You told

Emma I know about you guys, right? She's sorta brushing me off, like she wants to make it clear that she isn't interested."

"Yeah, she knows," I reply. "It's gotta be something else. I need to get her alone."

That's all I have time to tell him before Emma and Rachel join us with their food. A dramatized shootout has just started on the other side of the studio grounds, so the lunch crowd has pretty much cleared out. The table we're sitting at is a tight fit—half the length of a regular picnic table, and on its own behind an old wood-planked restaurant called The BBQ Shack, where we've just snagged some ribs and fries.

The weather is nice today, not too hot, and trees shade the table— but Emma still doesn't take off her sunglasses. Maybe she just wants to watch my reactions without Rachel noticing? I put my own sunglasses on so I can do the same thing with Emma.

Devin and I devour our barbecued ribs and fries in five minutes flat, leaving us to sit and watch the girls pick at their plates. "I know who Jimmy Stewart is, but who's the Bergman chick?" I ask, just to make conversation.

Rachel looks at me like I've grown a third eye.

Ten minutes later, I'm well educated on all things Ingrid Bergman, and Rachel caps off her lecture with, "Basically, anyone who hasn't seen her in *Casablanca* should be shot."

Devin coughs, and I almost say, "*Casa*-what?" but I'm afraid Rachel will make me watch it with her tonight, snuggled on a couch with a box of tissues.

Rachel's next party piece is even worse. "Let's play movie trivia!" she says. "Jake, who won the 1972 Oscar for Best Actress?" I only stare at her. "Oh, c'mon! Liza Minnelli. This one's easier: what film won Best Picture for that year?"

Seriously? "Sorry," I say, "but you've *really* gotta dumb this down for me."

Emma laughs, which snaps me out of my stupor. "Maybe something more on this level," she says. "What classic movie is about a theme park with dinosaurs?"

"*Jurassic Park*!" Devin and I reply together.

"Lucky guess," Emma says. "Which species of dinosaur ate the lawyer?"

"T. rex!" I tie with Devin again, and we high-five like we're brilliant.

Emma's face has life in it again, and she's about to say something else when someone kicks me—making me jolt—so her focus goes to my reaction instead.

"Oh my gosh!" Rachel says, apparently the one who delivered the deathblow to my ankle. Her hands are all over me now. "I'm so sorry! How did I kick *you*?"

Emma and I straighten up at the same time. I've been trying to cheer her up by playing a game of footsie, so our feet were twisted together like pretzels when Rachel apparently tried to kick *her*, not me. "It's okay," I reply. "I was just . . . stretching my legs."

"Oh, cute!" she says, looking at me as if I'm a newborn kitten. "Anyway, I was about to tell you that if I had little brothers like Emma does, I'd watch more adventure shows. But my acting coach encourages a study of *serious* films I can benefit from. You know, professionally."

"*Jurassic Park* made a serious load of cash," Devin says. "Doesn't that count?"

"I guess, if you're only concerned about the bottom line," Rachel replies. "But I just remembered something super funny! Emma had the biggest crush on a boy in fourth grade who was obsessed with dinosaurs. She made me sit through a full day of dinosaur movies so she could impress him with prehistoric talk. She even took notes."

Emma buries her head in her hands, laughing, and I bust up too.

It will be a few days until I can see her again so it's killing me to be on the opposite side of this table. Devin brought my mom down here for the premiere, but I'm taking her back to Phoenix tonight and staying there until Rachel leaves. Then we only have five working days left before a two-week hiatus, when Emma is going home to Arkansas.

"Emma's parents would've died if they knew she liked this kid because he was such a troublemaker," Rachel says. I laugh even harder now, imagining Emma studying about dinosaurs behind closed doors to impress a pint-size punk. "But she's always had a thing for bad boys—it's that wild streak in her, which is why McGregor hired her. Only, McGregor thinks it's more dormant than it really is."

"Whatever," Emma says, forcing a laugh. "His 'second nature' casting is loony."

"You told me just a few months ago that you thought the theory was brilliant," Rachel says. "That it explains why you always go after guys you should stay away from."

Since I'm one of the guys Emma has tried to stay away from, I'm curious to see where this topic will go. McGregor is definitely right about *me*. I do wish, at least sometimes, that I could listen to the devil on my shoulder and not care about anyone but myself.

And every once in a while, that's exactly what I do.

"I don't *go after* bad boys," Emma tells Rachel. "I *don't*," she adds, and looks at me. Then, as if she suddenly remembers who her real date is, she turns to Devin. "I just happen to find out they're wild after I start dating them. So . . . um, Devin, is there anything dangerous I should know about *you*?"

Devin glances at me. "Jake and I accidentally started a field on fire once, with a stray bottle rocket. Is that dangerous enough?"

I've already told Emma that story, but she smiles big anyway and starts to say something else, when Rachel cuts her off. "Sorry, Devin, but *accidentally* doesn't count. You pretty much need a Surgeon General's warning slapped on your chest to turn Emma's head. I mean look at the list . . ." Rachel ticks off a few of Emma's pre-Hollywood crushes, then moves on to the two jerks she dated before Troy. Then she says, "Troy was a total player too, and now there's Brett—well, sort of. Emma's already liked him *forever*, but she's playing hard to get now. She's a real tease when she wants to be."

There's a whole lot of crap for me to process in that last part, and I'm not the only one at a loss for words. Emma's mouth is half-open. "Rachel, can you, um . . . come with me?" she finally says, sliding off the bench. "Please."

"Why? Ten-one-hundred?"

"Ten-what?" Devin asks.

Rachel giggles. "That's set talk for using the bathroom."

She's been spouting off industry terms all day, and I haven't understood half of what she's said—how could Devin? "Darn it, Dev," I say, pushing my hands down the sides of my jeans. "I forgot my *Movie Star Pocket Dictionary*, or I'd let you borrow it."

"I doubt even that would help me understand what's going on here," he replies.

Emma ignores both of our jabs and speaks to Rachel again. "I just need more ketchup, and it looks like you do too."

"I'm fine, thanks," Rachel says. So without another word, Emma leaves the table.

I gulp down the rest of my drink. "Dang, I'm out of water. Keep Devin company, will ya, Rachel?" I take off before she can reply.

Devin covers for me as I walk away. "Yeah, tell me more about *Stars in Their Eyes*."

I find Emma inside The BBQ Shack, looking into a plastic tub of identical ketchup packages as if she isn't sure which one she wants. Besides a woman who's scrubbing a grill with her back to us, we're the only ones in here. When Emma notices me, she looks around, all panicky. "What are you doing?"

I step up to the soda fountain beside her and refill my cup with water. "Devin just asked Rachel about her new show. That will buy us some time."

"She isn't *always* this obnoxious. She's nervous, so she's saying stupid things."

"Forget what Rachel said," I reply, telling myself the same thing.

"You were so right about this," Emma says. "It was a dumb, *dumb* idea. I don't want to go back out there."

I set my drink down and turn her toward me so the lady cleaning the grill can't see her. Then I take off my sunglasses as a hint for Emma to do the same, and wait until she catches on. She looks away as soon as her glasses come off, but not fast enough for me to miss how bloodshot her eyes are. She obviously didn't sleep last night either.

"What happened at the premiere?" I ask. "I thought if I danced with Rachel it would take a bit of pressure off you, but—"

"Jake, it wasn't just her." She swallows. "I can't do this any longer. I'm telling Rachel everything *tonight*, and she'll probably leave. Then . . . I need to talk to you. So can I meet you in Phoenix sometime tomorrow?"

"Tomorrow?" I glance around before giving her a quick kiss. "That's a yes."

We return to the table separately.

Rachel gets a call during our drive back to Sabino Canyon, which she relays to the rest of us one line at a time: Her mom is flying to L.A. in the morning to find them a place to live. She's already put their house up for sale. Rachel has to cancel her spot as an extra on *Coyote Hills* and leave tomorrow, instead of Tuesday, because she has too much to do for *Stars in Their Eyes*.

Emma has to be as happy as I am to hear all this, but it also means that she's cornered into doing what she told me she'd do—tell Rachel about us *tonight*.

Once we enter Emma's community, Rachel starts talking about the "next time" we go out—yeah, right—and Devin and Emma say their good-byes when he parks in front of her town house. He keeps the car running and walks around it to open the door for Emma. I'm about to do the same, but Rachel stops me. "Stay a minute, will ya?"

When Emma is out, Devin closes the passenger-side door and traps me in the backseat with a stalker. It doesn't help that the last of the sunlight gives the inside of Devin's car a creepy orange glow. I keep my hand on the door handle.

Rachel sighs. "I'll be living in L.A. now. Do you go there a lot?"

"No. Not really." I don't want to be rude, but this has gotta end.

"Oh . . . okay," she says. "Then I'll have to come *here* more often."

This girl couldn't catch a clue with flypaper.

I finally know what to say. "Rachel, I'm sorry if today wasn't as fun as you'd hoped it would be. It's just that . . . well, I've fallen pretty hard for someone else."

Her eyes widen. "Um . . . all right. I asked Emma if you had a girlfriend, and she said you didn't. Or I wouldn't have . . . I mean . . . she should've told me. That's all."

"Don't blame Emma, okay?" I ask. "She wanted this weekend to be perfect for you. It's not her fault that I ruined her plans."

A sharp breath later, Rachel says, "I feel so stupid."

"No, please don't," I reply. "I just hope you realize that I'm not the same guy you've seen in all the ads—those smiles, the stupid smirks—they're all fake. I never even liked modeling, and I won't be acting long either. I'm in school now so I can move over to the business world. But Emma says you're a great actress, so I'm sure you'll do amazing in Hollywood. Good luck."

Rachel takes in another shaky breath, nods at me, and exits the car. I would have followed her out, but what would be the point? I've already said good-bye.

EMMA

Rachel storms past me on my front porch, and as much as I hope Jake hasn't let something slip, I also wonder if it might be better that way. She's done this type of thing before—torn me down to make herself look better—but she was especially ruthless today.

It's been almost impossible to function since last night, and Rachel isn't even the biggest reason. I didn't sleep, trying to figure out what happened with Brett and what to do about it.

As soon as Rachel is inside my town house, she runs up the stairs. Then I sprint back to Devin's car, and Jake tells me what he said to her. He had set up a good base for the truth, so I hope I'm ready to build on it. Rachel is about to learn a lot more than she wants to know about Jake's *girlfriend*.

Once I'm in my living room, I can hear Rachel crying upstairs. I tiptoe up to my bedroom and change into pajamas—I'll be sleeping on the sofa like I did the night before—then sit by the bathroom door for at least thirty minutes. She finally comes out with a roll of toilet paper, wiping her face. "You're out of tissues."

"Oh . . . kay," I reply. "Sorry."

Rachel leans against the wall opposite me and slides down it until she's sitting. "While you're apologizing, go ahead and explain why you made me look like an idiot today," she says. My jaw drops, and she rolls her eyes. "Let's skip right over the *bombshell* Jake just dropped on me, and start with the easy stuff: Did you know that Jake quit modeling and that he doesn't even want to act much longer? He likes business, Emma. *Business.* Those little details would've been really great for you to tell me."

I force myself to remain calm. "I told you to ask about his classes, remember?"

Rachel slams the toilet paper on the floor. "Only in a casual comment sort of way! You also told me to talk to him about the film industry, and *hello!* Jake doesn't know an Oscar winner from Oscar the Grouch."

Does she really think I wanted to sabotage her? "Rachel, I only said you should ask about his favorite movies, not *quiz* him on award shows from decades ago." I'll take the blame for keeping the truth from her, but I'm not responsible for her acting like a know-it-all. "Even I couldn't have guessed that stuff."

"You shouldn't have to guess!" she says, jumping up and heading for my bedroom. "If you were as serious as you should be about acting, you'd study this industry as much as I do."

Apparently the seven movies and two TV shows I've starred in don't count.

I scramble to my feet and follow her. "Memorizing film facts and reading tabloids is a far cry from *studying* the industry," I say, done with playing nice. "And nothing you've ever been taught in acting classes can prepare you for—"

"What? Hard work?" Rachel heaves her hot-pink suitcase onto my bed. "Try mopping floors at Papa's Pizzeria sometime, for minimum wage! It probably takes me a full year to earn what you're paid for a single day of sitting in your cast chair and sipping bottled water!"

I grab Rachel's other suitcase and throw open the top; the faster she packs, the better. "Oh yeah," I say. " 'Cause it's always that easy! You know those mindless things I say and do when I'm . . . um, what did you call it? *Acting*? Well, that stuff just magically pops into my head. I mean, with all the water sipping I have to do, how could I have time to study a script?"

Rachel tugs her clothes off hangers. "You think that justifies all the money and attention you get? Today was supposed to be my big chance with Jake, and *you* did all the talking! But you can't help but steal the spotlight, can you? Famous Emma Taylor always has to prove how cute and clever she is."

Every insult I've ever held back races to the tip of my tongue. "You have a very warped sense of reality," I shoot back. "The guys were bored to tears with talk of *Casablanca* and whatever film won whatever award in nineteen-whatever. The only thing I tried to do was save your butt!" I could've gone on. John Wayne and Clint Eastwood both starred in films made at Old Tucson Studios, but Rachel thought Jake would rather have his ear talked off about *Ingrid Bergman*? Seriously?

"You didn't save me! You totally ruined my setup for the next topic." Her face is so close to mine that I can feel heat leaping off it. "The Best Picture winner for 1972 was *The Godfather*. What guy wouldn't want to talk about that, huh?"

"Well . . ." I'm speechless—my mouth moving, my mind spinning, but no sound coming out. Had I really cut into her trivia game too soon? Am I really an attention hog? My heart pumps boiling blood through my veins as I try to recall the entire conversation at the picnic table. No . . . the only thing I'd wanted today was for time to pass as quickly as possible.

If I were selfish, I would have canceled the whole thing and taken the time I needed to tell Jake about what happened in the atrium. Our few minutes alone in The BBQ Shack would have been a seriously crappy place to say, "Oh, by the way, Brett kissed me."

Rachel zips a suitcase, bringing me back to the present. "I wasn't just rambling," she says. "I was trying to connect with Jake, even if it meant talking about the Mafia. But as usual, the whole conversation turned into something about you."

"*You're* the one who brought up the dinosaur movie marathon," I reply, "knowing how stupid I'd feel. And you didn't stop at simple teasing either. You had to bring in all that garbage about me liking 'bad boys.' That was intentionally cruel, Rachel, and it hurt."

"And you didn't mean to hurt *me*? Holding back all that stuff about Jake?"

"Trust me, whatever I've held back, it's been to *avoid* hurting you," I say, my voice failing a bit. I fold a shirt, one that I actually bought for her, and attempt to calm down.

Rachel plucks the shirt from my hand. "I don't need your sympathy. I'm done living in your shadow, begging for your crumbs. I'm not just 'Emma Taylor's friend' anymore, I'm . . ."

As she goes on, I realize I've been fighting for a friendship that's evolved into something that isn't good for either of us. And it changed long before I met Jake.

"Rachel, I never wanted you in my shadow. I wanted to do this *together*," I say. She's ranting right over the top of me, but it doesn't matter. I just need to get this out. "If I could duplicate everything I have, I'd hand it to you. In fact, I've tried. I've gotten you into auditions. I've taken you to every premiere and party you could come to. And I've felt so guilty for having yet another thing you wanted, that I almost gave it up."

What a mistake it would have been to lose Jake for this.

I finally have her attention. "Whatever. It all started with that *Mountain Home* role, which should've been mine, and you know it," she says. "If I hadn't been sick the day of the audition, I would've easily beaten you out for the part."

I want to scream, "That was six years ago! Get over it!" Instead, I glance at the photo of my smiling best friend on the wall, then look back to the girl in front of me.

"You're living the life that should've been *mine*," she says, but I'm already leaving the room, desperate to talk to Jake. "And you've loved every minute of rubbing it in my face!"

She slams my bedroom door, and I stand in the hall, fuming. I have plenty to rub in her face, so if this is the end anyway, why not? Shouldn't I just open that door and tell her how Jake and I kiss until we run out of breath, and how he wants me, not her?

Rachel is the one who opens the door again. "And about that *bombshell*: you also lied to me about Jake having a girlfriend, and I asked you about that at least three thousand times."

I don't even blink. "Yep."

"Yep, what? Are you admitting that you lied to me?"

"About three thousand times," I say.

Rachel huffs and her eyes narrow. "How long have they been together?"

"Officially, since last Friday," I say, at last feeling the weight of the moment. "Unofficially, since Labor Day."

"Labor Day?" she asks, and I can see the wheels turning. "Why . . . didn't you tell me?"

My mind races through the details—all the waiting, struggling against what I wanted so badly, making Jake feel like he was my last priority. "Honestly, Rachel, I can't even explain it to myself now, so I won't even try to justify it to you."

"Fine! I'll never forgive you anyway!" Rachel bellows. "Just tell me who she is."

I head toward the stairs. "It doesn't matter anymore."

JAKE

"Whoever coined the term 'drama queen' must've met Rachel," Devin tells me after dropping the girls off at Emma's. He stayed with me last night, along with my mom. "What's her damage?"

"Show business," I reply. "Sorry about the weird day."

My mom has been on her own and has probably inspected every inch of my condo to make sure I'm not living like a pig. I had a cleaner come a few days ago, but there's no way I'll admit that. Laundry is as far as my domestic skills go.

I had set Mom up with every *Star Trek* movie ever made, so I expect the sights and sounds of blasting lasers to hit me when I open my front door. Instead, Devin and I find a gloomy, silent living room, with only a paused image of an entertainment reporter on my big screen. My mom is just as still as the reporter is, so I race across the room. "You okay?"

"Yes . . . I'm, well . . ."

I lean over to look into her eyes. "Are you dizzy? Does your head hurt?" I reach for my cell, ready to dial 9-1-1.

"No, Jake. This isn't about me." She motions to my TV, and Devin and I turn to the screen again. "I was watching coverage of the premiere, and . . . goodness, I'm not sure how to . . ." She glances at Devin.

"It's okay, he can hear it." I think I know what's going on now. It's a total Mom thing to freak out about. "What did they say? That I'm a crappy actor?"

Mom touches the remote on her leg. "They had nothing but praise for you, Jake, which is wonderful. But . . . I don't know how to approach this without assuming too much, or—" I grab the remote and start the StarTV news from the beginning. "Jake," Mom says, "maybe I should tell you about it first. It might not be what it seems, especially considering—"

It's too late. The same plastic, bottled blonde who interviewed us on the red carpet opens the news segment with, "Rumors of a *Bremma* reconciliation are definitely true, my friends. At last night's premiere of *Coyote Hills*, two of its stars, Brett Crawford and Emma Taylor, celebrated the long-awaited debut in a stolen moment together."

As the reporter goes on, video footage takes over the screen. It shows Brett and Emma, alone in a white room with trees. Emma is in her red dress and Brett in his suit. They must've gone off together during the party . . . while I danced with Rachel?

The video has a strange glare to it, as if a camera took the footage from outside a window. The reporter's voice turns to static in my ears when the shot changes and Brett and Emma are now . . .

standing toe to toe. Then I hear nothing at all, feel nothing but blood pulsing through my veins . . . they're kissing.

The view is straight on. Their lips aren't just touching, they're locked.

I think of Brett chasing Emma down the hall, and him saying that he couldn't give her enough of what she wanted. So *this* hadn't been enough for her?

The reporter continues to narrate the scene, play by play. "Emma Taylor was so swept off her feet that she dropped her plate of cookies. How adorable! Brett must be great with those famous lips, huh? I wonder what sort of treat they have planned for their upcoming hiatus. More cookies, perhaps?" The reporter laughs as if she's a comic genius. "Whatever these two cook up, it's always delicious! We'll keep you posted! As for—"

I keep watching in a state of stupor until Devin takes away the remote. The screen goes black, but I still stare at it. The only light in the room is from a small lamp. "Jake," Mom says, "I'm sure there's an explanation. They've been doing all this silly publicity, and perhaps—"

I shake my head. "It wasn't publicity. It was real." I don't know what to grab first. "Let's just . . . get you home, okay?"

"Devin, would you mind driving me back to Phoenix when you're ready?" Mom asks. "I think Jake should stay here and sort this out."

"Look, Mom," I snap. "Emma's liked Brett *forever*—you heard Rachel today, right, Devin? She's even told me that herself. But she explained everything else away: a bad camera angle, a clueless onlooker who said they were all over each other. Because, you know, stories like that get attention, sell papers, create buzz."

Both my mom and Devin try to calm me down, make sense of it all, but they could've just as well been talking to solid rock. I help my mom into Devin's car, haul her suitcase and wheelchair out, grab the bag I already had packed for Phoenix, and take off.

Who knows where I'll go? Anywhere is better than here.

EMMA

Jake's voice mail picks up on the first ring, so I keep calling as I walk over to his condo—still in pajamas, because I can't return to my bedroom with Rachel in there—but his car is already gone. I go back to my town house, figuring Jake's phone is probably dead after our long day at Old Tucson Studios. He'll eventually notice on his way to Phoenix.

I call or text every few minutes until I drift off on my couch.

When I force my eyes open in the morning, Rachel's hot-pink luggage is just a few feet away from me. My home phone rings and I sit straight up—I only get calls on that line from Jake and the front gate. I stand to answer but hear Rachel pick up in the kitchen. "Actually, this is Emma's . . . um, guest," she says. "Yeah, I called a taxi. Tell him I'll be out in a few minutes."

I don't hear anything else for thirty seconds or so. Finally, there's a sniff, and I sink back onto the sofa. I don't want to get into another fight. The cruel words just need to stop.

Rachel enters the living room with her eyes as red and swollen as mine were when I woke up yesterday. "It's you, isn't it?" she says, followed by another sniff. Her voice is raw, surrendering. The fight is over. Everything is over. "*You* are Jake's girlfriend."

"Yeah," is all I say. There's no use telling her that our first kiss was only a week ago. Because, really, we've been together a lot longer than that.

Rachel sits on my blankets that are heaped on the sofa. "I knew it would happen, Emma, that Jake would fall for you. Every guy does. But I thought if you and Brett were dating, it might at least buy me some time to get here—to show Jake I was perfect for him. But you kept saying that you *didn't* like Brett anymore, so I . . . I tried to convince you that you should."

My breaths are shallow as Rachel sits and cries beside me. Everything I think of saying sounds so cliché: *I didn't mean for this to happen; I fought it; I didn't want to hurt you.* What good are those words now? I can finally see the real Rachel again—the girl I grew up with, dreaming of stardom and how great it would be to fall in love. We just happened to have the same dream, and fall for the same guy.

And I got both.

"This isn't just about Jake," Rachel sobs. "I mean, yeah, I'm totally mad that you lied to me, but there's so much more. You just don't get it. My Twitter followers don't care about my photography—they want to hear about *you.* For six years now, it's felt like people have only wanted to be my friend because I know *you.* I've lost track of how many guys have flirted with me, then dropped the line, 'So, can you hook me up with Emma?' I hate it. It's humiliating."

"I wish you didn't feel that way, Rachel," I say, my anger completely gone. "Because it couldn't possibly be true about *everyone*. But this was the talk we should've had last night—in fact, we should've had it a long time ago."

Rachel nods. "I'm sorry about what I said last night."

"Me too," I tell her, then have to force myself to go on. "The problem is, there's some truth to what we both said, and we don't have just a few easy issues to work through."

"Right," she replies. "I'm sure it's gonna take a while, but at least we got it all out."

I stand and peek through the blinds; Rachel's taxi is here.

"You'll be a big star," I say, my throat tight. I finally find the courage to turn back and face her. She's making sure her suitcases are fully zipped. "And I'll *always* be your very biggest fan. But I think we should . . . not be so close for a while."

Her line of vision rises to meet mine.

I have to push through this. "Thanks for not hating me for dating Jake," I finally get out. "But I can't talk to you about him, for obvious, awkward reasons. And he's only the tip of the iceberg when it comes to how guilty I feel about having so much of what you want—what you deserve." She's really taking this in, so I keep going. "*Stars in Their Eyes* will have its best season yet with you on it. But realistically, it will be a while until, you know . . ."

"I have anywhere near the fame you do," she says.

I nod, crying myself now, and reply, "You need some space to find your own happiness. And that will only happen if you're not comparing *your* life to *mine*."

Rachel swings her carry-on bag over her shoulder. "Well, I guess if you can't talk to me about your super-hot boyfriend, or your fancy job, *or* your big Hollywood parties, then you're just a boring friend anyway."

She hugs me, and we both laugh through our tears. It isn't a perfect ending, but it feels right. "I'm curious about one thing, though," Rachel says. "What does Jake think about all these fake publicity stunts between you and Brett? I mean, I get it that it's helping the show, but—"

"They aren't publicity stunts," I reply. "We've never meant to stir up any speculation about romance—the opposite actually. The media just keeps blowing things out of proportion."

Rachel's bag falls off her shoulder. "Then what was up with that kiss last night?"

Somewhat in a daze, I ask, "What kiss?"

"You know. With Brett. And the cookies."

Cookies? My entire body explodes into tiny pieces. "In the atrium?" I choke out. "You . . . *saw* that kiss?"

If she saw it, Jake could've seen it. *Anyone* could've seen it!

"Oh. My. Gosh," Rachel says. "You're gonna flip. You're gonna—"

"What, Rachel? Tell me. Please!"

"I couldn't sleep," she says, "so I watched your DVR recording of the premiere coverage on StarTV. And they showed it—you and Brett kissing."

"Wait, they . . . *what*?" I grip my hair by the roots. "How? *Who*?"

"It was a video, Emma, not just photos. I'd figured stuff out about you and Jake by then, so it sort of threw me off. But then I thought you must've been faking it with Brett, and—"

"But I didn't kiss him back! Wasn't that obvious?" I tear my blankets off the sofa and find my cell. Jake still hasn't returned any of my calls or texts from last night.

"Nooo," Rachel says. "It looked like you were totally into it."

"Holy CRAP!" I redial Jake's number—his phone still goes straight to voice mail—and race into the kitchen for my bag. "How's that even possible? Did someone tweak the footage?"

Rachel follows. "Jake doesn't know Brett kissed you? Oh, wow. This is bad."

I hug her again. "Go to L.A., have a great time, and let's e-mail in a few weeks."

"There's just one more thing," Rachel says when I step away. "I'm the one who told *Celebrity Seeker* about your longtime crush on Brett. They saw my Twitter feed and direct messaged me, asking for a fresh story no one else had. And they paid me *five hundred* bucks for it, Emma. You *know* how bad I needed that money. So please ask your mom to stop blaming my mom. She's really upset about it."

I stare at Rachel, my eyes burning. "Oh . . . kay. Thanks for telling me."

My flip-flops are by my front door, so I step into them and run outside, grabbing one of Rachel's suitcases along the way. I leave the suitcase on the curb where the taxi driver takes care of it—but not before he gives me a funny look that says, *Pajamas, flip-flops, and a Gucci handbag?*

I get my first speeding ticket ever driving from Sabino Canyon to the other side of the city, and my second on the freeway between Tucson and Phoenix. Both cops say it's great to meet me, but neither one gives me a break. *Hello?* Can't they see that I'm already having a bad day? I look like I was dragged out of bed by zombies.

So much for preferential treatment of celebrities.

I call Jake over and over, also trying his mom's house, but no one picks up. I leave a ton of messages on his cell—at first, just brief ones saying to call me. Then I finally spill everything, explaining to Jake how I'd ended up with Brett in the atrium, what happened, and that I hadn't told him about it yet because Rachel was staying with me. And that's why I had asked Jake if I could meet him in Phoenix, to tell him the whole story. But nothing. Not a single word from him.

Not one reason to stop panicking.

I had turned off my phone during our double date yesterday, and my voice mail was full when I turned it back on after my fight with Rachel. Timing wise, it wouldn't make sense for any of the messages to be from Jake, but I check anyway. It turns out that several are from my mom, one is from my publicist, and a bunch more are from friends congratulating me on the premiere. The last message is from McGregor. He says, "Ah, lassie, I think we need to talk."

I only listen to the first few seconds of each of my mom's calls, which pretty much start the same way. "Where are you? Can you *please* explain this?"

The message from my publicist begins with the usual: "Do you wish to comment on . . ." This is where she always fills in the blank with my latest adventure in stupidity.

The thought of Jake already seeing *the kiss* burns like acid trapped under my skin. I should've watched the premiere coverage before I left, at least to have an idea of how to explain why, according to Rachel, it looked like I'd actually kissed Brett back.

It's ten thirty by the time I reach Phoenix. Mrs. Elliott should be awake by now and picking up her phone. Is something wrong with *her*? Why haven't I thought of that sooner?

Jake used my phone to call Devin a few days ago, so I scroll through my call history and find his number. "Devin, this is Emma," I say when he answers. "I can't find Jake."

He doesn't reply for several seconds. "Well, I know he isn't in Phoenix. And I doubt he wants to be found. I was with him when he saw that kiss."

I pull to the side of the road, instantly sobbing and unable to drive. "But I didn't kiss Brett back," I say. "I promise I didn't. It was all him."

Devin groans. "Look, I shouldn't get in the middle of this, but if you want my opinion, it seemed pretty mutual to me too. So unless you sent a body double into that atrium, Jake's probably had enough of this crap between you and Brett."

"I get that, but—" I can't finish. Devin is right, I've run out of plausible excuses. "Just . . . please, tell Jake to call me. Or to at least listen to my messages."

We say good-bye, then I send Jake yet another text, and I head back to Tucson . . . to wait.

My cell rings during the long drive home, and I answer in a hurry. It's only my mom, calling to act disgusted with me. Dad isn't happy either, since it was just two days ago that I told them I like Jake, not Brett. I explain everything that happened in the atrium, but Mom just says, "Good grief, Emma. This is dating, not brain surgery. It shouldn't be so difficult."

"Do you really think this is *normal* dating?" I reply. "Most girls only have to defend their actions to their parents, but that's just the beginning for me. I'm expected to explain my every mistake to a publicist, a producer, and millions of strangers who somehow find out if a guy even calls me! And heaven forbid that I'm caught holding a boy's hand—everyone jumps to the conclusion that I'm already planning my wedding. Does that sound *normal* to you?"

My mom hesitates. "Emma, I realize you're overwhelmed by the pressure of living in a fishbowl—or in this case, a glass atrium—but that's why I'm always reminding you to be more responsible with your choices. You have a career to consider."

I let this sink in before I reply, so my words will sound as serious as they are. "I'm sorry, Mom, but I have to fire you. You never seem to know when I need a mother, not a manager."

I spend the rest of that Saturday making hourly trips to see if Jake has returned to his condo. I check almost as often on Sunday. By Monday—which I luckily have off from work—I don't go anywhere at all. It's over. I know it is.

My town house is a mess of empty water bottles, dirty cereal bowls, and tissues. I'd finally found some that Rachel missed, and I used up half the box going over the video of Brett kissing me in the atrium. I've seen it several times now, but it only took once for me to realize that the footage had been slowed down, making a three-second kiss look like a five-hour marathon. And all that stupid talk about me dropping my plate of cookies—as if Brett had stolen my strength with some kind of mesmerizing kiss—what a joke!

The StarTV cameraman must've been hiding in the hedges outside the atrium. That's the only explanation for why the video didn't capture me escaping Brett's hold—we dropped out of view when my plate fell. StarTV would have had a much better story if they'd known the truth about my freak-out. But truth is hard to come by and guesswork is painless, so why bother?

The more time that passes, the angrier I get that Jake has so little faith in me. But if he were to show up at my door, I would probably still throw myself all over him—which is why I jump out of my skin when someone finally *does* break the silence in my living room with a loud knock. I part my blinds and squint into the sunlight, certain I'm seeing a mirage. "No freaking way!"

I spin around and start stuffing my mess under the sofa. The knock comes again, followed by, "Sweetheart, we can see you running around in there."

It's no use. I can't shower, vacuum, *and* wash my pile of dishes before my family crashes through the door. So I finally open it.

"Surprise!" Levi says, squeezing me to death. Seven-year-olds have lobster claws for arms. Logan joins in on the screaming and squeezing. And now they're jumping in circles around me. I'm so stunned I can't speak.

My dad works his way in behind my brothers, his arms full of grocery bags. "That's enough, boys. Remember what we told you."

"Oh yeah," Logan says. His chestnut hair is sun-bleached from playing outside all summer, and his brown eyes have their usual mischievous gleam. Levi looks just like him, but with a few more freckles. "You're sad, so we have to *be-haaave*. That sucks!"

"Logan! Watch your mouth," Mom says. Her arms are full of grocery bags too, and she shuts the door with her backside. "Hello, Emma. We . . . your dad and I . . . well, here we are."

A baseball-size lump grows in my throat; my mom doesn't have a full sermon prepared? "Yeah, thanks. For coming. But . . . why?" I ask, and my parents both shrug at the same time, which is so weird. I look back to my brothers. "How did your tournament go?"

"We won!" Logan says, so I give them both high fives.

"Just the first game," Levi adds. "We lost all the rest." He throws open the doors of my entertainment center. "Why don't you have an Xbox?"

I shock myself by laughing. "Since when do you get to play video games?"

"Since Dad bought us a whole bunch!" Logan says as he leaps onto my sofa, shoes and all. He avoids my mom when she drops her grocery bags and runs over to stop him from jumping. Then he spins off the sofa and crashes on the floor. "He even plays with us sometimes."

"Only the fishing game," Dad says, snagging Logan before my mom can.

Mom grumbles something as she scoops up the groceries and heads into the kitchen.

"I don't have time for camping anymore," Dad goes on. "So this is the best I can do for the boys."

It's a lame excuse, but I guess virtual bonding is better than no bonding at all.

My dry lips crack when I smile. "In that case, I have something even better than video games. There's a river out my back door that's so shallow and slow right now, you can catch fish with your bare hands."

"No one is *fishing* for their food today," Mom calls from the kitchen, soliciting a chorus of groans from my brothers. "I'm making a nice family dinner."

"Jake must be an outdoorsman," Dad says in a hushed voice, guessing right. Obviously, I hadn't thought of the primitive fishing skill myself. Jake had talked me into trying it when we had a rare day off together. No one even seemed to notice us playing around in the river.

I wrap my arms around my waist, attempting to squeeze away the memory.

"Dad!" Levi says. "Mom told us we couldn't talk about boys, remember?"

I find it funny that they set ground rules before they came. "Jake is actually an Eagle Scout," I inform my dad, because he is too. "So, yeah, sorry I finally found a decent guy, then scared him off."

Dad looks like I've punched him in the gut.

He takes the rest of the groceries into the kitchen. The twins run in there too, where Mom is now blocking them from the back door. Dad tells me about their day of flying out, chasing the boys around baggage claim, and shopping at a nearby grocery store.

Meanwhile, Mom warns the boys about the dangers of rivers—shallow or not.

"Don't worry, Mom," I say. "In Tucson, you're safer in the water than anywhere else. On land you'll find rattlesnakes, scorpions, tarantulas, Gila monsters, coyotes, mountain lions, and bears. Even an occasional jaguar." I learned all this at the local zoo, where I will *never* visit again. "And, oh yeah, javelina."

"What's a hav-a-lee-na?" Logan and Levi both ask, their eyes round as quarters.

"It's a big hairy pig with razor-sharp teeth."

"Whoa!" Levi says. Logan has already slipped out the back door.

Mom puts a hand on her hip. "You should've told them about the lizards instead. They'll be looking for snakes and tarantulas all day." Levi takes off after Logan.

"Then they better have supervision," I say, scooting my dad

outside. It feels so good to smile—out of all my fans and famous friends, it's my *family* who showed up when I needed them most. I turn back to my mom. "I'm glad you guys came. Surprised, but glad."

It's only now that I recall the last time I spoke to her.

She takes out chicken and potatoes from a grocery bag. "You haven't answered your phone for two days." She stops still, with just her eyes moving to look at me. "Emma, we've been worried sick. We had no idea what to expect when we got here."

I hurry over to the sink, which is filled with dishes. "It doesn't usually look this bad," I say, hoping to dodge the real issues. "And neither do I. It might be nice if I showered, huh?"

"That isn't what I meant," she says, and I look back when I hear the catch in her voice. She pushes aside the groceries and comes to my side of the counter. "If you can forgive me for not being here for you in the past, I'd . . . well, I'd like to be here for you now."

I nod, taken aback. "I'm sorry I worried you. I haven't answered *anyone's* calls. And the one person I really need to talk to isn't calling." I can't fight my tears anymore. "Mom, I have to work with Jake in just a few days. And Brett too. How am I supposed to do that?"

Time has completely stopped this weekend, and I don't want it to start again.

"We've had far too many arguments for me to notice how happy you've been these past few months," Mom says. "Your dad noticed it, though, every time he talked to you. So if Jake had anything to do with that, I can understand why you're so upset right now."

I try to push my doubt aside. Could my mom really understand *any* of this?

"For once I felt like someone saw past the characters I play, both on and off set," I reply. "I'd convinced myself that Jake didn't care that I'm not as perfect as everyone expects me to be."

"Emma," Mom says, still seeming sincere, "you've turned out remarkably well for pretty much raising yourself. How many girls your age would spend a literal fortune of her own money to start a foundation for the disabled? Or worry so much about a friend's dream that she would put her own happiness in jeopardy?"

I don't answer.

"Trina told me what happened with Jake," Mom continues. "She's actually more upset than Rachel is, and she had planned to expose it all to the tabloids."

My stomach twists. "What did you tell her?"

Mom pulls a wicked face that I've never seen before. "I reminded Trina that the influence she's seen you have in getting Rachel *in* to auditions, can work in the opposite direction as well."

"You didn't!"

"I did," she says, entirely serious. "And I'll threaten her with worse than that if Trina whispers so much as your middle name to the press."

"What's wrong with my middle name?" I like it.

"Nothing," Mom replies, "except that you were named after your aunt who later tricked us into buying her daughter a new nose."

My laughter is cut off by a hiccup. "Oh yeah."

"As for returning to work. I have a suggestion, if I'm still your manager."

I hesitate for only a second. "I appreciate all you've done, Mom, I really do. But—"

"It's not working anymore," she says, and I nod. "I've been

thinking the same thing. It's just . . . difficult for me to hand you off to someone else's care. But believe it or not, I have exciting things planned for my *own* life—raising your brothers, for example. Perhaps even traveling with your dad. I hope, however, that you and I can still find . . . *time* for each other?"

"Yeah, of course," I reply, a wave of relief passing through me. "In fact, I've been wondering if maybe . . . you'd want to help more with my foundation? I need a really good organizer—someone who can take care of the details."

She would actually be perfect as the foundation's *director*, but we'll take it one step at a time. And this way, she can still be involved in my life without supervising my every move.

"Sure, I'd love to help," Mom says. Then we're both silent for a bit while we just smile at each other. Sort of awkward. But she eventually says, "Now, as only your mother, I have just a *thought* about Jake."

"Okay," I reply, the tightness in my throat returning.

"Simply put, even nice guys can be idiots," Mom tells me. "So if you're confident you didn't do anything to betray him, then this is his problem, not yours. And if he's worth all these tears, he'll figure things out and come back on his own."

A knee-jerk reaction. Isn't that what Jake had said sometimes happens to him? Is this all that's going on? Or has he heard, as Devin hinted, one too many excuses from me?

"You don't think I should try to talk to Jake before we go back to work?" I ask Mom. She has to know how crazy things might get on set if I wait. "I've already left a ton of messages, and I asked his best friend to tell him what happened, but—"

My dad opens the back door and pokes his head in. "Emma, do

you have a bucket?" he asks. "We'll also need a hose. And a few towels."

Mom and I walk around the counter to get a better look at him. He's wet all the way up to his waist. "I don't even want to *see* the boys," Mom says with a hand over her mouth.

I peek outside, too curious to resist. Logan and Levi are plastered in mud—from their toes to the top of their heads—and are chasing a flopping fish down the running path.

JAKE

It's better to just be numb, to forget about it.

I've been staying in a hotel since Friday night and plan to stay here as long as I have to. It's a given that I'll have to move, but my job is a serious problem. I can run all I want to from Sabino Canyon, but seeing Emma—being told to kiss her on cue, like I know will happen in upcoming episodes—will be impossible to pull off without losing my mind.

She's been right all along. We never should've crossed that friend line, so this is the angle I use when I e-mail her the day before returning to work:

> I don't want you to feel like you owe me an apology.
> I'm the one who pushed you into something that you
> told me, over and over again, you weren't ready for. So
> let's just remember the good times and move on. It
> isn't worth fighting over.

That one paragraph took me a full day to write. It's the easy way out, but I don't have time to handle it like a man. I'll have to work with her at least once before our hiatus begins, but it isn't until Monday night, when I get my schedule, that I know when that will be.

Tuesday and Wednesday, I'm working on some scenes without the principal cast. Thursday, I'll only be with Kimmi. Then Friday is the day: Emma and I are scheduled to be in a chemistry class scene together. The script features the early stages of dangerous flirting between our characters—art imitating life in the most agonizing way.

My only hope of getting through Friday is if I walk into the studio with a totally calloused attitude. But when I see Emma sitting in her cast chair, my heart detaches from the rest of me and starts thinking on its own. She doesn't look like herself. With her eyes lacking their usual brightness, she seems hollow. It's hard not to stare, so I head for the food instead.

Two crew members are already at the table and don't notice me before I overhear them talking about Emma. They say she's been despondent all week. McGregor catches me listening in, and says, "You look like you've been blindsided by a bulldozer."

"I'm fine, okay?" I reply, but he knows I'm full of it.

A few minutes later, while McGregor explains how he envisions the scene, Emma and I are practically face-to-face, but nowhere near looking at each other. I'd sent her the e-mail so we wouldn't fight in front of everyone at work, but why isn't she even *trying* to explain herself? I guess she might've already done that in one of the messages she left me, but I was so pissed off that first day that I erased every one of them without listening.

We start rehearsal, and right off the bat, the script supervisor corrects me on my opening line. "Jake, that's from the original script. Didn't you get a copy of the revised scene?"

"Uh . . ."

Tyler pushes stiff fingers through his hair. "It was delivered by express courier yesterday afternoon," he says. "We missed you at the studio."

I look down at my feet, but my eyes shift to Emma's instead. "Sorry, I haven't been home for a while," I reply, then realize that I forgot to grab the sides—copies of my lines and what scenes are being filmed—from my dressing room.

Tyler walks over to mumble something to a fuming McGregor, then finally speaks into his radio. "We need sides of the revised lab scene for Mr. Elliott."

"Copy that," is the reply. A PA swears in the background, probably because his head is on the chopping block for not double-checking that I saw the changes. No one usually has to.

"Sides flying in," comes from a nearby radio.

A PA runs onto the set and puts the miniature pages right into my hands. I scan the lines. "Wait, this is . . . totally different." There's still a lot of friendly conversation, but none of the touchy-feely stuff from the original script. Is the love triangle being delayed? Or even cut?

"Back to one!" McGregor shouts.

Emma has wandered off, fiddling with a wad of electrical tape. We return to our marks behind a lab table. "We just need to get this over with," I tell her.

"You made that clear when you broke up with me in an *e-mail*," she says. "But, gosh, I loved the personal touch at the end: 'Let's just remember the good times!' Where'd you get that line, your high school yearbook?"

"Quiet please, let's rehearse," Tyler says, and the set falls silent.

"I meant the scene," I whisper, almost knocking over a row of glass beakers. The whole table is covered with flasks and other breakable crap, all filled with neon-colored goo. It's a seriously bad day to be filming on this set.

McGregor doesn't take his eyes off us. "And action."

I read my first line, tripping over it like it's written in a foreign language. Then Emma practically coughs through hers. Tyler glares at us both before turning to McGregor.

"Regain your focus," McGregor says. "Let's go again."

"You're being *stupid*," Emma snaps, which isn't her line—it's meant for me. A mere second later she flubs her part again and looks to the script supervisor. "Sorry, what's my line?"

The script supervisor says, "Forget about *my* date, how was yours?"

Emma hesitates before nodding, and we start rehearsal over again. And again . . . and again. McGregor finally stops pacing the floor. "Let's add the Steadicam."

Tyler raises his brows. "We'll need twenty minutes to set it up."

"Just do it," McGregor tells him. "We'll film this one line at a time if we have to."

Adding a third camera isn't all that unusual, but the set has always been arranged for it in advance, and we only use the Steadicam when we're in a hurry to get a scene finished. I'd say this qualifies. We still have the other half of the scene to shoot with Kimmi and Brett later on.

The gaffer sends his lighting team running. PAs also race around the set, directed by radio commands. "You two, follow me," McGregor hisses at Emma and me. As we obey, Emma rolls the wad of electrical tape between her hands even faster. I need something to fiddle with too, like a stick of dynamite.

McGregor leads us to Emma's dressing room, opens the door, and extends his arm. "After you," he says. Emma steps in first, and I follow, but McGregor stays in the hallway. "You have exactly eighteen minutes to work this out, or you'll both find your characters taking a nosedive off a steep cliff. Understand?" He closes the door.

We spend at least three of our allotted minutes in brutal silence while Emma plays with her tape, and I mindlessly kick a metal leg on her chair. She finally looks right at me and says, "This is absurd, Jake. Stop pretending like you flipped a switch and shut your feelings off."

"I guess that's what happens when someone cheats on you. Right?" Emma squints her eyes at me like she doesn't know what I'm talking about, so I add, "Oh, I see—I'm overreacting. You *sure* there wasn't any kissing involved? Because it looked pretty darn real to me."

"Did you even listen to the messages I left?" she says. "I explained *everything*."

I fold my arms. "Let me guess, you were rehearsing a future scene?"

"We were just talking, and then he caught me off guard!"

"How could you say that? I told you *months* ago that Brett liked you—and McGregor told you too. And you want to know something even more interesting? Brett has been telling *me* for months that *you* liked him, that you were practically begging for a relationship."

"What?" she says. "There's no way he could've thought that."

"The only thing I *can't* sort out," I say, "is when you were acting and when you weren't. That seems to be a very fine line with you."

Emma pushes past me. "How stupid of me to think you were the only guy who ever knew the difference."

She leaves the room and slams the heavy door behind her. My heart is hammering so hard it feels like my ribs might crack. I sit in Emma's dressing room for another ten minutes, trying not to look at anything that belongs to her. McGregor finally comes to get me.

"That went well," he says. "Emma's flooding the ladies' room with tears, and judging by the look on your face, special effects had better hide the explosives."

"Funny you say that," I tell him. "I was just thinking about dynamite."

McGregor's face twists into pure fury. "There's not one bloody joke to be made about this!" he says, but *he* made the first joke, not me. Or at least I'd thought he was joking. "We have over a hundred employees working on this production, most with families to support, and we're all at the mercy of a childish love spat!" He continues to release heaves of breath until he finally drops his head. "My apologies. I'm rather volatile when my studio is in disarray."

Maybe I'm the one who needs to talk to special effects.

I'm back on set before Emma is, and I find Brett prowling around, hours before he's supposed to be here. It isn't the first time I've seen him this week, but it's the first time I've wanted to say something. And I have *plenty* to get off my chest.

My target must be obvious because McGregor blocks my path. "Jake, when I hired you, I hoped you'd bring a much-needed maturity to this group. Please don't prove me wrong."

I shake the tension from my arms. "Since when did right or wrong matter in this business?" I ask. "As Emma just informed me, I can hardly tell the difference anymore."

"Then we've given you a proper welcome to Hollywood." McGregor turns back to our audience and shoots a stabbing glare directly at Brett. "This is a closed set. If you're not in this shot or have a radio on your hip, get out!"

EMMA

The fact that only one chemistry flask has gone crashing to the floor today is nothing short of divine intervention. Jake and I have barely made it through filming the first half of the lab scene—it took us over two hours—when Brett and Kimmi arrive on set, and we're stuck with them for at least two hours longer.

Even on a good day, those guys can't be in front of the same camera without a SWAT team of crew members distracting them from killing each other. And now that I'm fighting with Jake, and Jake isn't speaking to Brett, and Brett is being all sulky with me, McGregor is acting like he would rather shut down the whole production than deal with us.

And maybe it would be better that way. We're only wrapping episode six, with sixteen episodes to go in the first season. Then there are three more years on our contracts after that . . . which makes eighty-two additional episodes to film . . . with eight to ten workdays for each. This means spending at least *seven thousand* more hours together.

I want out.

I was a minor when I agreed to do this series, so I should just plead teenage insanity, pack up, and hit the road. My lawyers can take care of the rest. I would rather walk away, ruin my career, and lose all of my money in a lawsuit with the studio, than wake up every morning and try to convince myself that I hate the guy I just spent the entire night dreaming of. And *then* come to work and have to be all flirty with him for the camera.

I can't do it.

"Last looks!" The shout rattles my head.

Kimmi is close by, complaining about her flat sneakers. "They make my ankles look fat."

"And don't forget that the camera adds ten pounds," Brett says from the other side of her. "Even to your ankles."

I would have told Brett to leave Kimmi alone, but we've hardly spoken to each other since the premiere. According to "someone close" to us, however, we "skipped off to San Diego last Saturday." I'm dying to call the tabloids and ask a few questions about our invented trip, such as: *Did we eat at a cozy restaurant? Did we buy a house together with a white picket fence? Or was it a beach villa, where I can splash in the waves while Brett surfs?*

As part of the curious public, don't I have the right to know this stuff?

"Martini's up!" Tyler calls. "First team, back to one! Then we're off for two weeks!"

We all return to our marks behind adjacent lab tables. An entire classroom of extras has just left. McGregor explains that this shot will be tight—only on the principal cast. The camera is closest to

Jake and will show our adjacent tables from the side. The angle is to capture a brief exchange between Brett and me, where he answers my question about our experiment.

All day long I've felt Jake next to me, been haunted by his familiar voice. And now to my right, just a few feet away, is the guy who somehow came between us. But how?

Production calls are made, and McGregor sits behind his monitor. "And action!"

"You *know* it was all real," I whisper to Jake, right over Brett's first line. Brett is the only one with a mic. "Deep down, Jake, you have to know that."

"Emma . . ." I hear him say, and his tone has changed. It's soft. Sad.

Probably my imagination.

"Cut!" McGregor says. "You missed your cue, lass. Let's go again, from the top." I try to focus, but there's a metronome inside me, making me *think, think, think* everything through. "And action!"

Brett leans back from his table. "What did you say, Eden?"

I turn my head, on cue this time. "What's the next step?" is my actual line, but I don't have to say it for this shot. The camera only has to catch my hair swishing from one shoulder to the other; Eden is nothing but a prop right now. A silent temptress.

But what am I?

A few lines later, McGregor calls "Cut!" again.

"Back to one!"

We're about to start over when a sound guy shouts, "We're picking up background noise!" And we all freeze, listening. There's a distant roar of military jets.

McGregor flies into a rage. "I built my studio in the middle of the Sonoran Desert, and . . ." He curses and commands us all to stay exactly where we are. Then he leaves the set for who knows what—to call the Pentagon?

My heart is throbbing, my eyes stinging. I turn to Brett, unable to hold back any longer. "Did you know?" I ask. "Did you kiss me *knowing* that I liked Jake?"

The crew scampers around and chats loudly, but I can still hear Jake breathing to the side of me. Brett looks over with a stunned, hurt look on his face, and for the first time, I realize he's faking it. "You like *Jake*?" he asks.

"Oh please!" Kimmi says, coming around Brett. "Of course he knew. I told you that forever ago. And he also knew there was a camera outside the atrium."

"Whatever," Brett tells her. "You're such a liar."

Jake stirs behind me, but my focus stays on Brett.

Kimmi steps closer. "Brett followed Payton and me into the atrium at the party, and then they started arguing because Brett doesn't want us getting back together—but I am *sooo* over Payton, anyway. Then Brett did a double take at the window and said, 'Chill, dude, someone's in the hedges with a camera.' So we all left."

The part about Brett chasing after them is for sure true. And if that's true, and Brett has been feeding *Jake* lies about me liking him, then . . . everything at last makes sense.

Brett laughs. "Think about it, Emma. Kimmi would say anything to make me look bad."

"You set me up," I reply. "You were coming into the ballroom to find me when we happened to pass. Then you lured me into the atrium, planning to kiss me and *knowing* it would all be caught on camera."

"Oh, come on! Why would—"

I slam my hands into Brett's chest. "I'll tell you *why*!" The set falls silent, and all heads flip toward us, but I can't rein in my emotions. "Even if I would've pushed you away after you kissed me, you still could've played it up in the tabloids and claimed that I'd broken your heart! And it's really no big deal that I've figured you out now, is it? Not when you can *still* say that I cheated on you with Jake. So either way, you win!"

Brett holds up his hands. "That . . . that isn't true."

"You've tipped off the press all along! Starting with the motocross."

Kimmi eases away. "Actually, that was me."

"See, just like we thought," Brett says. "So how can you—"

"It doesn't matter," I reply. "Our trips to L.A. didn't have anything to do with promoting the show. The publicity was all for *you*."

The veins in Brett's neck are purple and angry. "You're crazy."

"Yeah, I must be," I snap, "because I fell for every lie and sob story you told me. Well, bravo! Great performance."

"Really?" Brett says. "You want to talk about *lies*? Where'd you and Jake go for Labor Day, huh? When you were supposed to be with *me* in Tahoe? Or how about that scam of setting each other up with your best friends? That was a good one!"

Jake's voice is right by my ear. "Back off, Brett."

"You know, Jake, I thought we were tight." Brett takes a step forward, and someone shouts for security. "But do you really think I'm stupid enough to believe you *dropped* Emma's phone in the back of my truck? Not that I doubt furniture was involved at some point."

"I'm serious," Jake says. "Back off!"

"Please, Jake," I tell him. "Stay out of this."

"No," he says, sliding his arm around my back, strong and protective. My breath catches, but only for a second. "This changes everything."

I step away from him. "Is that what you needed? *Proof*?"

"Emma, I'm sorry. I—"

"Just leave your apology on my voice mail, all right?" I say, cutting Jake off as I walk backward, off the set. "Maybe when I'm in a better mood, I'll listen to it." I shrug. "Then again, maybe not." I look between Jake and Brett. "Why don't you two do me a massive favor and beat each other up? I'd hate to break a nail on one of your big heads."

I walk away, but I hear a slap seconds later and glance over my shoulder to see Brett rubbing his cheek and cursing at Kimmi. She shakes out her hand and says, "I don't mind breaking a nail for a good cause."

My only true friend here turned out to be Kimmi. How ironic.

I grab my handbag from my dressing room and race down the hall toward the parking lot, fully aware that McGregor may not let me return. But what is there to come back to, anyway?

Just as I reach the exit, footsteps pound down the hall after me. "Emma! Stop!"

JAKE

Security rushes the set with McGregor blasting in with them, demanding that I explain what happened, or I would have already caught up to Emma.

I didn't stick around for the fallout, but can hear McGregor shouting at Brett halfway across the studio. When I finally hit the hallway with our dressing rooms, Emma has just reached the exit to the parking lot. I beg her to stop, but it isn't until she's only a few steps from her car that she even acknowledges me. "Please, Jake . . . don't," she says. "Just let me go."

"I screwed up, okay? I'm so sorry."

"Want to know what I've done this past week?" Emma asks, reaching the driver's side just as I jump in front of her door. "I fired my mom, told my best friend to get a life of her own, felt ridiculously guilty over a kiss I was tricked into, and cried my eyes out while I *prayed* that you would call. What a complete waste of a sunny week in Tucson!"

"Emma . . ." I reach for her arms, but she takes a step back and then another—almost as if she's afraid of me. I realize then that this situation is way too similar to the one she'd been in with Troy last spring, so I stuff my hands into my pockets and give her some space. "I just assumed the worst because Brett had already been messing with my head," I say. "And you didn't tell me about the kiss, so I figured that you . . . wanted it. Picked him over me."

"That's insane, Jake," she says. "And when did I get a chance to tell you what Brett did? This wasn't a one-minute phone call I could sneak in. But I said I needed to talk to you, remember? I just didn't expect StarTV to get involved before we had some time alone."

"I get that now. I should've listened to your messages." The setting sun behind her sends me back to the first time we were in this parking lot together . . . the day that started it all. It can't end like this. "Look, as today went on," I say, "I realized I might be wrong and wanted to ask if we could talk after work."

"I needed you to believe me *before* today," Emma replies and steps closer, but only to go around me to open her car door. "I can't stop the press from broadcasting my mistakes to the world, so you'll always have reasons to doubt me, no matter what I do." She sits behind the wheel and fastens her seat belt. "It's never going to work, Jake. It just isn't."

I hold on to the top of the door so she can't shut it, understanding for the first time how Troy could've felt desperate enough to slam his fist through her window to stop her from driving out of his life. But I'm *not* like Troy. And yeah, I've cared about no one but myself this past week, but ultimately, I'm not like my character Justin either, who would also *make* Emma hear him out. I'm better than that.

After just one tug on the door, Emma looks up with pleading eyes.

I step back and watch her drive away.

The blowup on set happened at about six o'clock Friday night. By Saturday morning, the first day of our two-week hiatus, online gossip sites have already spread the story, and stunned fans everywhere light up the Internet—all taking sides: Bremma vs. Jemma.

By Saturday afternoon, we're breaking news on StarTV and I've been cast as the villain: "Brett Crawford accused fellow cast-mate, Jake Elliott, of borrowing his truck to romp around with Emma Taylor, who Crawford was seen kissing as recently as last weekend. Can you say *scandalicious*?"

There's no telling who leaked the explosion on set. It's all twisted to sound as juicy as possible, and missing the only details that really matter to me—that Brett is much more of a master manipulator than an actor, and that at some point in the past week, Emma and I broke up.

At least I think we did.

Liz says I have one week to hire a publicist, or she's forwarding all calls directly to my cell. So now I have to shell out some serious cash to have a publicist say just two words: no comment. I can think of a few short phrases I'd like to tell the press myself. For free.

I'm staying in Phoenix during our hiatus, and when my mom needs groceries on Wednesday, I make the mistake of thinking I'm still an anonymous nobody and head out. But the second I leave her community, I'm chased by a literal motorcade of random cars with their windows rolled down and cameras flashing.

I race into the store, but the freaks follow me. The management does nothing to stop them—I'm not even sure they can—they just get into the excitement like everyone else as photographers throw out questions like, "How did you get Emma to cheat on Brett?" When I don't respond, they get downright dirty, trying to provoke me into a response—*any* response. And if that includes me shoving one of them into a shelf full of soup cans, all the better. They'll have premium pictures, a killer front-page story, and an even better lawsuit.

These scumbags have nothing to lose, and the only choice *I* have is to ignore them.

What kind of story could they possibly make up from a grocery trip, anyway? *Jake Elliott was seen Wednesday morning buying milk and butter, confirming the rumor that he and Emma Taylor are hiding out in Phoenix together, since she's also known to like dairy products. We expect to catch them buying cheese any day now. Fruit and vegetables are sure to follow.*

It's Thursday night now—nearly a week after I last saw Emma—and I'm on my mom's couch flipping through channels while I wait for Devin to show up to watch the Suns game. It was his idea. He's been dishing out nonstop apologies—for not believing Emma, or even telling me that she called him—and a truckload of pity.

But my mom . . . not so much.

She comes out of her room and notices I'm not studying for a test like I'm supposed to be doing. My economics textbook is on the floor, well within reach, but I've already read three hundred pages in the last few days, and I can't recall a word of it.

"Has lying on the couch all day made you feel any better?" Mom asks.

"Nope," I reply, ditching my usual front of being *fine*. "I can't study. I can't sleep. I hate being stuck inside, but going out is a death sentence. Anything else you want to know?"

"Yes, actually," she says, maneuvering her wheelchair right up to the couch. "When do you intend to talk to Emma? I'm sick of watching you mope around."

"Thanks. That's just the shot in the arm I needed."

Mom is quiet for a sec, and then she releases a long sigh. "I knew falling for Emma would have its complications. I just hoped it wouldn't hurt so much."

"Well, it does." I've only told my mom enough to get her to stop bugging me every five minutes. "But I blew it, and she doesn't want me back. End of story."

"And you're okay with that?"

I sit up in a flash. "No, I'm not *okay* with it!"

"Then what are you still doing here? You've been talking up your big life plans for several years now, but it wasn't until you met Emma that you actually did something about them. So I think a girl who inspires you to go after what *really* makes you happy, and not just fame and fortune, is well worth fighting for."

I run a hand through my messy mop of hair. "I'm past debating that. It's just . . . I don't know. It all seemed too perfect, and whenever I feel that way, things fall apart. Always. So I guess I just jumped ship at the first sign that it might be sinking. It was stupid."

Mom puts a hand on my knee. "Your ships don't always sink. Yes, you once had a great dad who changed after making some bad choices. But that was his fault, not yours. And it's time the two of us accept my fate as it is now, bound to this wheelchair. My stroke was rotten luck, that's all. But I've hated how significantly it's altered your own life. So seeing you get back to doing what *you* want to do has been very healing—for both of us, I think."

She's never let me give up on anything. "Does that mean I have to stop pouting?"

"To be honest," Mom replies, "your smirk is cute enough to sell suits, but your pout couldn't sell socks. Groveling, however, might look good on you."

"Groveling," I repeat, a word I've been thinking about all day. "Right."

That will take a lot more than a phone call.

EMMA

I've been lying flat on my bedroom floor in Fayetteville—wearing a bathrobe and a towel wrapped around my head—for over an hour. I was already living in L.A. when my parents bought this house, so without my collection of teddy bears in one corner and my movie memorabilia covering the walls, this bedroom wouldn't feel any more personal than my whiteout bedroom in Tucson.

The real difference is the *Star Wars* theme music booming from the main floor below me. Along with all the movies, my dad brought home plastic lightsabers a few nights ago, so Levi and Logan are now Jedi freaks. Mom is probably thrilled, though, since the boys have a few days off from school this week and their new fascination is keeping them busy.

Dad is always at work, so he isn't much help. And I'm pretty much worthless too.

I had stayed in bed longer than usual this morning, reliving a dream—the kind where you keep closing your eyes again, trying to slip back into it. Jake was there, as usual, but neither of us were actors, and we were perfectly happy together. My first thought when I woke was, *See, you just need to leave the industry, and things will be much better.* And I was satisfied with that. But then I had this thought: *You were happy with Jake. Tabloids and all.*

But will I ever be less sensitive to gossip? Can I learn to just shut it out?

Leaving *Coyote Hills* this way would probably end my career; I'd drop to the D-list overnight. It might make things easier with Jake, but he may not even want me back, so I have to take him out of the equation. What do I want for myself?

Still flat on my back after my shower, I stare at the textured ceiling as if the random shapes might somehow give me crystal-clear answers. And crazy enough, it works.

I grab my phone and call McGregor.

"I don't want to quit," I say the instant he picks up. This is our third call since I stormed off set a week ago, in full costume. The first time we talked, I apologized for my behavior but suggested he kill off my character in a chemistry experiment gone bad, because I wasn't coming back. In our second call a few days later, I agreed to stay through the end of the season. But now, I decide to tell him, "I love acting. *So* much. I don't want to give it up just because a bunch of jerks think they own the rights to my life story."

I hate that the smallest corners of my world can be invaded at any time, but no amount of lies can change who I really am. And not *every* personal moment is spoiled by the paparazzi.

Jake and I were the only ones at that campground when we kissed for the first time. No one ruined it by twisting the details.

And even with all the cameras that were there the night I found the courage to face Troy at Club 99, not a single photo told the actual story of me overcoming my fear of him.

My life, as public as it seems, is still only mine.

"I figured you'd come to your senses," McGregor says, and I can almost see his crooked grin. "I'd hoped Brett would grow out of his shenanigans, but sometimes—only sometimes—I find my casting theory to be flawed. Not everyone has the hidden qualities I believe they have. I've given Brett until the end of the season to restore my faith, or his character will indeed be the victim of a sad accident. In the meantime, I've threatened to give him an exceptionally intimate scene with Kimmi if he doesn't behave. Have you spoken to Jake since last week?"

I swallow hard. "Not yet. But more than anything, Jake and I are good friends, so somehow . . . we'll be okay." His friendship is the biggest loss I feel.

"Then I won't expect any more problems," McGregor replies.

This isn't the only second chance I'm hoping for. I had wanted Jake to let me leave the studio in peace, but it now kills me that he let me go so easily. At the campground, though, he had said he couldn't give up on me even if I wanted him to, and I believed him.

I still do.

I wonder if he's seen any of those totally cliché chick flicks where the main character has an epiphany, a massive smile slides across her face, and then she dashes off to the airport to confess her love just in the nick of time. If so, Jake should know exactly what I'm about to do—race to my laptop and buy a ticket to Phoenix. But the next flight isn't until tomorrow.

Tomorrow? Ugh!

If I hadn't sulked in my room all day, trying to wish away my problems, I could've already been on my way to Arizona. All I can do now is start the twenty-three-hour countdown.

When I open my e-mail inbox to double-check the flight itinerary, I do the usual scan to see if anything is from Jake. Nope. But there are two other e-mails that grab my attention—one from Rachel, and one from Kimmi. There are also the same five e-mails from Brett that have been there for six days—unopened—plus five new ones from him. The subject lines are all identical: READ THIS IF YOU WANT TO KNOW EVERYTHING.

Everything? What I already know is enough to make me obsess about prying Brett's toenails off with pliers. But Kimmi has never e-mailed me before, so I open hers first:

> How Not to Be Pathetic, Lesson 305: Smart girls only
> get hurt once. Don't take this as a compliment, but it
> looks like you've finally learned something—Brett is a
> loser. You were stupid to think otherwise. But Jake is
> more like a wolf in a designer suit, so I'll cut you some
> slack this time. Just don't let him fool you with his
> apologies. Are you ready for my Lessons in Revenge?
>
> Your best frenemy forever,
> Kimmi

Our relationship is *so* weird. But after her well-placed slap last week, I'll admit that she's not a bad gal to have on my side. As for her Lessons in Revenge? I laugh out loud at the idea of Kimmi being my social mentor, then hit my reply button and write: How to

Make Your Own Decisions, Lesson 1: Thanks, but no thanks.
(Nice slap, though. I owe you a new set of nails.)

After I send that message, I open Rachel's e-mail. This is the first time I've heard from her since we agreed to give each other space. The e-mail says:

> Okay, so I HATE Hollywood!!!!! Kidding! I totally LOVE it!! There are four major hotties, and I'm not leaving this competition without at least one of them wrapped around my finger (even if I need to hog-tie him). There are super cool people here and everyone is asking me to take photos of them nonstop, cuz you know, I've got mad skillz! And guess what? I'm not the only freak who can name every winner for Best Picture, Actor, and Actress since the Academy Awards began! But I'm still gonna win this thing—no prob. I've found my happily ever after!! Speaking of, I know talking about The Bod is taboo, but if that big fight on set really happened (notice that I said IF!) I hope things are okay now. Anyway, I promise I'll just e-mail until . . . whenever. xoxoxoxoxo

I can't help but smile—an e-mail once in a while won't be so bad. When I write back, it's mostly about *Stars in Their Eyes,* and how to hog-tie a guy without hurting him *too* badly. I also say I'm not ready to talk about Jake yet, but maybe soon. Once that's off, I glance at the time . . . twenty-two hours and forty-five minutes until I land in Phoenix.

I need a new clock; time isn't going fast enough on this one.

So out of sheer boredom, I consider Brett's ten identical e-mails in my inbox. He'll never stop spamming me unless I reply, so I finally open one:

I doubt you'll even read this but here's the truth anyway. Yes, I did know something was going on between you and Jake. I just didn't think it was as serious as it obviously is—you've both seemed pretty messed up since the premiere. I'm sorry if things are still bad, but I really do like you, a lot, so this sucks for me too.

The problem is that you didn't just make me want to BE good, you made me LOOK good. People started thinking of me as a decent guy again. So when I saw the camera outside the atrium, I figured that could be my last chance to tell you how I felt, and at the same time make everyone believe you really liked me. And your friend had just told me you did, so I thought you might actually kiss me back. I know it doesn't matter now, but I really am tired of being a loser and of people saying I'm a washed-up child star. Acting is the one thing I KNOW I'm good at.

I hope you'll forgive me one day—maybe in twenty years when I'm fat and bald and flipping burgers at a fast food joint with the rest of the Hollywood has-beens.

I think all this through for a few minutes before I reply:

You're right, Brett. I lied to you about something I was
desperate to keep secret, but I never would've betrayed
you like this. So yeah, I might be on that 20-year plan
you mentioned. Meanwhile, I think we're both good
enough actors to at least pretend to get along,
especially at work. We owe that to McGregor.

P.S. That dude who kicked Troy's butt for me at Club 99
is actually a pretty decent guy. I doubt I'll see *him*
flipping burgers anytime soon.

Whoops and cheers are suddenly outside my bedroom. Levi
and Logan burst through the door and are all over me before I can
even stand up. "Whoa, whoa, whoa!" I wrap my bathrobe a bit
tighter. "What are you so excited about?"

Mom finally catches up and scolds the boys for not knocking.
"Dad just called," she tells me. "He wants to go out as a family
tonight—dinner and a movie. He'll be home at five."

I toss the boys a look of panic. "Oh no! I only have six hours to
do my hair!"

I decide to wait until after the movie to tell my family that I'm
leaving the next morning. I've already been home for a week, so I
hope they'll understand. I get ready, pack what I can, do a couple
of hours of homework, and come downstairs to find my brothers
beating each other with lightsabers. "We're gonna fight the greasy-
haired vultures," Levi says, referring to the name I've given the
flock of paparazzi outside my parents' gates. They've been here for
six days, and as far as I know, only left during the rainstorm that
blew in yesterday. Going out with my family tonight will be
crazy—*but* I can handle it.

Levi peeks through the living room curtains. "Why do they want so many pictures of you? Just give them one of those." He points to our family photos on the wall.

I rough up his hair. "They don't want a picture of me smiling. They want to catch me crying or making ugly faces at them."

"That sounds fun!" Logan joins Levi at the window and parts the curtains enough to show his whole face and stick out his tongue. Soon, all three of us are laughing and blowing raspberries on the glass. *Jake would love this.*

"Let's throw eggs at them!" Levi says.

"Great idea!" I reply, only half joking. And of course, that's when my mom walks in, shocked that I'd encourage such behavior. She's been vacuuming the entryway and dining room, which is strange because her cleaners usually do that.

"Why don't you pick up the living room instead?" Mom tells the boys, pointing out the mess of potato chip bags and scattered popcorn kernels on the rug. We've been getting along pretty well while I've been here—not perfectly, but much better. "Emma and I need to work on her foundation."

"You have a *federation*?" Logan shouts. The boys grab their lightsabers.

"Not quite," I say. "It's a *foundation*. But if you want to help people—like Luke Skywalker does—you can join it."

I pick up the living room with the boys and vacuum it while my mom cleans the kitchen. When she returns, we're all sitting on the sofa with angelic smiles.

To keep my mind off other things since leaving Tucson, I've plowed through a stack of homework and read through several early foundation applications I gathered from Mrs. Elliott's physical therapist. Arizona will be a great starting point because I can meet some of the participants myself to determine if the various benefits are working and if improvements need to be made. But it's difficult to choose which candidates to help first, so my mom and I have decided to organize the applications into priority levels, according to immediate needs.

She's also been keeping up managerial duties until my agent and I choose a new manager. I haven't been too into it this past week, but I finally feel some hope again.

As Mom and I sit together and go through the candidate profiles, we read about children as young as two and adults in their eighties—all capable of improving their circumstances and abilities if given a chance. I become particularly interested in a twelve-year-old girl who was injured in a car accident. She's recovered from her internal injuries, but needs extended therapy to help her walk and speak again. This girl is the same age I was when my dreams of becoming an actress came true, so I wonder what *her* dreams had been. Will she still get to live them?

Somehow, I want to make sure she can.

I suppose there's at least one good thing that's come from my face being slapped all over the tabloids: millions of people know who I am, and I have a chance with this foundation to take advantage of that.

As my brothers run in and out of the living room, my mom and I answer their questions about joining my *federation*. They now have fistfuls of change and dump everything into my lap. "Here's our money," Levi says. "Is that enough?"

"Plenty," I reply, and also tell them about the twelve-year-old girl whose face they've just piled their donation onto. "You can be the first ones to help her."

We work on the profiles for another hour or so, and when it's nearly five, Mom jolts and says, "The sheets! I forgot to . . ." She trails off when I look at her, and scurries toward the laundry room. What's up with her?

My dad will be home any minute, so I take the applications to Mom's office, freshen up, and peek outside to see that another beautiful rainstorm is pounding the paparazzi. They're all in their cars now and some are even pulling away. Looking up at the dark-gray sky, I pray for lightning—lots of it. My family will have a much better time tonight if we don't have a dozen strangers tagging along.

"Will you please make sure the boys stay on the sofa?" Mom asks as she goes upstairs. "I want to keep the house tidy."

I turn on the TV for them and fish my phone out of my bag. What if I get to Phoenix tomorrow and Jake doesn't want to talk to me? Should I at least give him a hint that I've been rethinking things?

I type and erase several text messages—lines I've rehearsed over and over again for when I see him—but they all say about the same thing: **I miss you**. So that's what I finally gather the courage to send. Then as I just stare at my phone screen, waiting for a reply, my brothers think I'm playing the quiet game, so they turn off the TV and join in. Mom appreciates the silence, but I'm drowning in it. One little chime could save my life right now, and . . . I get it. The message on my phone says, **I miss u 2**.

In a stupor of disbelief, I whisper, "Jake misses me."

The boys have heard enough to figure out that Jake is—or at least had been—my boyfriend, so they laugh and tease me while I try to decide what to text back. Or should I call?

I'm still debating a few minutes later when my dad's arrival through the garage door makes my brothers bolt from the sofa. "Dad!" Logan bellows. "Emma's boyfriend *misses* her!"

That's when I hear a laugh that makes me stop breathing. I look up from my phone, certain I've imagined it. "Who are *you*?" one of the boys asks.

I can't see into the kitchen, but I hear Jake again, introducing himself.

My hands fly to my chest. My heart thumps hard against my ribs, then begins to race.

Mom peeks into the living room with an enormous smile, but she quickly disappears to get my brothers under control. Then Dad enters the room. "I got a call this morning from a young man who thought I might know where to find you," he says, and Jake steps out from behind him. "Your mom and I are taking the boys to dinner and a movie. We'll be back at nine," Dad goes on, then turns to Jake. "Or sooner."

Could you be any more obvious?

Moments later, Jake and I are alone in the house. I stand from the sofa and lace my hands in front of me, then in the back of me, then in front of me again. "Hi . . . you're, um . . . in Arkansas," I say.

"Yep," he replies. His expression is tentative, as if he isn't entirely sure how I feel about this grand gesture. "And I'm freezing."

I can't help but laugh a little because I've never seen him this nervous. "That's because there's a storm outside. And you're wearing a T-shirt."

"Yeah, well, I forgot a jacket," he says, rubbing his bare arms. "It was warm when I left Phoenix. You know, like always."

We're just staring at each other now.

"Are we really talking about the weather?" I ask.

"Uh-huh." He takes a few steps closer. "I planned out a million things to say when I got here, but my mind went completely blank when I saw you."

Where are my own practiced lines? Where is that nagging feeling I've had all week to tell Jake how sorry I am? But I doubt he traveled all this way for an apology, so I close the remaining gap between us, slip my fingers into one of his hands, and say the three words I didn't have to rehearse: "I love you."

Jake offers me a smile I haven't seen for far too long. "I am *beyond* in love with you," he says, and then we kiss until all the space in me that felt so empty is full again.

JAKE

I could easily kiss Emma all night long, but we have a lot to talk about before her parents get home. I finally speak against her lips. "Uh, sorry to interrupt. I just need to say—"

She laughs. "I think this says plenty."

"Trust me, it isn't because I'm not enjoying this," I reply. "I've just got a pit in my stomach that I want to get rid of."

Emma gives me a look of disbelief. "You already apologized, last week. I'm the one who needs to say how sorry I am for having a totally psychotic meltdown. Because, really, it wasn't only because of you. Or even Brett. Everything just came crashing down, all at once, and you got caught in the middle of it."

I can't hold her close enough, get enough of how it feels to have my arms wrapped around her again. "But there's more to my own crazy behavior than I admitted to you," I say. "I've had a serious case of jealousy, pretty much since the day we met. But I didn't want you to think I'd be just another possessive creep in your life, so I didn't tell you how bad it bugged me that Brett somehow got the whole freaking world to believe that your love was written in the stars. And on top of that, he got to *kiss* you, take after take after take."

Emma's fingers trail up and down my back, giving me chills. Man, I've missed her hands. I've missed all of her.

"I should've realized you felt that way," she replies. "But I was too busy trying to keep everyone else happy, remember? From now on, though—thanks to Brett—I'll think twice about blindly assuming the best about someone."

"No, don't do that. You're the reason I'm giving my dad another chance, and we're talking again. So stay just the way you are— you're like my moral compass." I laugh. "Okay, maybe not always. Sometimes you tempt me into a heck of a lot of trouble."

Emma hits my chest. "Speaking of fathers, how did you end up with *my* dad?"

I explain how I called his office this morning to say I was at the airport in Phoenix, and had only bought my ticket late last night, or I would have asked sooner if I could visit Emma at their home. I figured he'd like it if I asked him first. Besides, I didn't know where they lived. And I'd planned on renting a car and staying at a hotel, but Mr. Taylor said there were too many photographers around, so he'd have to sneak me past them—just like Devin had to smuggle me past the paparazzi at my mom's gates today.

Then Emma's dad offered me their guest room.

"So I'm thinking Southern hospitality, right?" I say. "But your dad was all business once he picked me up at the airport. Only ten minutes into our conversation, he made it perfectly clear that if I ever make you cry again, he's coming after me—with like a bat, or a pitchfork, or whatever else it is you crazy hillbillies attack people with."

Emma has both hands over her mouth. "Yeah. Usually pitchforks."

"But we're cool now," I say. "I pretty much told him everything I just told you—raging jealousy and all—and he gave me a pat on the back for being so honest. In fact . . ." This is big. "Your dad just helped me think of a perfect career for when I'm done playing make-believe."

Emma looks skeptical. "You don't want to be a college dean, do you?"

"No way," I reply, "but I think I'd make a killer agent." I'm still kinda stunned that I didn't think of this before today. "I've been a model, and now I'm an actor, so by the time I'm through with my *Coyote Hills* contract, I'll have a ton of experience on the talent side of the industry. And I'll at least be close to finishing a business degree at that point. But here's the kicker: if I really want to be a force to reckon with, I'll have to go to law school. That's where your dad came in. He said it's common to get both a business and a law degree. So my brain finally put acting, modeling, and the buzz I get from negotiating contracts all together, and the idea to be an agent hit me like an arrow!" I'm so excited about this that my eyes are probably bulging out of my head. "I mean, think about it—my agent is great at her job, but she has the personal skills of an iceberg. So if Liz can be as successful as she is, *I'll* be amazing."

"*So* amazing." Emma goes on tiptoes to kiss me. "And the thought of going to law school doesn't intimidate you at all?"

"I can hardly wait."

We talk on the couch for a while, then my lips easily find their way back to Emma's, and I lose all awareness of my surroundings. But it only takes a split second of her brothers shrieking through the kitchen for me to snap back to reality.

I bolt off the couch so fast that Emma lands with a thump on the floor.

The twins run in just as I'm trying to tug Emma up—she's laughing too hard for me to get a grip on her. Emma's parents stop still under the archway between the kitchen and living room. Her mom's eyes are wide open, as if she's imagining what her sons just walked in on.

It wasn't as bad as it looks, I want to tell her. *I swear*.

Mr. Taylor studies me—not Emma, just me and my bonfire-hot face. Then he shakes his head with what I desperately hope is amusement. "I guess you two worked things out."

Emma is still laughing. "Oh man, that was funny."

"I'm sure it was," Mrs. Taylor says. She turns to the boys. "Pajamas, please."

They whine the entire way but finally make it up the stairs.

Mr. Taylor's face is stern again. "The photographers are gone for now because of the storm, but they'll be back. Do you intend to do something about this, or—"

"Not that we're rushing you," Mrs. Taylor says. "You'll need to develop a careful plan with your publicists. It's critical that these things are spun just right."

Emma tips her head, obviously bugged that her mom has kicked into managerial mode. But instead of saying something to her, she looks at me. "Any ideas?"

"Yeah, just one, but it's kinda shady," I reply, having already thought up a plan on my way here—hoping I'd have a reason to carry it out. "I figure if the paparazzi are this determined to get proof that we're together, the tabloids must be willing to pay a hefty price for it. So why not hand over the proof ourselves? We'll tell whatever story we want to, and offer it along with our *own* photos. Then we'll just play the media until we get the bid we want, and donate all the money to Emma's foundation. I don't know if that's ethical, but . . ."

"Well, it's hardly ethical for these creeps to interpret a person's every move in bizarre, embarrassing, and even vicious ways," Mrs. Taylor says with a more parental tone. "And this way, you'll have as much control over the situation as you can."

Emma's smile is as wide and beautiful as I've ever seen it. "That's perfect!"

"Impressive, Jake," her dad says. "But you missed an important element. If you each sell just half of the story under separate identities, the money you donate to Emma's foundation can be written off on each of your taxes as a charitable contribution." Everyone laughs. "You can even deduct your expenses for this trip. You're discussing business, aren't you?"

The twins come bounding back into the room. "You guys were kissing, huh!" one of them says. I'm not sure which one—they look exactly the same to me. "That's gross!"

Emma throws a hand over his mouth. "Who needs tabloids when you have little brothers?"

The other twin lifts my shirtsleeve. "You've got *huge* muscles."

That's apparently enough to win the approval of both boys because they climb all over me until Mrs. Taylor finally tells them to go to bed. She has to coax them back up the stairs one step at a time.

Mr. Taylor sticks around until his wife returns, then makes firm eye contact with me for the umpteenth time tonight. "I'll be in my office, right down the hall."

Once he leaves, Emma's mom reinforces his already-clear message. "He'll be there until Jake is ready to be shown to the guest room. No later than midnight."

Emma puts a stubborn hand on her hip, as if she's about to argue, but I say, "That's cool," and Mrs. Taylor seems to appreciate my immediate compliance.

Once she disappears up the stairs, Emma and I return to the couch. "Things will still be crazy for a while, but we'll be okay," I tell her. "We're pros at sneaking around."

Emma leans into me. "How can we blame people for wanting pictures of us? Look how cute we are together."

"What's not to love, right?"

We whisper back and forth like this, for no more than five minutes, before we hear Emma's dad from down the hall. "It's awfully quiet in there!"

"Sorry, Dad!" Emma hollers back. "We'll try to make out a little louder!" In the absence of a reply—what could Mr. Taylor even say after that?—Emma tells me, "A return trip to Arizona is sounding pretty good right now. And I've already booked a ticket for tomorrow."

I smile and stretch my arm around her. "Eh, this isn't so bad. If the network okays McGregor's idea for a new reality show, we'll be supervised a lot closer than this. But my guess is that the cameras will only be on us eight, maybe ten hours a day. So that gives us—"

Emma throws a hand up. "Whoa! McGregor . . . reality? *What*?"

"He said he told you. He's calling it *Beauty and The Bod*."

"Well, he's totally insane if he thinks . . . wait a sec," Emma says. "How would McGregor know to call you The Bod?"

I grab as many couch pillows as I can to hide behind. "I'm getting pretty good at this acting thing, aren't I?"

"You sure are!" Emma pries away one pillow at a time, preparing to clobber me. But then she pauses, smiles, and tosses them aside. "You know, I actually wouldn't mind having the past few hours on film. I'd watch this scene over and over. I'd never get tired of it."

"Yeah?" I say, and scoot a bit closer. "Then let's go again, from the top—make sure we get it right."

"But let's skip the part where we talk about the weather," she says, slipping her fingers through the back of my hair and whispering against my cheek. "Jake and Emma's awesome make-up scene . . ."

I kiss her. "Take two."

ACKNOWLEDGMENTS

All of my love and appreciation goes to Shawn, Aubrey, Kailey, and Ella, who have been both supportive and patient while I chased this dream. Also to my parents, Don and Ann Marie, and my in-laws, Wayne and Valerie. You've pretty much sacrificed your retirement years to help out whenever I've needed you. And I have to include Gabby Pribil among my family because she's cared for my daughters almost as much as I have over the past several years.

I offer my sincerest gratitude to my fabulous team at Bloomsbury, especially Caroline Abbey, my lovely editor who called me with the *best news ever* while I was at Costco, and turned out to be the best deal I ever got there. Also Laura Whitaker, who I was lucky enough to acquire along the way as both an editor and a friend (and it's an extra bonus that she likes a good romance as much as I do). Sarah Shumway, Cat Onder, and Michelle Nagler, thank you so much for the roles you each played in bringing *Not in the Script* to life. Ilana Worrell, Erica Barmash, Emily Ritter, Lizzy Mason, Courtney Griffin, Donna Mark, and Lisa Novak—few readers are aware of how hard *you* work to provide them with awesome stories, so this is your well-deserved shout-out. *Thank you!*

Erin Murphy . . . where do I begin? I would've never dared to dream that an agent like you existed. You have given me 24/7 customer service, nonstop encouragement, and a lifetime supply of new best friends—the fabulous EMLA Gango! You treat me like I'm your only client who matters (but let's face it, you treat *everyone* that way).

Joy Peskin, your unwavering confidence in this novel is the reason it finally escaped my laptop and is now on bookshelves. And your confidence in *me* has at times been the only thing that kept me writing. But it's our irreplaceable friendship I treasure most. By far.

Sara Watkins, how can I ever thank you enough for your late-night reading marathons, laughing at the same jokes over and over again, and putting up with my endless "Sorry, but I've gotta write" excuses? It's pretty fair to say I owe you lunch. Like, forever.

I've had many other friends and mentors who have cheered me on throughout these long years of learning (and hoping), especially Jessica Day George, Heather Moore, Kim Thacker, Kristyn Crow, Alison Randall, Jennifer A. Nielsen, Carol Lynch Williams, Ann Cannon, Jen White, and Amy Efaw. You are all exceptional writers and even better pals.

Many thanks to Rachel Parkin and Tyler Atkinson for helping out with the technical details that were needed to write this book, as well as reviewing the manuscript for accuracy. And my highest-pitched fangirl squeals go out to the cast and crew of *Parks and Recreation*, *Parenthood*, and *Melissa and Joey* for allowing me to tour your studios, watch you film, and best of all, bask in your glory!

I also owe a lot to the many friends I made on Kryptonsite.com, where strangers from all over the world knew me as ajfinn and made me believe that my writing could one day find an audience outside of the three people who previously liked it. A very heartfelt thank you to Cardinal, SVSlueth, MOOman0618, Binkys711, NYC300Z, Ketchup, escout, Dr. Jekyll, LuvClana, Mythos, Superman_lives_on, booze_is_me09, itsallinthespelling, iLuvClana, 4EverSmallville, Spacewalker_33.3, and the rest of my ever-faithful fan fiction readers. Long live Clana!

And a BIG thank you to the readers out there! I hope you enjoyed *Not in the Script* and will continue to be a part of my life. Please stop by to say hello on Facebook (Amy Finnegan, Author) or on Twitter at @ajfinnegan. I'd love to get to know you! And you can also follow the characters of *Not in the Script* on Twitter at @onlyhre4 thefood, @EmmaTayAllDay, @actorincognito, @SoooooOverIt, @Crazy4Hollywood, and @NotInTheScript. They'll follow you back and will often reply to your questions or comments. And since I'm obviously not ready to give them up, I will occasionally be posting extra scenes at AmyFinnegan.com, where you can also find news about author events and additional books. I hope to see you around!

WANT MORE OF WHAT YOU CAN'T HAVE?

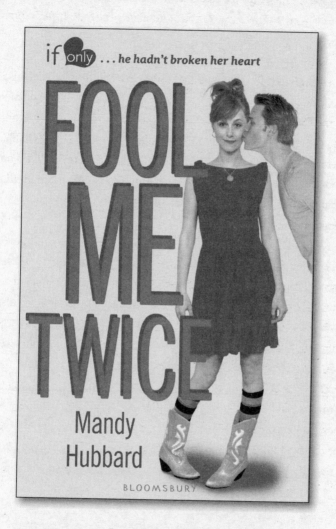

Read on for a glimpse at another romance featuring a gorgeous ex-boyfriend with a touch of amnesia and the most epic revenge plot in the history of everdom!

"I pledge allegiance, to the flag . . ."

I stiffen, my grip on the pitchfork, tightening so hard the wood bites into the still-developing calluses on my palms. The voice behind me is the very one I've waited to hear for the last week. . . . But he's *mocking me.*

I slice a glare in Landon's direction. He's standing in the entry to the empty stall, his lanky, all-too-muscular body a silhouette against the fluorescent fixture hanging behind him. The dust kicked up by my work swirls in the light hugging his body.

I wish I could make out his expression, to figure out if it's the same sneer he gave me that first day back at school last fall. When he broke my heart.

I smirk, saying, "Ha, ha, ha. You must think you're super clever."

"Actually, I do." He puts a hand to his heart. "You really wound my ego."

I roll my eyes. " 'No tears, please. It's a waste of good suffering.' "

He drops his hand back to his side. "Are you quoting *Hellraiser*?"

I blink. "Um, no?" I turn back to the pitchfork, hoping he buys it, and toss another scoop into the overflowing wheelbarrow. I should have emptied it already, but this is the last stall.

"Since when do you like classic horror movies?" His voice has that old familiar drawl to it, that same twang I loved when he whispered to me, his breath hot on my ear. His family is from Texas. They moved to Washington State six years ago, but he's never let go of the accent.

"Since when do you care what I like?" I scoop at a pile of manure near his toes, daring him to stand still as it slides dangerously close to his battered Justin cowboy boots. He doesn't move. "I mean, I was *just* getting used to the silent treatment."

"Meh, I got bored," he says.

Bored. I scowl. "I'm sure there's a *real* flag somewhere in desperate need of your allegiance."

I scoop up another forkful of soiled bedding. Maybe he thought he'd get away with just waltzing up, that I'd somehow forget what he did, like I'd fall at his feet at the first sign of his interest.

When I look up at him again, he hasn't budged, he's just chewing on his lip. He licks his lip, and for a second I forget I'm staring, thinking about how it felt when we'd kissed, when he'd traced his tongue across *my* lips. When he grins, I realize he's caught me.

Ugh. I should not be thinking of how good he is at kissing. Actually, scratch that. I should be thinking of how good he is at kissing *other girls.* That made it pretty easy to stay angry. Like he did in the halls the first day of school last fall. I wore this adorable Zac Brown Band T-shirt because he said they were his favorite band, and I was practically bursting with excitement to see him after a few days apart . . . and then I saw him, but it didn't go the way I'd pictured.

He was leaning in to kiss *her,* while I stood there dumb-founded. He knew exactly what he was doing because mid-way through their steamy makeout session, he saw me staring, a strange gleam in his eyes as he watched the way I unraveled. It was like he enjoyed watching me shatter, just like little boys love burning ants with magnifying glasses.

And it sucks to be the ant. I am *so over* being the ant.

"Nah, you're a little more . . . lively."

I snort, shaking my head. Lively. Yeah, I could show him lively.

"What?" he asks, crossing his arms and leaning against the doorway. The effort makes his muscles bulge. He probably practices the move in his mirror in the hopes of using it to ensnare his next summer fling.

I toss the pitchfork onto the heaping wheelbarrow. "Just leave me alone, okay?" I grab the cart's handle and yank.

But he doesn't move, and I back right up into him, our bod-ies colliding. Instead of stepping aside, he grabs my elbows to keep me from knocking him completely over, and then actually removes me from the stall and slides me into the aisle, like I'm a kitten that's run into his path.

Then he turns and easily pulls the overladen cart over the bump, onto the smooth cement of the aisle. The stall door screeches as he rolls it shut.

"I still have to put pellets in there," I start.

"I'll get it."

I stare at him, unwilling to believe he'd volunteer to take on even a tiny portion of my workload without wanting something in return. "Well, you just go zero to sixty in about five seconds, don't you?"

He flashes me a wolfish smile, the one that makes him seem half-dangerous, half-sexy. But now I know what really lurks beneath all those muscles and cowboy swagger, and his smile is no longer so attractive.

"What's that supposed to mean?" he asks, tipping the rim of his cowboy hat back far enough that I can see into his intense brown eyes. He's . . . irritated.

Good.

I narrow my own eyes and match his look. "The silent treatment, to mockery, to doing me favors," I say, ticking them off on my fingers. "Before you turned on the roller coaster, you could have at least warned me to keep my hands and feet in the car at all times."

He huffs. "Can't a guy do a girl a favor?"

"No." I laugh, and not in a pretty way. "Not you, anyway."

Dang. I had wanted to be aloof. Unaffected. I'm screwing it up.

He shrugs, totally unbothered by my visceral response. "Fine then. Do it yourself," he says. But he doesn't move out of my way or open the stall door either. Instead, his eyes sweep over my now-dirty polo shirt, down my legs, and then back up again before he smirks. "What's with the getup?"

I grit my teeth and check out my outfit. I'm in my Serenity Ranch polo, as required, along with my jean shorts, but I have lime-green leggings underneath, and my cowboy boots don't match any of my clothes—they're powder blue. It's like my outfit is a mullet—business on the top, party on the bottom.

"Can't wear plain old shorts in a saddle, you know that," I say, like he's being stupid. "It pinches."

"Right. And regular jeans would just be too . . ."

"Boring?" I say, throwing his words back at him.

"Uh-huh, and being a freak show—"

My anger explodes. "What do you want, Landon? Hurting me last year wasn't enough and now you've gotta waltz in here and insult me?"

Crap. I wasn't planning to admit how much he hurt me. I'm ruining all of this. Bailey's going to laugh me out of our cabin later.

In response, he crosses his arms and waits as if he was the one to ask the question and he's expecting an answer, but I have nothing else to say. And then he just shrugs and walks away, whistling an all-too-familiar tune.

Oh say can you seeeeeeee.

Ugh.

Photo © Heidi Ann

Amy Finnegan writes her own stories because she enjoys falling in love over and over again, and thinks everyone deserves a happy ending. She likes to travel the world—usually to locations where her favorite books take place—and owes her unquenchable thirst for reading to Jane Austen and J.K. Rowling. *Not in the Script* came about after hearing several years of behind-the-scenes stories from her industry veteran brother. She's also been lucky enough to visit dozens of film sets and sit in on major productions such as *Parks and Recreation* and *Parenthood*. This is Amy's debut novel.

www.facebook.com/AmyFinneganAuthor

@ajfinnegan